W9-CMF-056

Wildest Dreams

Wildest Dreams

Jennifer Blake

Fawcett Columbine

New York

A Fawcett Columbine Book
Published by Ballantine Books
Copyright © 1992 by Patricia Maxwell

Library of Congress Cataloging-in-Publication Data
Blake, Jennifer, 1942-
Wildest dreams / Jennifer Blake.—1st ed.
p. cm.
ISBN: 0-449-90617-5
I. Title.
PS3563.A923W55 1992
813′.54—dc20   91-58328
                                                              CIP

Design by Holly Johnson

Manufactured in the United States of America

First Edition: August 1992
10 9 8 7 6 5 4 3 2 1

For Loretta Theriot
who dreams of perfumes, and creates them.

ACKNOWLEDGMENTS

I am deeply indebted to Loretta Theriot, perfumer, of Creole, Louisiana, for the generous loan of a wealth of material from her huge library of perfume research, and also for the tale of a hundred-year-old bottle of perfume found in an old Louisiana plantation house which still retained its fresh floral scent. Most of all I'm grateful for an early-morning phone call from her that began, "Guess what? Last night I dreamed you wrote a book about a special perfume. . . ."

My gratitude also to Alessandra Lassabe, formerly of Bourbon French Perfume Company, New Orleans, for sharing information on her family's involvement in the perfume business, including the story of how her grandmother failed to pass on the formula for a valuable perfume before her death. Though *Wildest Dreams* is not the story of her family, the Bourbon French Parfum Shop, St. Ann Street, the French Quarter, did provide a much appreciated spark of inspiration.

The many references to the language of flowers as practiced by the Victorians were culled, in the main, from the wonderfully perfumed pages of *Penhaligon's Scented Treasury of Verse and Prose, The Language of Flowers*, edited by Sheila Pickles. *Wildest Dreams* would not have been the same without this lovely volume.

Other books that provided background on perfume and its manufacture were searched out for me by the staff of the Jackson Parish

Library, Jonesboro, Louisiana. As always, I would like to recognize their cooperation and swift answers to calls of distress.

Thanks a million to Sue Anderson for jogging my memory about views, flowers, mileage, and other details of a special trip to Europe in the spring, not to mention twenty years of dreams and other travels.

And a special thank-you to my two great assistants, Delinda Corbin and Katharine Faucheux—who also happen to be my daughters—for researching, editing, and generally making my life easier while the story was in the making.

Wildest Dreams

Chapter 1

The perfume shop was dim and still, lighted only by the street lamps beyond the front windows and the Venetian-glass chandelier left burning in the back. The corners and the spaces behind the glinting glass counters were thick with night shadows. Soft darkness concealed the opening to the rear work area.

Joletta Caresse made no move to turn on more lights. She closed and locked the tall entrance door behind her with swift care. Drawing out the old-fashioned brass key, she stood still to listen.

Footsteps sounded from down the street outside, coming along the sidewalk under the arcaded front of the building. Their cadence slowed as they drew nearer. Abruptly, they stopped.

Joletta peered through the wavy, antique glass in the shop door. Looking past the black-bowed funeral wreath attached at eye level, she could just make out the tall form of a man standing back in the shadows of the arcade.

Her heartbeat increased, thudding against the wall of her chest. In spite of the dimness inside the shop, she felt unbearably exposed. The impulse to run, to hide, blossomed inside her while at the same time her feet felt glued to the floor. She gripped the key in her hand so tightly that its ornate edges pressed against the bones of her fingers.

The man outside stood unmoving. He made no attempt to conceal himself further, but seemed to be looking straight at her with an intent and purposeful stare. There was in the set of his shoulders an impression of controlled power and alert senses.

Joletta had no idea how long he had been following her. She had noticed him only in the last block before she reached the perfume shop. Even then, she had not been sure he was not simply walking in the same direction. He had made no effort to close the distance between them, yet there was something in the close matching of his pace to hers that had set off alarm bells in her head. The dangers of the French Quarter of New Orleans at night were something she had heard about all her life, but this was the first time she had ever run into a problem.

Joletta's eyes began to burn from trying to penetrate the dimness under the arcade. She closed them tightly for an instant to relieve the strain. When she looked again, there was nothing but empty space.

The man was gone.

She leaned her forehead against the glass door an instant as she breathed a soft imprecation. She was not sure what she had thought was about to happen, but the relief that nothing had, made her feel weak in the knees. At the same time her nerves jangled with irritation at the cat-and-mouse game the man had played with her those few seconds.

It was possible, of course, that she was imagining things. It would not be too surprising; she had been through so much in the last few days that her reactions were something less than normal.

Then again, perhaps she was not.

Joletta took a deep breath as she tried to relax. In the semidarkness, the smell of fragrance was pervasive, reaching out to envelop her like the embrace of a familiar and well-loved presence. Joletta turned slowly, swallowing hard against the sudden ache of grief and loss.

Mimi. The scent was hers, the indelible signature of Anna Perrin, Joletta's grandmother. That rich mingling of perfumes had always clung to the older woman's clothes, to the soft white crepe of her skin and the silver waves of her hair. It had been a part of her, like the radiating warmth of her smile and the name Mimi that Joletta had bestowed on her as a child. That fragrance also invaded Mimi's rooms above, the living quarters used in turn by the four generations of Fossier women who had owned the shop. Over the years the smell had penetrated the fibers of the draperies and rugs, sneaked into the hidden drawers and age cracks of the antique furnishings, even permeated the plaster on the walls and the wood of the floors. Mimi had loved that constant aura of perfume. She had been lucky, she said, to live always among the souls of flowers.

There had been thousands of flowers at Mimi's funeral, the outpouring of friends and business associates and the many civic, social, and charitable organizations with which Mimi had been involved during her lifelong residency in the Vieux Carré, as the French Quarter was known among the descendants of the French Creoles. Their scent had mingled with the odor of sanctity during the service at St. Louis Cathedral and floated on the warm, humid air that stirred the gray moss on the live oaks of the cemetery as Mimi was laid to rest in the Fossier family mausoleum. Everyone had known how Mimi loved flowers; like the ownership of the perfume shop, it was a tradition of the Fossier women.

Joletta gave a slight shake of her head to dislodge the images. She wouldn't think of such things. Lifting her chin, she stepped deeper into the shop.

Her movements were assured; the place was such a part of her life, had been from childhood, that she could find her way through it in the darkest of nights. She knew the exact periwinkle-blue color that covered the walls. She had overturned the Parisian flower cart holding beribboned baskets of soap and potpourri during a rowdy game of chase with her cousins Natalie and Timothy, one rainy Sunday as they were all growing up. From the time she was twelve, it had been her duty to dust the antique armoires with their lace-swathed shelves filled with perfume containers of every size, shape, and color. Her first lessons in making perfume had been given on her thirteenth birthday, using the essences in the stoppered vials of brown glass on the vendor's cart. She had tripped on the threadbare antique Aubusson on the floor and turned her ankle while wearing her first pair of high heels. And she had cried out her anguish and confusion over the ending of her four-year engagement while lying on the old rosewood settee covered in cream shadow-striped silk.

The shop was full of memories, good and bad; it had been the center of her life after she had come to live with Mimi following the deaths of her parents when their car skidded off the road in a rainstorm and overturned in a canal. She sometimes thought that was the reason she had been so determined to get away from it when she left college; the smell of perfume had seemed to dominate her every waking moment. She had been sick of it.

She had wanted independence and personal privacy, had needed to get away from the cloying, indulgent, loving examination of her every movement, thought, and mood. She had been determined, then, to prove that she didn't need anyone, not Mimi, not the older women who worked in the shop and who had become substitute mothers, and especially not her ex-fiancé. It was the reason she had moved into her own apartment close to her job as historian in a research library and well away from the Vieux Carré just over six months ago.

Joletta reached the doorway at the back of the shop which led into the shelf-lined mixing room. As she stepped through, the perfume scent was even stronger, coming from the hundreds of glass decanters that shone in rows along the walls. In the center was a worktable with deep shelves underneath that held old-fashioned leather-bound ledgers and also newer ones covered with plastic. These ledgers contained hundreds of formulas for perfumes, some recording the various mixtures made under special label for the public over the years, but most with careful notations of the custom blends of customers. A large portion of the entries were recently made, though there were also notations dating back over a period of nearly a hundred and forty years, a melancholy listing of the ingredients for the favorite scents of women long dead. Each blend was set down in a complicated system of numbers and symbols developed by Violet Fossier, Joletta's great-great-great-great-grandmother, who had founded Fossier's Royal Parfums so long ago, just after the Civil War.

A frown of irritation pleated the skin between Joletta's soft brown eyes as she surveyed the ledger shelves. They were a jumbled mess, with the ancient books mixed helter-skelter with the new and all of them piled this way and that with their sheets crumpled and folded.

Her aunt Estelle Clements, Mimi's older daughter and sister to Joletta's mother, was responsible for the disorder. She had been in the shop earlier with her daughter Natalie, searching for a special perfume formula. Known as Le Jardin de cour, Courtyard Garden, it was the oldest perfume made by the shop, one that accounted for well over half its yearly sales.

There was a family legend that said that Le Jardin de cour, under a different name, had been the favorite fragrance of the Empress Eugénie of France in the days of the Second Republic. Eugénie, so the story went, had gotten it from a former serving woman of the Empress Joséphine, an elderly woman who had taken it when her mistress died. Joséphine had received it from Napoléon Bonaparte himself, who was known to be addicted to fine perfume. The scent was supposed to have been discovered by Napoléon during his Egyptian campaign, and prized by him because it was said to be the perfume with which Cleopatra had ensnared Mark Antony, one that had come to her from the Far Eastern deserts where it had been used in ancient times by the priestesses of the Moon Goddess.

This special formulation had always been closely guarded by the Fossier women, its exact ingredients known only to the owner of the shop in each generation and passed down from mother to daughter over the years. Mimi had been the last of the line to be entrusted with it. However, Mimi had failed to pass it on.

They had all watched Mimi make the perfume many times; they knew most of the different essences that went into it. Le Jardin de cour, however, was no simple blend. To put this one perfume together could take an hour or more of careful measuring and mixing. One tiny slip, a minute droplet too much of a single flower or plant essence, and the process would have to be begun again from scratch. The ruined batch might be perfume of a sort, might even be marketed at a reduced price, but it would not be Le Jardin de cour.

Mimi had tried desperately to give them the information they needed as she lay in ICU during the short hours between the time of her fall on the stairs and the moment when her heart stopped beating. It was impossible. She had sustained a stroke that paralyzed the left side of her body, including her facial muscles, so that her speech was croaking and slurred beyond recognition. The all-important formula was far too complicated, required too much detail and precision, to be communicated in the few sounds Mimi could manage.

One by one they had tried to understand—Estelle, Natalie, Timothy, and Joletta herself. One by one the others had turned away, exhausted by the useless effort. Then, near the end, Joletta had made out a single word, just three difficult and uncertain syllables.

Diary. That was what it sounded as if Mimi had said.

Joletta had told the others what she had heard, though she told them, too, that she could not remember ever seeing Mimi keep any sort of diary. Aunt Estelle and Natalie had practically run from the hospital. The doctors had warned them Mimi could not hold on much longer, but they would not wait.

Timothy had stayed behind to be with Joletta. He sat with his hands between his knees, interminably cracking his knuckles and sweeping his shock of overlong blond hair out of his eyes while he talked in a rambling fashion. He was loose-limbed and athletic, and might have been considered handsome if his personality had been more forceful. But he left the aggressiveness to his mother and his sister. Only a year younger than Joletta, he seemed less because he was so much under his mother's thumb. His manner was breezy, and his hazel eyes glinted with humor. He tried to distract Joletta, but saw it was useless after a time and slouched off down the hospital hallway in search of the cafeteria and an evening meal.

Joletta had been alone with her grandmother as the evening shadows closed in on the hospital and the hush of the dinner hour invaded ICU. She had been alone as Mimi's pulse grew weaker, as her breathing slowed, stopped, began again, then ceased in the unbroken silence of death. For long moments afterward, Joletta stood in the isolation of the curtain-enclosed cubicle, holding her grandmother's lax fingers with their bony knuckles and fine white skin marred by age spots, fingers that had baked and cleaned and soothed her childish hurts. She smoothed the soft silver strands of hair from Mimi's temples, hair that still seemed so alive. And warm tears pooled in her own eyes and slid slowly down her face.

Aunt Estelle had made a scene in the corridor outside ICU when she returned to find that Mimi was gone. She claimed Joletta had sent her on a fool's errand, that she had wanted her and her children out of the way at the last so she could be the only one to hear Mimi's final words.

Joletta had been so angry and heartsick at the commotion that she could not speak even to defend herself against such vicious accusations. Still, it would be a long time before she could forgive her aunt for making them.

Joletta didn't like to think of that moment, even now. Moving past the ledger cabinet, she continued on toward the heavy door in the far end of the mixing room. She reached for the iron bar that closed off entry to the courtyard beyond.

With the heavy bar in her hand, she hesitated, thinking of the man on the sidewalk. The courtyard was completely walled in, but there were two other entrances. One was a locked doorway in the great iron grate that closed off the porte cochere, or old carriage way, that led from the street, and the other was a small, wooden gate connecting to the courtyard of the building next door.

Joletta shook her head as she pushed up the bar and stepped outside. No one had used the other door or gate in years; Mimi had preferred that everyone come and go through the shop so she could keep an eye on them. They were probably rusted shut, but even if they were not, only someone thoroughly familiar with the place could find their way inside.

Joletta made her way along the arcaded loggia that protected the shop's back door toward the staircase that led up to the rear balcony of the rooms above. She smoothed her hand over the worn top of the newel post of the mahogany stair as she began to climb upward. Looking out over the courtyard beyond, she thought for a moment about Violet Fossier, the woman who had first established the perfumery.

Violet had taken as her shop the ground floor of the town house that had been built for her as a bridal gift from her husband. This town house, located on one of the most famous streets in the Quarter, had been designed by James Gallier at the height of his fame as an architect to Louisiana planters. The rooms were spacious and airy, with finely carved moldings. Their furnishings—the marble mantels, the paintings and sculptures, mirrors and costly silk-tasseled draperies, silver, crystal, and fine china ornaments—had been brought back from a grand tour of Europe taken as a bridal journey of sorts by Violet and Gilbert Fossier. It had been during this two-year ramble around Europe that Violet had conceived her passion for perfume. It was also there that she had come upon the formula for the special fragrance she had called Le Jardin de cour.

This perfume, as Mimi was fond of telling customers, had actually taken its name from the courtyard behind the shop. Unlike the house, which had been commissioned and furnished by her husband, the courtyard had been the creation of Violet Fossier. To Joletta it had always been the most serene and satisfying place in New Orleans. The high walls of cream plaster with Roman arches under the loggias along the lower floor of the house blended harmoniously with the geometric-shaped flower and herb beds lined with boxwood in the French style. These, with the paths radiating from a central fountain and a stone arbor covered with ancient grapevines, showed the influence of that long-ago tour of Europe. The plants chosen by Violet years ago were all scented, from the climbing roses and wisteria on the walls and huge old sweet olive and cape jasmine shrubs that filled the corners to the groupings of petunias, nicotiana, and early lilies in the beds. Their sweet fragrance, along with the gaslights that cast flickering shadows across the center fountain while leaving secret alcoves of pleasure here and there in darkness, gave the impression of a sensual, even seductive, retreat.

Joletta had always been curious about Violet, what she was like, what she had been thinking of when she built her courtyard garden, what had happened to her to cause her to open her shop with this fragrant haven behind it. As a historian, Joletta had a special interest in the Victorian period with its momentous events as well as its strict mores and conventions. Violet's conduct in that time had seemed so unusual, especially among the aristocratic Creoles of French and Spanish descent in the Vieux Carré, where trade was repugnant as an occupation for a man, much less a woman.

Joletta had asked Mimi about it several times, and her grandmother always promised to tell her the whole story when the time was right. Somehow, that time had never come, just as the moment had never been right to pass on the formula.

There were moving shadows in the far end of the courtyard. A whispering sound could be heard above the clatter and tinkle of the fountain, as if branches were scraping against the old bricks of the wall in the night wind. Or as if there were phantom lovers whispering in one of the shrubbery alcoves.

It was definitely eerie to be there alone in the dark; she should have waited until morning, Joletta thought. Even then, it would not have been the same with the shop closed for the funeral and the weekend afterward. There would be no cheerful ringing of the shop bell, no new perfume being mixed, no laughing greeting or loving scolding from Mimi, no smell of something rich with onions, celery, and garlic in a well-browned roux simmering in the upstairs kitchen. Strange to think that it would never be that way again.

Joletta really didn't want to enter the emptiness of the upper rooms. It was an intrusion, or so it seemed. And yet, what was one more? The others had already been there looking, thumbing through Mimi's books and papers, rummaging in her closets and drawers. Her own search could be no more of an invasion. Passing along the upper gallery to the narrow entrance doors, Joletta used her key to let herself into the town house.

She switched on the light in the parlor, but did not hesitate among the formal furnishings of rosewood and gilt, marble and ormolu. Skirting a square table centered under a Baccarat chandelier, she walked into the connecting bedroom.

It looked like something from a museum, with a Louis XIV

scrolled bed, a dressing table of similar design, and faded draperies of old rose satin over curtains of yellowed lace. Here, as in the parlor, was a fireplace mantel of Carrara marble that surrounded an ornate cast-iron coal grate. Against one wall was a tall chest of carved and gilded wood. In the bottom section of it were drawers of different sizes, but the top was made up of a series of small compartments hidden behind double doors painted in the style of Boucher, with pastoral scenes of amorous shepherds and shepherdesses and hovering cherubs.

Mimi had called this piece of furniture her memory chest. In it were the items she particularly cherished: a seashell she had picked up at Biloxi on her first trip there as a child; the gifts of fans and silver-backed mirrors and other tokens received from members of the Mardi Gras krewes who had called her out to dance at balls during her coming-out season; the red glass buttons from the dress she had been wearing the night her husband had proposed; a dried and disintegrating carnation from his funeral wreath, and many other such treasures. Somewhere among them, Joletta knew, was what she sought.

She found it in the third compartment, stuffed behind a baby's christening robe. It was in a bundle tied up with a frayed black ribbon, along with a miniature in a frame so heavy and iridescent with tarnish that it had to be made of solid silver.

What Mimi had called a diary was a boxlike book covered with worn maroon velvet and finished with discolored brass-bound edges that made square corners. Actually a Victorian traveling journal, it was thick with pages of heavy acid-free paper, each page covered with closely spaced lines of looping Spencerian script interspersed with sketches of dainty flowers, and a few small-scale figures and landscapes. Joletta had seen it once before, years ago. She stood now with the bundle in her hands, fingering the brass corners of the journal while she gazed down at the miniature that was uppermost.

The small painting, done in oil colors that were soft and delicate yet as clear as the day they had come from the brush, showed the head and shoulders of a young woman. She appeared on the verge of a smile, the look in her wide, pansy-brown eyes diffident yet inquiring, guarded but vulnerable. Her brows were delicately arching, her lashes long and full. Her nose was slightly tip-tilted and her mouth formed with gentle curves tinted a natural coral. Her soft brown hair was drawn back in a low chignon from which short tendrils escaped to curl at her temples and cheekbones. There were

garnet-and-seed-pearl eardrops in her ears and a matching brooch
at the throat of her flat lace collar. She was not beautiful in a classic
sense; still, there was something intriguing about her that made it
difficult to look away from her. The artist had drawn his subject
with care and precision, and also with a talent that made it seem she
might complete her smile at any moment, might tilt her head and
answer some question whose echo had long since ceased to sound.

Violet Fossier.

Joletta remembered the day she had first seen the miniature and
the journal tied up with it. Mimi had been in bed with a chest cold.
Joletta, thirteen or fourteen at the time, had been trying to take care
of her. Mimi, who always scorned inactivity, had declined to nap
or read. She had directed Joletta to the chest across the bedroom to
get her tatting. As Joletta searched, taking out the treasures one by
one in her quest for the tatting bobbin, Mimi had told her about
each item.

"Bring that to me, *chère*," her grandmother had commanded as
Joletta pulled out the journal.

The brass-bound book had been heavy, and its ornate hasp and
small dangling lock and key attached with a piece of black ribbon
had rattled as Joletta walked. Mimi took the book from her, han-
dling it with care, smoothing the worn places on the velvet. In answer to Joletta's plea to see inside, her grandmother had carefully
opened the lock and lifted the frontpiece to expose the yellowed
pages with their beautiful handwriting and delicate sketches marred
with small ink blotches.

"This belonged to your great-great-great-great-grandmother,"
Mimi said. "She once held it in her own hands, wrote in it every
day for the two years of her journey to Europe. She put her
thoughts and feelings onto the pages, so that to read them is to
know who and what she was. What a shame it is that we don't do
these things anymore."

Joletta, enthralled by the ornate script and faint mustiness that
rose from the paper, had tilted her head to read the first line.

"No, no, *ma chère*," her grandmother had said, snapping the
journal closed. "This isn't for you."

"But why, Mimi?"

"You're young yet, maybe someday when you're older."

"I'm old enough now! I'm nearly grown, not some little kid."
The frustration she felt was strong in her voice.

Mimi looked at her and smiled. "So ancient, then, yes? But there are still things that you do not know, nor should you until you are of an age to understand."

Joletta had looked at her with her lips pressed together. "When will that be?"

Mimi sighed. "Who can say? For some it never comes, this understanding. But put the book away for me now, then come back and let me tell you something."

Joletta had obeyed, though without grace. At her grandmother's gesture, she had climbed up to perch on the side of the high bed. Mimi reached out to touch her face, cupping her pointed chin in a smooth, timeworn hand.

"You were named for your grandmother Violet, did you know? Joletta is a Latin form of Violet. You are also very like her. Your eyes are not so brown and have little flecks of rust; your hair is a shade or two lighter, I expect from the sun—Violet probably never went into the sun in her life without her hat and parasol. Still, you have the same bone structure, the same brows and nose—especially the nose. *Le nez*, the nose of the perfumer."

"Do I? Do I, really?" Joletta was breathless with pleasure at the idea.

Mimi gave a slow nod. "I have noticed it. One day you will look almost exactly like her."

"But she's so pretty."

"So are you, *chère*; haven't I always told you so?" Mimi's tone was faintly scolding.

"Yes, but you would say it anyway." It was not Mimi's love Joletta doubted, but herself.

Mimi reached out then to smooth her hair. "Don't worry, one day you will see it. And you will have Violet's spirit, too, I think. You are such a quiet little thing most of the time, but you have wild dreams inside that will someday burst free. You can be led, easily persuaded with reason, but not pushed. You will give and give until it's that last tiny bit too much, and then you will turn and fight, fight without counting the cost, perhaps even without mercy. I fear for you sometimes, little one. You need so much to have happiness and a heart at ease, and you can be hurt so badly if you are not careful."

Looking at the miniature now, Joletta could not quite remember everything her grandmother had said, but she recalled enough to make her stare hard at the features of Violet Fossier.

Thinking back, she wondered, too, if there had not been more to Mimi's refusal to let her read the journal than she suspected at the time. She wondered if there wasn't something a bit shameful in the pages, some dark family secret that Mimi thought she was too innocent to see. Mimi had been like that. Because she had been convent school taught and gone chaste to her marriage bed, she assumed her daughters and granddaughters were just as pure. It was sweet of her, but an impossible image to live up to.

Was she really like Violet Fossier? Joletta tilted her head as she considered it. She was near the same age now as Violet had been when the miniature was done. There might be some resemblance, but the difference in the hairstyle, the clothes, and the expression made it difficult to be sure. If the resemblance was there, it was only superficial. Joletta knew with wry acceptance that she had never been so fascinating as the woman in the miniature. She was an independent female with a job she enjoyed, her own apartment, and no steady man anywhere in sight. The only thing definitely the same was the nose.

She stood still, breathing gently in and out, testing the accumulated scents of the room. Yes, she had the nose.

There was never a time when she had not been aware of the infinite variety of smells in the space around her. She had thought everyone must inhale them as easily as she did, must note them, catalog them, sometimes turn their heads to follow them. She knew differently now. Some people recognized the majority of the scents about them but not all, some caught no more than half, while still others seemed to notice only those smells that were actively bad or good.

Here in this room were the accumulated scents of dust and ancient coal smoke, furniture polish, and floor wax, plus the dry and acrid base notes of old silk and leather and wool and cotton from the contents of the memory chest. Overlying all these, however, were the myriad scents rising from the shop below, drifting in the damp stillness of the air.

The strongest of these was rose, that most ancient of perfumes and still the world's most popular. It was the one Mimi had let Joletta measure first, all those years ago, holding her hands steady around the decanter, wiping up the small spill with a tissue she had tucked into Joletta's pocket. "For luck," she had said with a wink and a kiss, "and for love."

Lavender, muguet, cinnamon: these came from the potpourri that was mixed fresh in the shop each morning. Joletta's mother had used it often in her own home, and Joletta associated the clean, faintly old-fashioned sweetness with memories of her.

A fruitiness mixed with orris root was an unwelcome reminder of Aunt Estelle. The older woman had a tendency to douse herself and her clothing in whatever perfume was newest and most highly advertised, so had moved these last few days in a miasma of some designer scent that smelled remarkably like imitation grape drink.

The blending of orange and other citrus scents conjured up Joletta's dorm room at college. She had used their freshness in that period of her life to cover the smells of old paint and gym socks. The smells had seemed brisk and modern yet with an undertone of wedding orange blossoms. She had lost her taste for them, abruptly, when her engagement ended.

The undertone of musk brought back the winter day when she and her cousin Natalie had knocked a full bottle of that essence from a shelf to the stone floor of the mixing room. Natalie claimed Joletta had done it. She had, but it had been Natalie who had pushed her into the shelf. Regardless, Joletta had had to clean up the broken glass, sop up the cloying liquid by herself. The smell, sickeningly strong in excess, had clung to her for days, lingering in the pores of her skin, hovering in the back of her nose. The worst of it, though, was that Mimi had been afraid to trust her in the mixing room again for months.

Joletta had tried to explain what happened that day, but Natalie had been louder, had burst into tears and screams when accused. Joletta had finally stopped trying to make herself heard. After all these years, Joletta was used to being overpowered by her older cousin. She still admired her cousin's forthright ways, her brash display of stylish clothes and expensive jewelry, her determination to have her own way and hang the consequences. Joletta knew that she had her own understated style, one based on a few pieces of quality clothing in neutral tones that could be put together in infinite combinations and made interesting by bright accessories and a few pieces of antique jewelry. Regardless, Natalie's display of the latest from Saks and Neiman Marcus made her feel dowdy, and somehow diminished by comparison.

The fragrance of cloves was a reminder of Timothy; the men's cologne he wore was heavy with it. He had a preference for strong scents, rather than the simple outdoorsy blends Joletta would have expected. Timothy's disposition was laid-back with an easy charm that came from extended summers around country-club pools or else taking part in some high-risk sport such as hang gliding or white-water rafting. Mimi's only grandson, the only male child to be born in the immediate family in the last two generations, he had been spoiled, but seemed to have grown out of it.

There were other scents, dozens of them. The most dominant of these, vying with the rose, was vetiver. The green, woodsy note, one not unlike eucalyptus, was used in many of the fragrances in the shop. Brought to New Orleans during the French colonial period, vetiver was native to India and had for many years taken the place of lavender in tropical climes where that English herb was difficult to cultivate. Lavender was a plentiful import these days, but New Orleanians were still partial to the distinctive fragrance blends that could be achieved with their old favorite.

Yes, she had the nose. For what good it might do her.

Taking the things she held to the bed, Joletta put them down and slipped the journal free of the ribbon tie. Unlocking it, she quickly flipped through the pages, scanning the faded paragraphs and sketches that went on and on, paying particular attention to the frontpiece and endpiece pages. There was no sign of a listing of numbers and measurements that might be a formula.

The corners of her mouth tightened with disappointment, then she took a deep breath. She should have known it wouldn't be that easy. She would have to go through the journal page by fragile page.

That would take time, and it was too late to start now. She would need to take the journal home with her, possibly make a photocopy so she wouldn't damage it, then do a thorough study. She could well have been wrong about what Mimi was trying to say, what she meant. The chance she was right was a slim one at best.

Joletta tucked the journal into her shoulder bag, then let herself out of the town house, turning the lights off as she went.

There was a spring wind stirring the trash in the street, one off Lake Pontchartrain with a smell of rain in its coolness. Joletta settled the strap of her shoulder bag higher on the shoulder pad of her jacket, pushed her hands into her pockets, and started walking in the direction of the parking lot where she had left her car.

The streets were nearly empty; the hour was late. Across the street were a pair of lovers with arms intertwined. The slow clip-clop of hooves signaled the passing of a tourist carriage in a cross street not far away. She met a group of college boys who whistled and yelled catcalls, drunk on beer and freedom and too young to be quiet about it. In the distance the wail of a jazz trumpet made a lament in the night.

New Orleans was winding down, finishing off the evening. She had been longer at the shop than she expected. The sounds trailed away behind her as she left the main streets of the quarter. All that was left was the clatter of her own heels on the uneven pavement.

She thought at first that it was an echo. Even after she realized the footsteps were heavier than her own, she hoped whoever was behind her would turn down a side street, enter a building, or else fall back as she increased her speed.

It didn't happen. The treads continued, steady, purposeful, so closely coordinated with her own it could mean only one thing.

She had almost forgotten the man who had followed her earlier. He had departed so easily. Besides, she had nearly convinced herself that she had been mistaken about him.

She had, apparently, been right after all.

Her throat was dry. There was an ache beginning in her side from the quick pace she was keeping. She could think of a dozen things she might have done to prevent this situation, from calling the police to staying at Mimi's place overnight. None of them was of any use now.

There were two possibilities: either the man wanted money or he was a weirdo who got his kicks from terrifying women. She could drop her shoulder bag and run, hoping that would satisfy him. On the other hand, if she hung on to the purse, the weight of the journal inside would make it a formidable weapon.

Without pausing in her stride, she swung to look back. The footsteps stopped. She could see the shape of a man in the shadow of one of the many balconies that overhung the sidewalk, but could not make out his face or enough of his clothing to tell anything about him. His general height seemed to match that of the man who had followed her earlier, though she could not be sure.

She faced forward, walking faster. The footsteps began again. The sound of them seemed to rattle among the buildings, fading and growing louder, coming and going in a curious, uneven rhythm. Or it could be the jolting pound of her pulse in her ears that made her think it.

All the things she had read about self-defense for the woman alone, all her good resolutions to take some kind of class on self-protection or buy a weapon to carry in her purse tumbled through her head. None of it was helpful. She had never followed up on her good intentions.

It was still two blocks to the parking lot. When she got there, it was going to be dark and the attendant would probably be asleep or gone for the night. If she got there.

She put her head down, stepping up her pace until she was nearly running. In a moment she would make a break for it. Behind her the footsteps increased in speed.

"Darling! There you are!"

The voice, warm and deeply masculine, rich with concern, came from just ahead of her. She glanced up, startled. She had a brief glimpse of dark hair and an intense gaze shadowed with appeal and daring, caught a whiff of night freshness, starched linen, and the clean sandalwood note of some excellent after-shave. Then the man was upon her in a rush, scooping her up, holding her against him with long, firm arms.

"There's a guy behind you, ma'am, and it looks like he has a knife in his hand," he said, speaking quickly, his voice urgent under its quiet timbre. "I'd like to be heroic and demolish him for you, but I'm not sure he doesn't have friends. Play along, and it may be all right."

Her nerves were too tightly strung to make sense of what he was saying. She only knew it wasn't all right, and wasn't going to be, knew it with an instinct that sent prickling gooseflesh over every inch of her body. She drew in her breath to scream.

In that instant, the man's hold tightened around her and his firm mouth descended on her parted lips.

Chapter 2

The kiss was heated and piercingly sweet, its hard pressure inescapable. Joletta felt the rush of warm blood to her head and the champagne froth of rising ardor in her veins. At the same time she moved her head in negation while a soft sound of distress caught in her throat.

A moment later the man raised his head. He stood still with his arms clasped around her, holding her against him. Joletta, meeting his gaze that appeared dark blue in the light of the street lamps, saw an arrested expression overlaid by wry fatalism.

It had been some time since she had been kissed. Too long, perhaps. A shiver of reaction moved over her, and there was an aching constriction in her throat. Disoriented by the swift turn of events, she stood still with her fingers resting lightly against the firm muscles of his chest under his suit coat.

The man who held her drew a sharp breath, then released her, stepping back with the taut, abrupt movements of extreme reluctance. He glanced beyond her. "Sorry, ma'am," he said on an uneven laugh. "I just—I thought that I might be more convincing as a bodyguard if it looked as if I had a personal interest. At least it seems to have done the trick."

Joletta glanced over her shoulder. There was no sign of whoever had been following her. Speaking with difficulty, she said, "That

may be, but I imagine you could have done the same thing without—"

"Yes, ma'am, but where would the reward be in that?"

She gave him a straight look. There was a hint of exaggeration
in the form of address he used and the drawl of his voice. She
thought it was deliberate, though she could not be sure. In the dim
light, his hair was the dark and shining brown of polished black
walnuts, its texture thick and not quite tamed to smoothness. His
features were clean-cut and nicely proportioned, dominated by a
straight nose and square chin with a hint of an indentation. The
curving lines on either side of his mouth suggested he smiled often,
and the glint of fast-moving intelligence could be seen in his eyes.
His shoulders, under the coat of a well-cut navy suit, were broad
without being bulky. He was above average in height, his manner
compelling without being overbearing.

After a moment Joletta said, "Must there be a reward?"

"Gallantry, southern style, isn't appreciated the way it used to
be. It should be practiced for its own sake, I expect, but I prefer to
collect on my own, given the chance."

Listening to the sound of his voice, driven by the rise of well-
developed curiosity, she said, "Where are you from?"

"Virginia, originally. Does it matter?"

"No," she answered, and repeated more firmly as she bent her
head to search in her shoulder bag for her car keys, "no, of course
not."

A faint whimsical note sounded in his voice as he said, "Were
you headed somewhere? Strike out, and I'll tag along to keep you
company."

It was a disarming suggestion, but she had no intention of encouraging him. She didn't trust most men she met in broad daylight,
much less one she had run into on a dark street at midnight in the
Quarter. She looked up as she took out her brass ring of jangling
keys. "Thanks all the same, but gallantry doesn't have to go that
far."

"My old nurse who taught me my manners would say it did."
His easy stance in front of her did not change, nor did he show any
sign of leaving.

"Well, she isn't here," Joletta said evenly, "and I don't know
you from Adam. You might be mixed up with the guy with the
knife for all I can tell."

"Good thinking, but you're still unmolested so far, aren't you— well almost. Be sensible. Let me walk you to your car."

"I appreciate your help, but I'm sure I can manage on my own now."

Joletta stepped around him, moving in the direction of the parking lot. "Maybe so," he said as he turned and fell in beside her, "but why should you have to?"

She gave him a swift glance. "Really, this isn't necessary."

"I think it is."

The parking lot ahead, a small square surrounded by the high walls of houses and courtyards, was like a dimly lighted well. The solid presence of the man beside her was not actually unwelcome, and there was no point in pretending otherwise. Since there seemed to be no getting rid of him anyway, she allowed her silence to signal her reluctant acquiescence.

After a moment, however, her own training in manners at Mimi's knee began to surface. What had seemed self-protective silence seconds before began to feel like ungracious sulking. She glanced at the man moving beside her, at his suit, so somber with its matching striped tie. He had the look, she thought, of some kind of executive with time on his hands after a day of intense negotiation. In an attempt to ease the moment, she said, "You're in New Orleans on business?"

"You could say so."

"Is this your first time here?"

He shook his head. "I come through now and again."

"A convention, maybe?" New Orleans was a major attraction for group meetings.

"Not this time," he answered.

Since he did not elaborate, Joletta did not pursue it. It didn't matter what he did or why he was in the city; she would never see him again. Still, the disappointment she felt at his minimal answers was surprising, even disturbing in its way. She had managed just fine without the tingling, visceral response to a man that she felt inside at this moment. It was a complication she didn't need.

"You don't have to break into a run," he said quietly. "I'm not going to jump you again."

Joletta slackened her pace. "I wasn't running."

"No, of course not." There was humor underlying the irony in his voice.

She came to a halt and turned to face him. "This is far enough," she said. "I'm thankful that you came along when you did; I don't know what I would have done if you hadn't. I don't even hold the kiss against you, but—"

"No?" he asked, the word quietly doubtful.

"No," she answered with firmness, perhaps more firmness than necessary. "Anyway, my car is just over there, and I'm sure I'll be fine now."

He studied her a moment. "So buzz off, huh? What if the guy with the knife is still behind us, waiting for your bodyguard to leave?"

"It doesn't seem likely." Joletta spoke with bravado instantly belied by her quick look over her shoulder.

"Right," he said, his voice dry before he went on with more purpose. "My car is here, too, since this is the only decent parking lot on this side of the Quarter. Let me run you home, then I can be sure you get there safe and sound."

She shook her head in amazement. "You must be crazy. I don't even know your name—"

"Tyrone Kingsley Stuart Adamson the Fourth, at your service. Is that enough name for you? If it's too much, call me Rone. And what can I call you besides 'darling' and 'ma'am'?"

"Nothing! Look—"

"No, you look," he said, his voice deepening to hard-edged certainty. "I'm not leaving you here at this time of night. If you won't let me drive you home, at least let me follow you. No, correct that. I'm going to follow you whether you want me to or not."

She stared at him for long seconds, at the firm planes of his face and the unwavering purpose in his eyes. "Why?" she demanded. "Why such concern?"

"It's my nature, a habit beaten into me with a peach-tree switch by a strong-minded black housekeeper who cared about that sort of thing. I also open doors and give up my seat to women; I just can't help it."

As an answer, it was not quite satisfactory. Regardless, Joletta could find no real reason to question it. Mimi had also been big on manners and moral obligations. She compressed her lips as she turned, but protested no more as he continued beside her to where her Mustang sat locked and dark.

The man called Rone took her keys from her and opened the door, leaning to check in the backseat for hidden passengers before he made a courteous gesture indicating it was all right for her to get in.

Joletta could not allow him to outdo her in graciousness. She held out her hand. As he took it she said, "Well, thank you for the rescue. I am grateful."

"In spite of everything? That's generous of you." He smiled down at her as he spoke.

"No, really—" she began.

"Never mind," he said, "I'm grateful myself for the opportunity."

It didn't seem wise to question his meaning. She withdrew her hand. "Good night, then."

He stepped back to allow her to enter the car. As she slid under the wheel he turned and walked off toward a silver Buick with a rental-company sticker prominent on the back bumper.

It made Joletta nervous to have his headlights shining in her rearview mirror as she drove, to know that he was watching the way she threaded through the narrow streets of the Quarter and turned back toward the lake. It also disturbed her, as she thought about it, that she was allowing a chance-met stranger to discover where she lived.

She need not have worried. As she pulled into the entrance drive to her apartment building, Rone Adamson blinked his headlights once, then drove on past without stopping. She would not, Joletta told herself, have had it any other way.

Regardless, she turned her head to watch the red taillights of his car disappear. Releasing her tight grip on the steering wheel, she reached up to touch the soft surface of her lips. They felt extra sensitive, a little feverish.

It had been almost six months since she had allowed a man to come close enough to kiss her like that. Six months since Charles, her fiancé, had kissed her good-bye.

They had known each other so long. Stocky and blond, Charles was playmate, friend, brother, the only boy she had dated through high school. The intimacy between them had evolved naturally, beginning with a chaste good-night kiss and reaching its high point some two years later, after they became officially engaged, on a sleeping bag beside the Mississippi River. When they started to college, Charles had wanted them to take an apartment just off campus together, but Joletta had refused. Mimi, she knew, would not have understood. Still, they had spent their every waking moment together. They had visited a doctor for birth control together, planned their future home and family and every detail of the wedding that would eventually take place. Together, always together. Joletta had bought her gown of champagne tissue silk sewn with pearls and iridescent beads. Their attendants were supposed to wear blue, to match the most dominant color of the stained glass in the little Victorian church on the River Road where the ceremony was to be performed.

Somehow, the wedding date was never set. Charles's parents wanted him to go with them on an African safari the summer after he and Joletta graduated. Then his grandfather had died after a lengthy illness, and Charles had felt it was selfish to think of their own happiness during such a time. He had suggested that they should save money for a down payment on a house, and maybe even put a little back for a Caribbean honeymoon. What was the rush, after all? They had the rest of their lives ahead of them.

Joletta had felt, after a time, that her life was on hold, but Charles's arguments for waiting had seemed so reasonable, so practical, that she had dutifully saved her money while living with Mimi.

Then Charles had used his savings to make a down payment on an electric-blue Mazda Miata convertible.

Joletta had walked around the sports car where it sat in front of the perfume shop. Her chest grew tight. She looked at Charles where he stood back with his hands on his hips and a proud smile on his face. Her voice wobbled a little when she finally spoke.

"You—you really don't want to get married, do you, Charles?"

"What do you mean?" he asked, taking a step back.

"Is there someone else? All you have to do is tell me."

"Nobody, I swear," he said, a high-pitched note of protest in his voice. "What is this?"

"I'm just trying to find out why you spent our future on a car."

He frowned. "It's my money; I work hard for it. I have a right to buy what I want."

"Yes, but you said—"

"I know what I said, but God, Joletta, we'll be married forever, and I feel like I've never been free."

"Are—you saying you would like to see other women?" She had known he always checked out any attractive woman who passed while they were together, but had thought it was a habit he would grow out of as he became more mature.

"Why not?" he said with a shade of belligerence in his tone.

"And maybe you should see other men. It might be a charge, who knows; I certainly never managed to turn you on that much."

"I haven't complained," she said, her voice low.

"Maybe you should have; it might have helped. As it is—" He shrugged.

She swallowed. "I never knew you felt this way."

"Now you do."

It was a long moment before she could speak past the ache growing in her throat. "Fine, then. I don't think I want to marry someone who doesn't care any more than that about me, either." She fumbled at the ring he had given her. It came off easily since it had always been too big. She grasped his hand, slapped the ring onto his palm, and closed his fingers over it. "Take it," she said, "and just go away. Now."

He stood staring down at the ring with a look of amazement and indecision on his face for long seconds. Abruptly, he swung from her and climbed into the car. The Miata laid down long strips of black rubber as it pulled away.

The sudden end of Joletta's plans and everything she and Charles had shared had been like a death. Her life had been so intertwined with his that she felt torn apart. The hurtful things he had said remained with her, eating away at her self-esteem.

Mimi had helped her, Mimi and time. However, even Mimi had not been able to convince her that all men weren't like Charles. Most of those she met had seemed exactly like him, ready enough to take her out, ready to jump into bed as if that were some kind of test for the future. Joletta had not been interested in being tested, didn't trust a future that had to be tried out beforehand. She had seldom progressed beyond the first date, and had become less and less likely to agree even to that.

Mimi had told her she was burying herself in the research library. It was possible her grandmother had been right. You could count on the past; it never changed.

Rone flipped his light switch off and on again as a farewell for Joletta Caresse, then drove on for a quarter of a mile before making a left turn and parking in front of a convenience store. He checked his watch before he got out and went in. Returning a few minutes later with a large coffee in a foam cup covered by a plastic lid, he started his car and drove back the way he had come.

At the apartment complex again, he pulled into the drive, found a parking space, and cut the engine and headlights. The complex was fairly new, built in separate buildings of two to four apartments each that were set at various angles around a central pool area. From where he was parked, Rone could see the bedroom window of the apartment he had checked out earlier as belonging to the woman he was watching. It was covered by mini-blinds that were tightly closed, though now and then he could catch a glimpse of a shadow passing over them.

He took the top from his coffee and tasted it. Grimacing, he shook his head. Too strong, it must have been simmering for hours, but he was going to need it to stay awake. Discarding the lid in the litter bag provided by the rental company, he shifted in his seat, trying to make his long frame more comfortable. He propped one wrist on the steering wheel as he took another sip of coffee and allowed his gaze to return to the lighted window above him.

He sighed as he shook his head in bemusement. The impulse to kiss Joletta Caresse had been irresistible. It had also been a dumb thing to do. He didn't care; it had been worth the risk.

His first night on the job and he had blown his cover, to use a phrase out of some mystery thriller. That might be bad or good, depending. One thing it had been was necessary; he couldn't have let the creep with the knife touch her. There had been a few bad seconds when he thought he was going to be too late. Next time he would be more alert.

Next time. God.

He hadn't been sure what he was doing was necessary. It had seemed so melodramatic, even paranoid. Apparently, it wasn't, not at all.

He felt like such an amateur. He had almost let her see him there at the perfume shop; he had thought the place was further along the street, hadn't expected her to be quite so wary. He would have to do better.

He hadn't been ready to find someone else on the trail either. He had tried to give both Joletta and himself some space by waiting for her near the parking lot, a big mistake. That creep. Where had he come from? Had he really had a knife? There had been a flash of some kind, and it had seemed best to have a good excuse for stepping in when he had.

But to kiss her? Unprofessional. Wrong. A clear case of taking advantage. He should feel worse about it, he really should.

Joletta Caresse was something else, not precisely beautiful but lovely rather, in a soft, old-fashioned way, a loveliness mixed with pride and swift-moving intelligence that made a man want to move in close, to find out if what he thought he saw was real. She was fragile looking but amazingly fearless, and with an obvious inner strength. She smelled wonderful; there had been the scent of roses in her hair. The way she felt in his arms, soft and silken but firm where a woman should be firm, rounded where she should be rounded, made the muscles in his abdomen tighten just to think of it. Something had been so right in the size and shape and touch and smell of her that it seemed she could, if she would, step right into his dreams and take up where his fantasies of the perfect woman had left off.

He must be crazy.

And God, no doubt about it, had a weird sense of humor.

There she was up there, just possibly the woman he had been looking for all his adult life. Here he was down here, waxing poetical about her like a lovesick teenager and burning his mouth on bad coffee.

Any day now, something was going to tip her off about him, and then she was going to dislike him intensely, even hate him.

It was guaranteed. It could be no other way.

Chapter 3

Mimi's lawyer of some twenty years' standing was a silver-haired charmer who had been refusing offers for political office for as long as Joletta had known him. He had tried to make a pleasant occasion of the meeting called in his office to explain the provisions of Mimi's will, ushering them into a paneled conference room and offering coffee. Aunt Estelle, seating herself on the opposite side of the long table from Joletta, with Natalie and Timothy on either side of her for support, had demanded that he get on with the legalities. He had complied.

There had been no surprises so far. The bulk of the estate, consisting of the French Quarter house, the perfume shop, and a certificate of deposit of no great size, had been divided in accordance with Louisiana's forced heirship laws, with half going to Estelle Clements as Mimi's elder daughter and the other half to Joletta as the only child and heir of her younger daughter, Margaret. Aunt Estelle's lips thinned with irritation, but she made no comment as she waited for the lawyer to set aside one page of the document in front of him and turn to the next.

"We come now," the lawyer said, looking from one to the other with a grim smile, "to the personal bequests."

He read them out: to Estelle, the family silver she had always coveted; to Natalie, a few pieces of jewelry of great style but no

28

great monetary value; to Timothy, the silver pocket watch and ivory shaving-brush set that had belonged to his grandfather and great-grandfather.

The lawyer cleared his throat before he continued in firm, even tones. "And the final items read as follows: 'To my beloved grand-daughter, Joletta Marie Caresse, I leave the piece of furniture known as my memory chest, along with its contents in their entirety. These contents shall include, but not be limited to, the brass-bound journal written by Violet Marie Fossier née Villère, dated 1854–1855, which shall be for the sole usage and ownership of said Joletta Marie Caresse, with the full right and permission to dispose of same in any manner which she deems suitable.'"

The lawyer placed the copy of the will on the desk in front of him and folded his hands upon it. His manner businesslike, he asked, "Are there any questions?"

Aunt Estelle drew a hissing breath before hitching the solid bulk of her body forward in her chair. Her tone was stringent as she spoke. "Do you mean the diary, this journal, was there in my mother's old chest all this time?"

"I assume so," the lawyer answered.

The older woman turned on Joletta. "You knew it, didn't you? Didn't you?"

Joletta felt an uncomfortable heat rising in her face, but she answered readily enough. "No, I didn't, not immediately. I guessed it later."

"This is outrageous," Aunt Estelle declared, turning on the lawyer. "That journal is the most valuable piece of property in the estate. My mother can't have meant to leave it in such a way that my children and I would not benefit from it."

"The will was drawn up to my client's specific instructions," the lawyer at the head of the table replied in dry explanation.

"Then she can't have been in her right mind," the older woman snapped. "I want it overturned, now."

"You can contest, of course, Mrs. Clements," the legal representative said with a trace of steel entering his tone, "but I should warn you that there is little ground for it. My client appeared perfectly aware of what she was doing when she dictated the terms set down here, and there is nothing irregular about the way the matter has been handled. I can't speak for the value of this journal, never having seen it, but I expect it is primarily sentimental in nature."

"You didn't know much about my mother's business if you

think so," Aunt Estelle returned. "But never mind. I believe that nothing specific was mentioned about the formulas to the perfumes. Is there any reason why these could not be sold, any legal obstacle to such a sale?"

"None at all—subject to the agreement of all parties concerned," the lawyer said in chill tones. "Since you and Joletta divide the estate between you, you would both have to sign the documents of sale and both share equally in the proceeds."

"I understand." The older woman gave a nod that made her fleshy jowls quiver.

"I'm not sure that I do," Joletta said slowly as she turned toward her aunt. "You can't mean to sell the shop?"

Aunt Estelle gave her a hard stare. "Why not, eventually? But I was speaking only of the formulas at the moment, especially the one for Le Jardin de cour."

"But Mimi would hate that. She would be so hurt if she knew you had even thought of letting it go."

"I don't need you to tell me what my mother would have wanted, Joletta, thank you very much."

"Without that perfume, the shop will be useless," Joletta protested, leaning toward her aunt. "The place is the heritage of the women of our family, a part of the history of New Orleans. You can't just throw that away."

Beyond her aunt, Joletta saw Natalie look at her brother with an expressive grimace. Timothy only shook his head, though there was sympathy in the glance he sent in Joletta's direction.

Estelle Clements gave her son a brief look before switching her attention back to Joletta. Through tight lips, she said, "I don't intend to throw anything away; I intend to sell it for a very high price. Much you should care, anyway. I'll be making all the arrangements while you sit back and take half the money."

"I can't believe you would do it," Joletta said, shaking her head.

The older woman's expression sharpened into dislike and her massive chest heaved under its decoration of gold chains and ropes of pearls. "While I'm at it, Joletta, there is something I've been wanting to say to you. You lived off my mother for years, worming your way into her heart. You may think you're going to push me and my children out of the way now while you take over, but I have news for you. As soon as that formula's found, it's going to the highest bidder, and there is nothing you can do about it."

Such shock at her aunt's animosity crowded in upon Joletta that she couldn't think what to say. She hadn't known her aunt felt that way about her.

It was Timothy who broke the taut silence. "Now, Mom, don't upset yourself," he said, drawing his lanky legs nearer his chair as he sat up straighter and brushed his hair back with a quick, nervous gesture. "I'm sure Joletta wouldn't want to take anything from us."

His mother glared at him. "When I want your opinion, Timothy, I'll ask for it. In the meantime I will remind you that your loyalty should be to me."

"I was just saying—"

"I heard you," his mother replied in quelling tones. "Please be quiet unless you have something to say to convince Joletta to see things my way."

Hot color rose under Timothy's fair skin. He met Joletta's gaze with a look of apology as he gave a light shrug.

Joletta sent her cousin a small smile in return. She had always felt closer to Timothy than to Natalie; he was nearer her own age and had something of her own uncertain disposition. It had been good of him to brave his mother's ill humor. His father, when Timothy was younger, before his parents divorced, had sent him to boys' camps and on Outward Bound excursions to toughen him up, make him more self-reliant. Timothy had always come back tan and fit, but no less dependent on his mother's approval.

Her cousin's intervention had allowed Joletta the time to marshal her thoughts once more. Keeping her voice as calm as possible, she said, "I really think we all need to think about this."

"There's nothing to think about," her aunt said with precision. "I happen to have a few contacts in the cosmetics industry. Lara Camors herself is interested; she's ready to put the marketing division of Camors Cosmetics behind Le Jardin de cour. She wants to run a huge ad campaign touting the old legends about Napoléon, Joséphine, and Cleopatra, calling it the perfume of women who want to get ahead, the perfume that increases a woman's power and influence."

"You've already discussed marketing?" Joletta couldn't keep the dismay from her voice.

"You needn't make it sound as if I couldn't wait for my mother to be buried. The possibilities in the perfume came up some time ago, when Lara and I were guests at a house party. That woman started with a cleansing cream and developed a company that is an industry giant, a billion-dollar conglomerate; there's no telling what she and Camors Cosmetics can do with the formula. Of course, there was no use saying a word about it while Mimi was alive."

"But—doesn't it bother you, the thought of ending everything, closing the shop?" Joletta reached out in a gesture of appeal.

"I never cared for the place, and I certainly don't intend to spend my days pouring perfumes together. Lara will pay at least two million, maybe more, for complete rights to the Fossier's Royal Parfums name and the formula for Le Jardin de cour. I don't intend to lose out on that money."

Joletta had always wondered why Mimi had never trusted the perfume formula to her eldest daughter. Perhaps she had had good reason.

Estelle had left New Orleans when she was in her early twenties, taking a job in Houston. It was only a few hours away on the interstate highway, but to a New Orleanian of Mimi's generation and insular outlook, it might as well have been the moon. A short time later Estelle had married a Texan, a man too tall, too loud, too wealthy, and too obviously sure of himself for Mimi's liking. Mimi had never gotten along with Errol Clements and had forgiven her daughter for marrying him only when Estelle had had the good taste to divorce him while Natalie and Timothy were small.

Afterward, Estelle had not come home, but had divided her time between Houston and the East and West coasts. She had grown extravagant and too much in thrall to designer labels, at least in Mimi's eyes. The excellent French-style taste instilled in her in her childhood had been corrupted, so that her appearance was regrettably overstated.

This was all bad enough, but Mimi's older daughter had also proven that she lacked the perfumer's nose, as shown by her deplorable taste in perfumes for her own use.

They were all waiting for her to say something more, her aunt and her cousins, even the lawyer who watched the byplay with an air of weary impatience, as if he had seen such family disagreements before and feared he would again.

Natalie, tall and blond, with the pouting expression of a runway model, appeared a little uncomfortable, but no less interested in the situation because of it. Joletta could not imagine why she should be concerned; her life-style could only be described as glamorous, filled with parties and jaunts to the Caribbean and the Riviera. She had married well, and divorced better, at least twice. Money could hardly be a problem, judging by her suit of silky-smooth black leather, the

Fendi handbag she carried, and her Ferragamo shoes. Joletta studied Natalie's carefully made up face with the delicately wrinkled skin around her eyes from the sun exposure necessary for a constant tan. There was nothing in her cousin's expression to indicate that family feeling held any interest for her; still, there was always the chance.

"What about you, Natalie? Wouldn't you like to try running the shop?"

"You must be joking," Natalie said with the nasal vowels of New York grafted to a broad Texas drawl. "Where would I find the time?"

"You don't work that I know of; why should it be a problem? You might even enjoy having some worthwhile use for your energy."

"Oh, right. Can you see me peddling perfume to grubby tourists in T-shirts and rubber thongs? Thanks, but I prefer to direct my energy, as you put it, to better things. Such as the marvelous man I met last week. You wouldn't believe him—stunning to look at, and the most darling manners. Money, of course. He's my idea of a career."

"Besides that," Aunt Estelle interrupted in resentful tones, "Natalie knows nothing about the shop; Mimi never saw fit to discuss it during her visits."

Joletta studied her aunt for long moments before she said quietly, "But I know about it."

"And just what does that mean?" The words carried a threatening edge.

"It means," Joletta answered, her gaze steady, "that I might run the shop myself."

An odd look crept into her aunt's eyes, one of half-concealed cunning. "You could do that, for what good the shop would be without Le Jardin de cour."

"You're forgetting something," Joletta said. "If Violet's journal is mine, and the formula is in it, then Le Jardin de cour also belongs to me."

"And you're forgetting that there is another way to find out what is in a perfume."

Joletta shook her head. "Chemical analysis? You know what Mimi thought of that."

A method without soul or accuracy, her grandmother had called it. Like most creative perfumers, Mimi had nothing but scorn for a process that was used, most notably, for making cheap copycat blends of famous fragrances. No machine, she said, could capture the finer nuances of a scent, could identify those minute quantities of rare oils that gave a great perfume its subtlety of character, its true essence and secret heart.

"It will serve the purpose," Aunt Estelle said shortly.

Joletta considered her aunt. At last she said, "I don't think it will, not without the journal."

Aunt Estelle made no answer, though the high color in her face took on an alarming darkness. Natalie stared for brief seconds at her mother before she turned toward Joletta. Her voice sharp, she said, "What are you saying?"

"It sounds to me as if Camors Cosmetics is interested in the whole package, journal as well as formula. Even if a chemical analysis should come close to the original, Le Jardin de cour is just another perfume without the background that goes with it. More than that, the government is picky these days about unsubstantiated advertising claims. Camors needs the journal to back up the legends."

Her aunt gave a humorless laugh. "Bright girl. But you know, I don't think you've found the formula yet, or you would be a lot more interested in the money."

Joletta made no answer, since she did not want to admit the truth.

"There's another thing," the older woman went on with hardly a pause. "If you want to own the shop, you'll have to buy out my interest in it and the house. Where do you think you're going to get the money? Who do you think will lend it to someone your age, with no business experience, no credit record to speak of, no collateral? You'll soon see how hopeless it is, then you'll come begging me to help you sell."

"I'll find a way."

Those words echoed in Joletta's mind long after she left the lawyer's office. Where they had come from, she had no idea. She had a little money saved, the money that was supposed to have gone on a house. Even if she added what would come to her from Mimi, it would not be nearly enough.

More than that, the thought of running Fossier's Royal Parfums, stepping into her grandmother's shoes, had never crossed her mind. Somehow, she had always assumed her aunt would do something, maybe bring in a manager, when the time came.

It wasn't going to happen. She would have to take over. But was it what she really wanted?

She had so recently taken charge of her own life, so recently stopped allowing things to happen to her instead of making them happen herself, stopped letting the people around her do what they wanted, walk in and out of her life without protest. Was it actually a decision, then, declaring that she meant to run the shop, or was she letting circumstances control her actions again?

She couldn't tell. And yet, what other choice was there?

It was the next morning that she was called to Mimi's house. The three women who worked in the perfume shop, and who had been keeping it going for the last few days, were upset; two of them were in tears. The shop and Mimi's quarters above had been ransacked during the night. Glass cases had been broken, perfume spilled, and pages ripped from the formula ledgers. Upstairs, antiques had been overturned, upholstery slashed, and the contents of drawers and cabinets thrown into a heap like so much trash. The destruction looked deliberate, the result of frustrated rage. The explanation seemed obvious also. Someone had been searching for the formula, but had not found it.

Who could it be, except her aunt?

Joletta acquitted the older woman of doing the actual damage. She must have hired someone to come in the night while the shop was empty, professionals with special knowledge of where things could be hidden and no sentimentality about fine old furnishings. That Aunt Estelle could set such people loose on her own mother's belongings was sickening.

Joletta, standing in the middle of the mess, looked down to see the miniature of Violet Fossier at her feet. She knelt slowly to pick it up. The frame was bent; the canvas had buckled and the oil paints were cracked and flaking. As she stared at the face of the woman in the small portrait, it seemed she could see gentle reproof in the painted gaze, and also a challenge.

Pain shifted under the anger that simmered inside Joletta, almost as if a real person had been injured. She felt such a kinship with Violet since reading her journal. She had devoured the closely written pages in a few short hours, and wished for more than the brief chronicle of desire and deception, love and loss.

As she stood there with the miniature in her hands, an idea began to form in her mind.

Violet had found the perfume she had named Le Jardin de cour in Europe; the journal detailed how she had come to own it and even how she happened to begin making it. Was there a chance that by visiting some of the same countries and scenes that Violet had seen, Joletta might be better able to make sense of any formula that was hidden within the journal's pages? Could it be possible that by following in Violet's footsteps, using the journal as a guide, she might see a pattern, some arrangement of scented flowers and numbers that bore a resemblance to what she knew of the ingredients in the old perfume?

Violet had been religious about describing the particulars of her journey. She had set down the exact distance covered each day and the time spent moving from one destination to another, had recorded the heights of buildings and bridges and mountains and the lengths of rivers and streams. She had given the sizes of ships and carriages and trains, of rooms and pieces of furniture, and the number and descriptions of paintings and statuary viewed in famous churches and old houses. In addition, she seemed to have mentioned every flower she saw blooming in every garden in five different countries, and had made drawings of most of them.

Joletta had not been able to decide if Violet simply enjoyed minute detail, if she had been afraid she was going to forget everything if she didn't write it down, or whether there was some significance to it all. However, the fact was that numbers were vital to the notation of perfume formulas. Most perfumers referred to separate essences, or their own special combinations of essences, by number rather than name, while the formulas themselves were set down in ratios or percentages.

The urge to travel, to get away, had been strong in Joletta since she had read the first few pages of the journal, pages where her great-great-great-great-grandmother spoke of her fervent joy at the prospect of leaving the numbing routine of her days behind and seeing new places and beautiful new things. The words had struck a response inside Joletta. As the pain and loss of Mimi's death sank in, she felt a growing need to get away from all reminders of it. At the same time all the things she knew—her job, her apartment, the unvarying cycle of her days—seemed dull and without interest. She was desperate for a change. More than that, she had been cheated of her promised honeymoon trip.

There was also the fact that it was spring. Though Violet had been abroad two years, the events covered in her journal seemed to have taken place in a single year's span, beginning in late spring of

1854 and concluding almost twelve months later, again in the spring. If Joletta acted at once, she could be in Europe at the same time of year that had been important to Violet, perhaps see some of the same flowers and trees blooming, the same greenery on the hillsides and crops on the farmlands.

Joletta noticed, suddenly, that her hands were trembling. It was no longer anger that gripped her, nor was it fear; it was excitement.

She would not let her aunt win. She wouldn't. She was going to decipher the formula, no matter what she had to do or where she had to go to get it. With the formula and the journal in her possession, she would be in a position of strength when the time came to make up her mind about what to do with the perfume.

She would go to Europe. She would go for Mimi, in an attempt to keep faith with the trust her grandmother had placed in her when she spoke to her about the diary. She would go to escape her aunt's maneuvering, at least for a short while. She would also go for herself. It would be a quest of sorts, a journey with a purpose. And if nothing came of it, at least she would have the memory of the trip.

It was raining when the plane landed in London, a fine gray drizzle that streaked back along the windows and spattered into the puddles on the tarmac as they rolled toward the gate. Inside Heathrow terminal, the cool, moist air smelled of damp wool, toasted tea buns, and a hint of saffron overlaid by the inevitable stench of jet fuel. Joletta, inhaling deeply, smiled.

England, she was in England. The sheer joy of it was a burgeoning pressure inside her. It was the first time she had felt the depression of Mimi's death lift more than a fraction, and it felt good. Until this minute the trip had been a goal and a duty. She had spent the short few days since she had booked it making arrangements for leave from her job, assembling a wardrobe, packing, and all the dozens of other details it took to be gone from her apartment for several weeks. There had been so much to do, so much to think about, that she had not been able to rest at night. Once on the plane for the late-evening flight, she had fallen into an exhausted sleep. This was the first moment that the trip had seemed real.

She had settled on a package tour. She might have struck out on her own if she had had any experience in traveling; as it was, she preferred to have someone else handle the arrangements so she could concentrate on the problem that had brought her. She had managed to find an itinerary that closely followed the route taken by Violet Fossier and her husband, Gilbert, so long ago, one that began in England, covered France and Switzerland, and ended in Italy. The main difference was that Violet and Gilbert had spent two years in their travels, while she would have to make do with considerably less.

The red uniform of her tour-group leader was a welcome sight. Joining a number of other American tourists, she allowed herself to be directed toward passport control and customs.

The lines were long. Joletta set her brown tweed carry-on bag at her feet while she searched in her shoulder bag for her passport. She looked up with it in her hand as a buzz of commotion began around her. Just beyond where she stood, there was a large group from some African country being ushered through the area by uniformed guards, the men solemn and the women intriguing in turbans and floor-length dresses of draped silk. A murmur of speculation began about refugees from yet another *coup d'état*.

There came the soft thud of quick footsteps on carpet just behind Joletta. As she swung her head a wiry young man in jeans and a ponytail slid past her. He bent without stopping and snatched up her carry-on bag.

"Hey!" she yelled, and launched herself after him. Stretching out her hand, she grabbed the strap of the bag and gave it a hard yank.

The young man jerked to a halt and swung around. His face twisted with malice and desperation as he drove his fist at Joletta's face. She saw the punch coming. She ducked away, but the blow caught the side of her head. It slid across her ear and the gold hoop earring that dangled from her lobe. She staggered back as her bag was ripped from her grasp.

Strong arms caught her from behind, arresting her fall. At the same moment the narrow-spaced eyes of the young man widened in alarm. He skipped backward and spun around. Fighting his way through the stream of refugees with the heavy bag dangling from his fist, he disappeared around a corner.

"Stop him," Joletta cried, pushing at the man who held her. "He's got my bag!"

The hold upon her remained firm, unbreakable. "Just let it go, ma'am," came the quiet advice from above her head. "Whatever's in it can't be as valuable as your safety."

She went still. Sandalwood. So clean and fresh yet so faint that it drew a person closer to inhale it. A shiver of awareness, acute and not quite comfortable, ran over Joletta. She straightened slowly, turning while the voice of the man echoed and reechoed in her ears. Her eyes widened as she saw his face.

"I don't believe it," she said, almost to herself.

"Try harder." Tyrone Kingsley Stuart Adamson IV made the recommendation with smiling irony before he went on. "I did a double take myself when I saw you get on the plane back in the States, but I never expected to be called on to do my gallant bit again. You all right?"

"Fine—I'm fine." Her answer was given automatically.

"Sorry I couldn't save your bag for you."

She gave a brief shake of her head. "It's all right, really. At least it will be until it comes time to brush my teeth."

It was a feeble attempt at nonchalance, but he accorded it the recognition of a nod. "I see you hung on to your passport; that's worth something. Let's get through customs, then I'll see you to your hotel."

She told him where she was staying, but pointed out that her tour group was providing transportation. He waved that away, saying that the buses would be long gone before she got through the headache of reporting the theft of her carry-on.

He was right. By the time Joletta had dealt with the endless explanations and the effort to remember every item in the bag for the paperwork, she wished she had written the whole thing off, not reported it stolen at all. There was nothing of any real value in it anyway. She had started to put the photocopy of the journal in, but decided against it since she wanted it closer at hand in her shoulder bag. The original she had left back in New Orleans, she hoped well hidden.

The rain had stopped and the sun was shining by the time she and Rone finally reached the city. To accept an offer for a combination breakfast and lunch seemed both practical and natural; it was difficult to stand on ceremony with a man who had heard a description of the extra nightgown and underwear she had packed in her carryon. Besides, he had been so helpful and understanding, and extended the invitation with such charm, that she couldn't think of any reason to refuse.

They dropped Joletta's luggage off at the hotel and picked up her key, then went on into the center of town. In a small restaurant with stained-glass windows, smoke-darkened wood paneling, and banquettes of green leather under florid Victorian wallpaper, they ordered rashers of bacon with scrambled eggs and a grill of sausages, mushrooms, and tomatoes, plus an unusual goat-cheese pizza.

"So," Rone said when the waiter had walked away, "are you just having a run of bad luck, or are you in trouble?'

It was a question that had occurred to Joletta. That her aunt might have set someone on her both in New Orleans and here was an idea so disturbing, however, that she didn't want to think about it.

"Bad luck, I suppose," she said with a wry smile. "I feel like the original green tourist after this morning."

He watched her for a long, considering moment, the light in his dark blue eyes assessing. Finally he said, "It happens. If anything else does, I hope you'll let me help you."

"I'll keep your rescue agency on file."

"I mean it," he insisted.

There had been a time when she had entertained the usual teen-age dreams of a protective knight. The man who sat across from her might well qualify; he radiated warmth and concern, and was even better looking than she had thought from their first brief meeting. The smile lines in his face were more pronounced and his hair an even darker and richer shade of brown. His suit was expensively cut and his shirt was of white silk. Regardless, he was a stranger, someone with his own problems. And Charles had cured her of foolish dreams.

She shook her head. "I appreciate your concern, but I'm on vacation, that's all. Everything's going to be fine."

"Knock wood," he said, then his lips twitched in amusement, "or maybe not. Your bad luck seems to turn out well for me."

"I don't think I want any more just on the off chance that you'll be around," she said, and rapped the table.

He sobered, then reached out to lift her hair away from her face slightly. "Do you know you're losing an earring?"

She reached up to touch the wide, eighteen-carat-gold hoop in the ear he indicated, then winced as she felt the soreness of the pierced hole in her earlobe. "It must have got in the way of that guy's fist. It's a good thing it did come loose."

"Let me fasten it for you." He didn't wait for an answer, but leaned close to take the hoop in his fingers and hook its gold wire closure into its catch.

He was so near that Joletta could see the way his lashes grew in thick, dark rows and the shadow of dark beard stubble under his skin. She was aware of an odd vulnerability. What he was doing was, in its way, an intimate thing; most of the men she knew would have run a mile to avoid it, or else have instantly become all thumbs at the mere idea.

The brush of his fingers against her cheek brought a small shiver of reaction and the memory of the touch of his lips upon hers. The deftness of his movements made her wonder, briefly, what other intimate tasks he might also be good at performing.

Heat rose in her face at such an unaccustomed mental detour. In an effort to combat it, she said, "You haven't told me why you're in England."

He gave her a direct look. "If I said you brought me, would you believe me?"

"Frankly, no," she answered.

"I thought not," he said on a sigh, though his gaze on the high color in her face was intent before he went on. "All right, the answer is business and pleasure; I decided to mix a little of one with a lot of the other."

"What is it, exactly, that you do?" She propped her elbow on the table edge and rested her chin on her palm as she waited for his reply.

"There are people," he said lightly, "who would tell you I do nothing at all, and do it very well."

"A playboy?" she commented doubtfully.

"Not quite."

"I thought not. I seemed to remember that you were in New Orleans on business."

"Ah, yes, I wasn't sure you would."

"That night stayed with me," she said with asperity. "It's not often I nearly get mugged."

"I thought, just for a second, that there might have been something else to make it memorable."

She gave him an inquiring look that was spoiled by the return of color to her face.

"I think you know what I mean," he said, propping an elbow on the table in his turn as he smiled into her eyes.

She was saved from answering by the arrival of their food. Rone sat back in his chair to allow his plate to be placed in front of him; still, she was conscious of his gaze upon her. When they had been left alone again, she was ready. Picking up her fork and attacking a mushroom, she said, "You were going to tell me about your job."

"Was I? Maybe I was at that. Actually, I deal in illusions."

"A magician?"

"I should have said filmed illusions."

"Right. A movie mogul then."

"Not exactly," he said with a wry grimace. "I produce commercials."

She wasn't sure whether she believed him; there was a mocking undertone to his voice that might have been directed at himself instead of her. Regardless, it was all too apparent that he was getting a kick out of teasing her. She said slowly, "Now, do you really?"

"It's a perfectly legitimate occupation."

"I'm sure it is, but I just expected you to be some kind of high-powered executive."

"Boring and restrictive. I prefer to be a free agent. Tell me again the places you mentioned to the police as being on your itinerary. I've just decided that I may need to visit them myself, maybe scout locations for a new European layout."

"Instead of a British layout, you mean?" she queried.

There was warm amusement and something more in his smile. "No, I don't mean that at all. The business that brought me here won't take long. But since I'm here, and so are you, I have this sudden urge to join forces, to traipse around behind you in your travels. Would you mind?"

She stared at him with her fork holding a bit of egg suspended in the air. His irresponsible attitude didn't sit right, somehow, with the forcefulness of his personality.

"Don't look so surprised," he said. "Have you never done anything on impulse?"

"I'm here with you at this moment. That's as close as I've come so far." She managed to keep the words light, though it wasn't easy.

"And even this is against your better judgment, isn't it?"

"Can you blame me? I don't know you any better now than I did the night we first met."

"At least I know your name now, even if I did have to get it off your luggage tags."

"That hardly counts."

"No, ma'am. I guess not, ma'am."

"Don't do that! I don't mind if you call me Joletta, really I don't. It's just that—"

"Right," he said with a shake of his head. "You're a conventional woman and you can't help it. So forget I said anything."

"Surely you didn't expect me to agree?" She should leave it alone, she knew, but something in his manner gave her the feeling that she had been too abrupt.

"There's always hope. But I'll say in my defense that I wasn't suggesting that I share your bed, or even your room."

The muscles in her abdomen tightened in pure reflex. Her voice tight, she said, "I didn't think you were."

"Good," he said, "I'm glad we settled that."

Was his voice a shade too affable? The thought that he might be laughing at her was an uncomfortable one. In an effort to retrieve the situation, she went on, "Anyway, you don't look to me like the kind of man who would be satisfied with a package tour."

"You would be surprised at what I can be satisfied with," he answered, his firm lips curving in a smile as he caught her swift upward glance. The bright look in his eyes dared her to comment.

She took the dare, though from a different angle. "Is that so? And I suppose you would just love an afternoon tour by double-decker bus, one that ends with a visit to the Tower of London?"

"Actually," he said with a judicious air, "a guided tour of the Tower is the practical choice. Advance ticket holders get waved in ahead of the regular tourists; you don't have to stand in line at the gates."

"Yes," she said heartily. "And I was thinking of a walk around Hyde Park first, for the exercise after sitting so long on the plane."

His gaze widened as he pushed back his plate. "All in one day?"

"I also had in mind getting to the park by the underground, just to see if I can figure out the system. No taxis."

"Right." His voice was hollow.

"I don't have much time to get everything in," she said, suppressing a smile. "Of course, I'll understand if you decide you'd rather not follow me around after all."

"Never crossed my mind," he said, the words deliberate as he waved a hand at her plate. "Eat up. We have to move fast if we're going to keep to the schedule."

She had been so sure he would back down. Now she was trapped into joining forces with him by her own badly timed levity. But what could it hurt, after all? They would be in public every step of the way, and far too busy for problems.

The biggest obstacle to completing her program was Rone.

He did his best to distract her with offers to rent a rowboat and row her about the lake in the park, or buy her a cup of tea and a cucumber sandwich for a picnic under the flowering horse-chestnut trees. He pointed out the unexpected color combinations of the pale, gray-white English office workers lying on the jewel-green grass and slowly turning lobster red in the unexpectedly warm afternoon sun. He lagged behind to listen to the doomsday preachers and anarchists at the Speaker's Corner, and insisted on taking a half-dozen photos of Joletta as she stood beside a thatched keeper's cottage where bluebells grew.

At the Tower, he whispered suggestions for making off with the crown jewels as they snaked past them in the endless queue. Falling behind the others as they looked at the ravens in the courtyard, ravens required by legend to remain in the Tower to keep it from falling, and England with it, he was all pity for the poor birds. They were, he said, modern prisoners suffering cruel and unusual punishment; because ravens mate on the wing, having their flight feathers clipped to keep them from leaving doomed them to celibacy.

Joletta laughed at him and did her best to ignore him by turns as she juggled her shoulder bag, camera, and notebook in the attempt to record everything she saw. She made careful notations of distances and times and anything else that could be numbered, from streets and roads to turrets in the Tower. It was some time before she realized that Rone, for all his foolishness, was helping her. He took over carrying the camera bag early in the day and often reached to hold the notebook when she was using the camera. Now and again he took her shoulder bag and slung the strap over his own shoulder when it appeared to be getting in her way. She was grateful, until she noticed him glancing over her notes, reading them.

As she took her shoulder bag from him outside the Tower once more, she gave him a long, direct look. He endured it for a moment, then lifted a brow.

"Yes, ma'am?"

"Nothing," she said after a moment, forcing a smile.

His helpfulness came from his ingrained courtesy, she thought, and it was no more than human nature that caused him to glance at what she had written as he held her notebook in his hand. That was all there was to it.

What else could there be?

They finished off the evening with steak and kidney pie and a bottle of cabernet sauvignon at a small restaurant in the West End.

Between them, they managed to involve two waiters, a busboy, and the cook in an argument over whether there was liver in the pie or if the kidneys themselves tasted like liver. There was apparently no answer to the question, and toward the end, Joletta discovered she was too tired to care.

Rone insisted on coming in with her when they reached the hotel. Joletta felt her stomach knot with tension as they neared her door. It had been a nice day; it would be a shame to have it ruined by a tussle over whether he could or could not stay with her.

She need not have worried. He opened the door for her and glanced inside. Swinging around, he held out her key. She reached for it, but he closed his fingers around it, retaining it for a long moment while he gazed down at her with somber consideration in his blue gaze. His lips tightened, then he gave a minute shake of his head and dropped the key in her hand. With a promise to call her next day and a quiet good-night, he was gone.

Joletta stood where she was when the door had closed behind him. He had not even tried to kiss her. For a moment she had thought—but no. It was surprising, after the way they had begun. But then, he was a surprising man.

Weighing the key in her hand, she attempted to decide if she was relieved or miffed. She didn't know; she really didn't.

Chapter 4

May 4, 1854

    Today I went shopping for kitchen toweling made of English linen as described to me by my cousin Lilith, who had found it at the emporium of Fortnum and Mason on her last voyage abroad. It was a trivial expedition, yes, but this toweling is all that Gilbert has so far permitted me to purchase. He suggested a subdued gray stripe before he left the hotel for a visit to the cabinetmaker. I ordered twelve dozen pieces in a bright blue plaid, and pray he may dislike them.

    Afterward, I was caught in the rain.

    How simple it is to write those bare words, but how confusing it was and how—I should like to say exciting, but that is not a state at all suitable to a staid married lady of six-and-twenty.

Violet wandered through the food courts of Fortnum and Mason, pausing now and then to look at the picnic baskets, the vanilla beans, or tins of tea, but refusing all offers of assistance. She would have liked to buy a few things, some cheese and wine perhaps, or a tart or jar of biscuits to take back to the rooms she and Gilbert had hired. She knew, however, that her husband would not approve. Gilbert was punctilious about appearances; he would be mortified if the hotel staff should think that he was pinching pennies by dining

46

in his room instead of going out to a restaurant. They were staying at Brown's Hotel, a hostelry established some years previously by Lord Byron's valet, a fact that was supposed to give it an added cachet. To Violet, it was merely stuffy.

Violet had felt somewhat conspicuous on the streets without her maid. The elderly black woman, Hermine, who always accompanied her when she so much as set foot outside the house in New Orleans, was laid down upon her bed with a chill brought on by the English climate. While it was true that most of the other women Violet saw were either in pairs or escorted by gentlemen, there was a goodly number of respectable-looking females who were alone. Certainly there were enough of them that Violet need not fear she was behaving improperly. There were compensations to being unchaperoned, she had discovered. She could move much faster on her own. And to be able to shop without Hermine looking over her shoulder, muttering disparaging comments and sighing over the weight of the market basket, gave her a lovely sense of freedom.

Leaving the store, Violet strolled along the street with no particular destination, simply enjoying the outing. She paused at a window display of souvenirs of Prince Albert's Great Exhibition, which had been held three years before, among which were cunning little boxes made of glass to represent the marvelous Crystal Palace and a brass trotting sulky like the one that had been exhibited by the United States. Entering a bookseller's shop to browse, she was tempted by an old hand-bound and beautifully illustrated booklet of William Blake's poems, but she came away without it. She had walked some distance when the sky began to darken and a dull rumble of thunder sounded overhead.

The parasol she carried had been designed to protect against the hot Louisiana sun rather than English rain. Its fringed silk was not only woefully thin, but was inadequate to cover the full spread of her gown over its crinoline. Violet looked around her for a hackney carriage, but there was none to be seen that was not already occupied. The native Londoners had been much quicker to note the change of weather than had she.

A chill wind blew up the street. It swayed her green silk skirts around her and swirled her sash of Balmoral plaid and also the matching plaid ribbons on her small jade velvet hat tipped forward on her high-dressed curls. She turned this way and that, in search of cover. A short distance away, across the street, was the arched marble gateway to a small park. There were great chestnut trees inside in full bloom with clumps of rhododendron under them that were footed by massed wallflowers. In the center was a cast-iron pavilion framed by the twisted trunks of ginkgo trees.

As the first spotting drops of rain began to fall, Violet put up her parasol, then lifted her skirts and stepped from the sidewalk into the street. Holding the flimsy sunshade before her to protect her face from the wind, with its freight of coal dust and bits of blowing straw from horse bags, she ran for the far side.

There came the clatter of hooves, followed by the shrill neighing of a horse and the agonizing squeal of a handbrake. A man shouted a curse and a whip snapped. Violet jerked her parasol aside to see a hackney looming down on her. The bewhiskered driver hauled on the reins while a powerful gray stallion reared up, almost on top of her.

Abruptly, an arm like an iron shackle fastened upon her waist. Her head whirled dizzily as she was half lifted, half dragged to the curb. The iron wheels of the hackney carriage passed inches away and she was buffeted by the wind of its passage. The curses of the driver floated back on the wind, mingling with the irate shouts of the gentleman passenger hanging out the window.

Between the hard grasp of the man's arm about her and the biting grip of her own corsets, Violet could not breathe. Shivering with reaction, her chest heaving as she tried to draw air into her constricted lungs, she stared with misted eyes at the cravat of the man who held her. The insignia on the gold pin that secured it, and the delicate fern design of his waistcoat into which it was tucked, did a crazed dance before her; still, she felt their patterns would be imprinted on her mind forever. When she was certain she was not going to faint from shortness of breath, she slowly lifted her gaze.

His eyes, that was what she saw first. They were so clear and kind and warm in spite of their crystalline blue-gray color. Set so the corners were turned down slightly, they were shaded by straight brows and edged by lashes so thick they gave him a secretive air. His cheekbones had a Slavic prominence on either side of a straight Roman nose. His jawline was square, and though his mouth was strongly molded, there was gentleness about its curves and smooth surfaces. He had lost his hat in the brief skirmish, and his close-cropped hair curled in wild, russet-brown disarray with the dampness and wind.

Violet, searching his face, grew aware of the heavy beat of his heart under her hands, which were trapped between them. The dark lavender-blue outer ring of her brown eyes darkened and her own fringe of jet-black lashes swept downward again.

She was released abruptly.

"Forgive me, my lady!" the man said, stepping back, holding his arms stiff at his sides as he inclined his head in a bow.

She had known he would speak with an accent, however slight, even before she heard him. "No, please," she said softly, "I must thank you."

"I beg you won't. What I did, it was nothing." He looked around him, his gaze lighting on his hat lying in the wet road with its crown crushed by a carriage wheel. Beside it lay her parasol with the handle in two pieces and its broken ribs poking through torn and fluttering silk. Around them, the rain began to quicken.

"Your umbrella is as useless as my hat, I think, or I would retrieve it for you."

"Please don't try," she murmured.

"No, but you must have shelter. Come."

With his hand on her arm, he pulled her with him toward the cast-iron pavilion. She went willingly enough, catching up her unwieldy skirts for the quick dash. Their footsteps skimmed over the wet grass, then they were pounding up the low steps and ducking under the water streaming down from the steep slate roof. Violet's skirts whirled around her, then settled as she came to a halt and turned back toward the open doorway.

It was amazing how dark it had grown there under the shadows of the trees with the closing in of the storm. The noise of the rain was like the rushing of a cataract as it assaulted the new spring leaves and pounded the grass, rattled on the slates overhead, and splattered on the pavilion steps.

Violet, watching the rain as if mesmerized, gave a small shiver and rubbed her arms with her hands. The chill came, she thought, from inside, for her arms were covered by the sleeves of her green velvet jacket with its peplum waist. There were drops of rain beaded on the velvet, and she stripped off her gloves to brush at them in distress. The fabric would be quite ruined and she had worn it no more than twice. Gilbert would not be pleased.

The man beside her spoke in low tones. "It is irregular, I know, but since there is no one to present me, perhaps you will permit me to introduce myself?" He inclined his head briefly. "I am Allain Massari, my lady, at your service."

"How could I be so ungrateful as to refuse to know you?" she said, giving him her gloved hand. "But you are not English, I think. French perhaps? Or is it Italian?"

Amusement sparkled in his eyes. "My mother was Italian and French; my father claimed no particular country as his own, but enjoyed many, especially England. I am many things, then, but prefer to think of myself as simply European."

Was that another way of saying that he had no right to his father's name, so had taken that of his mother? She could not embarrass him by asking. In any case it made no difference, since it was unlikely their acquaintance would be a long one. These thoughts ran quickly through Violet's head before she realized with a start that they were no longer speaking English. "Ah, you are very fluent in French, m'sieur."

"I felt you would be more comfortable. I am right, am I not?"

She assented, telling him of her Louisiana French background, before she went on. "And are you equally at home in Italian?"

"I have a lucky facility with languages," he said dismissively, then frowned a little as his gaze rested on her cheek. He reached to draw a handkerchief from his sleeve. "You will allow me one small privilege further?"

He touched her chin with the fingers of one hand, tilting her face toward the little light that was available. Using the handkerchief, he blotted the raindrops that stood on the skin of her forehead and the smooth planes of her face, and even those that clung to the ends of her lashes.

Violet knew she should have stepped back away from him or at least protested; instead she stood quite still. His hands, she saw, were beautifully shaped and well cared for, but carried hard ridges of calluses on the fingers and across the palms. They were the mark of one who practiced often with a sword. It was intriguing, that knowledge. She allowed her gaze to search his face, noting the strength of its bone structure, assessing his absorption in his task.

He accepted her quiet scrutiny, until, suddenly, he looked straight into her eyes.

What happened then seemed beyond belief, yet, at the same time, inevitable.

He let the handkerchief in his hand fall, so it drifted down to catch on her wide skirts, then glided in snowy folds to the floor. A softly whispered phrase that might have been a plea or an imprecation damning himself rose to his lips, though in what language she could not tell for the thunder of her heartbeat in her ears. With infinite care, he lowered his head and touched his lips to hers.

It was a kiss of such gentle sweetness, such reverence, that it touched her to the heart. She felt the rise of tears, tasted their saltiness, even as her mouth throbbed under his and her blood began to froth in her veins with the effervescence of champagne. She felt glorified, transfigured in some way, so that who and what she was no longer mattered. It was as if she had discovered a part of her that had been missing, as if that piece had just locked in place, so it could never be lost again. The only thing important was the moment, and the feelings that made it her own.

He raised his head, his gaze on the trembling, coral-pink softness of her lips. Slowly, as if exercising a perilous restraint, he stepped away from her until his back and taut shoulders struck the upright post of the pavilion. He turned from her then, grasping the post with one hand in a grip so tight that the tips of his fingers turned blue white with the pressure and the structure creaked somewhere in the metal beams above them.

"Forgive me," he said in ragged tones, "my manners—but I meant no disrespect, I swear it."

"Please, don't." Her words were so quiet he might not have caught them if he had not been straining to hear. "I—I was also at fault."

He shook his head. "You will think that I am a trifler who took advantage. It isn't so—or rather, it is, but it was not deliberate."

"I—realize." She glanced at his broad back, then back down at her clenched hands.

"Do you?" He turned to face her then, but kept his distance.

Her lips trembled into a smile. "I think that had you intended it, you—might have used more address."

Relief and laughter sounded in his voice as he said, "I would like to think so."

She met his gaze for a long instant. Turning slightly from him to stare out into the park, she said, "I am married."

There was a small silence before he answered. "I know. I saw the ring."

Violet looked down at her hand where a ruby surrounded by diamonds surmounted the shining gold circle on her finger, the traditional marriage ring of Gilbert's family. Closing her fingers into a fist, she folded her arms, tucking the ring away out of sight. At the same time a heated feeling moved over her as she wondered if she had assumed too much in telling this man of her marital status, as though it could make a difference to him.

He spoke again. "Where are you staying while in London?"

"Just a hotel," she said, without giving the name. "We will be here only a few days more before moving on to see other sections of Britain. Afterward, we cross the channel to France."

"Paris, of course."

She nodded her agreement. The quiet, made murmurous by the rain, which fell more gently now, stretched between them. She sent him a quick glance from under her lashes, but he seemed to be absorbed in some thought that made him frown. She swallowed. In stifled tones, she said, "My husband will be expecting me at the hotel. I should return as soon as possible."

"I will find a hackney for you when the rain stops."

"That would be very kind."

"No," he said, "only necessary, though I would prefer that it was not."

There was an odd, hollow finality in his voice. Still, he did not move for long moments. Nor did she. They stood gazing at each other instead with wide eyes and faces pale with strain.

Beyond the pavilion, the rain had begun to slacken. As the clouds moved on and the day grew brighter, the light took on an unearthly green cast, as if the misty atmosphere was made of atomized emeralds. Somewhere a bird called, a note of piercing supplication held achingly long. There was no answer.

He put her in a carriage a short time later. Violet gave him her address since it was necessary for him to call it up to the hackney driver. He stepped back then with a formal bow, perfectly correct, entirely respectful, though the gaze that held hers was dark gray with reluctance. Violet inclined her head in reply and lifted a gloved hand in farewell. As the carriage drew away she looked back to see him standing straight and still, staring after her.

Gilbert was not at the hotel after all when Violet returned. She was grateful for that small mercy. It allowed her time to change out of her damp velvet and silk with the help of a hotel maid, then send the costume to be dried and brushed in the hope of saving it. It also gave her a respite in which to ring for the tea she needed to banish the chill inside her, time to regain her composure while she drank it.

She was sitting in her blue wool dressing gown before a small coal fire in her bedroom fireplace when her husband returned. She set aside her cup in order to pour out tea for him. He came forward to press his lips to her forehead before turning his back to the fire and reaching for the refreshment she offered. He smelled of stale linen and smoke from the cheroots he knew she disliked. Unaccountably, her hand shook as she passed the cup over, so that it rattled in its saucer.

"Any success with the cabinetmaker?" she asked in haste to cover that moment of awkwardness.

"Very little. Most of the chests and sideboards being manufactured in England these days are designed for cramped little chambers like this hotel room. I cannot seem to make them understand that something on a more gránd scale is required for the higher ceilings and wider rooms of our Louisiana climate. They think in terms of low, closed spaces to combat cold rather than tall and open ones to escape heat."

"I would have thought that with the present interest in India, which has the same warm climate—"

"Ah, the English. They expect India to accommodate itself to their ways—which means their furnishings—rather than the other way around."

"But the beautiful screens and fabrics of the Eastern empires, not to mention porcelain ware and brass-inlaid tables, seem to be in fashion."

"Mere decoration, not furniture," he said dismissively. "I am thinking of looking for older pieces such as might have come from the large manor houses in the countryside. They should have a more workable scale."

"An excellent idea," she murmured since she knew it was what he expected.

He sipped his tea before he went on. "But it might be better to give up here and cross to France at once. With this war on, there is such confusion and congestion at the ports from the military supplies bound for troops in Turkey and the Black Sea that there could be serious problems in shipping furniture back to Louisiana. The general opinion seems to be that it can only get worse."

Her husband, Violet knew, was not displeased to be in Europe during this contretemps in the Crimea. He took a keen interest in the furor pitting the leaders of Great Britain, France, Austria, and Prussia against Czar Nicholas I of Russia, who was attempting to control the fate of Turkey, the country known as the "sick man of Europe." Each morning without fail, Gilbert went out for a newspaper in which to read the latest telegraphic reports on the war activities. The last news had been the disembarcation of British and French troops at the Black Sea port of Varna, sent to protect Constantinople from Russian attack.

"You think there will actually be fighting?" she asked.

"The English people seem to be caught up in the war spirit. It looks as if Aberdeen and his cabinet must order an invasion of the Crimea before summer to satisfy the public outcry, if for no other reason."

"An attack on the Russian naval base at Sevastopol?"

"Precisely." His answer was clipped short.

It annoyed Gilbert when she displayed too much understanding of subjects he considered to be in the male province. Violet knew it, still she persevered. "As England and France are allies, would we not have much the same problems shipping furniture from French ports?"

"Napoléon the Third is not so committed to depressing Russian pretensions in Turkey, therefore the French preparations for war are not as far advanced. There should be no great difficulty so long as we don't linger here."

Violet tilted her head. "I have no objection, of course; still, there is so much we planned to see, Bath and Brighton, the Lake District—not to mention Scotland and Wales."

"We can always return, perhaps late in the year, when war activities will slack off as the armies go into winter quarters. As for Bath, we can make a small detour in that direction. I believe that an opportunity for you to drink the water is of sufficient importance for the concession."

"Yes, of course," Violet said, though her voice was compressed.

"But what of your morning, *chère*?" her husband went on. "You found the toweling?"

She told him of her purchase, including a description of her near accident and the small garden where she had found shelter. She did not mention the man who had been with her. Gilbert was a sensitive man, one who understood, sometimes, more than was said. He was also capable of extreme jealousy. She preferred not to be forced to explain the events that had occurred in detail.

She found herself studying Gilbert as he stood before her. After nearly seven years of marriage, she still felt she hardly knew him. He was a rather remote person, one not easily given to confidences.

A part of the problem, she suspected, was the difference in their ages; Gilbert was some twenty years her senior. She sometimes thought he saw her as a child, someone who must be guided and directed in all things, protected from outside influences.

Gilbert Fossier was a wealthy man, owner of both sugar and cotton plantations, warehouses and steamboats, and a large block of land in the Vieux Carré of New Orleans. He had married as a young man, but his first wife had died from yellow fever in one of the many recurrent epidemics. He had devoted his energies to building his fortune, until he had seen Violet on her debut during a ball at the opera house. He had spoken to her father for permission to address her that same night.

Violet had not been opposed to the match. Though only seventeen, she was not frivolous. She had thought Gilbert distinguished, with his substantial form and jet-black hair that was dusted with silver at the temples. She had been flattered that a man of such power and wealth should choose her; she had been taught the value of such things from childhood. He had seemed wise and kind, assured and controlled compared with the clumsy, hotheaded young men her own age. She had accepted his betrothal bracelet with ready compliance and even a certain satisfaction.

But then had come her wedding night, and she had discovered that Gilbert was not controlled at all, that the mere sight of her in her nightgown could make him tremble. So great was his desire for her, and so fearful was he that he would fail to attain it, that he had pushed her down on the bed and taken her with painful, fumbling haste.

This performance would become more pleasurable for her in time, or so her mother told her. It had not. The few times she had thought she could feel the first stirring of response to her husband's passion, her tentative movements had driven him into such a frenzy that the exercise had been over before it well began. Her husband knew and regretted it, she thought, but could seem to do nothing to change matters. The result was that she had ceased to try to feel anything. She endured the brief mountings and was happy when she was left alone in her own bedchamber to sleep.

Regardless, she did not doubt that Gilbert loved her. His was an intense, possessive adoration that could make him rave for hours if she smiled at a man as he was introduced to her, or else bring him to kneel at her feet begging for reassurance if one happened to look at her twice as she passed by.

He was kind and generous, but could be dictatorial. He was

wise, but would brook no challenge to his knowledge. His self-assurance was certainly a part of him, but could become obstinacy if his authority was questioned. He had gained weight since their marriage, becoming rather thicker around the waist, while his hair had grown more gray and was sparser on top. His eyes, the light brown with splotches of green around the pupils known as hazel, had sunk further under his hooded lids, while their expression had become more cynical.

He was watching her now with heavy-lidded interest that might have been tainted with suspicion. She felt her heart jar against the side of her chest as she sought refuge from that look by concentrating on her teacup.

She had mistaken his expression.

He reached to take her tea from her, placing the cup and saucer on the mantel before he caught her hand and drew her to her feet beside him. "How intriguing it is to see you in your dressing gown in the middle of the afternoon, *chère*. I had thought you might be feeling unwell. I am delighted that it isn't so."

Violet's eyes widened as he touched the curve of her breast under the wool. "But Gilbert," she said in haste, "Hermine may decide to leave her bed and return to duty at any moment."

"She won't enter without permission."

"She'll think it strange if she finds us behind a locked door."

"What does it matter? Besides, she must know that this is one purpose of our journey, to have greater opportunity to get you with child."

It could not be denied. Hermine, a woman of lusty appetites, would no doubt approve wholeheartedly. She thought her mistress's nature was too cool, felt this was the reason she had not conceived.

The maid was also anxious for Violet to have a child because it would add to her consequence. It was already great enough as the maid to the wife of the master, but it would add that much more luster to her position if Violet also became the mother to the heir of the Fossier fortune. After so many barren years, Hermine's hopes had begun to lag, until plans were made for the European sojourn. She was sure that a course of the waters at Bath, or at Wiesbaden in Germany, would assure the outcome that was nightly in her prayers. If not, there was always Lourdes as a last resort. Hermine had great faith in water and shrines, particularly if Gilbert did his part. The last, she told Violet without even the hint of a smile, was essential.

Violet herself was just as anxious to have a child. It would give her someone to love, a warm, sweet, tiny being who would love her in return without conditions. Caring for it would fill the emptiness of her days, and perhaps give her reason to avoid Gilbert's visits in the night.

Her husband led Violet away from the fire and over the Brussels carpet strewn with cabbage roses to the heavy bed of rosewood with its brown-gold silk hangings. He unfastened her dressing gown and slowly stripped it from her, leaving her underwear. As she mounted the low steps and settled on the mattress, he quickly removed his coat and trousers and half boots, tore loose his cravat, and shrugged from his waistcoat and shirt. Still wearing his underdrawers, he bounded up beside her.

Obedient to his will, Violet lay still while he slipped the tiny buttons of her camisole from their holes and spread the edges wide. She felt his hot lips at her breasts, suckling, nibbling with hurtful, stinging persistence. As she made a slight sound of protest he jerked the tape of her own underdrawers free and slid them down her hips.

Quickly, he covered her, letting his male member protrude through the slit in his underdrawers as he thrust between her legs for his entry. She moved to accommodate him to spare herself pain. His quick and jerky movements above her made the bed creak in its frame and set the bed ropes to jouncing and the curtains to swaying. Then, almost before he had begun, Gilbert put down his head and clamped his mouth over hers while he pushed himself into her to the greatest depth with a hard shove of his hips.

Violet could not breathe, could not move for his weight. In discomfort and the grip of despair, she saw, suddenly, in her mind's eye, the face of Allain Massari. Tears came then, rising up from some well of desolation inside her that she had not known existed. They crowded under her eyelids, seeking release. As she made a silent cry of his name, heard it echoing in her mind, the moisture burned its way out and seeped slowly into her hair.

The following morning there was a spray of lilac on the breakfast tray that was delivered by the hotel maid and left outside the door of the bedchamber. Hermine brought the tray to Violet where she lay in bed, then moved away to pull back the draperies over the windows.

Gilbert, an early riser, had already gone out for his newspaper and morning walk. He would breakfast elsewhere, since he had fallen in with the English habit of hearty fare for the morning meal and their hotel could supply no more than a simple repast.

Violet sat up and surveyed the warm rolls and butter with coffee that was her morning habit. She would have preferred café au lait, but it appeared such a thing was not to be had in London, and so she contented herself with pouring extra cream into the weak brew.

She was stirring the cream into her cup when the lilac blooms aroused her curiosity. Putting down the spoon, she picked up the spray of flowers. It was softly lavender and still damp with dew, and the scent that rose from the hundreds of tiny, individual blossoms was as clean and sweet as the first breath of spring. She lifted the spray to her face to fill her lungs with the fragrance while a small smile of pleasure curved her lips.

It was only then that she saw the note that had been tucked under the lilac.

It was unlike Gilbert to be sentimental. She picked up the piece of paper with something like embarrassment, holding it a moment before she quickly broke the small, almost indecipherable seal.

The note was not from Gilbert.

There was no signature and no message beyond a few lines of poetry written in strong, black script.

> Love's language may be talked with these;
>> To work out choicest sentences
>>> No blossoms can be meeter;
> And, such being used in Eastern bowers,
>> Young maids may wonder if the flowers
>>> Or meanings be the sweeter.

She knew the poet, the lady author who had written the *Sonnets from the Portuguese*, Elizabeth Barrett Browning.

She also knew the meaning hinted at in the poem.

Searching the tray with care, she found the wax seal she had broken. Gathering the bits, she carefully fitted them together again. Yes. The insignia of the cravat pin she had noticed yesterday, the one worn by Allain Massari. He had impressed its design, one of a phoenix within a coronet of laurel leaves, into the wax as a seal.

Yes.

She took a deep, shuddering breath and let it out slowly, then caught her bottom lip between her teeth. He had remembered her hotel, had discovered the room she shared with Gilbert. He must have been somewhere outside the door only moments before, perhaps persuading the hotel maid to allow him to leave his token on the breakfast tray.

Oh, yes, she understood.

A spray of lilac.

In the language of the flowers so beloved by Shakespeare in his time and favored more recently by the Romantics, lilac had special meaning.

It stood for First Emotion of Love.

Chapter 5

Four days later Violet followed the porters carrying her trunks and boxes down the last flight of the hotel stairs and into the lobby. Gilbert had instructed her to wait inside while he supervised the loading of their baggage into the dray that would take it to the railway station, and also located the carriage he had ordered for their own transport.

"You are certain we left nothing behind, Hermine?" Violet said to her maid who trailed behind her.

"Yes, mam'zelle," Hermine said, her round, dark face patient. "I looked with great care."

"You packed my nightgown that was left in the dressing room?"

"Yes, mam'zelle. And I have the case with your scents and lotions and pomatums and also the box with your jewelry. Be calm; we have everything."

The voice of the maid was soothing and also a little weary. Violet felt a pang of remorse. Hermine was feeling better, but still had a hacking cough from her chill; it was unfair to fret her. Violet's jitters over packing and leaving the hotel this morning were unusual. She was ordinarily more composed about the business of travel.

She had not been herself for several days. For one thing, her monthly courses were upon her and she was not happy with this proof that she had failed yet again to conceive. Also, Gilbert had refused to put off leaving because of her indisposition, saying the tickets had already been bought, and besides, riding in a railway car could be no more fatiguing than sitting in a hotel room. He seemed to have little comprehension of the potential difficulties and embarrassments in attending to her needs in the cramped toilet facilities provided on trains.

It was also true that she felt a distinct reluctance to leave London behind. She had been forced to admit, when pressed by her husband, that she had seen the important monuments and historical exhibits, had visited the major museums and art galleries, and had drunk a sufficiency of tea. She could give no logical reason, therefore, for her wish to stay on.

Regardless, she knew why. It was simply a reason Gilbert was not likely to accept. She didn't, in truth, find it acceptable herself. There was no earthly good that could come of a respectable married lady keeping anxious watch for a man she had seen once in a rain-swept pleasure garden.

She couldn't help it. She had scolded herself for continually thinking of those few idyllic moments and vowed a dozen times that she would stop. She had told herself she was being foolish, that the incident had meant nothing to Allain Massari except a diverting flirtation. She had tried to be dutiful and pleasant toward her husband and find satisfaction in the long years that stretched before the two of them as man and wife.

In spite of everything, her mind returned again and again to the words that had been spoken between Allain and herself, to the look on his face as he held her and the desolation in his eyes as they parted.

She had kept the lilacs though they were limp and faded; they were in the case Hermine carried, pressed in her journal on the page where she had written every meaning for flowers that she could bring to mind. And she had pinned the bouquet of pansies that had been on her tray this morning to the lapel of her traveling cape.

Pansies, which meant You Are in My Thoughts.

At the far end of the room, beyond the circular ottoman seats and potted palms that marched in a line down the middle of the lobby, a gentleman stood with his back to her while he spoke to a liveried servant. He held his hat of fine nut-brown beaver in one gloved hand at his side. His camel's-hair coat, cut along the austere lines made popular by Victoria's consort, Albert, fitted his broad shoulders to perfection, while its collar and lapels of rich brown velvet gave it an added elegance. Even as he spoke he shifted his position, turning his head slightly, half smiling, to stare for an instant in Violet's direction.

Allain.

Violet drew in her breath as a small shiver moved over her. The look he had given her was fleeting, the briefest possible appraisal from under his lashes across the busy lobby; still, Violet felt it as the most intimate of greetings. It said to her that he had been watching for her, had been aware she was there from the moment she arrived, and that he took pleasure just from the sight of her.

A flush began at the soles of her feet and rose in fiery heat to her hairline. She could no more prevent herself from smiling than she could have stopped the swift beat of her heart. A sweet, insidious joy invaded her senses, singing in her veins, though she lowered her gaze to the carpeted floor to hide it.

Dear God. This would not do. It was wrong, it was foolish.

It was also wonderful, as if she had wakened to delight after a long and dreamless sleep.

The need to speak to Allain Massari was urgent inside her. Surely there could be no harm in a final farewell. Their lives that had touched so briefly would part here, and that would be the end of it. One day she would do no more than smile at the memory of her innocent London escapade.

"Stay here a moment, Hermine," she said, "and I will see what is keeping Gilbert."

She moved down the room with her skirts whispering over the carpet and dipping gently around her. She reached to touch the cluster of pansies she had thrust into a tiny pewter flower holder with a minute amount of water and pinned to her lapel. As she neared the group of men where Allain stood, she placed her thumb on the catch of the flower holder and pressed hard. The small bouquet came free and tumbled to the floor.

She stopped with a low cry of feigned surprise, then bent as if she would kneel to retrieve the flowers.

Allain was quicker. He stooped to scoop up the pansies, presenting them to her with a bow of impeccable grace.

"Thank you," she said in almost inaudible tones. "I had hoped you would—"

"I know, and I am all admiration for your cleverness." Laughter made his eyes bright as he met her gaze. "I was at my wit's end, trying to devise a way to approach you."

Her smile in return was fleeting and troubled, though she was warmed by his instant understanding. She said, "I only wanted to say good-bye. We leave for Bath today for a fortnight. Afterward, we are going straight on to Paris."

"Ah, so soon."

She nodded. "The war preparations—"

"Yes." He paused, then went on in hesitant tones. "I have been thinking about your sojourn in Paris. I wonder—has your husband given any thought to having a likeness of you made while you are in the city?"

"A likeness?" Her gaze was alert.

"A portrait. What better place to have it done? I can recommend Delacroix as an artist. He is not only gifted in portraiture, he also happens to be a valued friend of mine as well."

"Delacroix? But he is renowned for his scenes of war and—and odalisques in the harem." There was a trace of disapproval beneath the puzzlement in her voice.

"Indeed. But he does portrait studies when it pleases him. He is secure in his profession—he's the natural son of old Talleyrand, you know, so official patronage has always been his, leaving him free to pick and choose. It's true that he scorns to paint vapid society ladies, so you may have to go to his studio to persuade him. Once he has seen you, however, he will be enthralled."

"You frighten me," she said, her voice not quite steady.

"It was not my intention," he answered quietly. "It would never be my intention."

She drew a quick, painful breath against the constriction in her chest. "Yet if—if our paths should not happen to cross again after all, would you believe, please, that I wish you good fortune?"

He was silent a moment, then he shifted his shoulders in a slight shrug. "Good fortune? Good-bye?" he repeated musingly. "Such words, *cara*, are far too final for us."

He took her hand, saluting it with the lightest possible brush of his lips and with promise in his eyes. Releasing her, he turned away with precision just as Gilbert strode into the lobby. By the time her husband had made his way to where she waited, Allain had moved to the desk of the concierge, where he was apparently immersed in an amicable and familiar discussion with that individual.

"Who was that speaking to you?" Gilbert asked with a quick glance in Allain's direction.

"No one," Violet answered without looking at him as she refastened the holder of pansies. "Just a gentleman kind enough to retrieve my flowers for me when I lost them."

A scornful expression passed over her husband's face as he surveyed Allain's elegant form, but he said no more. Raising a hand to beckon Hermine toward them, he took Violet's elbow to guide her from the hotel.

Just before she passed through the portal, Violet looked back. She should not, she knew, but she could not help herself.

Allain was watching her. He lifted his hand in the graceful gesture, placing it over his heart as he inclined his head in the most minute of bows. There was yearning in the somber cast of his face, and doubt. But there was no resignation.

He, Allain Massari, was a fool. It was criminal of him to continue to seek to involve himself with the beautiful American lady; he should be shot for his thoughtlessness, if not for his effrontery. But she was so sweet, so lovely, and had fit so perfectly into his arms. He could not help himself.

He would protect her, at all costs, but he hated having to be so careful. He would like to simply drive away with her, take her to Venice. There, in a palazzo with the moonlit waters lapping on the old stones below a window open to the soft air from the lagoon, he would—

But no. It was impossible.

If it was only the husband in the way, he might dare.

There was also this other business. He wanted no part of it; what need had he for such complications, such a dangerous undertaking? These fools who sought to persuade him would not believe it. They had involved him whether he wanted it or not. Or perhaps it was his father who had involved him, long ago.

He would disentangle himself. Then who could say what might happen? It depended on what transpired in Paris. And that depended on the will, and perhaps the courage, of Violet. What a fine name for her, his shy and sweet lady of the flowers. Modesty, yes, so it meant, his Violet. But she had no need of it. None at all.

Bath seemed dreary to Violet, though it might have been the rain that fell without ceasing, making it impossible to walk about the town as she would have wished. Regardless, she drank the requisite three glasses of the warm, mineral-tasting water every morning in the pump room with Gilbert at her side to be certain she did not skimp on the fullness of them. She dipped her fingers into the King's Bath, saw the head of the goddess Minerva, and was shown some of the tombs of those whom the water had not cured. She admired the abbey with its lovely fan vaulting, viewed the remains of the old Roman aqueduct, and was driven past the Royal Crescent and also the homes of notable past residents, including the exiled Louis Napoléon, who was now Napoléon III. None of it could hold her interest for long.

Everything irritated her, from the cool dampness that made her shiver and the food without noticeable seasoning to the measured drone of her husband's voice as he read to her from the guidebook he had purchased. In fact, nothing about Gilbert pleased her: the way he combed his hair with slatherings of pomade made it lie too flat to his head, the noise he made as he drank his coffee embarrassed her, and the methodical and endless round of trivial tasks he performed each night before he got into bed set her teeth on edge.

The reason for her state was perfectly apparent, or would have been if she could have brought herself to admit it. She refused. A well-brought-up young woman, once she was wed, did not look at another man, did not think of another man or dream of another man. To compare the person she had married with any other male was vulgar and degrading to both her husband and herself. Women of her kind were expected to devote themselves to their homes, their children, and the extended circle of their families, and to seek solace for any lack in their lives in the rites of the church. She knew the code, had heard it propounded and repeated her life long; it was unthinkable that she should break it.

Yet the endless round of her days made her want to scream, and the nights brought her to the edge of rebellion.

Gilbert, once her monthlies had passed, seemed determined to test the supposed efficacy of the Bath waters for conception. He not only came to her each evening without fail, but remained with her through the night, waking her as often as he was able. Her body grew sore from his repeated usage, her spirits sagged, and dark shadows appeared under her eyes from lying sleepless, thinking, waiting for the next onslaught. She prayed that her husband would become exhausted from his efforts, prayed that he would have the kindness to understand her lack of ardor and spare her, prayed that she might conceive quickly so she could plead the illness of pregnancy to escape his attentions.

Praying did not help.

Then one night she discovered something that did.

Gilbert had reached out for her, closing his hand over her breast. As she felt the heat of his touch the image of Allain flitted through her mind with the vague question of what it might be like if the hand upon her was his, if it was he who lay beside her. She wondered how he would touch her, if he would speak low in her ear, what he would say and do as they lay together on the bed. As Gilbert reared above her she pretended that it was Allain who parted her thighs, whose strength and warmth she took inside her, whose arms held her in a rocking embrace.

She gasped in the sudden intimation of pleasure then, moving by instinct with the rhythm of the joining. She continued moving for long seconds after Gilbert had stopped, seeking some nebulous joy that remained just beyond her reach, just beyond true comprehension.

He rolled from her abruptly, lying in absolute stillness on the mattress. Then he twisted around, sliding from the bed. His footsteps padded across the floor in heavy retreat. The door of the connecting bedchamber closed behind him.

Violet lay staring into the darkness, waiting for her breathing to quieten, waiting for guilt to make its way through the turmoil of her emotions to reach her. It did not come. Slowly, her lips trembled into a smile. The tears came then, rising from a well of desolation deep inside that she could deny no longer.

By morning she was composed again, and though her face was pale, there was a new firmness in the way she held her head, a new directness in her gaze. As she sat at the breakfast table with Gilbert, presiding over cold buns and lukewarm coffee, she sought for a way to bring up the subject in her mind. He gave her no openings; he was singularly quiet, almost ill at ease in her presence. At last, seeing that he had nearly finished making his meal, she spoke.

"I have been thinking of Paris this morning. You know, I suddenly have such a longing to be there."

"Only a few days ago you were reluctant to leave England," he objected.

She managed a light laugh. "Indeed. Fickle of me, isn't it? But I have decided that French furnishings will exactly suit me, if you can find them. How lovely it would be if we could be on our way today."

"That isn't possible." Gilbert looked at her closely, then away again. He took a long, black cheroot from his pocket and sat turning it in his fingers, though he did not light it.

"Tomorrow, perhaps, then? Everyone in New Orleans talks of Paris and its wonders. Everyone seems to have been there except me, and I'm tired of only hearing about the shops, the theaters, the gaiety of the court under Napoléon and Eugénie; I want to see them for myself. I can't wait to walk on the Rue de Rivoli or in the garden of the Tuileries. And I would adore having my portrait done."

"You might have mentioned a likeness earlier. I could have arranged to have one of the new collodion photographic images made of you while we were in London."

"But they have no color," she protested, "and they are so stiff and small. I would much prefer to have a portrait."

"It would take time," her husband said in heavy objection. "It might be better done in New Orleans; there are any number of painters in the city who would be happy to have the commission."

"Mere daubers," she said in a ruthless condemnation of which she was far from certain. "I'm sure you would not like to hang a mediocre likeness in the beautiful salon you are planning."

Gilbert pursed his lips. Wrapping the front of his dressing gown of gray brocade closer over his chest, he said only, "I believe there's a draft coming from the windows. I'll have a cold."

"No doubt," she answered guilelessly. "English weather is notorious for being unhealthy, is it not? But about the portrait; I was informed that Delacroix is the finest artist in the city, though I suppose it would be useless for you to try to engage him. I understand he is discriminating in the clients he accepts."

"I'm sure that he would not be so discriminating as to refuse my money," Gilbert said with testiness overlaid by irony.

Violet hesitated, secretly aghast at her own deviousness. She could sense that only a little more was needed, however, if only she could find the right words. She lowered her lashes. "I believe the man is also shockingly expensive."

"The best usually is."

"He may not be in Paris past the spring. Some say he is a great traveler, with a preference for new and different locales for his landscapes."

A thoughtful frown drew Gilbert's brows together, then he

shrugged. "There is something in what you say. Perhaps we should move on after all."

Violet kept her eyes lowered as she lifted the coffee carafe with a graceful gesture to pour the last of the weak brew into her own cup. Her reply was soft. "It shall be as you choose, of course."

Gilbert hitched his chair closer. Reaching out as she set down the carafe, he took her hand. "I will be just as well pleased to be in Paris. I was there as a young man and enjoyed it tremendously; I know it will be congenial to you. As for the portrait, it will give me pleasure to have one of you, *chère*, just as you are now."

Compliments did not come easily to her husband. She was touched in spite of herself, torn between a reluctant affection and remorse that she could feel no more. At the same time, however, she felt strangely remote from him. She had changed in some basic fashion. Because she no longer cared what he thought of her, because she had learned that she could influence his actions by willful design, she had escaped his dominion. She was, in some small degree, free.

Chapter 6

Rone, trailing Joletta at a respectable distance through the underground maze of the museum at Bath, thought that it was possible he had found his calling. He liked following women, or at least this woman. It was no hardship whatever to check out the natural, athletic swing of her walk, the way her hair shone in the dim lights of the subterranean baths, or the pure line of her profile as she stood gazing at the display of the head of the goddess Minerva.

She wasn't your usual tourist, skimming quickly through exhibits and points of interest while on the way to the shops and restaurants. Joletta stood and read signs, she made notes on a pad she took from her ridiculously large shoulder purse, and now and then she stopped and closed her eyes for an instant, as if listening to the trickle and rush of the waters that had been flowing under and through Bath for centuries. The expression of fascinated pleasure on her face caused a strange stirring inside his chest. He wondered what it would be like to recreate that look in a different, more intimate setting, bringing it to life with his own urgent touch.

He had come so close to taking her in his arms the night before. It had been all he could do to force himself to step away from her and take himself out of her room. He had no right to do more.

Even if he had the right, it would have been dumb. Impulses like that, as enticing as they might be, were not likely to help his

mental alertness. He needed to keep his mind on the job. One way
or another.

At the underground pool known as the spring of Minerva, he
saw Joletta take out a coin and, like countless others before her,
beginning with the Romans, fling it into the rippling pool.

Moving without haste to stand at Joletta's shoulder, he said,
"Did you make a wish?"

She turned her head with startled inquiry in her eyes. An instant
later a smile curved her mouth. "Of course," she answered.

"To Minerva?"

"It seemed the thing to do. There's something pagan about the
place, don't you think?" Her gaze was a little challenging.

"I expect to see the shade of some old Roman any minute now,"
he said.

"I'm sure," she said in dry recognition of the humor in his gaze
before she went on. "What are you doing here?"

"Watching you." He had not intended to say that, but since it
was perfectly true, he let it stand.

She gave him a quick, questioning look, then apparently decided
to treat his comment as mere banter. "Have you no appreciation for
history and culture, not to mention mythology?"

"You're much more interesting," he answered, on his mettle.
"I'm also trying to place the perfume you wear. Tea Rose, isn't it?"

She shifted to face him, giving him her full attention. "How did
you know?"

"I have a good nose," he said, and was immediately aware of
how dangerous those words could be.

"You must have also smelled a great many kinds of perfume.
I'm amazed."

He looked away from her as he said, "Actually, it was a fluke.
I—had a great-aunt who liked old-fashioned perfumes. My mother
gave her Tea Rose every year for Christmas."

She lifted a brow. "Are you suggesting my taste in perfume is
old-fashioned?"

"Good Lord, no!"

"No?" The look in her eyes was teasing. "You know, men don't,
as a rule, have quite as sensitive a sense of smell as women. When
you find one who does, you tend to take notice."

"I'm glad there's something about me that interests you," he
returned, then went on before she could say something depressing.
"I suppose you're with a tour group again?"

"In a manner of speaking. I came with a group on the bus, but we've been turned loose on our own until after lunch. You came alone?"

"Rental car," he said in agreement and explanation. "Would you mind if I joined you for lunch? I'll spring for the meal as an inducement." He gave her his most boyish smile.

"Now, how," she said with a lifted brow, "could I possibly refuse an offer like that?"

Rone thought of a bright answer, but decided not to press his luck.

An hour later Joletta lay stretched out on the grass with her face turned up to the sun. Her thoughts drifted back and forth between the past and the present, between the man who lay beside her and her own ancestress who had once passed this way.

It was too bad the weather had been so dreary when Violet had been in Bath; she might have found it more to her liking. Or maybe not. The company a person saw places with made a lot of difference.

Rone was a surprisingly pleasant companion. He was not only ready to see whatever there was to be seen without complaint, but he could make her laugh. He had said that it was impossible to understand the mentality of a people who had allowed Roman innovations such as self-cleaning bathrooms and steam heat to fall into disuse. He had also been amazed at gentry so at loose ends that they let a land speculator and ex-gambler like "Beau" Nash become social arbitrator of Regency Bath, dictating how they entertained themselves while in the town.

It was Rone who had chosen their food, from the Sally Lunn buns with cheese and the hot meat pies to the apricots that he claimed would be perfect with a bottle of Veuve Cliquot champagne. He had sworn that he would treat her to a five-course lunch at the pump room if she didn't like his menu, but there had been no need. The buns were yeasty and light, the meat pies suitably rich, and the flavor of the apricots had melded wonderfully with the champagne. Joletta even had to approve the setting he had found, a stretch of incredibly green grass they shared with a small flock of grazing sheep as fluffy and white as the clouds that drifted slowly overhead.

She didn't know why she was surprised to find herself enjoying Rone's presence. He had practically labeled himself a playboy, and men of that stamp made a career of being entertaining. Or so she had always assumed; she had never really met one.

Regardless, the idea of Rone being at loose ends, ready to forget his own obligations, was off somehow. He didn't seem the type; there was nothing lightweight or frivolous about him. The little he had said about his job made it sound unimportant and that was also hard to believe. Not that she thought him a hard-driving captain of industry; that wasn't quite right either. Why she should think so, she couldn't say; she was no expert on men and their occupations.

It was odd, but Violet had also known very little about her Allain. It had not been the thing, back in those days, to come right out and ask a man, "Hey, what do you do?" A gentleman did nothing; that was the whole point. Moreover, a man's status was supposed to be evident without a person having to ask. Life must have been full of pitfalls then.

Rone was so quiet, as he lay beside her, that she thought he had fallen asleep. She turned her head to look at him, allowing her gaze to follow the strong line of his jaw, the firm molding of his mouth, the wiry thickness of his brows. He was an attractive man, more attractive, even this close, in such clear light, than he had any right to be.

His features were relaxed, as if he had let the guard he kept on them at most times slip for a few moments. The lines at the corners of his mouth and beside his eyes were shallow, almost gone. He had shaved so closely there was a tiny nick at the indentation of his chin. His hands, well shaped, with square-cut nails kept short and scrupulously clean, were folded on his chest.

The hair around his ears and just above the collar of his shirt of soft gray pima broadcloth was perfectly trimmed. On his wrist was a flat gold watch by Juvenia with a severely plain face.

There was a neat and classical correctness about his grooming and style of dress that was curiously appealing. It was also, she thought, far from cheap.

As he opened his eyes to stare straight into hers, Joletta felt a small leap of her nerves. He had not, apparently, been as relaxed as she thought.

Wariness made his gaze opaque for an instant before warm appreciation surfaced there. He said, "Was I snoring?"

She shook her head. "Not at all; I was jealous. I'm still trying to recover from jet lag myself."

"Join me," he offered. "I've got a shoulder you can use for a pillow."

"Can't. Too much to see and do." She softened the refusal with a smile, at the same time aware of a pang of regret. The idea was amazingly enticing. To distract herself, she looked around where she was seated on their paper tablecloth for her guidebook, pushing aside a notebook and pen and a handful of tourist brochures to find it.

"I have to ask," he said, "what's with all the notes. You mentioned being a research librarian, I think. Are you doing some kind of paper on the monuments of Britain?"

"I just like details, and you never know when they might come in handy." She answered easily, since it was a question she had already heard a few times from the people on her tour.

"While I'm at it, it's also been puzzling me why you're traveling alone. There must be a man in your life who could have come with you."

She flipped the pages of the guidebook, giving it her attention as she answered, "Not really."

"No?"

"No."

He was silent a moment, as if analyzing the timbre of her voice. Finally he said, "You have something against men?"

"Why would you think that?" she asked, surprise standing in her eyes as she looked up.

"Most women your age, especially women who look like you do, are married."

"I was engaged," she said lightly. "It didn't work out."

"The guy was a jerk, right? And you wasted so much time with him, and were so wrong about what he was like, that you don't trust your judgment anymore."

She considered it for a moment. "I don't know about that."

"It's the only thing that makes sense."

Annoyance crept into her tone. "He might have died in an accident or turned out to be gay."

"But he didn't, did he? What happened?"

"We dated for six years, and were engaged nearly that long. He thought we should save for our future, you understand. Then he decided he would rather have a new convertible."

"Just like that?" Rone asked, frowning.

"Not quite, but close."

The description Rone applied to the man who had been her fiancé was short and profane.

"Exactly," she agreed.

"But just because he was a jerk doesn't mean all men are like that."

"I know that, thanks." The words were dry.

"But it doesn't help? Care to hear my sad tale?"

She gave a small shrug, her mind busy with trying to decide why she had spoken about Charles. As a rule, she never mentioned him.

Rone sat up and reached for the wine bottle. Dividing what was left in it between their two glasses, he handed Joletta hers and took a sip from his own. "My wife," he said evenly, "didn't stay around a full three years, much less six. She fell in love with her scuba instructor on a trip to Bora-Bora, and got involved with whale songs and Greenpeace and the fate of the oceans. She told me I was boring and my life was decadent before she went off to live with her beachboy in a grass shack on stilts."

"You made that up," Joletta accused him as she watched his face for the beginnings of a smile.

"I didn't. Word of honor." He held up a hand in a Boy Scout's salute.

"I don't believe it."

"She sent me a picture of the shack. There was a monster crab the size of a small dog that lived under the back steps, and they could swim off their front porch or catch aquarium fish from it for breakfast."

Joletta looked at the wine in her glass. "You don't sound as if you mind."

"I was a little hot for a while, but it passed. We both knew it wasn't working. If two people aren't right together, it's better to find it out after three years instead of thirty."

"I suppose," she said slowly.

"Tell the truth, do you miss the guy you were going to marry?"

"Not really, not anymore." She drank the last of her wine.

"Yes, and the sex couldn't have been that great, either. He sounds too self-centered."

She gave him a look from the corners of her eyes, but made no answer. He was more right than he knew.

"So forget him. He can only matter as much as you let him."

"I'll do my best not to go into a decline," she answered in dry tones.

They were still while the grass around them blew in the wind and the spring sunshine grew warm on their faces. Joletta let her mind wander, thinking of old relationships, not necessarily her own. And about cravat pins that modern men never wore. It was some time before she spoke again.

"Rone?"

His response was a few seconds in coming, as if he had to rouse himself from his own long thoughts to make it.

She frowned a little before she went on. "Do you know anything about the Foreign Legion?"

"The what?"

"The French Foreign Legion. You know."

"*Beau Geste*, holding the desert fort to the last man, all that Hollywood stuff?"

"I was wondering when it was established."

"The middle of the last century at least, I'd say, going by the movies. What year, I couldn't begin to guess."

A slow nod was her only answer as she narrowed her eyes in concentration. Rone set aside his empty wineglass. "Want me to find out for you?" he asked after a moment.

"No, no," she said with a quick smile, "it isn't that important. I was just—thinking about something I read—and about a ring I saw once in an antique shop, one with an insignia that I was told was a symbol of the Legion. The design was a phoenix, the bird that rises from its own ashes. But I can't quite remember if there was anything else around it, a coronet of leaves, for instance."

"You mean laurel leaves, like the old Roman victors?"

"I suppose," she agreed.

"I see the phoenix, for the renewed lives of so-called lost men. But I don't know about the rest."

"Never mind; it doesn't matter."

He sat looking at her with a suspended, almost bemused look in his eyes. She could follow his gaze as it touched her hair, the shape of her mouth, the curves of her body as she relaxed beside him, then returned to rest once more on her lips. Tension crept in upon them, holding them still. Joletta had the feeling that if she breathed too deeply, if she twitched a muscle or inclined her body even a fraction of an inch toward Rone, she would be in his arms.

The trouble was that she could not be sure whether the impulse was his or her own. Or whether she was wary of it or wanted it.

One of the sheep lifted its head and bleated.

A faint shiver ran over Joletta. She felt her heart give a small throb as she looked away. After a moment she glanced at her watch.

Rone drew back as he followed her gesture. "Yes, I know, time to play tourist again."

"Afraid so," she said, her voice subdued.

Joletta had thought that Rone might offer to drive her back to London, and she searched her mind for an excuse to refuse. She didn't need one after all. He returned her to the square where the tour bus was parked moments before the buses began to reload. His manner distracted, he said something about looking for a place to make a phone call, told her he would see her the next day, then turned and walked away.

Joletta was relieved, but she was also irritated. Shaking her head at her own lack of logic, she settled back for the bus ride. She meant to catch up on her notes, but spent most of the time staring out the window, watching as the bright yellow fields of blooming rape and squares of new-plowed ground, the hedgerows and manor houses of England, glided past.

It was later, while she was dressing to go out on a pub-crawling tour, that the phone rang.

"This is your twenty-four-hour information service," Rone said, his voice deep and shaded with humor as it came over the line. "I thought you might want to know that the French Foreign Legion was founded by King Louis-Philippe in 1831. Recruits, all foreign volunteers, sign up for five years; when they complete their hitch, they become French citizens. Names and pasts are forgotten, kept entirely secret. It was, and still is today, a mercenary force which swears allegiance, not to France, but to the Legion. Anything else you want to know?"

"The ring design?"

"Only a phoenix. No crown. Happy now?"

"Ecstatic."

"I'll be around early tomorrow. For my reward."

He hung up before she could answer.

Joletta overslept the next morning. It wasn't just because of the late hour she had returned to the hotel or the various kinds of ale she sampled at the different pubs, nor was it the walk around London's West End in the wake of their cheery, red-nosed Dickensian guide. She had lain awake for a long time after her return, thinking about Rone and the coincidence of his being on the same plane arriving in London, and also his persistence in seeking her out.

Such things did happen, of course, chance meetings, powerful attractions. Still, it bothered her. Her vanity was fairly healthy, but she found it hard to believe someone like Rone was so enamored of her that he would follow her around on the kind of touristy outings she was enjoying.

She need not have wasted her energy. When she hurried downstairs, breakfastless, he hadn't arrived. She kept watch for him until the bus for Westminster Abbey was ready to roll out of the hotel parking lot. When there was still no sign of him, she shook her head with a slightly crooked smile and went on as planned.

She missed him, missed having someone to exchange quips and irreverent comments with, someone to exclaim to or to soothe her complaints. In the afternoon, as she explored the terra-cotta splendor of Harrod's on her own, she discovered that wandering through the various courts with their molded ceilings and marbled splendor was not the same without him. Tea in the Terrace Room on the emporium's fourth floor was a fine way to satisfy the cravings caused by staring at the candy and cakes and cheese and bread below, but would have been better if Rone had been there to show her how to pour the Betjeman & Barton mango tea without knocking the silver strainer off the top of the small silver pot. And deciphering the mysteries of the London bus system on the way back to the hotel was a chore instead of an adventure.

He was also absent the following day.

Joletta was determined not to think about him; still, she would have liked very much to have someone to share her pleasure in the gardens and to listen while she moaned about how short her time was compared with the weeks Violet had spent wandering in them. She needed another person to help her rhapsodize over the massed plantings of rhododendrons and azaleas and the huge lilac shrubs in full bloom, and to understand why she stood bemused before great beds of vivid, windblown pansies.

She wanted to tell Rone about the journal.

It had been on the tip of her tongue that afternoon in Bath to explain to him about Allain and the phoenix ring, but some remnant of discretion had held her back. The impulse was crazy, she knew, and yet she thought he would understand and maybe even be able to help her search out its secrets. It would, at the very least, have been nice to have his unbiased opinion.

She wondered what he would think about the language of the flowers that Allain had used to such romantic effect. Would he consider it a gesture of charm and grace, or only corny sentimentality?

It was sentimental; she had to admit it. But what was wrong with that? It seemed that the Victorians of Violet's era, with their unabashed reveling in the heights and depths of their emotions, were less restricted, in their own way, than people were today. No one had time, now, for sweet and delicate indications of growing affection or for gentle enticements; no one risked their lives for love, or pined away for lack of it. Sentimentality had become an embarrassment. It was mushy and lacking in sophistication. It had been repressed, much as the Victorians had repressed sexuality. The situation was exactly reversed these days, so that love was now expressed as sexual attraction, with heavy breathing and the quick grab. It was depressing.

In a strange sort of way, Joletta envied Violet. Her ancestress had come to Europe in search of distraction and fecundity, and had found a romantic adventure. It hadn't been that way for Violet's descendant and her chance-met stranger. Joletta didn't know why; maybe it was her own fault. Maybe she should have been more open, more forthcoming. Maybe she should have grabbed.

It didn't matter, not really. She wasn't going into a decline for lack of love. In fact, she didn't need the complication of a man tagging along behind her when she crossed the channel to France the next day. She was just as well off without Rone.

As she strolled along the paths of Regent's Park, Joletta found herself turning often to look behind her, or else searching the faces of the people nearby. At first she thought she was, almost unconsciously, expecting Rone to appear. After a while she began to feel on edge, not quite at ease. There was a prickling awareness in the surface of her skin, as if she were making herself conspicuous, or else was being watched.

Her pleasure in the gardens evaporated. She put away her notebook where she had been scribbling descriptions of the running roses, clematis, wisteria, and other old-fashioned flowers that Violet had mentioned. She took a few more pictures of annuals in massed beds, but her heart wasn't in it. When a large group of schoolchildren came along, all in uniforms, she followed close behind them until she reached the gate. She headed then for the underground that would take her back to the hotel.

There was a note waiting for her at the desk. It was from Rone. She read it quickly in the elevator, then again more carefully once she had reached her room.

There was certainly nothing sentimental or romantic about it; it was, instead, brisk, slightly humorous, and matter-of-fact. He apologized for not appearing as threatened, but a business problem had come up, one that still required his attention. He had tried to call several times, but she was always out. He was keeping his fingers crossed for a smooth channel crossing for her, and he would catch up with her in Paris.

It wasn't exactly a kiss on the hand and a promise of a secret rendezvous. Joletta, struggling with a variety of feelings from gladness and amusement to irritation, shook her head. She wanted too much, no doubt. The question was, did she really want it from Rone Adamson?

She had had a late lunch, on top of which her body had not quite caught up with English time; going out to dinner seemed more trouble than it was worth. She had bought a little of the beautiful fruit and cheese and bread at Harrod's the day before. She would take a hot bath, read a little, nibble a little, and call it a night.

It was when she opened the drawer to take out her nightgown that she discovered her room had been searched. Her underclothes might be made of nylon and synthetic satin, but she liked them neatly folded, not in a rumpled pile. The books and pamphlets she had been gathering over the past few days were stacked wrong, and the clothes left in her suitcase had been rearranged, with the sweaters she was saving for Switzerland on top.

It might have been a maid exercising her curiosity, though Joletta thought the maids in most hotels were trustworthy. It could have been a petty thief looking for loose cash, or someone from a passport-theft ring; she had been told before she left home that American passports were worth several thousand on the black market. If it was any of these things, however, the intruder must have been disappointed. Everything valuable or interesting she had with her stayed with her every moment, either in her shoulder bag or in a safety pouch inside her clothing.

That included the journal.

She didn't want to think the journal might be the cause of the search, hated feeling that she would now have to be on her guard.

She had just begun to feel safe, to feel distant in time and space from her problems. She had begun to hope that the episode at the airport was a coincidence, that it had nothing to do with New Orleans. None of that was acceptable any longer. It was difficult to readjust her thinking.

It was even harder to admit that there was another connection between London and New Orleans, another unacceptable coincidence that had cropped up since her arrival.

That was Rone.

Chapter 7

She would always remember the poppies of Flanders, Joletta thought. One reason was their brilliant blood-red color as they lay in thick swaths between the green of the spring grass and the soft gray blue of the French sky, but the main cause was their tour director, who joined them with their Belgian bus and driver at Calais after the channel crossing. The director, a Welshman with a voice as rich and smooth as natural honey, read as they rode through the countryside from the poem "In Flanders' Fields."

Violet had described the poppies in her journal. Their hardiness in spite of their apparent fragility had impressed her, as well as their color. It seemed deeply satisfying to Joletta to think that she was seeing so much that her ancestress had also seen. That was the whole point of the trip, of course, but it was amazing how much was still there, still basically the same, from the old landmarks to the plants.

She had dreamed of Violet and her Allain since Bath, vivid, disturbing dreams that she could not quite recapture when she woke. In them it seemed that she herself was, somehow, Violet. Her subconscious at work, no doubt. She wished she could remember the details; it might well be helpful.

She was one of the few people on the bus who was traveling alone. Most of the others were retired couples who had escaped their children and grandchildren, or else honeymooners or widows traveling in pairs. There were two single men in their fifties, one a tall, thin professor of psychology who kept his nose in a guidebook, and the other a short balding travel writer with a great regard for his own crude jokes. Joletta had so far avoided the writer by pretending to be extremely sleepy, but she was afraid she might have trouble with him eventually.

Their tour director was fluent in French, Spanish, Italian, and German. He was pleasant and erudite, but his instructions concerning time spent at stops and payment of excursion fees definitely had something of the policeman about them. But he was good at his job, which was to make sure that the group got where it was going on time and that everyone enjoyed the trip.

The chestnut trees were blooming in Paris, not only the white, candlelike horse chestnuts, but also the rust-red Spanish chestnuts. They towered over the traffic of the motorway and lined the avenues in pruned perfection. The River Seine, as they crossed it to the Left Bank, wound like an iridescent ribbon of brown and green and blue under its many bridges, while buildings Joletta had only seen in photographs loomed above it in dingy limestone majesty.

The hotel was not large or grand, but was comfortably quaint, with a tiny lobby and white marble stairs that flanked an elevator the size of a broom closet. Joletta's room faced on the avenue and had twin beds with down coverlets and pillows set over extremely hard bolsters. The casement windows behind white lace curtains actually opened, exposing a minute balcony railed with decorative cast iron. The white-tiled bath had yellow fixtures, which included a bidet. Some of the tour group complained about the accommodations; Joletta was charmed.

There were, she supposed, still Fossier relatives living in Paris. Mimi would have known their names, would have written letters of introduction and insisted that Joletta deliver them. That wasn't the kind of stay that Joletta wanted; her time was too short for it. She had read and heard so much about the famous sights of Paris that she was hungry to see them, to touch them, to stand in the middle of them and know that she was there. She would enjoy as much of Paris as she was able in the time available, and hope someday to return for the rest.

On the morning of the third day, she left her hotel, strolling past brasseries, banks, and trendy furniture stores, pausing to stare into the windows of antique shops and check out the offerings of flower stalls. She was on her way to the Seine; at least that was her first destination.

Crossing the river, she moved along its Right Bank with the Louvre looming above her. The sun felt good; the air was pleasant with the smell of green growing things, with the dank scent common to rivers everywhere, and also a whiff of baking bread. There was an acrid undercurrent of exhaust fumes from the traffic rushing past, but Joletta was able to ignore it.

Imperceptibly, she felt her spirits lift. She had nothing to do except please herself for this whole day; she had done the tourist things and meant to concentrate now on the journal sites. She would, eventually, arrive at the Jardin de Luxembourg, which Violet had mentioned with special emphasis, but she was in no hurry. She wanted simply to be in Paris, to sample the good things to eat offered by street vendors, to watch the artists along the river, to stand on a bridge and stare. She wanted to feel the city around her, and to know that she was in the heart of it.

It was late afternoon when she reached the metro stop nearest her hotel, on a cross street just down from it. She made her way along the ceramic-tile-lined exit tunnel that was so much cleaner than the London underground and walked up the steps. She was tired, but happy, and ready for a bath and a quiet meal somewhere before bed.

Emerging into the slanting daylight with the rest of the metro passengers, she stood waiting for the light to change before she could cross the street toward the hotel. She glanced in that direction as her attention was caught by a woman and a man coming out of the tall and narrow entrance doors. They were talking as they descended the wide steps.

Natalie.

The light changed. Joletta started walking, then kept on. She moved with the knot of people across to the opposite curb, then continued along the sidewalk flanking the cross street without turning. Within seconds she was out of sight, but still she did not stop.

There was a tight feeling in her chest. She thought she might be sick. Her footsteps, quick and purposeful and gathering speed, rang in her ears. She didn't want her cousin in Paris. It wasn't simply that Natalie might interfere with what she was doing; her cousin's presence felt like a violation of her privacy and a curb on her freedom.

It had to be Aunt Estelle who had set Natalie to following her.

Perhaps she had pulled some strings, or hired some kind of investigator to track her down. As incredible as it seemed, it would have been just like her.

It was funny, really. Her aunt and Natalie probably thought she knew exactly where she was going and what she was doing to get the formula. Even if she tried to tell them differently, it was doubtful they would believe it. Fine, then. But she wasn't going to be harassed. Let Natalie catch up with her if she could.

"Hey, slow down, will you? Do you know you passed your hotel?"

The voice, warm with laughter, came from just behind her. It belonged to Rone.

Joletta broke stride, but before she could turn, her arm was caught and she was swung around. She put out her hand instinctively to ward him off as she spun to face him. Her open palm pressed for an instant against the warm muscles under his yellow polo shirt, imprinting their firm resiliency, their hard strength, upon the sensitive inner surface. She snatched it away as if she had touched a nuclear reactor.

Relief, suspicion, and quick, furtive pleasure clashed inside her, leaving her confused. She glanced swiftly beyond him, but Natalie was nowhere in sight.

"What are you doing here?" she asked, the words tight.

"I said I'd meet you. Didn't you get my message?"

"Yes, but I really didn't expect—" She stopped abruptly as it came to her that if Aunt Estelle knew where she was staying in Paris, she might also have discovered her hotel in London. If her aunt had sent someone to search the perfume shop, why couldn't she have found someone to search Joletta's London hotel room also?

"You have too little faith, Joletta," Rone said quietly as he released his hold on her arm. "In yourself, and in me."

Warm color rose in her face at the implication of his words, and also at the memory of the things she had thought about him. She looked away, unable to meet his steady blue gaze. She should have known he could not be so low and sneaky. What reason did he have, really? He knew nothing about her.

He was speaking again. "Are you sure everything's all right? No more bag snatchers or other desperate types after you?"

There was no point in telling him about the search; her problems were her own. And if she started talking about it, he might realize that her coolness toward him had come from suspicion.

"Of course not," she said with an attempt at a light tone. "I've learned a thing or two about taking care of myself."

"I'd be impressed, if I didn't know you've lost your hotel."

The teasing amusement in his eyes was distracting; still, she thought rapidly. "I'll have you know I know exactly where I am, and where I'm going."

"Oh, and just where might that be?"

"There's a little pastry shop a couple of blocks down, and I have a craving for éclairs."

"Now that you mention it, I can feel a yen coming on, myself— for éclairs, of course. Mind if I join you?"

He was asking for more than just permission to walk along with her to a pastry shop. He was also questioning his welcome. She said simply, "Why not?"

"I thought I might be in trouble." He indicated with a quick gesture that he was ready to continue in the direction she had been headed. Joletta hesitated, glancing behind him once more. There was still no one there. She turned and they moved off together.

"Why would you think you're in trouble?" she asked after a moment.

"Several reasons," he said, his tone a shade more serious than before. "I stood you up in London and left you alone nearly three whole days in Paris. Major crimes. I may also have appeared to take it for granted that you would care whether I showed up or not."

"I have no claim on your time, just as you have none on mine."

"All right, I probably deserved that."

She gave him a level look. "I wasn't trying to get back at you."

"You mean it was just a lucky shot?" His words were wry.

"Don't be ridiculous," she said, trying to be severe, but failing.

"How about dinner later, then, to celebrate the truce?"

"Fine," she answered. Let him make what he could out of that.

"Good. Then I'll tell you that I would have been here sooner, but I've been trying to tie up loose ends so I could have a few weeks of uninterrupted time to spend with you. That may not be important to you, but it is to me."

She walked on a few steps before she spoke. "You don't owe me an explanation—or anything else. We had fun in England, but I do have my own agenda—"

"If this is where you tell me you'd rather I got lost, it's too late," he said, his blue eyes dark with satisfaction. "I've already signed up for the rest of the tour."

She stared at him for a stunned instant. "You mean—the bus and everything?"

"And everything," he repeated with emphasis.

"Isn't that going a little far to prove a point?"

The planes of his face creased in a smile that seemed to hold extra warmth as he gazed down at her. "Is that why I'm doing it?"

"Why else?" It was hard to believe it was because of her, no matter what he seemed to be implying.

"I could be persuaded to cancel," he said with no more than an instant of hesitation. "Just say the word, and I'll rent a car and map out an ABC tour for us both like none you've ever seen."

"ABC tour?"

"Another Blasted Cathedral. Don't tell me your group hasn't discovered that joke."

"I don't think so."

"Cathedrals, museums, restaurants, quaint little inns, you won't miss a thing. I might even get you to Rome for your return flight." He tilted his head as he paused. "Then again, I might not."

"How did you know I would be returning from Rome?" It was easier to concentrate on that issue than to think of missing her flight home because of him.

"Easy. I got the number of your tour off your luggage tags at the same time that I got your name. When I spoke to the tour company, I just told them I wanted the same tour. There I was."

"Enterprising of you."

"Wasn't it," he said agreeably. "But you haven't answered. Would you like to rent a car and plan your own itinerary? Keeping in mind that we've already established the ground rules."

"Such as separate rooms?" she queried.

"Exactly," he agreed, though the light in his eyes also had an audacious glint.

It was tempting, especially since she now had some experience of the regimentation and compromises necessary in a group. It would also be tempting fate.

She gave a regretful shake of her head as she said, "I don't think I can afford it."

"I can." The comment was calm, without pressure.

"Thanks," she replied in firm tones, "but I prefer to pay my own way."

"A liberated lady?" he queried.

Her brows drew together as she thought about it. "It isn't that, exactly."

"You don't accept diamond bracelets, either," he suggested.

She flashed him a bright look. "Now you've got it."

He gazed down at her with an odd half smile curving his mouth. The look in his eyes was considering, but undefeated.

They bought the éclairs, rich with chocolate and cream, then walked idly along until they found a sidewalk café. When the waiter had brought the coffee they ordered, they sat in the last light of evening, eating their sticky treats and drinking from the tiny cups of incredibly bitter brew. The table was not much bigger than the cups and wobbled on the uneven sidewalk. A light wind rustled the leaves of a plane tree nearby. A sparrow hopped here and there on the sidewalk in search of crumbs. The traffic on the wide thoroughfare was beginning to pick up as Parisians headed homeward for the evening; its roar was punctuated regularly by the cranky horns of the boxlike little cars. The waiter who had served them, in his white shirt, black pants, and his apron almost down to his ankles, busied himself wiping tabletops and stacking chairs just inside the café's door.

"I don't think," Joletta said judiciously, "that you and I have improved our waiter's opinion of American manners."

"You mean by bringing our own eats into his fine establishment? Don't worry about it; that supercilious look doesn't mean a thing. The guy's probably thinking about his fallen arches."

"You think so?"

He nodded. "In Europe, nobody really cares what you do so long as you don't involve them or make a big noise about it. The trick to getting by—whether it's sitting in a Paris café or crossing the street against Rome traffic—is to be perfectly courteous but oblivious. Do what you like, do it with composure, and never make eye contact."

"You're joking."

"I promise you'll look like a native."

Rone watched Joletta as she sat so poised and alert beside him. Her attention appeared to fasten for an instant on a blond woman, obviously an American, who was coming toward them along the street. Her body tensed, then relaxed as the woman moved past them without a glance.

He wondered, then, if Joletta had seen Natalie back there at the hotel. She must have; something besides pastries had diverted her down this side street. It would be like her to say nothing to him since he was still a virtual stranger.

There was a great deal, he was discovering, that went on under the surface she presented to the world. She was a private person, self-contained, almost too much so. It wasn't that she was timid, he thought; timid women didn't walk down dark streets at night or set out for Europe by themselves. Rather, she used wariness and the repression of her natural impulses as a shield against personal pain. He would give a great deal to be on hand when she came out of her shell.

The evening light filtered through the top layer of her hair and reflected with a pearl sheen in the translucence of her skin, so she seemed to glow. There was a tiny smudge of chocolate icing on the tender curve of her bottom lip that made him want to kiss it away. The urge was so strong that he sat perfectly still, willing his self-control to kick in, as he leaned back in his chair with his fingers cradling his coffee cup.

He wondered at the rightness of his decision to join her tour. He was doing it to make his job easier, or so he told himself, but it was going to be a strain, no doubt about that. The question was whether he could stand it. Principles could be a pain—if principles was a word that could be applied to a situation of this kind.

He wished with sudden fervor that everything about this trip were as simple as he was pretending to Joletta. He would give a great deal to be able to amble with her around Europe without a care or worry, to have no constraint in his relationship with her except that imposed by common, decent behavior. Well, fairly decent.

He could still feel heat in the place on his chest where her hand had rested so briefly. Before he could prevent it, his mind flashed an image of what it might be like to have her touch him of her own will, with affection, even with desire.

The scent of her drifted to his nostrils, that gentle blending of Tea Rose and her own unique female fragrance. Most women smelled to some degree of vanilla, a kind of universal feminine smell. Not Joletta. He thought that was a part of the fascination she held for him, a part of his need to come closer to her, so he could decipher that fragrance. It was a little like the jungle orchid that created the vanilla bean, along with a blending of sun-ripened pear. Or maybe it was like a cross between a dark red plum and a night-blooming jasmine.

What it was, was maddening.

He was going to have to think of other things if he ever wanted to lift the napkin from his lap and stand up from behind this table without embarrassing himself.

He was becoming far too involved.

And he was beginning to be afraid of what was going to happen when this trip was over.

They started back toward the hotel as dusk began to gather. There were more people on the sidewalk at this hour, shop assistants and secretaries wearing ponchos and scarves, businessmen in trench coats with newspapers weighting their pockets, and elderly women carrying string shopping bags with baguette loaves of bread sticking out of the tops. The number of cars on the streets had increased also, while their respect for marked traffic lanes had decreased. Horns blared in a near-constant cacophony, and riders on bicycles wove in and out of the traffic with insouciance, apparently never looking at the drivers.

Joletta and Rone walked along, letting the other pedestrians push past them while they talked of the excursion to Versailles the next day. Joletta had signed up for it earlier; it was something she had not wanted to chance missing. She thought Rone could still make it if he cared to try.

As they reached a cross street they heard the rise and fall of the two-note police sirens coming from somewhere to their right. The steady flow of cars slowed, then braked to a stop. As foot traffic was cut off also people began to gather around the two of them on the street corner. The pedestrians grumbled among themselves, stretching their necks to look.

Rone, able to see over most of the Frenchmen and women around them, identified the cause of the commotion first. "Police vans, three of them."

The vehicles were painted a rich blue seldom seen on the other side of the Atlantic on anything except luxury cars, and were flanked on both sides by outriders of motorcycle police. They fought their way through the stalled cars, detouring now and then by way of the sidewalk to get around them. As the vans neared, the rising and falling tones of their sirens were deafening.

It was, apparently, some routine police movement, though it

might also have been a response to a terrorist attack; in Paris anything was possible. Joletta had been wakened by other calvacades just like it at least twice per night since she had been in the city.

"That sound always reminds me of the gestapo coming to get Anne and her family in the movie of *The Diary of Anne Frank*," she said.

"Wrong city," Rone answered, his voice even.

"I knew that," she said dryly. She glanced at him, but he made no answer as he looked right and left at the people crowding around them.

The last of the vans went tearing past. In the midst of its noise and rush, Joletta was jostled from behind. She stumbled a few steps away from Rone, but did not try to move nearer again. The mood between them had changed somehow, and she was a little chilled by the distance she sensed in him. Besides, the signal light on its side pole was flashing, indicating that it was almost time to cross.

Engines were gunned and tires squealed as the traffic surged forward again. It was like a raceway as drivers tried to beat the incipient change of the light. The flow seemed interminable, as unstoppable as a flooding river.

Then suddenly brakes screeched and engines geared down, rumbling to a standstill once more. Joletta, moving with the traffic-wise Parisians around her, stepped off the curb.

The roar of an accelerating car ripped through the traffic's hoarse grumble. Women screamed, men yelled. Joletta whipped her head around. She saw the red sports car spinning around the corner straight at her, noted its sleek, expensive shape and its power.

She was hemmed in on all sides. There was a wall of bodies between her and the curb. Terror beat up into her throat.

Abruptly, the crowd scattered. She saw an opening to one side and spun around, leaping toward it.

Her movements felt inconceivably slow. She flung herself forward with every ounce of her strength, struggling to attain height in an atmosphere that seemed made of glue. Her body was airborne, arcing deliberately, hovering in midair with the grace of a hang glider before plunging down toward the surface of the sidewalk. She thrust out her arms to absorb the jar of the landing.

She never felt it. Something struck her hip, a glancing blow that brought a vivid explosion of pain. She spun, tumbling like clothes in a dryer. Her head brushed something upright and hard.

Silence and darkness reached out to catch her.

Chapter 8

May 28, 1854

Everything in Paris is either boring or ugly. I am weighted down with ennui from listening to Gilbert's ancient relatives extol the beauty and aristocratic glory of the departed Bourbon regime and deplore the atrocities committed by Napoléon III as he seized the title of emperor last worn by his uncle—this while they live in tasteless and thoroughly petit bourgeois comfort.

Gilbert has become a tyrant. He decrees that I cannot go out without Hermine, since he is known in Paris and I must protect his good name. Known? He? Such pretension. Or perhaps it is no more than an excuse to keep me close?

A lavender twilight lay over Paris. It touched the gray, smoke-stained limestone buildings and cobblestones with a purple glaze and reflected amethyst in the puddles of water that lay here and there in the sunken stones of the rear stableyard outside Violet's window.

She stood at the open casement with her head resting on the glass, watching as a stable lad drawing water from the central fountain flirted with a maid hanging out of a window opposite. The air was damp and cool, and smelled of horses and decay, with now and then a whiff of the Seine that lay not so far away. Somewhere carriages rattled along the streets and boatmen and street hawkers

called, but the sounds were muffled by distance and walls. A church
bell clanged in discordant appeal, then fell silent.

It had been raining, but had stopped in time for the dull evening
to be colored by the sunset. Gilbert had been gone for hours, looking, no doubt, for the perfect rococo mirror or Louis XVI chair. He
was becoming fanatic about such pieces, talking endlessly about the
stories behind them. He was buying history, he said. Since it seemed
to make him happy, Violet did not argue with him.

She had been reading most of the day, the lugubrious *Dame aux
camélias*, by Dumas *fils*, the son of the famous writer and roué Al-
exandre Dumas. The book had been published some time ago, but
had been brought back to popularity by the production of the play
of the same name just over a year before, and also by the recent
performance in Venice of Giuseppe Verdi's opera *La Traviata*, which
had been based on the story. The tale, a tragedy about a courtesan
who gives up the love of a rich and handsome young man to save
him dishonor, then dies of consumption and a broken heart, had
lowered Violet's spirits to such a degree that she could no longer
continue. It would make a marvelous opera; she could see that, one
she would no doubt cry over at the French opera house in New
Orleans in some future season, but for now it left her restless and
impatient. She was in no mood for tears and self-sacrifice.

Gilbert had not contacted Delacroix. The artist was too elusive,
he said. He was also too important; hadn't he, just the year before, completed the ceiling of the Salon de la Paix of the Hôtel de
Ville, the seat of government for all Paris itself? Violet, Gilbert said,
was very pretty, but this great painter at the height of his fame
would certainly not stoop to putting her image on canvas. His darling young wife must accept the disappointment and think of another artist.

Violet refused to accept it.

What would happen if this single avenue of contact between
herself and Allain were allowed to wither away? Would the few
words of parting they had exchanged in a hotel lobby be final?
Would they never look upon each other again?

Perhaps that was what she should allow to happen.

Perhaps this sweet fever in her blood would pass. Perhaps in
time she would no longer call Allain's face to mind, no longer wonder
where he was, what he was doing, and if he was thinking of her.

No.

And no again.

Gilbert had been going out at night. He had been dining out with some of his male cousins, so he said, though he had returned to the hotel intoxicated and smelling of cheap wine and cheaper perfume. Violet was not so innocent that she did not realize how he had been entertaining himself. The Théâtre des Variétés where women appeared half-naked, the society of the demimonde, which included courtesans, mistresses to famous men, and other loose women, was talked about in whispers among the ladies of New Orleans. Its attractions were supposed to be powerful; it was not to be expected that a man visiting Paris would ignore the chance to sample them.

Violet had locked her door and pretended to be asleep when Gilbert returned, covering her head with her pillow to keep from hearing his knock. She had claimed in the morning that she had shut herself away because she had been frightened at being left alone. Gilbert had retreated into frustrated and sullen silence.

There had been a time when such silences disturbed her. She had felt them as a punishment, had been anxious to restore ease between her husband and herself, to find some concession she could make to regain his favor. Now she welcomed them.

This afternoon she had put on a gown of silk in rose and green stripes on white, and with nosegays of roses and greenery embroidered between the striping. Hermine had dressed her hair with a mass of ringlets falling at the nape from a high knot and with tendril curls at her temples. A dish of bonbons had been set out.

No one had called. She would have welcomed any visitor, Gilbert's relatives, his newly made business acquaintances, anyone.

The rain had begun two hours before and continued with thunder and great silver-white streaks of lightning above the chimney pots of the houses. When it had stopped, the streets had steamed.

Violet had watched each slanting raindrop and found a small thrill in every one of them. Rain had become for her an aid to memory.

And she had made a decision.

Now she moved to where a secretary-desk sat against the wall. Seating herself, she drew a thick sheet of paper toward her. She uncapped the inkwell, took up her pen of malachite and gold, and looked at its nib. She sat for long moments with the point of the pen hovering over the paper. At last she began to write.

A few minutes later it was done. She held the square envelope of cream vellum containing the letter by one corner, as if it was dangerous. The impulse to tear it up and retreat once more into apathetic safety rose strong inside her. It was folly, what she was doing; she knew it. More than that, it was a betrayal.

She had never thought she would come to this, seeking for something more than the comfort and stability of her position as Gilbert's wife. She had never thought she would need it, never thought she could be enticed by the transient excitement of seeing another man. Everything was not perfect between her husband and herself, but there was much to be said for the quiet predictability of their days together, for his generosity, his care for her welfare, the respect and homage he accorded her when they were in public together. If there was no great stimulation for her in their moments of closeness, perhaps it was not all her husband's fault, perhaps it was also due to her coolness.

Oh, but how could she ignore the turmoil of pleasure only the thought of being with Allain again gave her? She could not. This sweet joy might never come again. It must be seized. She would be discreet; she did not mean to injure Gilbert in any way or do anything that might harm her marriage. A light flirtation, that was all she desired. What could it hurt to speak to Allain, to learn something of him, to grasp at a few, innocent memories to warm the long years ahead? It was such a small thing, really, so small.

For two days there was no reply to Violet's letter. On the third day there came an invitation for an afternoon visit at the house of Delacroix.

"You wrote without consulting me?" Gilbert said as he stood holding the invitation in his hand.

Violet had been expecting precisely this reaction. "We have spoken of it any number of times, you and I, but you have been so busy. I was thinking of it again the other evening while you were out and I was alone. It seemed we would never know if the great Delacroix would agree to our request unless we asked. To think was to act. I may have been impulsive, but only look at the result."

He sighed, looking at her from under his thick, iron-gray brows. Finally he said, "You want this a great deal, do you not?"

"Yes." She let the answer stand without embellishment.

He tapped the invitation against his thumbnail while a frown of consideration hovered about his brow. Finally, when she thought she would choke from holding back all the pleas and reasons she had marshaled to convince him, he spoke. "Well, then, so be it. We will go."

———

Sherry and olives together, Violet discovered, made a wonderful blending of flavors, each canceling out the bitterness of the other. These two things were only a small taste of the marvelous food and drink that was served during the late-afternoon salon at Delacroix's house; there was something for every palate, every nationality.

It was Allain who introduced her to the odd combination. He was able to do it because the rooms where the gathering was held were crowded with people, all of them talking at the top of their lungs about politics and art and philosophy and a thousand other things, and most of them gesticulating like mad people.

Allain also pointed out to her the famous and infamous who came and went: the jovial and wild-haired mulatto Dumas the elder, who had recently published his memoirs in ten amazing volumes; the poet, novelist, and literary critic Théophile Gautier; a number of government officials, several actresses. Then there were the painters, the rebels Corot and Courbet, Daumier and Millet, with also a few of the more correct members of the academy.

Delacroix was a handsome man, Violet found, one who had designed his surroundings to suit his own severe yet exotic personality. He was wearing, on this occasion, a short, open robe of dark blue brocade over a perfectly normal shirt and trousers, while on his head was a drooping turban. He should have looked ridiculous, but appeared magnificent instead, and totally uncaring of what anyone thought of him. He had taken Gilbert in hand, presenting him to many of the more interesting people in the room. Gilbert looked to be a little dazed at the honor.

The evening advanced, and nothing was said about the portrait. Violet began to be a little concerned. She also began to wonder, as she watched the deference with which their host was treated by everyone present, if Gilbert had not been right, if she had perhaps been presumptuous in thinking the artist might consider painting her.

She sat erect upon a velvet-covered divan with lyre-shaped curved arms and tasseled bolsters, watching Delacroix and Allain and all the others as they talked nonstop. They exchanged ideas, each with its own catchwords and phrases, volleying opinions and conclusions at each other as if they were weapons in some demonic war of the minds. She was unable to decide if they really believed the things they said, or if they took a particular stand because it was popular at the moment or gave them reason for a debate.

Allain held his own among them; indeed, he often seemed to be at the center of the most heated exchanges. His arguments were persuasive, with sudden slashing comments that displayed wit and intelligence and more than a shading of humor. He seemed to know everyone, and to be known by everyone, particularly the ladies. All treated him with warmth and friendliness, yet with a subtle deference that seemed as instinctive as it was unusual.

Violet tried not to look in his direction too often. It was difficult. He was so dynamic, so alive, compared with the other men in the room. The warmth in his voice, the bright, shifting laughter in his eyes, was impossible to resist. He was so very attractive in his dark and formally correct clothing and with the fluttering light from the gas jets of the chandelier overhead shining in his curling hair. The slight bronze of his skin, in contrast to the pallid complexions around him, added to his air of untamed vitality.

There was a rustle of silk and a whiff of lily of the valley as a woman moved to sit on the sofa beside her. Violet turned to smile in greeting. It was one of the actresses; she thought her name was Clotilde. The title of actress might have been a polite euphemism for her, however. The afternoon gown she wore was cut so low in front that when she leaned forward, it was possible to see her breasts in their entirety, nestled like two plump partridges in a nest.

The woman surveyed Violet with sparkling curiosity before she leaned forward to speak. "So," she said, "you are the mystery woman."

Violet gave a quick shake of her head. "Oh, no, I think not."

"Oh, yes. Our Allain has not taken his eyes from you for hours, even when he is trying to be circumspect by leaving you alone. We all guessed there must be someone; he has been in Paris again for ages but has not been to the theater once."

"You—sound as if you know him well."

"But of course; everyone knows Allain. There is no place in the world where he isn't at home."

The woman's tone and the encompassing gesture she used seemed exaggerated. Violet lifted a brow as she said, "No place?"

"Did you think I meant all the beds in Paris? No, no, I promise you, though it's possible if it pleased him. But I speak of London, Geneva, Brussels, Rome; he has the entrée to all Europe's capitals, not to mention their courts. I've never quite understood how that is, except that his charm is formidable. Don't you find it so?"

"Yes, indeed," Violet said, her voice chill.

"Forgive me, please. I should not say such things to you, though you are so stiff and serious that you practically compel me. Tell me, will you let him paint you?"

"M'sieur Massari?"

"Oh, dear, I expect he meant to surprise you, and now I've ruined it. He will be displeased. But you won't tell him, will you?"

"I don't know that there is anything to tell," Violet said with dampening politeness.

"How wise you are, and much better at discretion than he. Allain is excellent with brush and palette—he could be one of the great ones if only he had more time and less money. Friends and ample funds are the enemies of art, you know; they smother the fire."

There seemed to be no answer to this. Fortunately, none was required. The woman went on with hardly a pause.

"But you will allow him to speak for himself, yes? It would be too cruel not to permit him to astonish you. Besides, think of the fun of letting yourself be persuaded; I'm sure his blandishments will be delightful."

"Indeed?" Violet said with as much composure as she could manage.

"Don't frown so, *petite*, or he will think I'm saying terrible things to you. Perhaps he does already, for here he comes. *Alors*, such devotion! I quite envy you, madame."

The actress rose, making a light comment to Allain as he approached and touching his shoulder in a brief caress as she moved away. He seemed hardly to be aware of her, however. Seating himself beside Violet, he demanded, "What was Clotilde saying to you?"

He really had been watching her. Gratitude to the actress for pointing it out made her inclined to generosity. She said, "Nothing of importance, except for one small thing. Are you really an artist?"

Light, like the flare of a sulfur match, ignited in his eyes, but he only said, "I paint."

"I suppose there is no reason that I should know it. I am barely acquainted with you after all."

"A situation it would be my great pleasure to remedy," he said, smiling a little. He hesitated. "I would like very much to paint you. Delacroix is recommending me to your husband as his replacement even now."

"You planned it this way all along?"

He inclined his head in a brief assent. "Are you disappointed?"

"I had thought," she said, giving him a quick glance from under her lashes, "that I was to be immortalized by the great man who only deigns to paint likenesses of himself and his friends."

"So you will be, if that is your desire," he said, springing to his feet at once. "Only let me go and find Delacroix—"

"No! No, please sit down," she said hurriedly, reaching out as if she meant to clutch at his coat, though she drew back before she actually touched him.

He sank back into his seat. Abruptly, he smiled. Catching her hand, he said, "You are being the coquette with me. This is promising."

"No, it was silly. I only meant—"

"You trust me enough, and understand me enough, to tease me. This means you have thought of me. I am amazed, and honored."

She was left with nothing to say as the blood flooded in suffocating heat into her face.

His smile faded. "Forgive me. Now I am teasing you, and it's too soon. I meant to go slowly, and with the greatest care, beginning with the portrait. Will you allow it?"

"Yes, of course," she said, her voice scarcely audible.

"Even though you know nothing of my skill?"

Her gaze resting on her gloved hand that was still caught in his, she said, "I expect you're very good. M'sieur Delacroix would not recommend you, otherwise."

He sat watching the feathery shadows on her cheeks caused by her lowered lashes, and the soft creaminess that was added to the oval of her face by the gaslight overhead reflecting in the pale yellow of her silk velvet visiting costume. His attention lingered longest on the small nosegay of yellow and purple pansies that was pinned at her throat. Violet, discerning the direction of his gaze, wondered if she had been too bold in wearing a fresh reminder of his last hidden message to her. She looked up, meeting his gaze with difficulty. The expression she saw kindled there stilled her fears.

"I will try," he said after a deliberate instant, "to be worthy of your trust—and consideration."

She smiled as she released her hand from his grasp; she could not help herself. There was seductive pleasure in being so easily understood.

"Allain, *mon ami!* I see you've made the acquaintance of Madame Fossier?"

It was Delacroix who spoke as he neared them with Gilbert at his side. Violet's husband was scowling slightly as he glanced from her to the man with her. Allain rose to stand at ease as the two other men came to a halt. He said, "I took the liberty of presenting myself, since you were so kind as to hint at the possibility of a commission. Madame is a challenging subject. She has excellent bone structure, luminous skin tones, and near-perfect facial proportions, but her character is subtle, sensitive. It will not be easily captured."

"I thought you would be intrigued," Delacroix said, a twist to his mouth beneath the luxuriance of his mustache.

Gilbert, the frown still between his brows as he stared at Allain, said abruptly, "Have we met, m'sieur?"

"I think not," Allain answered, his smile polite. "I believe you are from America, yes? I have thought many times of traveling to your young country, but the occasion never arose."

There was a small pause, which Delacroix filled by making formal introductions. Allain, his manner politely inquiring, began to ask questions about Louisiana and the length of time they intended to be in Paris. The moment of awkwardness passed.

It was later, as Violet and Gilbert were riding back to their hotel, that Gilbert broke a long silence to ask, "This Massari fellow, he is satisfactory to you? You wouldn't like me to look around for another painter?"

"There is no need to trouble yourself," Violet replied. "Since he has M'sieur Delacroix's recommendation, I am sure that he will be—more than adequate."

Gilbert reached out and patted her hand before settling deeper into the carriage seat. His voice heavy, he said, "As you wish, *chère*, as you wish."

For an instant the duplicity of what she was doing was an ache inside Violet's chest. Then she thought of being with Allain for the length of time necessary to have her portrait painted, of the long hours they must spend talking, becoming known to each other. Only two days, then the sittings would begin; this was the arrangement settled between Gilbert and Allain. Anticipation mounted inside her, growing until it banished the guilt.

The morning of the first sitting dawned fair and fine. Violet had slept little during the night. She lay in bed, watching the light glowing brighter by the moment beyond her window curtains. The sickness of nervous anticipation quivered in her abdomen, threatening to rise.

She wouldn't go; she would write to say she was indisposed.

The thought of sitting still while Allain looked at her as closely as an artist must made her heart beat with the heavy thuds of terror. She would be alone with him for ages. What would she say? What could they talk about for so long? What did he expect of her? Had she led him to think that he could take liberties? Was that what he wanted of her?

Was it what she wanted? She turned her head on her pillow and flung her arm over her eyes.

How could she have thought that this was her most fervent desire? How could she have imagined there would be pleasure in it? She could see nothing ahead except perils and pain. Too soon, the portrait would be done, and then what?

She wished that she knew her own mind better, wished that her nature was not so vacillating. She envied the women like Clotilde who could throw themselves wholeheartedly into a liaison with a man and never look back, never question the morality or wisdom of what they were doing. How wonderful never to be tortured by these doubts, never to be forced to lie and wonder if it was possible to put joy and pain in a balance and discover which outweighed the other.

How nice it would be if she could simply say to herself that she couldn't help herself, that what she felt was more powerful than her will to resist. She wasn't sure it was so, not yet at least.

If she didn't go, she might never see Allain again.

It was this last thought that roused her enough to leave her bed. By thinking of what dress she would wear and laying it out with its petticoats, its lace collar and jewelry, then discussing with her maid how she would dress her hair, she was able to get through the morning. Actually dressing carried her through to the moment when she must depart from the hotel with Hermine. The need to keep her composure in front of her maid allowed her to reach Allain's lodgings without calling up to the coachman to turn back.

The house was located on the Ile de la Cité, the island in the Seine that was shaped like a great mud-filled barge anchored forever in the river. Lying so near Notre Dame it was almost in its shadow— an ancient limestone building, narrow and dark, whose carved gargoyle rain spouts had nearly melted away with age.

A plump and sharp-eyed woman dressed in the plain clothes of a housekeeper admitted Violet and Hermine and showed them up the winding interior staircase. She opened a door leading off a large anteroom fitted out as a salon, announced Violet, then stood aside for her to enter.

The room was long and narrow, with tall windows on two walls letting in the clear white light of their northern exposure. The ceiling overhead was carved and gilded between its heavy beams in the style of two centuries before, and darkened from the smoke of the thousands of fires that had burned in the cavernous stone fireplace that filled the far wall. The furnishings in the room were heavy, almost medieval, consisting of a few chairs, several tall candelabras, and a wide divan, almost a bed, that was covered with fringed silk shawls whose patterns resembled Persian gardens, plus a long refectory table against the inside wall. A dais had been built in the center, and on it sat an armchair upholstered in a rich wine brocade. An easel had been set up before the dais with a fresh canvas in place upon it.

Allain turned from the refectory table where he was poring over a series of sketches. With an exclamation of pleasure, he came forward to greet them. He offered them refreshments of tea or wine and cakes. While the housekeeper went away to fetch a tray, he drew Violet toward the table where he had been working.

"Before we begin," he said, "there is something I want you to see."

The sketches were of her. They showed her somber and laughing, wary and trusting, with raindrops on her lashes, and afterward, when they had been dried away. There was a view of her looking down at a bouquet of violets, and another with a rose in her hand. There were studies of her mouth, her ear, the tilt of her chin, the shape and positioning of her fingers as she held out her hand. They were each of them precisely drawn, carefully labeled and dated.

"These," he said quietly, "are the ones I considered worth keeping."

Violet took a deep breath. "I can't believe you were able—but I see that you lied to me. You are indeed an artist."

"These were done for my pleasure alone, from memory. I show them to you now only that you may know, perhaps, that you have not misplaced your trust."

There was a low and sincere note in his voice that seemed to invade her senses, vibrating deep inside her, setting off waves of heat that mounted to her head. She said with difficulty, "I never thought otherwise."

"You are very gracious, though I might have expected it. I pledge that you will not regret coming to me."

He was interrupted by the return of the housekeeper. Allain indicated that the food and drink she carried should be placed in front of the fireplace. Turning with a warm smile for Hermine, he said to Violet in matter-of-fact tones, "The presence of another person during a sitting is a distraction to me. Perhaps your maid would like to visit downstairs with Madame Maillard, enjoy a few cakes and wine also? She would be within call if you should need her."

Violet met his gaze for a long instant. It would have been wrong to say that it was guileless, but there was nothing mirrored in the clear gray blue of his eyes that made her afraid to be alone with him. She agreed, then moved with him toward the fireplace as the housekeeper led Hermine away. The door closed softly, but decisively, behind them.

The wine splashed as ruby red as blood as Allain poured it out. He handed one of the glasses, of fine crystal banded with gold in concentric rings, to Violet, then waited while she seated herself before he took the chair beside her.

He sipped from his glass, watching her above the rim. The bronze column of his throat moved as he swallowed. His fingers tightened on the crystal stem in his fingers, so it seemed that it must break. At last he said, "I can't believe you are really here."

"Nor can I." Her lips moved in a hesitant smile. She wanted to drink her wine to steady herself, but feared she might spill it if she tried. She could not quite meet his gaze, but looked beyond him to where a silver dish on the fireplace mantel was piled high with what appeared to be invitations in thick vellum envelopes.

He followed her gaze in bemusement, then glanced back at her again. "There is so much I want to say, but I hardly know where to begin. I see you sitting there, and all I want is to look at you, and go on looking and—"

"Please—" she protested, her voice no more than a thread of sound.

"I didn't mean to distress you. It's just that I never dared think that you would come to me. I hoped, but no more. And I thought that I knew every pore of your face and individual hair on your head, but I was wrong. You are more beautiful than I imagined, yet more elusive. Suddenly I'm afraid to begin painting you, afraid there will always be more and more that I have failed to see."

Her face was flaming and she couldn't breathe. The wine in the glass she held trembled across its surface. She could not speak for the tightness in her throat. She did not know what she had thought might come of this meeting, but it was not this declaration. She would swear it.

"Forgive me," he said on a swiftly drawn breath as he set down his wineglass and got to his feet, turning to place a hand on the tall mantel that was just above his shoulder height. "I didn't intend to say these things—I meant to be calm and courteous and only a little gallant. You'll think I'm insane."

His perturbation seemed to ease a little of her own. "No," she said in low, vibrant tones, "but I am not used to hearing such things said aloud. I don't know how to answer you."

He looked at her over his shoulder, and the warmth of his smile was like an embrace. "There is no need to answer. You are not responsible for what I feel or what I say in my ramblings. But come, drink your wine. Then we had better begin your sitting before I say something we may both regret."

This passage between them set the pattern for the sittings that followed. Allain behaved toward Violet at all times with deference and exacting courtesy relieved by flashes of caressing humor. The compliments he made her in a constant flow caused her cheeks to burn, yet were so detached, so applied to the work he was doing, that she could not take exception to them.

He placed her on the dais each afternoon, arranging the folds of her dress, adjusting the position of her head, her hand, or her shoulder with gentle touches whose heat seemed to linger for hours. His nearness at such times made it difficult to breathe, and impossible to meet his gaze. She wondered if he ever noticed the way the fabric of her bodice trembled with the beating of her heart, or if he knew that the reason she could not relax as he instructed was because she felt so exposed under his intense scrutiny.

Perhaps in the attempt to ease her tension, he talked of many things, bits of gossip about clashes of temperament in the art community and rumors of intrigue at the court of Napoléon III; tales of the mismanagement of the funds for the rebuilding of Paris, or stories of the heroic efforts in the preparations for the war in the Crimea. He spoke of problems already with the royal marriage, less than a year and a half old, caused by the emperor's penchant for trying to conquer every attractive woman he met.

He spoke so easily, with such humor and so much tolerance for the weaknesses and mistakes of others, that Violet began to look forward to their conversations with the keenest of pleasure. His attitudes and opinions seemed to match her own as perfectly as could be expected of another human being. There was something infinitely seductive in that meeting of the minds.

One day, after almost a month of sittings, they were speaking again of the empress.

"I saw Eugénie driving in the Bois du Boulogne yesterday," Violet said. "She is so striking with her auburn hair and deep blue eyes, so truly lovely, that I can't believe the emperor would look at another woman."

Allain, concentrating on the canvas in front of him, did not look up as he answered. "There can be no doubt that he loves her; as ruler of France he might have looked higher than the daughter of a Spanish count and an American woman. They say, in fact, that Louis Napoléon tried to make Eugénie his mistress, but was so charmed by her refusal that he offered marriage instead. However, for some men who gain power, the chase is paramount, more important even than love. Louis Napoléon requires further conquests to allow him to revel in his feeling of power."

"It seems a weakness to me," Violet said slowly, "to need the sense of power so badly."

A shadow passed over Allain's face, leaving it somber. "Agreed," he said. "It can become an addiction as destructive as absinthe." A moment later he glanced at her with amusement rising in his eyes. "I hear, though, that Eugénie is not inclined to accept her husband's philandering without a struggle. She is supposed to have bribed an old crone who was once maid to another empress, Joséphine, for the recipe for a perfume known to have been used to retain the favor of the first Napoléon."

Violet shook her head with an answering smile. "How do these things become common gossip?"

"Servants will talk, and of course the empress could not go herself to speak to Joséphine's old maid."

"I suppose. But this perfume, how could she possibly expect it to matter, what could be in it to make her think it would be beneficial?"

"Who can tell? Something exotic, perhaps. The tale told by the old maid is that the perfume was brought to France from Egypt by Napoléon himself. Supposedly, his soldiers unearthed it from an unmarked tomb which he was told was that of Cleopatra, along with a tablet which proclaimed it the source of great power because it contained the oils used in the secret rituals of the priestess-queens of Isis who ruled in the days before the pharaohs."

"And has the perfume helped Eugénie?"

"It's too soon to tell, I think, but she has great hopes."

Violet shook her head. "I can't see why she should. The first Napoléon was not precisely known for his faithfulness."

Allain hefted the brush in his hand. "And yet, Joséphine was his supreme love for many years, a woman older than he, with bad teeth and no great reputation for faithfulness herself, one to whom he wrote thousands of letters protesting his devotion. He might never have divorced her at all if she had been able to give him a son. It makes you think, doesn't it? But the amazing thing is that he didn't wear it himself; they say he practically bathed in scent every day, especially the combination of bergamot, lemon oil, and rosemary known as Hungary water, eau du cologne."

"Perhaps Cleopatra's scent was too sweet and womanish for him?"

Allain smiled at Violet. "It's always possible, though I somehow connect rituals with the smell of incense in a cathedral, woody compounds such as cedarwood and sandalwood. A quirk of mine, I expect."

"You seem to know a great deal about scents," she commented, her tone inquiring.

"I have a friend who is a perfumer on the Rue de la Paix." He picked up a little shell-pink color on his brush and carefully stroked it on the canvas in front of him.

"Ah, I suspect that is where you heard of Cleopatra's perfume."

"Lately, yes. But I knew it long ago, from my mother."

"Really," she said, intrigued. "And how did she happen to have it?"

"As a gift from my father. And like Joséphine, my father had it from Napoléon himself."

"He knew him well?"

How odd it seemed, to speak so easily of so legendary a man. To Violet, Napoléon Bonaparte had always been a hero. He was viewed in that light by most people in New Orleans, in spite of the ignominy of his ultimate defeat. For a short few years it had seemed he would bring back the glory of France, just as it appeared that Napoléon III might do the same now.

Allain inclined his head slightly in agreement to her question, though his manner was abstracted as he stared at the canvas before him without offering to apply more paint. He said, "The scent, and the rather complicated directions for assembling the many different oils that go into it, was presented to my father as a token of friendship. But that was when he and Napoléon were young men, nearly forty-seven years ago, a long time in the past."

"Your father fought with Napoléon, perhaps?"

A brief smile came and went across his face. "My father admired him extravagantly in the beginning, but opposed him in the end. There were many who did so."

He put down his brush and palette, then wiped his hands with deliberate movements on a rag dampened with turpentine. Setting it aside, he moved toward her with lithe grace. He seated himself on the dais at her feet, turning to place one booted foot on the edge of the low platform and to rest his arm on his bent knee.

"Madame," he began, then stopped. His eyes, more gray than blue in the cool northern light of the windows, were wide and vulnerable as he searched her face. The openness of his expression touched something deep inside her, so she felt a strange mingling of pain and pleasure and loss of will.

"My name," she said quietly, "is Violet."

"Violet," he repeated with soft satisfaction. He drew a slow breath, which swelled his chest, then began again in quiet tones. "Madame Violet, you must know that your portrait is nearly finished."

She swallowed a little. "I knew it could not be long before it was done."

"I might, had I wished, have made the last stroke a week ago. I could do it now."

It was an admission that took her breath; it was, in fact, nothing less than a declaration. With it he had placed himself in her hands.

She said softly, "Could—could you?"

"The question is, shall I?"

His voice was even as he spoke, without further appeal. It was her decision. If she said yes, then he would accept his dismissal. He would complete the portrait, and the sittings would be at an end. And if she did not?

"I suppose," she said slowly, "that there is no great hurry."

The gladness that sprang into his face was like a shout. It crinkled the skin around his eyes and curled into the corners of his mouth. He made no movement toward her, yet she felt the warmth of his elation engulf her like a storm. She could not prevent the smile that rose into her eyes in return.

"Madame Violet," he said in stringent entreaty, "will you walk with me, then, since I have no work to occupy the afternoon? Will you stroll out on my arm while we pretend that we are simply a man and a woman in search of air, and perhaps, someplace to sit quietly and take a glass of wine?"

Did she dare? What if someone saw and reported it to Gilbert?

Oh, but how could she refuse when everything inside her longed for the pretense he suggested, responded in barely contained joy to the suppressed passion she sensed inside him?

She couldn't.

"Yes," she whispered, "I will."

Chapter 9

Violet and Allain left his house by a side door to avoid being seen by Hermine, who was sitting again with the housekeeper; the two women had become close friends, since they both enjoyed less than robust health and had a similar variety of complaints. Violet was not certain the maid would inform on her, but Hermine had been Gilbert's nurse as a young boy, and there was no point in placing unnecessary strain on her loyalty.

It was a magical afternoon. Wandering away from the *Ile de la Cité*, Violet and Allain strolled along the Right Bank of the Seine. They talked of many things, though there were also times when they fell silent to gaze at each other. There was no purpose to their meanderings, they paid no attention to how far they walked. It was enough that they had escaped, together.

The feel of his arm under her fingers, the restrained power of the firm muscles beneath the sleeve of his shirt and coat, made Violet's heart beat high in her throat. The brush of her skirts against his trousers seemed incredibly intimate, as if her clothing carried some extension of her own acute sensibilities. She was so aware of him, of his upright bearing, his gentle glances, and the stringent control he maintained in his manner toward her that it was nearly unbearable. Regardless, she never wanted this walk to end.

As the afternoon shadows grew longer they found a café at the edge of a garden with a table shaded by a plane tree. The cast iron of the table and the chairs was cold. The chill seemed to creep inside Violet, in spite of the *café au lait* Allain ordered for her with her wine to combat it. As she looked around her it appeared that the tables near them were all occupied by courting couples; they had that air of absorbed attention for each other about them. She said something about it to Allain.

His smile was wry. "Look closer," he said.

As she followed his recommendation she saw that most of the women were younger than their escorts, though there were a few couples where the lady appeared older and decidedly more prosperous.

"Oh." She sought somewhere else, anywhere else, to turn her gaze.

"Yes. I hope you aren't too distressed." He took her free hand, which lay in her lap, caressing her knuckles with his thumb that was hard with fencing calluses. "Dalliance is the custom in Paris."

"I see," she said, her tone pensive.

"I don't think you do, not if you believe I brought you here solely to expose you to this kind of atmosphere. I only thought you would not like to risk being recognized, as you might be at a more fashionable café."

"You needn't explain," she said, meeting his gaze. "I do trust you."

He watched her a long moment before he spoke with rough abruptness. "Don't. Please. It's more than I deserve. I would like nothing better than to corrupt you completely."

"But you won't," she said, her lips curving into a slow and tremulous smile.

"Won't I?" He waited a taut moment before answering his own question on a sigh. "No, not without permission."

His words were an admission in themselves. It was one that should have repelled her. Instead, it thrilled her to the center of her being. He wanted her, he did want her. Yet here was a man who did not seek to impose his will upon hers, made no demands, claimed nothing as his manly right. Did he realize the allure of the vow he had made, know the tantalizing headiness for her of recognizing that the choice of the direction their affair would take was hers?

Their affair. How odd to use such words.

What, then, did she want?

Was it possible that a safe, platonic affair was all she cared to risk? Would she, could she, venture anything more, even with this heat in her blood? Would it change what was between Allain and herself if she did? Was it possible that his view of her was so romantic that he would be disillusioned if she indicated that she desired more?

How complicated it was, so complicated that she felt paralyzed by the warring fears inside her.

There were other walks on other days, as the sittings became no more than an excuse to meet.

They ventured further into the center of Paris. Allain knew the best dressmakers, the finest milliners and most skilled makers of gloves and shoes, and he took pleasure in acting as her escort while she visited these places. His taste was refined, his eye for color and line unerring. He did not seek to press his ideas upon her, however, but rather urged her to develop her own. She had, he said, a natural sense of style, a quiet elegance that suited her to perfection. All she needed was to learn to depend on her own instincts.

He made only one attempt to pay for an item of apparel for Violet's use. Her refusal was so firm and unhesitating that he retreated at once. In return, Violet did not often buy the things that caught her fancy when she was with him, but returned for them later. It was difficult for him, she realized, to stand aside while she paid for her own purchases.

Allain was amazed at Gilbert's failure to consult her wishes in the furnishing of their house and castigated him for a dolt for excluding her from the shopping excursions involved. In the next breath, he praised her husband's cavalier attitude, since otherwise her time would have been spent visiting shops and combing through warehouses and attics with Gilbert, instead of being with him.

They set out one afternoon after a thunderstorm. Water still ran in the gutters and the sky was mottled with gray, but the need to be alone and abroad together made them careless of the wet weather. Allain, poking with the tip of his dress cane at bits of torn, apple-green leaves from the plane trees that were stuck to the damp sidewalk, broke a short silence. "The Comtesse Fourier will be giving a ball in a few days' time. Would you care to attend?"

"I would like it very much," she answered, "if Gilbert has no other plans. He has been much occupied in the evening of late."

"The occasion is a diplomatic gala in honor of the recent improvement in relations between France and Belgium. Most respectable, though a little stuffy. I will be happy to serve as your escort if your husband is unavailable."

She tilted her head a little, looking at him from under the rolled brim of the rather dashing hat of periwinkle-blue straw she wore. "I doubt he would consider that proper."

"Many married ladies are escorted by gentleman friends. No eyebrows are raised so long as they remain in public view. You might explain this to him."

The thought of an evening with Allain, even one spent where everyone could see them, was too enticing to be refused. "I suppose you could have the invitation sent, and we will see what Gilbert says."

He pressed his arm, where she was holding it, closer against his side, and the look in his eyes made her feel that she was equal to any explanation that might be required.

The air was dense with moisture. Violet's skirts felt damp with it, while their hems were becoming heavy and bedraggled from the puddles on the sidewalk. The light seemed to be growing dimmer.

Allain looked up, surveying the lowering sky. Frowning a little, he said, "Perhaps we should turn back?"

Thunder rumbled in a basso warning. A cool mist swirled around them. A moment later the deliberate and civilized French rain began to fall.

It was too late to return to the studio. Ahead of them was the blue-and-white-striped awning of a café. They increased their pace, making toward it. Then as the raindrops began to pelt down in earnest, Violet released Allain's arm and picked up her skirts to run. They dashed under the awning just as the heavens shuddered with an enormous crack of thunder. Laughing and breathless, they turned to each other.

Allain took her into his arms, holding her close as the rain drummed on the canvas overhead and ran down in streams to splatter on the sidewalk. Gazing down at her with his face alight and softness in his eyes, he whispered, "Remember?"

How could she forget? Their first meeting. The rain-drenched garden. The pavilion. She smiled up at him until, by slow degrees, her joy became anguish.

It was becoming intolerable, these brief episodes, the stolen moments together, being so close yet so far apart. Violet was perilously aware of how unfair it was to ask Allain to endure it, did not know how much longer she could bear it herself.

Unable to sustain the dark pain that shadowed his eyes also, she turned her head. Through the gray haze of rain, she saw the figures of two men huddled under the inadequate protection of a chestnut tree. As the rain grew harder still they broke and ran toward a housefront just down the street, where they crouched in its projecting doorway.

Violet's eyes narrowed as she tried to see through the rain. She had noticed the two men earlier, dawdling along behind Allain and herself. They did not have the look of gentlemen out taking their leisure, and still less that of merchants going about their business. There was something furtive about them in their dark, nondescript clothes and their idleness.

"Those men over there," she said to Allain in low tones. "I think they may have been following us. Do you suppose they are thieves?"

"I very much doubt it," Allain said. His voice was grim, though he barely glanced in the direction she indicated.

Something in his manner disturbed Violet. She looked up at him, saying quickly, "You don't think they mean us harm?"

"Who can say?" He answered with the smallest of shrugs. "Anything is possible."

"Oh, but surely not. It is broad daylight after all."

"Don't upset yourself," he said, smiling a little as he smoothed his hands along her silk-clad upper arms. "I expect those two wretches were only enthralled by how lovely you are. Believe me, I well understand the impulse to become your shadow."

He was, she thought, trying to distract her, to spare her anxiety. "More likely they are only traveling along in the same direction."

She was apparently correct. When the rain stopped and she and Allain set out for the return to his studio, the men trailed behind them only a few streets before they were lost from sight.

Gilbert, when the promised invitation to the ball arrived, was highly gratified at the notice accorded them by the Comtesse de Fourier. He would not dream of missing such a grand event, he said; his relatives, he was sure, would consider it quite a coup when he told them. He was astonished, however, that Massari should be on the comtesse's list; he would not have thought such an important hostess would have a mere artist among her acquaintances.

It did not, apparently, occur to him to wonder how their own names had become known to the lady.

So elated was Gilbert at the prospect of the gala that he suggested Violet order a new ball gown, one with the deep, lace-edged flounces of the current mode. Blush pink, he said, would meet with his approval. Violet feigned pleasure and enthusiasm and promised to make the gown her project of the morning. She did not tell him that her ensemble had not only been already chosen while in Allain's company, but was already due for a fitting. She was becoming far too good at dissembling.

Gilbert had been dressing to go out as they discussed the occasion. He dismissed his valet and stood adjusting the set of his coat across his shoulders and the exposure of his shirt cuffs below his coat sleeves. He studied her for a moment where, already dressed for the day in a gown of blue-and-cream-striped lawn, she sat at the secretary-desk penning a description of the day before in her journal.

"This artist," he said, "he isn't becoming too familiar, is he?"

She looked up with her pen poised in her hand and an eyebrow lifted in surprise. "Why," she said, "what can you mean?"

"His offer to squire you to this ball seems presumptuous, to say the least. I'm not sure I care for it."

"He has been the complete gentleman," she answered. "No one could be more respectful than M'sieur Massari."

"I'm relieved to hear it. I would be even more relieved to be told that this portrait will soon be finished."

"It progresses slowly, I agree, but it's really useless to try to hurry an artist." She tried the effect of a whimsical smile.

"It's as well he's being paid for the completed work rather than by the day. I'm sure these sittings are growing tedious for you." He gave her an intent stare.

Violet was aware of the heavy beating of her heart under her rib cage. She thought of the two men who had been following her and Allain. Perhaps there had been something in it after all; perhaps Gilbert had sent them. She raised a slim shoulder and let it fall again before she answered. "I don't mind. I have nothing better to do with my time."

"The man is an accomplished flirt, quite the Casanova," her husband went on, his words ponderous. "He has had more than one passage with sword and pistol on the field of honor for the sake of his amours, or so rumor has it. You must be careful not to let your head be turned by him."

Violet had suspected Allain was a favorite with the ladies, but it was distressing to hear it confirmed. It was also an indication of her hopeless state that she was more concerned about Allain's past than about Gilbert's suspicions. She said, "I'm sure there is no danger."

"Are you. It seems to me there is not the respect there should be for marriage vows here, that more wink at them than keep them. I would not like to see you drawn into such a trap."

"Really, Gilbert—"

"I would not mention it, but you have been different of late. You have gained that certain look of the Parisian in your dress, but also, it seems to me, in your manner. You must not go too far."

Violet gave him a long look. "And you, Gilbert? What of your evenings at the restaurants and theaters?"

"That is not at all the same thing."

"Possibly not, but it makes your reproaches seem strange."

"I am not a young man, Violet; I know this full well. To come to Paris at my age, after years spent in a backwater, is difficult; there is much I feel I have missed. However, this has nothing to do with you."

"I must not question your escapades, but you are free to accuse me?"

His frown was heavy as he stared at her. "You would never have said such a thing to me before. I don't like it. I don't like it at all."

"Everyone changes," she said.

"Yes, unfortunately. But I don't accuse you, Violet, I only warn you. I realize that youth calls to youth, that I am not, perhaps, as handsome or as gallant as some, but I am still your husband and a jealous man."

Violet could find nothing to say to that, either in protest or in reassurance.

The ball began at quite a late hour by Violet's standards, though no one else seemed to think so. She and Gilbert were among the first arrivals, but not, thankfully, the very first. The house where it was being held was in the old and no longer fashionable district of La Marais. A relic of the sixteenth century, the building had a certain appealing romantic grandeur in its decrepitude.

They mounted a gritty marble staircase whose enormous width had been designed to permit easy passage by ladies wearing farthingales, a convenience in the present era of ever-widening crinolines.

Their progress was monitored by liveried footmen so rigid of countenance and immobile in stance that they might have been effigies in wax. They were received by their hostess under the blazing candles of the first of a line of four crystal-and-bronze chandeliers, all of which were fuzzy with dust, then stepped out onto a parquet floor that had been sanded to silken smoothness by the dirt from countless feet.

For the next half hour Violet and Gilbert stood about while the orchestra sawed away at chamber music. Couples of every shape and size and every conceivable variety of ball dress promenaded slowly around the huge chamber in the effort to see and be seen, or else wandered in and out of the card room and inspected the dining-room setting for supper. The pace of conversation was faster, the range of subject matter wider, and there were a number of titled guests announced, but the ball was not so different, in all truth, from those of New Orleans. Gilbert exclaimed over this fact with great satisfaction more than once. Violet was disappointed.

The dancing began with the arrival of the emperor. Violet had not realized that royal protocol was the cause of the delay, had not known Louis Napoléon was to appear. She watched with interest as the great man led their hostess out onto the floor. He was, apparently, alone; there was no sign of the empress.

"Good evening, Madame Fossier."

She started a little as Allain spoke at her side. She had not heard him approach for the music, the shuffling steps of the dancers, and the babble of voices. A warm flood tide of pleasure crested in her veins as she met his gaze. It crept higher as she saw his attention rest on the rosebuds of deepest rose red set in a lace-edged holder that nestled at the corsage of her gown, exactly centered between the gentle curves of her breasts. The flowers, Roses for Love, had been delivered in the late afternoon. Violet had told Gilbert that she had ordered them for herself, to match her gown of rich rose chiffon whose flounces were edged in lace shot with silver. It was not so, any more than it had been true of the half-dozen other blooms and posies she had brought home with her in the last weeks.

"Well, and what is your opinion of our imperial leader?" Allain asked in soft tones when the proper greetings had been exchanged.

The dry acerbity of his tone caused the corner of Violet's mouth to indent in a smile. At the same time she saw her husband frown, as if he thought it irregular that the artist had addressed his query to his wife rather than himself. Violet was in no mood to efface herself at that sign of Gilbert's displeasure, however. She studied the emperor as she considered her reply.

In his midforties, of medium height with thinning ash-brown hair and the large eyes of the Bonapartes, he might have been attractive if his smile had not been quite so set and without warmth. He also lacked animation, as though keeping watch on his every word and facial expression had become such a habit that he was incapable of any form of spontaneity.

Violet leaned toward Allain a little as she whispered, "The man is very stiff, isn't he?"

"Stiff? No, no," he answered immediately. "That's no more than a natural manner bequeathed to Bonapartes at birth, a matter of imperial dignity."

"Just so," she agreed with a wise nod. "And who trims his beard and curls his mustaches in that ridiculous manner?"

"You don't find it handsome? Most females are impressed by the devilish quality. You have no appreciation."

"I suppose not." She gave a mock sigh.

"You will notice that the style has gained favor among the conservative male element, too." Allain tipped his head toward several other men who were sporting the Napoléon-style facial adornment.

"What a coincidence," she said, "since men don't, of course, follow fashions set by others."

Beside her, Gilbert cleared his throat with a harsh rasp. He was rocking on his heels with his hands clasped behind his back, a sign of perturbation. "I think it would be wiser," he said, "if we talked of other things."

Violet had almost forgotten Gilbert in the enjoyment of her banter with the other man. As she realized it, consternation moved over her in a wave.

Allain considered Gilbert with unimpaired humor. "Are you counseling caution, sir, or suggesting more respect is required for the ruler of France?"

"Both," Gilbert replied in stiff tones. "We are guests in this country."

"True, as am I," Allain agreed. "Yet if a man insists on the trappings of majesty, he must accept the slings and arrows which go with it. Of these, the most indefensible is quite often laughter."

Allain glanced at a dowager in a turban of silver lace decorated with nodding ostrich plumes who was waggling her fingers to attract his attention. He looked back to Violet, holding her gaze for an instant with what appeared to be apology in his eyes. Inclining his head, he added, "You will excuse me? I must speak to this lady."

His retreat, Violet thought, was for her sake, to remove himself as an apparent irritant. She watched as he was welcomed by the dowager and her friends. In a quiet undertone, she said to her husband, "You might have been a little more cordial."

"Why, when you were cordial enough for both of us?"

"To compensate for your lack of conversation," she answered, stung to heat by the censure in his tone.

Gilbert drew breath through flared nostrils. "I rather think it was otherwise, but in any case, I need not be overly polite, I'm sure, to a man who is trifling with my wife before my eyes."

"Trifling?" The accusation was so unexpected that she felt breathless, as if the wind had been knocked out of her.

"Precisely. And you encouraged it by giggling and whispering with him in a manner more suited to the bedchamber than to a public gathering."

"You—you must realize we have spent a great many hours together of late. It is natural that we should be on terms of friendship. Why should we not be, after all?"

He gave her a hard look. "I'm sure I have no need to explain the answer to you, Violet."

The heavy sarcasm in his voice was enraging. Her head high, she said, "I should also have no need to explain that you have little cause for your jealousy."

"I would much prefer to have none."

He turned on his heel and left her standing alone. That desertion was a social solecism so glaring compared with his usual punctiliousness that Violet could only think it a deliberate punishment for her defiance. She was doubtless supposed to be cowed at finding herself isolated among strangers.

Her husband, Violet thought rebelliously, would discover his error. She scanned the throng that shifted like a kaleidoscope of jewel-colored silks and satins as the music came to an end. Her gaze sought and found Allain. He looked up at that moment as at a silent command. Seeing her standing unattended, he moved at once in her direction.

The music was beginning again, the lovely strains of Strauss's "Lorelei" waltz, as he came to a halt in front of her. She gave him her hand. It was indiscreet, but she no longer cared. The look that sprang into his eyes warmed her, caressed her, applauded her. Her lips curved in a slow, soft smile.

Without words, they moved out onto the floor. His touch was lightly compelling as he took her into his arms. They whirled gently with her skirts billowing about their feet and his hand clasped at her waist. The rise and fall of the melody seemed to lift them, to bind them each to the other with its rhythm. She could feel his thighs moving powerfully against her through her crinoline, sense the tensile strength in his hand even through her glove. He danced as he painted, with precision and grace and unhindered instinct.

The night had seemed cool before, but she grew flushed with exertion and something more that she tried to hide with downcast lashes. Trepidation hovered in her mind, clashing with the reckless and half-stifled impulses that floated there. The lilt of the music was in her blood, and generosity in her heart.

The dance ended. Violet and Allain stood still, breathing in quick, uneven rhythm. She opened her fan, which was attached to her wrist by a silk cord, and plied it while turning her gaze to the milling dancers. She could not bring herself to look at Allain for fear of what he might discover in her eyes.

In that moment she noticed a uniformed aide-de-camp moving toward the emperor as if summoned. The man received instructions, then turned and began to make his way in their direction. He was almost upon them, however, before she realized that his objective was to speak to Allain.

"M'sieur le comte," the aide-de-camp said with a deep bow. "I present the compliments of His Imperial Majesty. He requests that you approach him. With the lady also, if you please."

Though couched with politeness, it was a royal command. The aide-de-camp stood aside to allow them to precede him. Allain offered Violet his arm and she placed her hand upon it.

As they moved toward the emperor she leaned her head toward Allain with a whispered query. "Comte?"

"A courtesy title, one extended to my father by the state of Venice many years ago," he said stiffly. "I never use it."

Violet studied the taut lines of his face. She said in quiet tones, "Is something wrong?"

"I don't like this."

"But why?"

"Louis Napoléon has not the slightest interest in talking to me.

Listen, carefully, *chère*. Whatever you do, don't allow yourself to be enticed away from the ballroom with the emperor."

"What? But why?"

There was no time for more; another two steps and they were standing before Napoléon III. Allain made his obeisance. Violet dropped into a formal curtsy. As the emperor extended his hand, palm up, she placed her own in it, though she wondered even as she did so if she was expected to kiss his ring or make some other gesture of subservience.

Louis Napoléon carried her fingers to his lips. "Charming, perfectly charming," he said. "We are enchanted."

"Thank you, Your Majesty," Violet responded with only a slight hesitation.

Allain breathed an imprecation too soft for anyone except Violet to hear.

The royal plural employed by Napoléon was a little comical in its pomposity, especially since Violet was aware of the short span of time the man before her had enjoyed the right to use it. Regardless, there was an air of burnished grandeur about him. It might have been the uniform he wore with its decorations, the power he wielded, or his inherited sense of noble purpose, but he seemed far from ordinary.

Violet, impressed against her will, was vaguely conscious of the emperor's invitation to dance and her own acceptance. In less than a moment she was on the floor, doing her best to match her steps to Louis Napoléon's sweeping, grandiose movements.

He held her so tightly that his medals and other insignia were in danger of becoming entangled in the chiffon flounce at the neckline of her gown. Looking into his face as she essayed a small comment on the progress of the ball gave her an excuse to draw back a little.

They exchanged a few more observations and Violet was searching for something else to say when there was a disturbance at the door. A gentleman of imposing appearance, decidedly handsome in his evening clothes, was just arriving. Judging from the fervent greeting of their hostess and the rapidity with which a number of other guests descended upon him, the man enjoyed a greater than average degree of popularity.

"Ah, there he is; I wondered when he would appear," the emperor said under his breath.

"Who is it?" Violet asked.

"Morny, of course. Have you not met? We must present you later; he will be indebted to us."

Violet had heard of the Duc de Morny; he was mentioned now and then in the news sheets, and Gilbert had spoken of seeing him briefly on the street. The illegitimate son of Queen Hortense of Holland and her lover, supposedly the Comte de Flahaut, he was the half-brother of the emperor. A man of singular charm only three years younger than Louis Napoléon, he was known as a bon vivant and connoisseur of women, in spite of his marriage to a natural daughter of Czar Alexander I of Russia. He had done much to bring his half-brother to power and held a prominent place in the current government.

"My husband and I," Violet said, "would be honored by an introduction."

"We will present your husband also, if you must have it so. Ah, but this nice discretion, this delicacy, recalls something to our mind. You must be the lady of the flowers."

Violet sent him a swift upward glance. "Your Majesty?"

"Massari has been scouring the hothouses of Paris and badgering the flower-market vendors for choice blossoms. He demands unblemished perfection and will accept no substitute for the species he desires. Everyone knows there is a married lady of great beauty and greater propriety in the case, though he will not speak of her. There has been much speculation."

She lowered her gaze to the braiding on his coat. "There is nothing to say I am that lady, Your Majesty."

"The thing is obvious, if you notice how Massari is regarding us. We should be wary; he will be ready to assassinate us."

"Surely not."

"He has a temper when pressed."

"You sound as if you know him well?" She could not resist turning the comment into a question.

"Europe is like a village in some respects; from Rome to London and Vienna to Marseilles, everyone knows everyone else, at least in certain circles. And everyone talks. Massari has a great number of friends, but is enough of a mystery man to maintain the interest of those easily bored."

"Mystery?"

"You are not aware of his background? He and Morny have a great deal in common; you would be amazed. Come with us to a small room where it is quieter, and we will tell you."

It was done so smoothly, his sweeping turn, which brought them to the edge of the dance floor as the music ended, his hand under her arm guiding her toward the direction he wished her to go. Violet was concentrating on the implications of what the emperor had said about Allain rather than on what he was doing. She was inside the door of the small withdrawing room before she remembered Allain's warning.

Her skirts swirled around her ankles as she came to an abrupt halt. "Wait," she said in haste."Perhaps I—had better not leave the ballroom, after all. My husband will not be pleased."

"But your husband has left you to your own devices for some time now."

"Yes, and for that reason may be looking for me even now. I had best go and see."

"And waste such a perfect opportunity for a passage at arms? Don't be shy; come to us!"

He was stronger than she would have guessed, and bolder. Thrusting an arm about her waist, he swung her away from the door and kicked it shut. In the same movement, he dragged her against him and sought her lips.

She turned her head sharply, pushing against his chest with both hands. "No, Your Majesty! Please—"

Her defense almost broke his hold. He gave a laugh of surprise before he redoubled his efforts. Catching the back of her neck, he slid his fingers under the knot of ringlets at the back of her head to tilt her face upward. She twisted in his hold as his mouth grazed the corner of her lips.

The door opened, letting in a gust of warm air and music. Allain stepped inside, then closed the panel behind him. "Your Majesty," he said in quiet tones. "You will, I trust, pardon the intrusion."

Violet pushed away from the emperor with a gasp of relief as Louis Napoléon's hold loosened with his surprise. The emperor whipped around to face the other man. His voice grating on the order, he said, "You will leave us!"

Allain moved without haste to Violet's side. "Not," he said succinctly, "without the lady."

Napoléon drew himself up. "We will not support this interference."

"I'm afraid you will have to," Allain answered, his attention on Violet as he offered her the support of his arm. "We bid you good evening, Your Majesty."

The emperor opened his mouth as if he meant to either protest further or call his guard. Abruptly, a gleam of humor rose in his eyes. He shrugged with elaborate casualness. "Very well, pluck the flower yourself, Massari. But I warn you, there may be thorns."

"I am aware," Allain answered, his voice grave and his regard steady as it rested on Violet's flushed face.

Turning, he led her from the room.

They had taken only a few paces into the ballroom when Violet began to speak in jerky, disjointed phrases. "I am so grateful you came. I never dreamed—I know you said—but I couldn't imagine that he would—"

"He is a goat."

Allain's tone was so savage that it sent a flicker of terror through her. She was not certain if it was possible for an emperor to receive a challenge to a duel, but she had heard that timbre in a man's voice before, in New Orleans, and knew it portended pistols for two, and breakfast for one.

She made a small sound of distress as she put a hand to her head. "I would really like to leave, if I could. Perhaps you might help me find Gilbert. I can't think where he can be all this time, unless he is in one of the card rooms."

"Yes, but are you all right?" he asked.

"I have a little headache, only. I promise I don't intend to swoon."

"I have no objection, so long as I'm here to catch you," he said, his mood lightening slightly as he smiled. "But it's impolite, you know, to leave a gathering before the emperor. You will have to slip away by a side door, and without bidding your hostess good-bye."

"I hadn't thought. Perhaps I had better stay."

Reluctance was heavy in her voice. It wasn't just the headache that drove her. The tensions of the last hour, the contretemps with Gilbert as well as Louis Napoléon, and now the idea that people were watching and gossiping about her and Allain, had become too much. There was no one she knew at the ball, none of Gilbert's relatives and acquaintances; everyone was a stranger and, in spite of the French tongue, foreign to her. She had been taught all her life to think of herself as French, but she was beginning to realize that she was something different, an American of French extraction.

Allain studied her pale face, then shook his head. "Never mind. I'll make your adieus. Let us go in search of your husband."

They found Gilbert at a faro table with a stack of gold coins in front of him. He barely looked up as she approached, and took no time to consider her request. He was winning, couldn't she see? He could not go while the cards were in his favor. Besides, he had been certain she was enjoying the dancing.

Violet, watching the tightness of her husband's mouth, thought he was glad to have a reason to refuse her. She would not lower her dignity by asking more than once. She turned away.

Allain, who had been standing just behind her, did not move. To Gilbert he said, "Your pardon, m'sieur, but have I your permission to escort Madame Fossier in your stead?"

Gilbert turned deliberately to face him. There was a heavy frown between his brows as he met Allain's clear gaze. He held a gold coin in his hand, turning it slowly between his fingers.

A soft silence descended as the cardplayers glanced at each other, then toward the two men. Allain, sustaining Gilbert's stare, slowly raised his head. His features congealed in implacable challenge, and there was an intimation of steel in the gray blue of his eyes. His trim, broad-shouldered form took on an imposing, almost regal stature. The force of his anger, perfectly controlled yet unremitting, was palpable.

Gilbert inhaled with a soft, hissing sound through his teeth. The frown dissolved from his face. He blinked rapidly.

The fear that Violet had suppressed earlier returned with renewed force. She put out her hand to touch Allain's arm in a calming gesture. Her voice tight in her throat, she said, "Your permission, Gilbert?"

He moistened his lips before he answered. His voice was hoarse as he said, "As you like."

"Thank you," Allain answered for Violet with brusque courtesy. Drawing her hand through the crook of his arm, he turned and led her from the room.

Violet glanced back at her husband as she went. Gilbert was watching them with angry bewilderment in his face. It was apparent that something he had seen in Allain's eyes had decided him against crossing the artist.

She turned her head to look up at the man who walked beside her. His manner was assured, relaxed now. She thought of leaving the house, of entering his carriage and driving through the dark and empty streets of Paris with him. Alone, with him.

Anticipation and an odd dread fluttered in her veins, swelling around her heart.

This ball had not, Allain admitted to himself, been the best of ideas. He had wanted to give Violet a night of pleasure, to see her shine among the best of Paris society, and yes, to have an excuse to hold her in his arms. It had not turned out precisely as he had planned.

He was embarrassed. It had been a long time since he had felt the need to annihilate another man. That it should happen with one older and less experienced, one whom he had wronged in thought if not in deed, was ignoble. He should never have forced a confrontation. His anger and concern for Violet did not excuse him. He had no right to chance making matters worse for her merely because his blood was at a boil.

It was the emperor whom he had wanted most of all to spit on his sword like the strutting turkey-cock that he was. The insufferable conceit of Louis Napoléon, to think he could sully Violet's lovely purity by tumbling her in a dark corner like some kitchen maid. Discretion had made a challenge unwise. He should have offered it anyway. What did he care for discretion, or for France if it came to that? He was only a transient, a chance visitor. His interest, like his danger, was elsewhere.

It had been Gilbert's misfortune to cross him too soon after the confrontation with Louis Napoléon. Humiliation or death, that had been the choice Violet's husband had been forced to make. He would not soon forgive his wife for being the cause of it, or for witnessing his coward's retreat.

If Gilbert had found the courage to stand up to him, what would he have done? The honorable thing would have been to delope, to fire into the air and allow the wronged husband his just shot. But would he? Ah, no. He would have killed Violet's husband in cold blood and for the most base of motives, to make her a widow. At least he would have tried. God forgive him.

He glanced at Violet as she moved behind him from the ballroom and down the narrow backstairs. She walked like a queen, or an empress, with her head high and back straight, deaf to the whispers that followed them. She was formidable in her pride and virtue. The courage her husband lacked was as natural to her as breathing. To treat such a woman as a child to be cosseted or punished at will was the act of a stupid man, one who deserved to lose her.

Amazing, to think that she would risk everything by going with him. He had not expected it. He had watched her struggle with the bounds prescribed for women of her class in these last weeks, and had respected her for it even while he made his delicate attacks upon her will. He would not have been surprised if, tonight, she had chosen the safety of remaining with her husband even in his defeat. Or perhaps because of his defeat.

She had not. She had chosen him.

Nothing had ever made him feel so proud.

Nothing had ever made him feel so humble.

Gilbert Fossier was not worthy of this woman. The trouble was, neither, perhaps, was he.

Chapter 10

Joletta opened her eyes with slow care. There was a pounding ache in her head, and every joint in her body felt as if it had been jarred loose from its moorings. She was lying on the sidewalk. A number of people were clustered around her. There was something soft under her head, possibly a rolled sport coat. Rone, in shirt sleeves, knelt on one knee at her left shoulder. He held her hand in his warm clasp, rubbing it a little as he frowned down at her.

At her other side was a darkly handsome man in a tan leather jacket, a shirt of cream silk, and with dark aviator glasses pushed on top of his head, pressing into the crisp black waves of his hair. His gaze upon her was brooding and concerned, though his rough-cut features lightened into a smile as he saw that she was conscious.

"My apologies, signorina," he said, his voice low and deep. "I should not have pushed you so hard, except there was no time for care."

Italian. She recognized the accent, the bronzed tan of his skin, the inimitable style of what he wore, without real surprise. There was a curious rightness about it. It was a moment before she realized why, and then she grinned a little to herself, at herself. A near street accident. Violet's Italian. Ridiculous. Her brain seemed to have gone a little haywire.

She lifted her free hand, to touch her head. There was the wet stickiness of blood in her hair. "The—car," she said, her voice a little uncertain.

"Long gone," Rone said. "It never touched you."

"The driver could have stopped; he must have seen what happened," the other man said, his thick brows meeting over his nose in a disapproving scowl.

"You saw him?" Joletta winced a little as her probing brought a throb of pain.

The Italian reached to take her fingers. Drawing a handkerchief from his pocket, he wiped away the bloodstains as he spoke. "Unfortunately not. There were people running everywhere, you understand? And I only had eyes for you who were in the imbecile's path. Ah, signorina, believe me, please; I would not for the world have been the one to hurt you."

"I'm—glad you were around," she said. "It would have been all right, I think, if the pole hadn't gotten in the way."

"Exactly so. But I should introduce myself. I am Caesar Zilanti, at your service, signorina."

Rone's gaze was sardonic as it rested on the other man. To Joletta he said, "It might be best to save the introductions until later. Right now I think I should get you to a hospital."

"Was I out that long?" she asked.

"Only a few minutes, not that the time means anything."

"It's just a bump; I'll be all right in a minute. I don't think I need—"

"You may have a concussion," he said, his voice firm. "It won't hurt to see a doctor to make certain you're okay."

"He is right, signorina," Caesar Zilanti said in tones of caressing persuasion.

"But I don't want to sit around all night in a hospital waiting room," she protested.

"It should not take so long." The Italian's dark gaze was earnest. "I'll be happy to drive you; my car is just along the street here."

"That won't be necessary," Rone said shortly. "We can find a taxi."

The other man raised a brow. "At this hour? You must be joking. Allow me to do this much, please, to soothe my conscience."

There was something in the atmosphere between Rone and Caesar Zilanti that troubled Joletta. They were too polite, the way they looked at each other across her was too wary. She wondered if there had been some kind of confrontation between them while she was out, if maybe they had had words over the way the Italian had pushed her.

She could not worry about it just now. The sound of their voices seemed to echo in her head, making it ache. She also felt foolish lying there on the sidewalk while they argued across her.

"All right, all right, I'll go to the hospital," she said, struggling to sit upright, "only let's get it over with."

"*Benissimo*, in my car?"

"Whatever is fastest," Joletta answered.

Rone's expression was grim, but he made no objection.

The hospital visit did not take as long as Joletta had expected. The process was efficient and the female doctor who saw her seemed glad to have an opportunity to use her English. Joletta had a very slight concussion, the woman said, hardly enough to show up on the X-ray film. There should be no need for hospitalization so long as she took reasonable care of herself: no long hikes, fast games of tennis, or anything of that nature. The usual over-the-counter headache remedies should suffice, though they would give her something a little stronger now. She should, of course, contact a doctor at once if the pain grew worse, if she experienced any dizziness or change in her vision. Otherwise, she should enjoy her visit to France; that was the prescription.

"Perhaps you will now allow me to take you both to dinner," Caesar Zilanti said when they were outside the hospital once more. "I would feel better, if you would. It's early, yes, but we could go somewhere and relax over a drink until a more suitable hour."

"I don't know," she said, glancing at Rone.

"Sorry, but I can't," Rone answered. "I have some calls I need to make."

She thought he had told her he had his business arranged so he needn't keep in such close touch. He might, of course, only be using that as an excuse. Regardless, she was not sure she wanted to cope with making conversation with a stranger just now without him.

Joletta turned toward Caesar Zilanti with an apologetic smile. "I think it might be better if I have an early night. I appreciate the invitation, really."

"Perhaps tomorrow night?" The Italian's dark gaze held appeal.

"It won't be possible, I'm afraid. We leave in the afternoon for Lucerne."

"Too bad," he said, "it would have been a great pleasure. But you will permit me to drive you back to your hotel, yes? Good."

The silver Alfa Romeo he was driving was parked not far away. As they walked toward it he went on. "Many tourists go on from Switzerland to Italy. Do you visit my country by any chance?"

"We'll be there four or five days," Joletta said.

Caesar gave her an incredulous look and a shake of his head as they reached the car and he opened the door for her. "Too little, far too little. There is so much I could show you, if I were there."

To have a guide who knew the small, out-of-the-way places, or who could sort out what was worth seeing from what was not, might have been nice. Joletta's smile held a shade of regret as she said, "I suppose we'll have to make do by ourselves."

Caesar slid into the car. "A shame," he said, his dark eyes somber with regret as he turned the key in the ignition with only the briefest glance to see if Rone was in the vehicle. "A terrible shame."

The Italian drove with verve and a total disregard for the dangers of the Le Mans–like Paris traffic. He did slacken his speed somewhat when Joletta reached for a hold on the dash as they rounded a corner. A few minutes later, however, he was racing again, and using his horn to intimidate less aggressive drivers.

He was, she supposed, the kind of man who might be called dangerously handsome, with heavy-lidded eyes, a sensually wide mouth, and thick hair that grew low on his neck. That he was aware of it was obvious, for there was an inner assurance about him and a faintly humorous challenge in the way he looked at her—and at most other women, she suspected. That manner, with his car and clothing that appeared to be on the forward edge of fashion for men, added up to a continental glamour that had an undoubted appeal. It was not the kind of looks that attracted Joletta ordinarily; still, it might have been interesting to get to know him a little better.

Or perhaps not. The last thing she needed just now was another complication.

She thanked the Italian for everything again when they reached the hotel. There was such disappointment in his dark eyes as he said good-bye that she might have changed her mind and agreed to dinner from sheer guilt, had Rone not taken her arm to draw her away.

"You're a softy, aren't you?" he said with amusement shading his voice as they walked into the hotel.

"Probably," she agreed, her own smile wry. "I'm also beginning to think I need a keeper. I've never had so much bad luck in my life; it's downright embarrassing."

"You shouldn't have been hurt this evening. If I had been more alert, it wouldn't have happened."

The self-blame in his voice disturbed her. She said, "You aren't responsible for me. I was joking about the keeper."

A corner of his mouth lifted. "What if I would like the job?"

"It's a thankless position, as you should know by now." There was a tight feeling in her throat, but she ignored it.

"My favorite kind."

"In that case, you've got it," she quipped, and was self-aware enough to wonder if she was really joking. She refused to consider that he might be serious.

She also refused to think that it might not have been an accident that she had come so close to serious injury this afternoon. The number of people who could have known where she was at that instant was so few, and foremost among them was Rone. Some things were best left unexplored.

There was grandeur and glitter at Versailles, just as Joletta had expected, but there was also something depressing about the huge, chill rooms, the mirrors endlessly reflecting emptiness, and the preserved fragments of lives that had been rudely interrupted, crudely terminated. The stagnant fountains in the unnaturally regimented gardens appeared forlorn, as if waiting for laughter and merriment and wicked, pleasurable decadence that would never come again. She was ready to leave when the bus pulled away for Lucerne.

The drive was long, though the motorway they took to the southeast was excellent. Joletta's head had begun to ache again, though she had been fine during the morning. She took a couple of aspirins and leaned back in her seat, closing her eyes.

After that, the trip became a blur of small villages of cream stone clustered around gray-roofed church steeples, of clipped hawthorne hedges and vineyards with the grapes pruned to knee height, and of bright fields of yellow rape and blue-green rye like giant patchwork quilts. The blue-and-white road signs, the rest areas labeled AIRE STOP, and the mechanized tollbooths that sped past her window had a surreal quality; they were not what she was used to seeing, and so seemed not quite what they should be.

She woke once to find her head pillowed on Rone's shoulder. Since he was asleep also, and the muscled firmness felt good under her cheek, she stayed where she was.

Lying there with her eyes closed, she thought of how easily he seemed to have made his decision to join her, and how easily she had accepted it. That he would want to be with her was gratifying, yes, but somehow she was also disturbed by it. He was congenial company, natural, easygoing, entertaining; somehow they found a great deal to talk about. Still, there was something in his attitude toward her that bothered her. He seemed to be attracted to her, yet he seldom touched her beyond the most casual contact. His comments might be mildly amorous, but his basic behavior was more brotherly than loverlike.

It wasn't that she wanted him to make mad, passionate love to her. She was glad to meet a man who didn't try to push her straight into his bed. It was a privilege to be with one who had the decency to realize that a woman with a concussion, however slight, would appreciate a kiss on the forehead and a quiet good-night at her bedroom door.

Regardless, when she thought of the way he had kissed her on a dark street in New Orleans, it didn't seem quite right. It was as if he was deliberately restraining himself, almost as if he was wary of offending her.

Nor did she fully understand her own reactions toward him. His presence, his attentive and protective attitude gave her a secret thrill, yet there was also something inside her that counseled caution. She was used to that in her dealings with men, used to questioning their motives, yet this seemed different.

She thought of her suspicion of him in London. It had not lasted, especially not after she realized her cousin, and possibly her aunt, was also in Europe. She wondered, however, if he might have sensed it. He was a man of such finely honed instincts that it seemed possible. She did not like to think there had been anything in her manner toward him that might have caused it.

She was not going to make too much out of this joint trip. In the first place she didn't have the time, and in the second it would not be smart. She had not asked him to come. On the other hand, she could not prevent him from joining the group, even if she wanted to. She would enjoy his company and the odd sense of security it gave her, taking the situation as it came. And if nothing much came of it, she would not be disappointed.

It was late when they arrived at Lucerne. The town was dimly lighted and the mountains no more than dark outlines looming beyond the starlit sheen of the lake. Their hotel was located down a side street only a few blocks from the lakefront. The room Joletta was given was small and quaint, with a many-armed art nouveau lamp with glass tulips for shades and walls paneled with alpine scenes in sepia tones. There were no sheets or blanket on the twin beds, only pillows and fluffy duvets. The big casement windows, though covered for privacy by electrically operated blinds, could be opened to the cool, pure mountain air. Breathing its freshness, Joletta fell once more into sleep.

She awoke ravenous and bored with being an invalid, ready for anything and everything. Immediately after breakfast, she and Rone took the cog train with the group to the top of Mt. Rigi. It was an exhilarating journey through meadowlands where the chocolate-brown cows of Switzerland grazed near wooden chalets on rich green grass starred with yellow alpine flowers, all against a back-drop of blue, snow-dusted peaks and steep-walled valleys. The day was gloriously clear, so the entire panorama of Alps, the sailboat-studded lake, and Lucerne itself was visible from the mountaintop. Perhaps for that reason, and because it was the weekend, families of Swiss, from grandmothers to the smallest chubby baby, were out in force.

The hang gliders were there, too. Joletta could not bear to watch them launch themselves into space with such terrible élan with only the flimsy support of nylon and aluminum tubing. She could not see how anyone could possibly enjoy such a sport and could not be-lieve that anyone actually did. Rone teased her about her squea-mishness, but she noticed that he made an effort to remain always between her and the edge of any precipice, even if it meant blocking her view.

They lunched on bratwurst and rosti potatoes with a dessert of raspberry ice, all while watching a folklore show. Afterward, Joletta and Rone roamed around the town. They window-shopped for Ro-lex watches and Swiss knives and snapped pictures of the ornate frescoed designs on the walls of the houses. They wandered along to the Lion of Lucerne, monument to the slain Swiss guards of Louis XVI, which, Rone informed her, had been called the most touching memorial in Europe by Mark Twain.

It was at the monument that Joletta discovered she had left her notebook behind at the hotel. There was a certain freedom in not having it; she could enjoy the civic plantings of pansies and tulips and English daisies, also the white lilacs, spireas, and mats of alpine rock-garden plants in the small, neat gardens before the small, neat houses, without feeling that every plant had to be recorded.

The sun was setting in rose-and-lavender luminescence when Rone and Joletta came finally to the covered footbridge. It snaked across the River Reuss at the point just before it flowed into Lake Lucerne. Appearing narrow only because of its long length, it was only partially closed in on the sides yet massively built, so much so that it made the covered bridges of New England seem puny by comparison.

Joletta and Rone craned their necks to look at the scenes from the history of the town that were painted on the roof-support sections in rich colors touched with gilt. It was a progression of events beginning in the Middle Ages, one they followed as they walked along with their own echoing footsteps and the whisper and gurgle of the clear, green-tinted river in their ears.

"Look, swans," Joletta said as they stopped to lean on the bridge railing near the water tower that loomed near the middle of the span.

"A mated pair." Rone followed the progress of the big white birds as they glided, touching their long graceful necks together, with their feathers tinted pink by the afterglow.

The water smelled a little of fish and cold-weather algae and melted snow. To their left lay the picturesque green onion domes of some church, while the mountain peaks lay in the distance behind them. They could just hear the brass band from a restaurant in the town. Lights were beginning to come on as the dusk deepened, small, glowing points of brightness that were reflected in the water at the river's edge.

The evening breeze blowing over the river was cool. Joletta pulled her cardigan of cream cotton closer around her. As she gazed at the lights along the riverbank and the organized patchwork of rooftops that made up the town, she wondered if Violet had stood here, had seen this view.

Thoughts of Violet had been easing in and out of her mind since the day before; she had even dreamed of her again while dozing on the bus. Joletta was beginning to admire the way her ancestress had dared to go after what she wanted. Violet had accepted the fear, the guilt, and the dangers, and acted anyway. That was not the kind of behavior one might expect of so thoroughly Victorian a woman. Or was Violet that Victorian? Had New Orleans been as affected by the prudish precepts taught during that era as had the more northeastern portion of the United States, where puritanism had its sway?

Thinking of herself and her long engagement to Charles, Joletta suspected that she had not been as deeply involved in that relationship as she had believed. It had never occurred to her to go after him, to risk rejection and humiliation for what she wanted. Though she had never quite admitted it to herself before, she had felt a quick, hastily suppressed relief when she knew Charles was gone forever from her life.

Given another chance, what would she do now? She wished she knew. She wished, in fact, there was some way to tell just how much of Violet's blood flowed in her own veins, how much of her spirit had been transmitted with Violet's genes.

"Tell me something," Joletta said into the long quiet that had fallen. "Do you think that history repeats itself?"

"You mean in the sense of people making the same mistakes others did before them?" Rone asked.

"I was thinking more along the lines of—not reincarnation exactly, but of events taking place in a later generation in much the same way they happened in an earlier one."

He gave her a quizzical look, his gaze resting on the sunset flush on her face. "I think you'll have to be more particular if you want an answer out of me."

"Never mind," she said with a smile that did not quite reach her eyes. "It was a crazy idea, anyway."

He watched her for the space of time it took a frown to come and go between his eyes. He ventured a reply of sorts anyway, then. "Strange things happen all the time, I suppose. As for reincarnation, there's a good portion of the world's population that considers it a perfectly reasonable idea."

"But not you?"

"I don't intend to rush into anything until they prove it."

"Which may be too late," she suggested.

His lips curved in a wry smile. "That's the trouble with most beliefs."

The pair of swans floated toward them, delicately courting with rhythmic twining of their long necks. They drifted under the bridge and out of sight. Joletta turned her head to look at Rone. He was watching her, his gray gaze dark and unreadable in the dimness. He straightened slowly, turning toward her. She came erect also. Her senses tingled with alertness as she sensed some change in him.

He reached for her with slow deliberation, closing his hands on her upper arms as if touching her was a pleasure to be savored. He met her gaze without evasion, the expression in his own open, yet somber, almost driven. She met his eyes, her will suspended and uncertain. As he moved closer she lowered her lashes, resting her gaze on the sculpted curves and smooth surfaces of his lips.

Her breath was suspended in her chest. She could hear the accelerating strokes of her heartbeat whispering in her ears. The scent of him, compounded of fresh air, clean clothing, warm skin, and sandalwood, drifted around her. The radiating warmth of his body was enveloping; it destroyed thought, annihilated will. Her eyelids fluttered down as she lifted her face ever so slightly in consent, in expectation.

His mouth was firm and gentle, the pressure inviting. She spread her hands over his chest under the lightweight canvas windbreaker he wore, sliding them upward to trail her fingers through the silky thickness of the hair growing low on the back of his neck. The surfaces of her own lips tingled with heated sensitivity as she allowed them to part in invitation.

It was a delicate exploration of will, a blind revel of the senses, a gentle prelude. Unhurried, they tested the physical bonding of the kiss, feeling its swelling power, and its promise.

Heat gathered under Joletta's skin, so she ceased to feel the evening coolness. His tongue touched hers. She met it with her own, enticed by its gentle probing. With a soft sound in her throat, she joined the sensual discovery of tender inner surfaces and the glazed-smooth edges of teeth. His hand at her back, smoothing the taut muscles, drawing her closer, was an incitement to surrender.

She lowered one hand, letting it drift down over the planes of his chest and under the edge of his windbreaker to the trimness of his waist. The leather of his belt was smooth, and cool in contrast to the wafting heat of his body. She followed its circular path to the center of his back, where the ridged muscles left a slight hollow that seemed a perfect opening for her fingers. She tucked them inside, pressing with her palm to hold him firmly against her.

His indrawn breath was soft, yet deep. He shifted slightly, cupping her face in his hand. With the side of his thumb, he traced the turn of her jaw, the delicate softness of her earlobe. Trailing his fingers lower, he brushed the slender turn of her neck, outlined the fragility of her collarbone, then slowly, gently, closed his hand upon the globe of her breast.

Anticipation burgeoned inside her, a steady, heated promise that spread in waves, until her skin tingled and the blood ran fast and warm in her veins. She shivered in instant reaction as his thumb smoothed across the exquisitely tender crest of her nipple. Her grasp tightened in a slow contraction of muscles as she pressed closer. She could feel the firmness of his lower body against the yielding softness of her own.

Footsteps clattered in approach. Voices murmured. They were no longer alone on the bridge.

Joletta went still, then began to withdraw by slow degrees. Rone's chest rose and fell in a silent sigh as he let her go just as slowly. He kept his arm at her waist as they glanced at the three Swiss students, two boys and a girl with waist-length blond hair, who tramped past them.

The young trio did not even look in their direction.

A rueful smile curved Joletta's lips. How American of her to be concerned over being seen kissing a man. There had been couples embracing with varying degrees of intimacy everywhere she had been so far, from Hyde Park to the top of Mt. Rigi.

She looked up at Rone, but the light had grown so dim that she could not make out his expression there under the roof of the bridge. It appeared grim, but it might have been only the deepening purple gray of the twilight slanting across his face, for a moment later he gave a rough-edged laugh and swung with her to walk on toward the bridge's end. Turning at that far side of the river, they retraced their footsteps back toward the hotel once more.

Most of the rooms of the tour group were on the same floor; Rone's was located near the staircase, a few doors away from Joletta's. He did not stop there, however, but walked on down the narrow hall with her. Joletta glanced at the room key she had picked up at the desk, trying to see it in the dim light given off by a wall sconce left over from the twenties.

Abruptly, Rone clamped a hand on her wrist, bringing her to a halt. As she looked up at him he put a finger to his lips for silence, then nodded toward her door.

"Did you leave the light on in your room?" he asked, his voice pitched just above a whisper.

"I don't think so," she said with a slow shake of her head.

Taking the key from her hand, he eased to the door and inserted it in the lock. Joletta started forward, but he indicated with a quick one-handed gesture that he wanted her to stay back.

The light went off inside the room.

Rone immediately shoved the door open. He swung back for a

cautious instant, then, a fraction of a moment later, plunged around the door frame and dived into the room. There came a hard grunt, followed by the shuddering thud of bodies slamming into a wall. A chair overturned with a skidding thump. Feet scuffled. Voices cursed in breathless strain.

Joletta ran forward. Just inside the room, she paused. There was the acrid lime harshness of an unfamiliar after-shave on the cool mountain air coming through the open window with its raised blind. In the light coming from the street, she saw two figures like dark, struggling shadows.

Her reaction was instinctive. She reached for the overhead light switch.

Brightness exploded in the room. A man in black with a ski mask over his head swung his head toward Joletta. He growled, then wrenched violently away from Rone and leaped toward the window. He sprang to the sill, hovered a split second on one knee, then jumped.

Rone sprinted to the casement, leaning to look out. Joletta ran to join him. All she saw was a dangling rope that still swayed against the brown plaster of the outside wall. It came from the roof two stories up, and ended near the ground that was two stories below.

"Gone," Rone said.

There was disgust and anger in his voice. Joletta sent him a brief glance before she looked back at the rope. "A cat burglar," she said in hollow tones. "I can't believe it."

He spun around, his gaze moving swiftly over the room. Folding his arms, he said, "Try harder."

She turned slowly. The room was a shambles, with drawers pulled out, the contents of her suitcase dumped on the floor and its lining ripped out, mattresses off the beds and springs hanging from the frames, the duvets torn open. Down stuffing covered everything with its feathery softness, blowing, rolling into gentle drifts in the cool draft from the window.

"Dear God," she whispered, her arm closing protectively around the heavy purse hanging from her shoulder, the purse that contained the journal.

"Right," Rone said in agreement, his eyes narrowing as he watched her. "Now, tell me one more time about your terrible luck?"

Chapter 11

The hotel manager, viewing the destruction of Joletta's room, was aghast, apologetic, and affronted. Such a thing had never happened before in any hotel he had managed. Theft, yes, but not this wanton violence. He could not imagine why it should have occurred now; such a thing was foreign to the nature of his countrymen. The young lady was not, of course, Swiss. Was it possible that she had angered someone from her own tour group?

The manager's attitude did nothing to help Joletta's feelings. Her experience so far on this trip made her reluctant to report the incident, especially since she had no intention of going into details concerning the journal or her family. Rone had insisted, however, and there was the damage to hotel property to be considered.

The police, when they arrived, were efficient and not unsympathetic. They wrote a thorough report of the damage, took down the description of the intruder, and promised an exacting search. They were unable to hold out much hope for capturing the man, however; the random nature of most hotel break-ins made them difficult to trace.

The manager did not linger after the police had gone. He would send a maid to replace the damaged bedding and make everything tidy again, he said. He would like to offer Miss Caresse another room, but it was not possible. The high season was beginning. The hotel was full; not even a closet was available. He would understand if she wished to go elsewhere, but he could not promise she would find other accommodations at that hour.

Joletta, assuring the manager that she would be fine where she was, closed the door upon the man and his excuses. Answering the endless questions, denying that she had any idea what the intruder wanted and keeping to the lie, had brought a return of her headache. She was in desperate need of a couple of aspirins.

"You can't stay here," Rone said, watching her with a frown between his brows.

"I have to," she said in a wobbly attempt at humor. "You heard the man."

"My room has twin beds, too."

Joletta glanced at him as she moved to pick up her shoulder bag from the end of her bed. There was nothing in his face to suggest anything other than concern and practicality. "That's very considerate of you," she said, "but I don't think it's necessary."

"You can't be sure. I don't like the way this place is torn up; there was a knife used on most of this stuff. What would you have done if you had been alone this evening? What would you do if the guy came back?"

She pressed the fingers of one hand against her pounding temple. Closing her eyes, she said, "He won't be back."

"What makes you think so?"

She couldn't think straight. The pain in her head was making her feel a little sick. She searched in the bag she held for a headache remedy, at the same time avoiding Rone's narrow gaze.

He moved from where he had been sitting on a table edge with his arms crossed over his chest. Taking the bag from her, he found the aspirins and shook two of them into her hand. "This what you were looking for?"

She nodded in mute gratitude. He walked to the bathroom and returned with a glass of water as she put the pills in her mouth. He watched her drink it before he went on. "You were saying about this guy with the knife."

She looked at him, then away again, before she sighed. "All right, maybe he will."

She hadn't intended to say that; the words had just come out. As Rone made no reply, she looked up at him. She expected questions, a demand to know why she hadn't mentioned the possibility to the police, anything except his intent, considering silence.

She moistened her lips before she added, "At least the man didn't find what he wanted, so he may have figured out that I've got it with me."

"Right," he said in stringent irony. "That does it. Come on, gather up what you need and let's go."

"No, I'll just lock the window and the door. I'll be fine, really." Shaking her head was not a good move; she stopped abruptly.

He met her gaze, his own level and a little hard. "I won't pounce on you, you know. You'll be perfectly safe."

"I'm sure I would be, but I prefer—"

"I really won't, you know. In spite of what happened on the bridge."

She swallowed, looking at the wall behind his head, the floor, anywhere except at him. The low timbre of his voice did strange things to an area at the center of her abdomen. "I—never thought you would," she said finally.

"It's settled then." He swung toward the bathroom, where he began to rummage among her belongings. "What do you need? A toothbrush? Hairbrush? What else?"

It was a relief, in a way, to have her hand forced. Joletta would have stayed in the room, but it was doubtful she would have been able to rest. On the other hand, she wasn't at all sure about her prospects for a peaceful night with Rone. She believed that he had nothing underhanded in mind in offering her a bed, but she could not forget that moment of closeness on the bridge. He had not, she thought, intended that to happen, either.

The room Rone had been given was more Spartan than Joletta's, but otherwise much the same. The twin beds were arranged at right angles to each other against two walls. He pointed out the one that he had used the night before and placed the things he carried on the foot of the other.

There was a moment of awkwardness as he turned to face her. Joletta wondered if he felt it, too. She wished she was more sophisticated, had more experience of situations of this sort. She searched her mind for something light to say to ease the tension, but came up with nothing.

"It's been a long day," he said. "You can have first chance at the bathroom, if you like."

She glanced at him from under her lashes, but made no effort to follow his suggestion. Instead, she moved to sit down on the bed.

She took a deep breath and let it out in a long sigh before she spoke. "There's something I think I should tell you."

As she paused, searching for words, he moved to take a seat in one of the stiff armchairs beside the minuscule table under the windows of the room. He said quietly, "About your visitor this evening, right?"

She nodded. "It seems you ought to know—especially if you're going to keep running into trouble because of me. The only thing missing is the notes that I've been making since England."

She went on quickly to outline what she was doing, and why. There were a few details she left out, such as her suspicion of her aunt.

Rone heard Joletta out in silence, though there was a pucker of concentration between his eyes. He was quiet for a long moment when she stopped speaking. Finally he said, "And that's all?"

"What do you mean, all?" There was a hint of disbelief in his voice that puzzled her.

"I mean are you sure that's all this guy wanted, the notes and the copy of the journal."

"What else could it have been?"

His dark gaze was watchful, assessing as he answered. "You tell me—remembering that he turned out the light and waited, knife in hand, when he heard you coming."

"You mean, you think he—" She stopped, unable to put it into words.

"He didn't know, apparently, that you wouldn't be alone."

"No," she said in a decisive tone after a moment. "He can't have meant to hurt me. He just figured out that I must keep the journal with me."

"You mean—I thought you said you left it in New Orleans?" There was a curious blend of disbelief, irritation, and amusement in his voice.

"I brought a photocopy," she said with a small curl of satisfaction at one corner of her mouth.

His gaze upon her was impenetrable as he studied her, though it lingered on the delicately tucked spot where her lips joined. He said finally, "So, I suppose you will go on just as before?"

"I don't know what else to do. The notes can be reconstructed, though the more I write down, the less all the facts and figures I've been gathering seem to mean."

"You're sure there's nothing more concrete in the journal about the formula?"

"Fairly sure."

He lifted his hands and let them fall again. "I don't mean to be discouraging, but that part of this trip of yours sounds like a forlorn hope to me."

"I suppose," she agreed. She tried not to think of Mimi's trust, or what it would mean if she was unable to find the formula.

"On the other hand, someone doesn't appear to be taking it that lightly. I'm thinking about you having your bag snatched in London and being nearly run down in Paris."

She looked away from him, fixing her gaze on the leaf-patterned carpet on the floor. "I try not to think about it, myself."

"That won't make it go away," he said, a trace of anger in his voice.

"No, but maybe they will give up if it gets too hard."

"They who?"

She shrugged a little without meeting his gaze. "Whoever."

Rone said nothing for long moments, then abruptly he asked, "Have you given any thought to quitting and going home?"

"I can't do that."

"Why not?" There was the sound of controlled impatience in his voice.

She turned a look of defiance upon him. "I don't know. Pride, stubbornness, curiosity maybe. Or maybe it's just something I have to do."

His dark blue eyes held hers. For long seconds he looked as if he wanted to argue further, then he inclined his head in a slow nod. "Fine, then. I'd like to help."

"You already have. It's amazing, the way you've been there when I've needed someone."

"I didn't mean that. I meant I'd like to help you on this crazy quest."

She gave him a skeptical look. "Such a forlorn hope can't be interesting to you."

A smile came and went across his face. "You interest me and I have a weakness for lost causes—and nothing better to do just now."

"It isn't a game," she said slowly.

"I didn't think it was."

The expression in his eyes was earnest and open. There was something so rock solid, so dependable yet relaxed about him as he sat across from her with a long leg thrust out in front of him, that it seemed foolish to remain on her guard.

Joletta gave him a slow smile. "Well, if you're sure—and since you're along for the ride already—I don't see how it can hurt."

A shadow seemed to cross his face, and for a long moment it looked as if he might make some comment. But he only said, "We'll start in the morning then. Now about that bath. Ladies first."

Rone, as he heard the water begin to run in the bathroom, got slowly to his feet and moved to the window, where he propped his shoulder against the frame. He punched the power button that raised the metal blinds so he could look out. His face set in lines of morose dissatisfaction as he stood staring at the ornate cornices on the buildings across the side street. He had what he had wanted all along. Why didn't he feel better about it?

She was so trusting. Or was she? There had been a flicker of something in her straight gaze that gave him a distinct feeling of uneasiness. He wondered what she saw when she looked at him with those huge sherry-brown eyes, wondered what was going on in her mind.

There wasn't much he didn't want to know about her.

He didn't want to hurt her. There had been an instant there, just now, when he had felt an almost overwhelming urge to explain himself, to tell her everything. It had not lasted long. The risk was too great.

What was he going to do?

For one thing he was going to keep his hands off of her. He was going to stay in his own bed, stay on his side of the room. He was not going to watch her too closely. He was going to come near her only when necessary, and as briefly as possible. He was going to pay no attention to mating swans.

That had been a mistake, this evening on the bridge. He had known it at the time, but had not been able to resist. It was dangerous, getting too near her. He would remember that if it killed him.

The man in her room earlier had taken him by surprise, had done so only because he had not foreseen that possibility, had not prepared for it. He should have walked Joletta on past the room, then returned by himself.

Whoever had been in that room was crazy, a definite menace. Somebody was going to hear about that when this was over.

In the meantime he should remember to attend to the cost of the damage in the other room. It was his responsibility.

So she kept the journal in her shoulder bag. He had suspected as much. He turned his head to stare at the big, soft leather purse that lay on the foot of the twin bed she was going to use. He moved to pick it up, glancing first at the bathroom door to be sure it was well closed. Rummaging inside, he took out the thick sheaf of paper held together by large rubber bands.

He lifted the cover sheet with tentative fingers. The writing appeared old-fashioned, almost indecipherable. Curious, that such a small thing could cause so much trouble. She might let him read it, later on. If not, he would make an opportunity to do so.

The sound of running water in the bathroom ceased. He returned the journal to the purse and moved away. He sat down on the other bed and lay back, clasping his hands behind his head on the pillow. He was lying there, staring at the ceiling, when Joletta emerged from the bathroom in a cloud of steam.

She had brushed her hair, so it curled around her face and shoulders in damp tendrils. Her face was flushed and moist and innocent of makeup. Her feet were bare, and so far as he could tell, she had next to nothing on under the turquoise silk sleep shirt she wore. The soft, shining material draped itself with miraculous fidelity to her tender curves as she moved to fold the clothes she held, placing them in a neat pile on the dresser.

"It's all yours," she said cheerfully.

He had to remind himself that she was speaking of the bathroom. He thought of turning on his stomach, but was afraid the movement would be too obvious as a cover-up for the effect she had on him.

This was insane. It was never going to work. But since he had begun, he had to go ahead with it.

He debated about whether he should or should not take a shower. It might be better if he simply lay here on this bed without moving, stewing in his own stale sweat. She was so clean, so sweetly wholesome and infinitely desirable in her freshness, that he would not dare approach her in all his dirt. Any deterrent was a good deterrent.

No, he couldn't stand it. It would be all the same if he made the shower cold.

Joletta was asleep when he came out of the bathroom again. Or at least she was giving a good imitation, lying with one arm flung above her head, her lashes shadowing her cheeks and her chest rising and falling in even cadence.

He had forgotten to take his pajamas into the bathroom with him. Fastening the towel he wore more firmly at the waist, he padded across to his suitcase that sat on the floor at the foot of his bed. Keeping an eye on Joletta, he searched out the pajamas that were still folded in sharp creases; pajamas he packed only for emergencies.

With the pajama bottoms in his hand, he eased to his feet again. Then, as if drawn, he approached the bed where Joletta lay. Moving with slow care, he went down on one knee beside it.

The light from the bathroom slanted with a yellow gleam across her face. She looked so vulnerable lying there. The shadow of the bruise and the small, bandaged cut at her hairline affected him with aching tenderness. He put out his hand to touch it, then stopped with it poised in the air. The softness of her skin, the sweetly curving lines of her mouth were an incitement that sent waves of heat rising to his brain. He wondered what she would do if he lay down beside her and kissed her awake.

He swore softly. So much for good intentions.

He rose to his feet so swiftly that a tendon in his knee cracked like the snapping of a whip. He went still, afraid that she would open her eyes and discover him standing there.

The minutes ticked past. He swayed a little, there on his feet. He was so tired. It had been years, it seemed, since he had last slept soundly. It might be aeons more before he could manage it again.

He retreated to the bathroom. There, he stepped into the pajama bottoms. He snapped off the light and came out again, walking quietly to his own bed. Sliding under the duvet, he stretched out.

He lay listening, but he could not hear her breathing. Was she that quiet? Or had she gone? He raised his head, his eyes wide in the dark.

She was still there. Still sleeping. Still beautiful.

Still untouched.

It was in the nature of things that two of the most talkative widows on the bus should see Joletta and Rone leaving his room together on the following morning.

It wasn't that it couldn't have been avoided. By that time Joletta and Rone had been to breakfast and taken an early-morning walk around the block. They had also gone down to Joletta's room to retrieve her suitcase and the rest of her things, since they would be checking out of the hotel that morning. She could, Joletta thought, have gone on ahead, taking her own luggage. But no, Rone had insisted on carrying her brown plaid bag as well as his own heavy black leather case.

There were more than a few knowing smiles when they reached the bus. Rone seemed oblivious to the interest they had aroused, but Joletta could not be quite so casual about it. It bothered her to know that people were speculating about her love life, perhaps even picturing her and Rone in bed together. She had few hang-ups about sex, but there were some things that deserved a decent privacy.

As they settled into their seats Joletta thought one or two of the older women watched Rone with a certain bright appreciation in their faded eyes. He was worth looking at this morning, with the lean planes of his face freshly shaven, his eyes still heavy-lidded from sleep, and the warm charm of his smile on display as he exchanged greetings with first one and then another.

He took up a bit more than his share of the seat with his wide shoulders and long legs, but he was so apologetic about it that it didn't matter. Joletta, feeling the press of his shoulder against hers for an instant before he moved away, and affected against her will, perhaps, by the speculation around her, could not prevent a vagrant curiosity about what kind of lover he would be. A gentlemanly one, she thought, courteous, humorous, and just possibly inventive. One corner of her mouth tugged upward a little at the analysis.

"What is it?" he asked.

"Nothing," she said quickly. "Are you too warm? No? I must have put on too many clothes this morning, or else it's the sun shining on this side of the bus."

They were heading for Italy. Lugano, near the Swiss border, was their destination for a late lunch, and they reached it in good time. The bus driver let them out near the lake while their guide pointed out a number of small restaurants and cafeterias along the streets in either direction. Rone and Joletta had a quick meal of eggplant Parmesan and a red wine from Tuscany in honor of their approach to the Italian frontier. Afterward they strolled across the street to explore a nearby park.

Hidden by a stone wall and a hedge of evergreens, this public park appeared to have once been a private garden surrounding a solid manor house. It curved to follow the lakeshore, a quiet retreat where the sound of bird songs was louder than the traffic noises beyond the wall. Studded with ancient trees in infinite variety, it was lapped by the chill alpine waters and made serene by the view of cloud-cloaked mountains through a soft gray-blue haze.

The sun was warm in contrast to the coolness that lingered in the shade of the trees. The scent of the massed beds of annuals drifted in the light air. Out on the pellucid blue of the lake, a motorboat sped, dragging a white arrow of foam behind it.

Joletta, wandering among the towering rhododendrons and azaleas, pausing to take pictures of the curving beds of pansies and wallflowers, wondered if Violet had ever seen this garden, if it had been there a hundred years before. She should know, but she didn't. She had skimmed over some portions of the journal in her first reading, meaning to study them in more depth later. Somehow, she had not found time, with her headaches and Rone's company.

They had a little over a half hour before they were supposed to rejoin the group. They would have to be back at the appointed meeting place promptly on the hour if they didn't want to be left behind, but for the moment there was no hurry. They sat on one of the many benches placed to take advantage of the lake view, enjoying the feel of the sun and the breeze in their faces. Joletta opened her purse and took out a few pages of the journal, squinting a little in the bright light as she tried to find the right section.

A scene unfolding between Violet and Allain snagged her attention. It was one of haste and longing changing to desire. Violet's pen had faltered over descriptions of passionate caresses, silken whispers, and crushed roses; she had splattered ink and left long spaces marked with single words and strings of quick dashes, places where imagination had to be exercised for understanding. It was absorbing, if somewhat frustrating reading.

It was long minutes before Joletta realized that Rone was reading over her shoulder. She jerked the pages from his line of sight, holding them against her chest.

"Why did you do that?" he asked as he straightened from where he leaned with his arm along the back of the bench. "I was just getting to the interesting part."

It had been purest reflex action, an instinctive protectiveness not unmixed with embarrassment. She got to her feet, putting the journal away as she answered. "I don't know—habit, I guess."

"If I'm going to help, I have to know what's in there."

"Yes, I know. But it will be better when we have more time."

He didn't push it, for which she was grateful. They walked along until they came to a long bed of deep purple pansies, so dark they were nearly black. Joletta stopped for a moment beside them, enjoying the sight of the velvety petals ruffling in the wind.

With some vague idea of introducing Rone gradually to the journal, she said, "Have you ever heard of the language of the flowers?"

"You mean as in, 'There's rosemary, that's for remembrance, pray, love, remember'?"

"Exactly," she said, smiling in surprise, both for his quick understanding and the Shakespearean quote. "It seems the Victorians were big on such things. The flower language was used in the journal for secret communication, a sort of code, by the man my great-grandmother became involved with. Pansies stood for Thoughts, or Thoughts of Love."

"You think this flower code might have something to do with the perfume you're after?"

"It crossed my mind, though I can't really see how it would work."

"No, but it does make you wonder about the meaning of roses." He gave her a quizzical glance that plainly showed he had been reading the journal for some time before she noticed.

"Love, of course. What else?"

"Oh, right," he said in dry disparagement for the evasion.

She gave him a caustic look. Nevertheless, his lack of serious attention for the contents of the journal was comforting. He was, apparently, content to wait for her to tell him as much or as little about it as she wished.

They had regained the path beside the lake and were strolling along it. Ahead of them a few hundred yards was a tall shrub with dark, shiny green leaves and bright clusters of blooms colored a brilliant coral.

"Is that an azalea?" Rone asked, moving toward the shrub.

"It's possible."

"Let's see," he said, picking up his pace.

Joletta glanced at her watch. There was time. She moved after him.

It was a rhododendron, and beyond it was a mass of lily of the valley, and past that was a rock garden where mats of yellow and magenta blossoms tumbled over mossy stones. Near the rock garden was a small boy, hardly more than a toddler. He stumbled this way and that, talking to himself as he played with a large blue ball. The child's hair curled in a wild platinum tangle, and there was devilry in his clear blue eyes. He was fast on his feet, and when his laugh rang out, it had the piercing clarity of near-unbearable joy. His parents sat not far away, holding another baby in a carrier between them on a bench while they ate towering cones of ice cream.

The little boy kicked the ball. It spun toward the water of the lake. Rone ran to intercept it, scooping it up and tossing it back. The little boy laughed and kicked the ball again.

What followed was a hilarious game of pitch, one Rone played while kneeling and lunging this way and that in the damp, emerald-tinted glass. Joletta, laughing at the sight, did not look at her watch again for some time.

They missed the bus. The place where it had been parked was empty. Though they had seen one or two of their tour group in the gardens earlier, there was now none of them in sight.

They had been warned that lack of punctuality was a discourtesy to the whole group, one that must alter multitudes of complicated arrangements and reservations. Anyone who failed to be at the appointed place at the required time would be left behind, to catch up with the group later. There would be some small amount of grace allowed, but no more than ten minutes.

They were nearly a half hour late.

"Never mind," Rone said. "We'll rent a car and catch up with them in Venice. Or failing that, in Florence."

"Our suitcases are on that bus," Joletta reminded him.

"We'll buy what we need."

"I've already done that once." His comments were so facile that she looked at him with suspicion rising in her eyes. "You're not heartbroken over this, are you? It's what you wanted to do all along, leave the others, rent a car, and go off on our own?"

"The idea had a certain appeal." There was wariness in his tone as he faced her.

"I think," she said deliberately, "that you did this on purpose."

He looked at her a long moment before he answered. "What if I did?"

"Why? Why would you do such a thing?"

"Correct me if I'm wrong," he said, his gaze speculative, "but I had the feeling you weren't exactly comfortable on the bus with me there."

"Oh, I see. It was all for my sake."

"Not entirely."

The calmness of his voice did nothing for her irritated nerves. "Anyway, whatever I may have felt, it didn't mean I wanted to leave the group."

"Too late now," he said.

The words he spoke were pleasant, without rancor. And why not? she thought irascibly. He had what he wanted, didn't he?

Chapter 12

June 16, 1854

I once considered myself virtuous. I have since discovered that within the heart of every woman of virtue lies a courtesan. I am a passionate female. Also a guileful one. How could I have ever thought otherwise?

What folly it is to suppose that we act of our own accord, that we make decisions from independent thought and with recognition for only our own desires. I thought that if ever I went to Allain, it would be in loving necessity. I did not guess it might also be, in some small degree, in anger.

Violet saw the two men as Allain was handing her into the carriage that would take her back to the hotel. They were standing in an arched opening of an arcade just down the street from the house of the comtesse. One of them turned to stare in their direction. He nudged his companion and pointed. Immediately the two of them set off at a run toward a low-slung black carriage that waited further along the way. When Violet and Allain's carriage pulled away from the entrance of the house, the driver of the dark vehicle picked up his whip. He had to jockey for position for a few seconds among the equipages of the other guests that were lining the streets. As the carriage Violet and Allain were riding in reached the corner, the other vehicle pulled out and then fell in some distance behind them.

"Did you see?" Violet asked, turning to Allain. "Those two men again, following us."

A grim expression settled over Allain's features as he shifted position to look back through the small oval window set behind the seat.

"You don't think—can it be that Gilbert sent them?" Violet went on hesitantly, then answered herself. "Perhaps not, since there has been so little time. Yet who else would have reason?"

He made no answer, though he met her gaze for long moments there in the darkness of the carriage. Facing forward once more, he reached for her hand, taking it in his warm clasp, holding it as if he meant never to let go. To Violet, his silence increased the sense of peril that hovered in the moment.

She could feel the quickening beat of her heart, sense the fine weave of his coat as a roughness against her arm. The heat of his body seemed to penetrate the layers of cloth, the silk of her gown and petticoats, which lay between them. Longing beat upward from somewhere deep inside her, rising with the pulsing of a headache behind her eyes. She felt a little giddy with it, even a little reckless. Thoughts chased themselves in confusion across her mind, narrowing to a single impulse. Slowly she opened the fingers of the hand he held, until her palm pressed against his.

"You are trembling," he said, a trace of concern laced with wonder in his voice.

"Only a little."

"Are you cold?"

"No," she answered, "I'm not cold at all. Is—is the other carriage still behind us?"

He turned his head to look, then gave a short nod of assent.

"What if," she began, then paused to clear her throat of an unaccountable obstruction. "What if Gilbert has had someone watching us before tonight?"

"I suppose it's possible," he said in low tones, "though I would rather not think it."

"Nor would I, and yet some things must be faced," she replied. "The question is, what must we do about it?"

"There are many things we could do," he said, his voice hard-edged with despair. "I could finish the portrait and we could bid each other adieu. You could become a dutiful wife and remain in your assigned place except when escorted by your husband. I could leave Paris. Or you could go."

"No," she said sharply.

"Then, if these men are in truth hirelings of your husband, we can let them report what they may. There is little enough they can say."

"Or," she said softly, "we can elude them."

"For what purpose? They will soon discover you are only returning to your hotel."

"Unless I do not return."

A stillness came over him. His fingers upon her hand tightened in a painful grip, then relaxed as he realized what he was doing. His gaze as he watched her in the dim light given off by the outside carriage lantern was penetrating. Quietly, he said, "Where else would you go?"

"That is the question," she said, her voice dropping to a whisper and her lashes flickering downward to conceal her eyes. "Can you think of nowhere that I might be hidden and safe?"

"Violet—"

That single word was taut with passion and denial.

She moistened her lips. "Please. I—I cannot bear that Gilbert shall control what I do, who I see or where I go, a moment longer."

It was long seconds before he replied, and then his voice was brusque, almost harsh. "I will no doubt be damned for it," he said, "but neither can I."

Allain leaned forward to give an order to the coachman that sent the carriage rattling at a faster pace along the street. As he leaned back again Violet caught his arm, holding tightly. She took a deep breath, feeling the tight press of the bones of her corset into her ribs. As he reached to hold her she turned her face into his shoulder, closing her eyes.

Violet had no idea how Allain intended to outdistance their pursuers; the winding streets of the older portion of the city allowed little in the way of evasion. However, he directed their passage through the intricate ways, with clear commands. At last they came to a tree-lined thoroughfare near the outskirts of the city. It was wider but still hardly less constricted than the older streets, for it was as crowded with carriages as had been the avenue before the house of the Comtesse de Fourier. There appeared to be a soirée in progress at the imposing mansion set back among the plane trees.

As the carriage slowed to thread its way through the vehicles, Allain ordered it to a sudden halt.

"What is this place?" Violet asked.

"The home of the Pontalbas. The daughter-in-law of the baron is entertaining tonight also, and was kind enough to send me a card of invitation."

Before Violet could speak, he opened the carriage door and stepped down. Reaching inside, he lifted her out bodily. He directed the coachman to drive on and find a place for his rig as if his master and guest had decided to descend and go inside. As the carriage rolled on along the street Allain guided Violet quickly among the other standing equipages.

She could hear the noise of the black carriage approaching behind them. It was a relief when Allain stopped beside a maroon barouche. He pulled the door open and guided her inside even as he called over his shoulder to a man in livery who had stepped forward from among a cluster of drivers.

"Tell your master I have need of his barouche, a matter of urgency. He may have the use of mine, provided he returns it in good time tomorrow."

"Ah, M'sieur Massari, I should have known it was you!" the man returned in low tones. "My master will be honored to be of service."

Allain sketched a brief salute and stepped inside, closing the door behind him. "This carriage belongs to a friend," he said to Violet in a hurried undertone, "a man of understanding."

"He must be, if he won't mind you borrowing it," Violet answered.

"He has taken mine before, with less reason."

They both fell silent, drawing back into the darkest corner of the seat as the black carriage drew nearer. It rolled past with the two men inside sitting forward, their attention on the other carriage, which Allain's coachman was drawing to the side farther along the street. Some distance away, the vehicle carrying the two drew up. No one emerged. The men apparently assumed, as Allain had intended, that their quarry had been put down at the house entrance to attend the second social event of the evening.

Long minutes crept past. After what seemed a small eternity, Allain's coachman, who had climbed down and vanished toward the back of the lighted house, materialized out of the darkness from the opposite direction. He climbed ponderously up to the box of the maroon barouche. A few seconds later the vehicle began to move. Their pace sedate, they pulled away from the Pontalba house and rolled off down the street.

As the barouche rattled past the black carriage sitting in darkness, Allain turned his broad back to it, taking Violet into his arms. The embrace would serve, he whispered, to block them both from view while making it appear that they were lovers bound for a tryst.

And wasn't that true after all, Violet thought as she lay in his arms with her forehead pressed against the strong column of his neck. Wasn't it?

The thoroughfare where Allain lived was empty when they reached it. They left the carriage several doors down from his so as not to draw attention to it. It seemed strange to walk slowly arm in arm to his door after the haste and excitements just past; at the same time there was a naturalness about it, like a homecoming.

The housekeeper opened the door for them. Her eyes widened as she saw Violet, but she spoke only to say that refreshments of wine and cheese with nuts had been set out in the studio against her master's return. As Allain dismissed her she moved away toward the green baize door that led to the nether regions of the house, though she glanced back once with concern in her eyes.

Together, Violet and Allain climbed the stairs. Their footsteps on the treads were neither quick nor dawdling but deliberate, as if they were there for a purpose they both knew and accepted. His hand under her elbow steadied and supported but did not urge her.

Violet did not question what she was doing. That the two of them should be here at this late hour seemed inevitable; everything that had gone before had been but a prelude.

There was a single candle burning on a table against the wall next to the fireplace. When the door had closed behind them, they turned to look at each other in its wavering light. Violet felt her breath trapped, encased in the whalebone cage of her corset. Her eyes were wide and pensive, purple-edged with trepidation, yet as resolute as those of a novice before the altar. She waited.

Allain turned sharply from her. Moving to the candle, he picked up a handful of tapers from a box that sat beside it. He kindled one in the flame before moving to place it and the others in the tall corner candelabra. The blossoming flames as he touched the full row of candles to light enameled his face with gold and blue and orange, giving it the hard and lifeless look of an effigy in bronze.

Violet felt the first stirring of doubt. She took a step forward.

"Don't," he said, the word slicing even in its softness. "Please don't."

"What is it?" she whispered.

He moved back to where the tray was set with glasses and a dusty bottle of wine. He gave her a tight smile before he picked up the bottle and began to pour. His gaze on what he was doing, he said, "Second thoughts. An attack of conscience, or shame. I should be stripped and beaten for bringing you to this."

She watched him for long moments while her pulse thundered in her ears. At last she said, "If there is shame, I share it."

"No. I set out to seduce you from motives pure and impure, but most of all from base, overwhelming desire. I should have conquered it; I have no excuse for that failure."

"Must there be one?" She beat about in her mind for some hint of what he was trying to tell her, but could find few clues.

"It is required, when so much is at risk."

"Is this risk mine or yours?"

"Yours," he said with roughness rising in his voice. "Yours alone, for mine was accepted long ago."

She gave him a wavering smile. "Can I do less, then?"

"You must. Your safety depends on it."

Did he think Gilbert would harm her if they were discovered? Somehow she did not think it was a consideration so mundane that moved him. What it might be, she could not imagine. Regardless, it made no difference.

"How can I think of safety when I am here?" she asked in low and strained tones. "How can I, and still be worthy of—of your roses?"

She put her hand to the blossoms at the corsage of her gown as she spoke, feeling their cool petals against her fingers. He caught her meaning, for he took a quick, uncontrolled step toward her.

"It's I who am unworthy of your love," he said, the words unsteady, "though you will always have mine."

She reached out to him. As she moved her hand the roses she had touched shattered, the petals loosening, falling, sliding down the full sweep of her skirts in a rain of rose red. They settled to the carpet, where they scattered at her feet, shimmering in the dimness like droplets of blood.

She cried out with the sound of pain and loss and unreasoning fear.

A spasm crossed his face of resolution hard pressed, defended, and then abandoned.

An instant later he caught her close, murmuring softly as he leaned to lift her high in his arms. "Never mind, my heart, I'll make you a path of roses, a bed, a bower. You will have roses all your days."

"And my nights?" she whispered.

Carrying her toward the divan, he answered, "Especially the nights."

He placed her among the Persian garden of silk draperies that softened the couch. Her hair, as he loosened the pins that held it one by one, uncoiled and trailed down her shoulder, mingling with the fringes of the draped shawls. He spread the long, curling tresses around her, his gaze soft with wonder and appreciation as he watched the candlelight shimmer in prism gleams among them. He cupped her face in the warm strength of his hands, then leaned to touch her lips with his own.

It was a benediction of sweetness, a salute of honor. Withdrawing a little, he held her gaze with the promise of his own while he lowered himself to recline beside her. She reached to press her fingertips to his mouth, tracing the line of his lips, their smoothness, their firm resilience.

"I wish," she said with a sigh catching in her voice, "that I could be pure and untouched for you."

"And would you have me untutored? It's better as we are; we need neither of us fear pain or penalty, but can come to each other with only pleasure."

She loved him then as she had not before, as she allowed him entry to a portion of her innermost self where no other had ever been. He saw it, and caught her close with his face against the silken hair at her temple. They held each other tightly, breast to breast, thigh to thigh, while the beating of their hearts shook them with the hard, uneven strokes of despairing elation.

He released her by slow degrees, murmuring in wonder as he brushed her forehead with his warm lips, touched them to the fragile skin of her eyelids, and explored the delicate ridges of her cheekbones. He sought the moist corner of her mouth, testing its sensitive folds before probing the sweetness within.

She met his gentle foray, touching her tongue to his in conscious daring. She wanted to taste him, to know him, to encompass him with her body and mind and to become lost in him. The urge was so strong, so vital inside her, that she feared to shock him by permitting him to see the strength of it. It spread through her with the fiery potency of fine wine, so she shivered and her hands closed convulsively on his shoulders.

His chest swelled as he took a ragged breath. He moved his hand to her back, where he began to free the tiny buttons of her bodice from their loops. His touch on her cool skin as it was slowly bared was incredibly intimate, unbelievably tantalizing. In the need to give him something of the same sensation, she trailed her fingers down along the collar of his coat and under its edge to reach the buttons of his waistcoat. She slipped them from their holes one by one.

He drew down the sleeve of her gown, exposing the slender column of her neck and the slight hollow at its base. He pressed his lips to that depression, tasting its sweet frailty, testing with his tongue the pulse that throbbed there as he freed her arm, then clasped his hand slowly upon the gently swelling curve of her breast. Her lips parted as she gasped. Spurred by that small sound, he brushed a trail of heated kisses along the lace-edged line of her camisole, which enclosed the warm curves rising above her corset. He moistened the thin lawn over one gentle mound with his tongue before taking a taut nipple into his mouth.

Drowning, drowning in too poignant pleasure and the rise of her own unbridled need, Violet pushed her fingers into the vibrant waves of his hair and exerted stringent will to prevent herself from clutching him to her. She hardly knew when he pushed the gown sleeve from her other arm and untied her petticoats, sliding the mass of cumbersome, silken, rustling clothing from her body. As he eased from her to strip away his own garments, she made a soft, inarticulate protest. She watched him with lash-shielded eyes, however, absorbing the strength and virile beauty of his body. This, too, she wanted to know.

She had to help him with her corset, pressing it at the narrow span of her waist while he unfastened the hooks. He breathed a soft curse as he saw the red ridges it had left in her skin, though he soothed them with caresses as she lay naked against him. His kneading, stroking fingers moved lower, skimming across the flat surface of her abdomen, coming to rest at the soft triangle at the apex of her thighs. His kisses followed.

She closed her eyes tightly, trying to turn away, to close her thighs, but he would not permit it. Relentless in his fervor, delicate in his passionate exploration, he took her with him into unknown, unguessed realms of delight. By degrees, she gave him unimpeded access, and he took it, and in return gave unrestrained enchantment. Made bold by the totality of her surrender, she reached for him with urgent hands.

He came to her in rampant grace, entering her in a controlled onslaught of purest, aching necessity. For long moments they were utterly still.

She was full, but not complete, filled, but not sated. Passion burgeoned inside her, spiraling up from some deep internal well. She shivered with it, trembling as she spread her hands upon the muscles of his back. Under her sensitive palms she could feel the ripples of tension the restraint he was keeping upon himself caused. They fueled her desperation, so she made a soft sound of distress deep in her throat.

He raised above her then, drawing ecstasy to its outermost limits as he remained poised, shuddering and continent, at the edge of his control. She caught him with both hands, dragging him down, so he plunged into her, deep and deeper, sounding sanity and dreams, bringing the explosive, breath-destroying glory of surcease.

Later, wrapped in silk-fringed shawls, they stood at the open window, breathing the fresh air and watching the night sky over Paris. Pinpoints of light glimmered in the darkness. Some, strung in rows and loops like exotic gold and silver beads, were the gas lamps along the streets and edging the Seine, while others were more scattered, appearing either vigilant or secretive. They gave a diffused glow to the night sky, shading it to gray blue in which the dimmest outlines of buildings could be seen. It was like a false dawn, though the real one would come soon, too soon.

"I want to remember her like this, our lady Paris," Allain said, his voice low and somber-edged with pain, "and I want to remember you just as you are—warm and beautiful, with your hair down your back—"

"Don't," she said, turning her head that lay on his shoulder so she could look up at him, reaching at the same time to place her fingertips on his lips. The words he spoke were a reminder of the parting that must come, and she was not ready to think of it.

He caught her hand and pressed it to his lips before holding it close against his heart. His chest expanded with the deepness of the breath he took, one it seemed he would never let go. When at last he did, he released her hand and reached to place the flat of his palm at her waist, spreading his fingers wide and then closing them gently on her flesh as if he needed to grasp and hold the very essence of her.

"You are so lovely, so very loving and lovely," he murmured

in husky confession, his warm breath brushing her forehead. "I love you, I do love you, I have loved you these many long weeks. Believe me, please, believe me. Sometimes, when I stood putting paint on canvas and looking at you on the dais, I had to stop and turn my back and remind myself of many truths—or else I would have gone to you and ravished you there on the floor."

She rubbed her forehead gently against his chin. Her voice not quite steady, she said, "Sometimes, as I sat there on my pedestal, I wished that you would."

"And shall I?" he asked, his hands moving upon her in firm entreaty.

"Would you?" The flush that spread through her body was one of anticipation.

"If it is your desire. If your desire is the same as mine." The words were a vow.

"Now," she whispered in anguished longing. "My desire is the same as yours now, at this moment, and ever after."

Repeating her name like a paean, he carried her to the dais and, placing her there, lowered himself beside her.

Decadent, immoral, immortal; they were all those things, and more. In lust and love, they used the fleeting minutes, and could not tell the one thing from the other, so fine was the line that separated them.

Regardless, the night ended.

Allain helped Violet to dress, tightening her corset, buttoning buttons, straightening her skirts over the width of her hoop. He used his own silver-backed brush to straighten the tangled mass of her hair while she stood still with her back to him and her head held high so she could breathe against the constriction around her heart.

Holding the warm weight of her shining tresses in his hands, he said abruptly, "Come away with me."

"Oh, Allain," she whispered. Tears gathered behind her eyes, crowding into her throat.

"Will you? If it's my desire?"

She turned slowly to face him. "I do love you," she said with difficulty.

He watched her, his blue-gray eyes limpid with the pain. He looked down at the ends of her hair that he still held, then slowly he let them go, so they drifted in a soft skein to lie against her skirts. His voice near cracking, he said, "You love me, but you are married to him. And this, among my many desires, is not possible."

"Gilbert loves me, too." She could not look at him.

"Oh, yes; how could he not? But as much?"

She shook her head in slow denial. "Yet there were vows made."

"Until death parts you," he said, adding with quiet surety, "I could remove him—on the field of honor."

Her head came up. Holding his gaze, she took his hands in hers, brushing the swordsman's calluses on his hands with her thumbs. She said, "If you could, you would not be the man I love—any more than you could love me if I disregard a sacred promise."

"You underestimate us both, I think."

"That may be, but it doesn't change anything."

He sighed, the tension going out of his body. "No, but perhaps I will be lucky, and he will have returned before you. And he will be—unloving."

For that, there was no answer.

Silent, his face chiseled to still restraint, Allain walked with her down the stairs and handed her into the carriage. He held only her hand through the short drive back to the hotel. And he seemed not to notice the dark carriage that sat before his house, and that followed them, at some distance back, until they reached the hotel. Violet did not speak of it, either. It made no difference, now.

Allain wanted to go inside with her, to see her safely to her room. She would not permit it. She had not forgotten the prospect of a duel. Alone, she might prevent it; it would be much more difficult if Gilbert and Allain should come face-to-face.

He went because she begged him to go. She watched him get into the carriage, watched it pull away, then she turned to enter the door that was being held for her by the night porter.

The door of the sitting room was unlocked, the room itself dark and still. Violet stood listening for long moments. Then her heart leaped in silent dread as she noticed the smell of tobacco smoke.

The red end of a cheroot glowed in the direction of a chair near where the open casement windows looked out over the courtyard. Gilbert's solid form was outlined against the increasing dawn. When he spoke, his voice rasped with contempt.

"You are up in good time, my darling wife," he said.

She hesitated. "Yes, I—"

"Spare me the explanations, please; there's no time for them. It's as well you are wakeful. I have been thinking in these past hours that it's time we moved on to Switzerland. We leave today, as early as it may be arranged."

Chapter 13

Gilbert did not mention the night of the ball on the journey to Switzerland, nor would he permit Violet to speak of it. Each time she tried, he either changed the subject or else rose and left her. It was as if he wished to pretend it had never happened. He was, in public, as attentive to her comfort and generous with trifles as he had ever been. In private he punished her with cold politeness, brooding silences, and his ever-watchful presence.

In Geneva he bought carpets and a gold pocket watch for himself that was engraved with a scene of the Alps. He bought a great carved box like a coffin, actually a marriage chest, which he said would be perfect for Violet's bedchamber. He bought a cuckoo clock that was supposed to be for her pleasure, though she thought the thing monstrously ugly.

They took a small chalet outside Lucerne, and every day they walked across the flower-strewn mountain meadows. It should have been peaceful there, in the pure air where the sound of cowbells echoed against the transcendent blue of the sky. Gilbert would not allow it. He made their mountain walks endurance tests, striding ahead with long angry steps, slashing at the grass and flowers with his stick, calling back at her not to dawdle. When the clouds rose above the mountains and the rain showers came, he refused to take shelter, but marched onward through the mud and wet without looking back to see if she followed.

In the evenings they ate in restaurants, adequate but bland meals totally without the flavor or spice of conversation. Afterward, they returned to their room, where Violet read or did needlework while Gilbert sat pretending to read a newspaper and staring at her, constantly staring, over the top of it. At times she sustained that gimlet observation for long hours, determined not to permit him to overbear her. On other nights she retreated to her bed, where she lay gazing wide-eyed into the dark, trying not to think, trying not to feel, trying not to remember.

Now and then in the evening Gilbert went out, staying late at the taverns, drinking great liters of beer and eating greasy sausages. On those occasions Hermine was instructed by him to keep watch and only allowed to go to her bed when he returned to relieve her. He was often drunk and morose on such nights, with grease on his face and garlic on his breath. Violet avoided him when she could at those times, for he was loud and indelicate then, comparing her unfavorably, feature by feature, with the bar maids he had seen.

He did not approach her bed, touched her only when it was unavoidable. She was made to feel, by the subtle alteration of his expression when he saw her partially clothed, that she disgusted him. She wondered why, if that was so, he had seen fit to drag her away with him. It appeared to be sheer possessiveness, to establish his right of ownership.

There were times when she could not bear the thought of going on and on like this, enduring her husband's silent rage. She had at first been as contrite as he could have wished, consumed with guilt and quite ready to admit her fault. As the weeks wore on, a stubborn resentment began to crowd out contrition. She grew angry in her turn at this attempt to make her regret her infidelity, to isolate her in her shame until she began to feel unworthy of the regard of other people. She was not a child to be petted and pampered when she was good, but chastised when she misbehaved. She was a human being, with feelings and needs, ideas and opinions. If Gilbert could not, or would not, recognize these things, if he persisted in his treatment, then she could no longer respect him, no longer feel herself bound to him.

So they made their way slowly around the lakes, from Lucerne to Como and on to Lugano. It was there they learned that the British cabinet had ordered its forces to invade the Crimea, and that a meeting of the allied commanders to discuss strategy was imminent. And it was in Lugano that the portrait painted by Allain caught up with them.

Gilbert had sent for the painting on the morning they left Paris. When it had not arrived by the time they left for the train station, he had ordered it shipped on after them. Their movements had been so sporadic since, that it had been some time in arriving.

Gilbert left it in its shipping crate, propped against the wall of their Lugano pension. He rested his gaze on it now and then with a baleful glare, but did not go near it. It seemed to fascinate yet repel him. Violet thought that, like herself, he wanted to possess it since he had commissioned and paid for it, but that he was determined to despise it.

Violet waited until he was gone one day, then sent for hammer and chisel to open the crate herself.

Looking at the portrait was like seeing herself as Allain had seen her. It renewed her.

The colors were magnificent in their rich purity, the flesh tones luminescent and vibrant with life. The form and composition were perfect in their symmetric grace. The draping of the material and delicate delineation of the lace collar of her gown had been done with exacting fidelity.

The eyes of the painting followed her, sensitive eyes shadowed with painful self-awareness, apprehensive yet resolute, only half concealing a tenuous joy and delicate, flowering desire.

It was a reminder of all she was, and of all that had been.

The pain of the loss spread from her heart, creeping through her with the intolerable ache of poison. There was no part of her that did not feel it, no single fiber that did not cry out with yearning. She had tried to suppress it, to hold it inside her. She could do it no longer.

Gilbert had been right not to look at the portrait.

But she would not crate it up again.

She was still standing before the likeness of herself, with the hammer and chisel in her hands and pieces of boards and burlap wrapping around her feet, when she heard her husband return. She did not move.

Gilbert paused in the doorway, then closed the door and came forward. His voice heavy with sarcasm, he said, "So. You had to see the handiwork of your lover."

She looked at him over her shoulder before she turned and walked to place the things she held on a side table. "Yes, why not?"

"You don't deny that he was that," he accused, the words rough. He looked beyond her at the painting, and his face tightened to the density of carved wood.

She heard the sudden hint of anguish under his tone and knew an unwelcome compunction. She moistened her lips before she answered. "I didn't know you doubted it."

"Stupid of me, wasn't it? I preferred to think that you had been merely indiscreet, not depraved."

"Indeed?" she said, her tone stiffening. "Then you might have saved yourself the price of your spies."

"Spies? You think I would pay anyone to witness my humiliation?"

"No, only to document it so there could be no mistake."

Anger flared in his eyes and he breathed quickly through his nose. "I would be more likely to have hired someone to thrash your paramour."

"To discourage him?" she asked, raising her chin. "I doubt it would have been effective."

He took a step toward her, then stopped. He said, his voice hushed and sibilant, "Then I would have been forced to have him killed, and you with him."

"A hired murder," she said softly, "would have been so much easier than meeting him on the field of honor, wouldn't it? I noticed you were not anxious for that."

"He had seduced my wife, persuaded her to dishonor my name; why should I give him the right of a dueling ground? I could have killed him like a dog and no court in Europe would ever have convicted me, particularly no French court. They understand these things here."

"Oh, yes. How wise, how just it is of them," she said in weary disdain, "to leave women no answer for the insults of their husbands."

He advanced toward her with his fists clenched. "I gave you everything!"

"Everything you wanted me to have, with no concern for what I myself might want."

He looked taken aback for an instant before scorn crowded out consideration. "You are too young to know your own mind; your taste is unformed."

"What you mean is that you are afraid my taste may not be the same as yours. You are right. The things I want and need, the things which give me pleasure, are not at all the same."

His face twisted, becoming purplish red as he stared at her. "You are thinking of your artist? You won't have him; I'll see to that. You can forget him, everything about him!"

He stepped to take up the chisel where she had put it down, then lunged toward the portrait. He slashed the blade across her painted face and throat in a shower of dried paint flecks. Hacking at the canvas again and again, he tore the portrait half out of its frame.

Violet stood frozen with horror for long seconds. Then she cried out, springing to grab his arm. "No! Don't, oh, please, don't! You can't!"

He swung his hand at her, catching her along the jaw in a back-handed blow that snapped her head around. She staggered away from him. He turned, dropping the chisel. It clanged to the floor, rolling under their feet as he caught her upper arm with one hand while he sank the fingers of the other into the thick mass of her high-piled hair. He dragged her toward him, clamping her tight against him.

"Yes," he said, his voice suddenly thick. "Oh, yes. Yes, I will. I can."

He pulled her with him toward the bedchamber. She pushed at him with her hands flat against his chest as she stumbled along. It did no good; he was too strong in his rage. She tried to claw at his face, but he snatched her wrist in a grip so numbingly painful that the strength left her knees. Catching her off balance, he half carried, half dragged her the last few steps to the bed.

"You're my wife," he said in grating triumph as he flung him-self across her. He pinned her to the bed while he clutched at her skirts, pulling them upward.

What happened then was painful and degrading, and completely unforgivable.

Violet endured it with tears running from her eyes, streaming into her hair in hot paths, wetting the mattress under her head. She made no sound except for the harsh and difficult gasps of her breath-ing. After a few moments she did not try to move, fought no more. She left him only her inert body while she retreated deep inside herself, where he could not reach, had never and would never, touch.

There she was unyielding. There she did not forget. There she was free.

Later, when he had rolled from her to lie heavy and still on his own side of the bed, the tears still flowed, so she used a corner of the sheet to wipe them away. The moments ticked past, measured by the cuckoo clock he had bought, a noisy method of marking them in the shuttered afternoon stillness of the room.

"Don't cry," he said, his voice low and drained of emotion. "I didn't mean to hurt you."

She did not speak or move.

"I would ask forgiveness, but you brought it on yourself with your defiance and lack of repentance."

She made no answer.

"Perhaps I did leave you alone too much, should have taken you with me while shopping, or consulted your taste in furnishings, but that was no reason to dishonor your marriage bed."

"It—wasn't just that," she whispered.

He ignored that small plea. His voice tired, yet with an undertone of iron, he said, "There will be no repeat of this affair. If you had a child, there would be no time for such foolishness. I will give you one if it kills us both."

She closed her eyes tightly and brought a hand to her mouth to stifle the cry that rose inside her.

It was the following day that Allain came.

One moment Violet was walking along the shore of the lake, trying to find peace in the beauty of the small garden she had discovered laid out along its verge; the next, Allain was beside her, strolling with his hands clasped behind his back and his face turned up to the sun as if merely joining her in a common morning ritual.

The scent of pansies drifting on the wind seemed suddenly sweeter, the sky bluer, and the clouds floating above the distant mountains more whitely perfect. Tears rose in Violet's eyes even as she tried to smile.

He glanced at her, the look in his face teasing. It vanished abruptly as he stopped rock still in the middle of the path. His voice grim, he said, "Has it been so bad then?"

"Yes—no," she said, brushing at the moisture with trembling fingers. "I'm only glad you're here."

His gaze traveled quickly over her walking costume of old gold linen twill trimmed with pine-green braid and worn with a small bonnet of plaited straw with ivy twining around the flat crown. It lingered on her pale face and the bruise that shadowed her jawline. The quiet sound of his voice did not match the deadly look in his eyes as he said, "I would have come sooner, but had no idea of your direction. I've been following on the trail of the portrait, shamelessly bribing its handlers."

"I would have sent word, said good-bye—but was given no time." Violet tilted the parasol of cream silk she carried so it shaded the bruised side of her face more deeply.

"I guessed how it must have been. My greatest fear in coming after you so quickly was that I might miss some message sent later to my house in Paris."

Bleak distress surfaced in her eyes. "I have been allowed nothing for writing except my journal, no access to a posting office."

"It doesn't matter now." He reached to take her gloved right hand, his grasp warm and sure.

"Today is the first time I have been out alone," she said with an attempt at a smile, "and that is only because Gilbert had an appointment to see a four-hundred-year-old armor chest and Hermine claims the mountain coolness has brought on her rheumatism." It was also, she knew, because of Gilbert's feelings of guilt over what had taken place between them, but she could not speak of that.

"I know; I've been keeping watch, waiting for a chance to see you alone. It appears I should have hammered down your door."

She shook her head, her fingers clenching his in convulsive dread. "It's better this way, but—you should not have come."

"How could I not?" he said simply. And from behind his back he brought forth a wallflower, pale yellow and cream, fragrant and perfect with the dew still on its petals. Turning up the palm of her hand that he held, he placed the flower in it.

A wallflower, which signaled Fidelity in Adversity.

She went into his arms then, could no more have resisted it than he could stop himself from gathering her into them. They held each other tightly, lips meeting in desperation, while Allain reached to tilt her parasol to shield them from the gazes of passersby.

Later, with arms still entwined, they found a bench facing the lake and sat in close embrace, staring out over the water. Violet thought with regret of how severe she had been toward the lovers she had seen in Paris in just such situations. She had not then realized the difficulty of finding privacy and safety for such couples, or the depth of the need that drove them.

It was some time before she and Allain were satisfied with the renewal of the touch and taste of each other. Finally Allain spoke, his words muffled where he rested his lips against the hair at her temple.

"I came, you know, to take you away."

She had hardly dared allow herself to hope he would follow after her in these last miserable weeks. She had known, however, that if he did, there would be a decision to be made. It was upon her now, here in this beautiful garden with the sun warm upon the grass and the scent of flowers in the air.

She wasn't sure she was ready. She disengaged herself slowly from him. Turning her head, she looked across the lake at the distant mountains lying like dreams of coolness against the sky.

"Away where?" she asked quietly. "Back to Paris?"

"I think not," he said. "It's the first place your husband will look."

"Yes. He—has made threats, you know."

"I don't fear them, but I would prefer that you not be troubled by him. I would like—I want very much—to live with you in peace and content. Perhaps, if it pleases you, it could be in Venice."

Venice. With Allain.

To go with him would be to leave behind not only her husband, but her family, friends, the place where she was born, even her country. She would be embracing a tenuous future with a man she barely knew.

She gave a small shake of her head. "Gilbert won't give up easily, I think. He is determined to—determined that I have a child."

"I pray," Allain said deliberately, "that any child you have will be mine."

She turned to face him. Her face was somber, her eyes opaque yet measuring as she met his steady gaze. The unfathomable depths of love she saw there, and the promise, caused her heart to shift achingly in her chest. The summer wind ruffled the waves of his hair and stirred the ends of his silk cravat. He narrowed his eyes a fraction against it, but did not move as he waited for her answer.

A slow and lovely smile curved her mouth. Her voice chiming with soft gladness, she said, "When shall we go?"

He got to his feet, standing straight and tall. Reaching for her hand, he drew her up to stand beside him. His gray-blue gaze, the same color as the mountain lake, held hers as he spoke.

"Now," he said. "At once."

Allain hired a carriage to take them over the mountains to Milan. He demanded the best available and the fastest horses. The fee was exorbitant, but he made no complaint. He even added a generous *pourboire* to encourage the keeper of the inn where the arrangements were made to forget that he had seen them.

From Milan, they traveled by train. The journey seemed intolerably slow to Violet. She could spare little attention for the waterfalls that cascaded down the mountain slopes, the vistas provided by the rolling hills, or the views of fortified towns perched above the valleys. She could not be easy in her mind, but turned again and again to look back the way they had come. What Gilbert would do when he discovered she was gone, she hardly dared imagine. She did not consider for a moment that he would do nothing. His pride, if nothing else, would prevent it.

Allain, taking her hand as they rocked along the winding roads, said, "Calm yourself, *cara*. Your husband may guess you are with me, but he can't know it. By the time he becomes certain, we will be far away."

"I know," she said, "but still—"

"Don't think of it. Put him from your mind. Think instead of what we will do in Venice. You have left so much behind—clothing, jewelry, keepsakes. You have my word that they will be replaced, insofar as I am able."

"I don't care for those things," she said.

"I do," he said, his voice serious. "I would not have you deprived because of me."

"You have given me so much more," she answered, and meant it. The bargain was a fair one in her view: all she owned in exchange for this chance at happiness. It had been offered to her before in Paris and lost, refused because of duty and misplaced adherence to a code she had not made. Now it was in her hands.

Allain had not mentioned marriage. Children, yes, but not the state of grace that made them legitimate. It was not possible, of course, would never be possible while she was tied to Gilbert. If there were not religious constraints, there would be the difficulties of persuading her husband to parade his marital failure in full view of friends, community, and even the legislature of the state of Louisiana, which presided over such dissolutions.

She and Allain would be forced to live in sin. Strange, how little meaning those words had in her mind, when once they had spelled scandal and ruin. It could not be helped. Words could not hurt her; only people could do that.

They stopped for the night at a small inn on the outskirts of Milan. Too keyed up to sleep, they made love in the moonlight streaming through the windows, then lay in each other's arms while the hours crept past.

By midmorning they were on the train as it puffed its way past red-tile-roofed villas surrounded by vineyards whose leaves shone in the sun, past straggling stone-walled villages alive with chickens and children and goats and edged with cemeteries studded with the dark green spires of cypress. They left the hills for the fertile plains. The air blowing in at the compartment window smelled of coal smoke, and also of blooming grass and farmyards. The sunlight streaming in was almost hot. Dust motes shaken from the velvet side curtains turned lazily in its golden shafts.

Violet had been impressed by the ease with which Allain had slipped from French to German, then into the dialect of Venezia, as he dealt with the various agents and officials at the train station. When she said as much, he only smiled. "It becomes necessary when there is no country you call home. Venice comes closest, perhaps, to deserving the name. I have relatives there still, my mother's people."

"Will we—that is, did you intend to visit them?" She was not sure she was ready to meet these relatives, whoever they might be.

The understanding in his face was disturbing as he answered, "Only if you wish it."

"It's because of your father that you have no true home?"

Allain agreed absently.

She shielded her eyes with her lashes as she asked, "Was he some kind of diplomat, then?"

"Why would you think that?" he asked, his gaze indulgent yet penetrating.

"You seem to have such official connections and—have lived in many places."

He shook his head with a smile. "My father had a prominent position for some years, though not in the diplomatic corps; actually he left it before I was born. Any recognition I receive is merely because my ancestors tended to marry well."

"Ah, because of wealth, then," she commented. He spoke, and acted, as if money were of no consequence.

He hesitated only a fraction of a second before he said, "You might say so."

"If the benefits of it are now yours, then I suppose your father is no longer alive."

"Both of my parents are dead, or so I believe. My mother, once a diva of the opera, died in England only a few years ago. My father departed on a pilgrimage of sorts a short time after I was born. He was to return, but was never seen again. We heard rumors for a few years, then—nothing."

It happened, men who were lost at sea, or else were robbed and killed on some lonely road with nothing left on the body to identify them. Sometimes men lost themselves on purpose, too, to evade family responsibilities or situations they could no longer endure.

"I'm sorry," she said.

He smiled a little. "Don't be. It was long ago."

"But your mother? Why was she in England?"

"It was her home, where my father had established her and where she had special friends in the social and theatrical circles. She would not leave it except for brief visits to Italy. She thought, you see, that he might return."

A chill moved over Violet as she considered the implications of what he had said. His father had apparently taken his mother from her home, her people, and established her in a foreign land. Then he had left her. She was going away with Allain, leaving everything. Would he, could he, ever desert her in the same callous fashion?

"Don't look like that, *cara*," he said, reaching to take her hand. "I will never leave you. But I am flattered that you would care, just as it pleased my conceit that you have thought enough about me to be curious."

Soft color seeped under her skin, though she met his dark gaze without evasion. Her voice soft, she said, "You have no idea how much I long to know."

"Know it you shall," he said in quiet avowal, "all of it."

Soon afterward, he changed the subject, speaking of the countryside through which they were traveling and the uneasy situation of the Italian peninsula. Violet enjoyed listening to the deep timbre of his voice, was interested in his analysis of area politics, but she could not help wondering if his sudden loquacity was not a diversion. He might intend to reveal himself to her, but the time for it, perhaps, was not yet.

The northern section of the Italian peninsula, so Allain said, had been for centuries the battleground where the kings of Valois and Bourbon in France and the Habsburgs of Austria had settled their differences. Control of various portions of it had been traded back and forth a dozen times over. Since the Congress of Vienna after the defeat of Napoléon I, however, France had been excluded from the area. Venezia, with Lombardy, was still under Austrian rule, but the remainder of the peninsula was occupied by a number of smaller states, including the Kingdom of Sardinia, the Kingdom of the Two Sicilies, the Duchies of Parma and Modena, the Grand Duchy of Tuscany, and, of course, the papal dominions.

There were a great many titles, old and new, associated with the many different regions, and a great deal of jockeying for position among the holders of those titles. In addition, as with the rest of Europe since 1848, there were constant rumors of revolution in the air. It was Allain's opinion that something, or some man, would eventually galvanize the peninsula into forming itself into a single strong republic. In the meantime the paramount faction, led by the King of the Two Sicilies, was hovering on the brink of committing itself to the allied cause in the war in the Crimea. There was no escaping the effects of that faraway conflict.

They reached the terminal station for Venice in late evening. Everyone surged from the train with much yelling and clanging of compartment doors. Baggage had to be collected and transfer made quickly to the ferry that would take them across to the city in the lagoon, as it was the last one of the day. Violet and Allain had little luggage to concern them; Allain carried his own small portmanteau that was all he had brought with him from Paris, while Violet grasped her rolled parasol in her hand. They had no choice, however, but to join the crush of people. It was the only way to get to the ferry pier.

They were leaving the station gateway in the midst of a crowd of a score or more when Violet was suddenly jostled to one side. She staggered, nearly falling as she tripped on her swaying skirts. There was a scuffle behind her. She spun around to see the crowd scattering while women screamed and babies cried. A small space had been left free. In the middle of it Allain was struggling with two men.

Terror washed over her. Hard on its heels came a rage more white-hot and blinding than any she had ever known. The parasol in her hand was sturdily made, designed for use as both sunshade and walking stick. Its straight silver grip was attached to a steel shaft, and the iron ferrule that finished the other end had the pointed shape of a spear. She sprang forward, swinging it like a sword.

Her first blow caught one of the assailants across the cheek and neck in a welling streak of blood. He turned on her with a growl.

Allain, snatching a glance in her direction, sank his fist into the abdomen of the other man to the wrist, then jerked free, lunging away from him. He caught Violet at the waist, whirling her behind him as he deftly plucked the parasol from her grasp.

The two attackers were lean, with dirt embedded in their skin and the scarred faces common to waterfronts the world over. One was short, the other taller and wider. Cursing, they closed in.

Allain never let go of his portmanteau. A faint smile hovered at the corners of his mouth, while his eyes were silvery with the fierceness of his intent and feline in their watchfulness. He attacked.

The first man gave a gurgling cry as he reeled backward. A stiletto fell from his lax grasp, glinting as it skidded over the paving stones. The second assailant swooped to grab for it. The parasol whipped the air with a soft-edged whine as Allain extended his reach. The man grasped his flopping wrist, stumbling backward.

Allain edged forward, the parasol level, steady.

The two broke and ran, stumbling over each other, clutching their wounds.

There was a ragged cheer from one or two in the crowd; the rest melted away with hardly a backward glance. Violet, reaching for Allain, gripped his arm so tightly that he winced.

"You're hurt!" she said, her voice hardly more than a whisper.

"My own fault; they caught me off guard." His smile appeared strained around the edges.

"Let me see—" she began.

He shook his head, indicating that they should proceed in the direction of the ferry landing. "It will wait until we reach some kind of lodging. I don't think it's much more than a slice."

"Were they after money," she asked in low concern as she walked beside him, "or was it—something else?"

"That is the question, isn't it?" he said. "But if they were sent by Gilbert, he must have the devil's own luck."

They sought lodgings in an ancient palazzo just off the Grand

Canal. It belonged to an elderly widow, the Signora da Allori, Allain said, a building of four stories built of mellow golden stone that was stained gray green at the waterline with the inevitable rise and fall of the water level. The facade facing its side canal featured double loggias on the second and third floors, with Gothic arches ornamented with stone lacework, which gave it an Oriental air.

Allain left Violet sitting, gently rocking in the somber black gondola that had brought them, while he went to speak to the widow's majordomo. By that time Violet had ceased to wonder how he knew where to go, how to get there, or whom to ask for shelter. Nor did it occur to her that he might be refused.

He was not. By nightfall they were ensconced in a large, square room with long windows that opened onto one of the front loggias. A tin bath had been wrestled up the stairs by a pair of grinning manservants directed by the majordomo, a middle-aged man with a nice smile but a long nose and longer chin. He was harried in turn by the housekeeper, an older woman with a sharp tongue, fine black mustache, and ample shape who turned out to be his wife. Water to fill the bath appeared soon after; it was plentiful, though not particularly warm.

A nightgown, a wisp of batiste edged with exquisite handmade lace, was laid out on the great bed with its dusty silk brocade hangings. With it was a dressing gown only slightly more substantial. The housekeeper had brought them, though when Violet asked her where they had come from the woman only nodded in Allain's direction, winked, and bustled from the room.

The majordomo, Savio, brought a doctor, a man of grave visage and sage opinions. The doctor looked at the slash in Allain's side with pursed lips, but did nothing more than wash it with soft soap, dust it with a white powder, and wrap it with clean linen. Bowing over his fee with consummate grace, smiling a little as he stepped, quite unnecessarily, to kiss Violet's hand, he departed. Allain frowned as he watched him go.

A man of many parts, Savio also provided an evening meal, one brought to them, on Allain's order, immediately after they had bathed. This repast, consisting of pasta and salad greens followed by pork roast with new potatoes and cabbage, was cooked by Savio's wife and served, with passable competence, by the two manservants who were their sons.

Later Violet and Allain carried the last of their wine to the loggia. They sat enjoying the evening air and entertaining themselves by watching the water traffic plying up and down, counting the different kinds of boats and the different cries of the boatmen that served as warnings against collisions.

The moon came up. It slanted its silver beams across the water, gilding the rooftops with their baroque chimneys, cutting the square buildings with their rows of columns into odd foreshortened cubes and angles with the look of a drawing in black and white made by a madman. Somewhere, in some ancient courtyard garden, a nightingale trilled. A musical ensemble two houses away was practicing Mozart's Concerto for Clarinet in A, playing that slow, melancholy piece over and over again, so it drifted across the rooftops, coloring the night with its bittersweet refrain. A gondolier out in the Grand Canal sang a snatch of song with the caressing lilt and rhythm of a love ballad. The water lapped at the poles at the landing below the loggia and slapped at the palazzo's old stone walls.

A gondola, gliding past, carried the yellow gleams of its prow lantern before it as it went. Violet, turning her head to look at Allain in that brief yellow glow, saw his face turned toward her, his eyes like dark, glinting pools of desire as he watched her.

She reached out her hand to him.

Chapter 14

It pleased Joletta to think that the route she and Rone were taking by car to reach Venice was not so different from that taken by Violet and Allain by carriage and train. The placement of roads had changed little in that part of the world, and the train embankment ran beside the autostrata for miles.

The car Rone rented, the only one available at the agency, turned out to be ancient and cranky, a standard-transmission compact that trailed a blue vapor of oil smoke and had no air-conditioning. Joletta knew without being told that few cars came equipped with air in Europe, but couldn't resist pointing out that the tour bus had been.

Rone listened to her acid comments and watched her trying to keep the wind from tearing the hair from her head for half the morning. When they stopped at a pharmacy for their toiletries, he bought a white silk head scarf and a pair of oversized white-rimmed Italian sunglasses. As he handed them over, Joletta was too surprised, and irritated that she hadn't thought of them herself, to offer more than a muttered thanks.

Regardless, when she tied the scarf over her hair, put on the glasses, and propped her arm on the open window as they whizzed down the road with the wind in their faces, she felt very European. She did not, of course, mention that to Rone.

Joletta had never learned to manage a standard transmission.

Because of it Rone had to do all the driving. Less than ten minutes over the Italian border, she was delighted to have an excuse not to get behind the wheel.

The Italian drivers were demons on the road, charging forward with a disregard for safety that bordered on suicidal, or possibly homicidal. An automobile could at any moment become a weapon of aggression in the war of the motorways. When it happened, they took no prisoners.

The frantic traffic, streaking along at one hundred and forty kilometers per hour and beyond, nearly eighty-five miles per hour, didn't seem to bother Rone; he merged with it with competence and élan. Hands rock steady on the wheel, senses alert, he held his own and did not flinch or give way to any man or vehicle.

By default it became Joletta's task to act as navigator. Following the strange road signs and distances in kilometers was not as difficult as she had feared when Rone first tossed the map into her lap. The highway system itself was little different from the interconnected roads and interstates of the United States, and the method of marking the different routes was possibly even better. Her instructions as she guided their progress were short and to the point, and usually in answer to some request from Rone.

He whistled as he drove, snatches of some Italian folk tune, Joletta thought, though she didn't know the name. Apparently he was happy because he had gotten his way about leaving the tour group. She was also enjoying the change. It was so much nicer to be speeding along at their own pace, slowing when there was a village worth seeing, or even stopping to take a photograph of a patch of wildflowers or a vista. The wind whipping through the open window felt good on her face. Free of the hermetically sealed and air-conditioned bus, she could catch the scents of the countryside, savor the privet scent of the vineyards, the whiff of herbs in newly mown grass, even the faint odor of a herd of goats.

She began to wish that the drive could go on and on. Still, she would not have admitted it to Rone under torture. She was in no mood to be reasonable. She was mad at him, and she wanted him to know it.

She reached out to switch on the radio.

Rone glanced at her, then abruptly stopped whistling.

She fiddled with the dial, trying to tune in a station. After a few minutes she frowned in irritation. She was sorry that she had put an end to his whistling. The sound of it was preferable to the rock music and soccer games that were all she could find on the radio, and was certainly better than his strained silence. Embarrassed to switch off the radio again so quickly, she left it on a rock station and leaned back in her seat.

It was a shame she wasn't talking to him, really, she thought as an hour passed and then another. There was history and romance and endless fascination in the very names of the places they were passing through, and Rone was one of the few people she had met who might have been able to appreciate these things. More, there were new green leaves on the trees, and the yellow gorse and red poppies along the roadsides seemed bigger and brighter than in England and France. She turned toward him once or twice to mention such things, but always subsided again without speaking.

She was staring out the window when he spoke in flat tones. "How long are you going to keep this up?"

"What do you mean?" The question was an automatic defense as she faced him.

The corner of his mouth twitched in a faint smile as he said, "The silent treatment."

She had not considered it in that light. It was an uncomfortable reminder of Gilbert's silence toward Violet in the journal. She didn't much like that image of herself, didn't care for the idea that that particular method of dealing with anger might be a family habit.

She said, "I'm here because you arranged it. I don't have to like it, or be nice about it."

"You don't have to sulk, either. If you don't like it, tell me about it. I can't read your mind."

"That," she said sweetly, "is a very good thing."

Laughter deepened the lines at his mouth as he looked at her where she lay back, relaxed in the seat, though his eyes were concealed by his dark glasses. His tone meditative, he said, "I wonder."

"Yes, well," she answered, straightening in some haste, "civilized people don't finagle others into doing things against their will."

"Even if it's in their best interests?" He glanced up into the rearview mirror, then across at her for an instant before returning his attention to the road.

"There was some difference of opinion over that, as I remember," she said. "But yes, even then."

"I would like to point out that it's only for an afternoon, not a lifetime. Unless there's a change of plans."

She lowered her sunglasses to stare at him over the rims. He appeared unruffled by her scrutiny, sitting at ease behind the wheel with the wind through the window fluttering the open collar of his polo shirt against his tan throat and sculpting his straight, dark hair into windswept waves. His ease and the sunglasses gave him a look that was cosmopolitan, if not European—and far too attractive for comfort under any label.

"Meaning?" she inquired in astringent tones.

A smile came and went across his face. "Meaning you might find you like striking out on your own. What else?"

"Kidnapping crossed my mind there for a second." She refused to mention the other idea that had flitted past first.

"You've been reading too many spy novels. But at least we got all that cleared away. Now will you talk to me?"

She reached to turn off the radio, where the soccer scores were being given again for what seemed like the tenth time in the past half hour. She wasn't so pigheaded as to spite herself. "I'll be glad to," she said. "What shall we talk about first?"

They bypassed Milan on the four-lane autostrata, the E30, streaking along past ancient villas of sun-warmed stone and long stretches of fruit trees in bloom and vegetables growing under protective plastic. They were making good time; there was no reason they shouldn't be able to rejoin the group in Venice for dinner at the latest.

One moment they were skimming along, talking about finding an aire stop for an afternoon snack; the next they were in trouble.

It was just a transport truck, one made on a slightly smaller scale than American models, but with nothing unusual about it; they had seen dozens similar during the day. It overtook them in the left lane in a perfectly normal manner. It seemed to be crowding them a bit, not a pleasant feeling in the lightweight compact, but drivers of big trucks in the States also had a tendency to think they owned the road.

Rone's soft curse came first. Joletta heard it distinctly. She swung her head. He was frowning in concentration as he stared into his side mirror. He pressed his foot hard on the accelerator.

The bump with its metallic thud was like being hit by a giant padded fist. The car fishtailed with tires squealing. Rone held the light vehicle on the road with main strength, steering into the spin. They straightened. Joletta, regaining her balance, grabbed for the dashboard with one hand and her taut seat belt with the other.

The truck slammed into the rear of the compact. It swerved off the highway, plunging down the embankment. The front tires struck with teeth-jarring force. They bounced and bucked, rolling, sliding. Dust and gravel flew. A row of plane trees rose up before them. Rone wrenched the steering wheel over, the muscles in his arms standing out like carved stone. They slewed around, skidding. The right side of the car struck with a solid, grinding thud.

Leaves showered. Metal groaned. Steam hissed in release. The car shuttered to stillness. The engine roared. It died as Rone cut the ignition.

"Out," Rone said in hard command. "Now!"

His seat belt clicked. He pushed at the door on his side, slamming against it with his shoulder as it stuck. Dazed, Joletta saw there was blood streaking down his face. She fumbled with her own seat belt with fingers gone stiff and clumsy. It seemed an eternity before she could spring the latch. She tried the door on her side, but it was welded shut by crumpled metal.

Rone caught her arm, pulling her toward him. She needed no other urging. Propelling herself across the seat, she caught the door frame to help drag herself out.

Rone's grasp was so strong as she pushed to her feet that she stumbled against him. He steadied her a scant instant, then took her hand, whirling with her away from the car.

Hot metal, burning wires; she could smell them.

They broke into a run, stumbling over the dry, weeded runnels of water drainage, tripping in the ivy escaping from the embankment ground cover, getting as far away as they could while the seconds counted down.

Behind them they heard a soft, fluttering rumble, almost like a gas furnace igniting. Then came the roar.

The concussion, with its crackling, searing, suffocating heat struck their backs. They ducked, diving forward, falling headlong. They covered their heads, hugging the ground.

The worst was over in only a few moments. Sitting up with caution, they shielded their faces from the incredible heat with their arms and turned to look. They had to; they couldn't help it.

The orange-and-yellow flames leaped upward, licking at the fresh green of the plane trees, whipping the sky with black tails of smoke. The interior of the car was a caldron of boiling red heat.

Almost, almost, they had been in that car. Breathing in harsh, lung-wrenching gasps, they sat watching.

On the motorway behind them, cars were slowing, a few stop-

ping. An argument broke out with loud voices and much waving
of arms. A man stepped from a red car and made his way down to
where Joletta and Rone sat.

"Well, my friends," Caesar Zilanti said as he approached within
hearing distance, "a lucky escape, yes?"

He leaned to offer his hand to help Joletta stand. She took it
automatically, her face blank as she stared at him. Glancing beyond
him at his car, she said, "Where did you—"

"He was following us," Rone said as he got to his feet unaided.
"I've been watching him for miles."

"Kilometers, perhaps, but otherwise, yes," the Italian said with
the lift of a shoulder. His dark gaze rested on Joletta. "The signorina
is so beautiful that I did not like to lose sight of her so soon."

Rone put his hands on his hips as he faced the other man. The
look on his face was harsh with skepticism. "It would be interesting
to know how you managed to catch up with us today."

"These tourists buses," the Italian said with a shading of disparagement, "they are very predictable. At your hotel in Paris I talk
to the driver who told me your tour director always tries to stop
for lunch at the Movenpick cafeteria near the lake in Lugano on this
route. I finish my business in Paris, I go to this place, but the signorina is not alone; I see her go into the park with you. The bus
leaves and you two are not on it. I walk in the garden. The rest was
easy."

"If you saw the bus leave us, why didn't you offer a lift?" Rone's
tone was neutral, but the chill in his eyes was not.

Caesar smiled, his eyes hooded under his dark and heavy brows.
"How could I know what game you were playing? It seemed possible you wished to be alone with the signorina, and who could
blame you?"

It was plausible, Joletta thought, but whether it was likely was
something else again. Rone seemed to think that Caesar might have
been following them more closely than he was willing to say. Could
the Italian know something of the break-in at the hotel in Lucerne?
Yet how could he? What earthly connection could he have with it,
or with this accident?

She was suddenly beginning to feel weak and her hands were
trembling. She not only felt terrible, she looked terrible, she knew
it, and all she could think about was the fact that she was going to
have to talk to another set of police from another country before
she could lie down and rest.

"However you got here," she said to Caesar in slow weariness, "I'm glad to see you, since this is your country. Maybe you can tell us what we do now?"

"There are two possibilities," he said, lifting a hand to rub at his chin. "The first of these is to drive away with me, at once."

Joletta blinked. She glanced at Rone but could tell nothing from the set expression on his face. To Caesar, she said, "But—aren't we required to file a report with the police, notify the rental company of the damage, things like that."

"Why give yourself the trouble? This is Italy; you do what you like, and hope the carabinieri and rental-car people don't find you to ask questions."

"I think we'll give ourselves the trouble anyway," Rone said deliberately.

"As you like," the Italian said with a smile and a shrug. "Leave it to me."

Rone said nothing, but the look on his face was sardonic.

The carabinieri were courteous and gallant and sartorially impressive in their perfectly tailored blue uniforms; they were also in no hurry to end their investigation. They regretted they would not be able to apprehend the truck driver instantly, but with so little to go on—anyone could see the difficulty. They were sorry that such a terrible accident had to take place in Italy; it was to be hoped that it did not give them a bad impression of their fine country and that the rest of their stay would be happier. How fortunate it was that no one had been seriously injured; Signor Adamson was certain his cut had stopped bleeding? *Va bene.* Then there was only the towing charges and the indemnity for the damage to the rental automobile. They had insurance, of course? *Bene, bene.* Ah, well, it was only a matter of signing a few dozen forms then.

It was late when they reached the quay in Venice where Caesar had to park his car. They were not so far behind the tour bus, as it happened; they recognized it parked on the quay and saw their luggage being unloaded onto a conveyor, which was sending it along to be piled onto a water bus for the trip to the hotel. It was possible, Joletta said as they walked toward the hotel, that they would be able to make the gondola ride and dinner that was included with the tour.

"Excuse me, please, but no," Caesar cried as if in pain. "I beg you will dine with me, instead, both of you; I have a cousin who owns a restaurant renowned for its food. Afterward, there will be time, if you like, for the gondola. Not this tourist business, a flotilla of boats racing around a few short turns and then back to the landing with hardly time for the gondolier to break into a sweat. No, a true gondola journey, very dark and romantic, this I promise."

By this point Caesar had proven himself a valuable ally, arguing their case with the carabinieri with all the passion the circumstances seemed to demand, putting Joletta and Rone into his car with tender care, and offering to guide them the short distance to the hotel while fending off the other guides and offers of water taxis they didn't need. Joletta, glancing at Rone, found him looking at her.

She indicated his shirt that was marked with rusty drops of dried blood. The suggestion tentative, she said, "It's possible you and I may need more time to clean up than the others in the tour group."

"I can't say I'm looking forward to having dinner quite as early as the older folks," he agreed.

"How early?" Caesar inquired, then lifted his brows in disbelief as he was told. "No, never! This is Italy, I tell you. Nothing decent is ever served before ten, eleven o'clock."

Rone nodded. "Your cousin's restaurant it is, then, but I insist on buying."

Caesar argued vociferously, offering every reason why they should take advantage of his hospitality, but the outcome was never in any doubt. Rone would pay. Caesar would pick them up in a water taxi at the landing near the hotel in a few hours.

Watching them shake hands as they parted, Joletta thought the two men had come to have a certain respect for each other, if no real liking. That did not explain why they were having dinner with Caesar. She wondered if Rone wasn't expecting to have time to pump Caesar, to discover if he was what he seemed.

The keys to their hotel rooms had large brass weights in the shape of a bell attached, a potent reminder that they were to be left at the desk on leaving the premises. Joletta expected to have trouble with Rone, expecting him to insist that she share his room. To head it off, she began to state her case as they walked up the narrow stairs to the second floor, where it was located.

"There's no need to say anything else," he said before she had half begun. "I know you were embarrassed at being seen coming out of my room this morning, and I wouldn't want that to happen again."

"Really?"

"Really," he answered in firm tones.

She gave him a grateful smile as she neared her door. "I didn't expect you to be so reasonable, but I'm glad you understand."

"I'm a reasonable man," he said, and went on without pausing as he took her key from her to open the door, then stepped inside. "I'll stay with you."

She stood still for an instant. Following him, she closed the door behind her with more than necessary violence. "That isn't what I meant!"

"I know," he said over his shoulder. Moving to the window, he swung the two glass casement panels wide, then flung open the wooden shutters. Beyond the opening was a jumble of cream stone walls, red tiled roofs sporting television antennas, a verdigris green church dome, and a small bell tower, while down below was a lapping canal. He left the shutters open as he turned to face her. "I do know," he repeated, "but I wouldn't leave you alone after this afternoon if you had a SWAT team hanging from this window and your own security guard outside the door."

She met his hard gaze for a long moment before she turned and dropped down on the foot of the bed that took up most of the room. Sighing, she said, "I was afraid you were going to make something out of the accident."

"I thought we disposed of the accident theory in Lucerne. You might easily have been killed this afternoon."

"And you."

"Yes."

Something in his voice made her send him a quick glance. He was watching her with what appeared to be bafflement overlaid with respect in his eyes. She looked down again, speaking almost to herself as she reached out to smooth the blue-and-gold tapestry bedspread on the bed. "It's hard to believe."

"That just shows what a blameless life you've led. It's always hard for honest folks to recognize the sheer meanness of other people."

She took a deep breath and let it out slowly. There were things she had been turning over in her mind that she had not mentioned, things he had a right to know if he was determined to stay around her. Yet how could she suggest to him that the people most likely to want to harm her were her relatives? She couldn't believe it herself.

Abruptly she lifted her hand from the bedspread. Swinging her head, she stared behind her at the wide expanse of mattress, the long headboard, the two pillows nestled side by side. She turned her wide gaze on Rone. Her voice was a note higher as she said, "This is a double bed."

"Queen size," he answered without a flicker of expression.

The air between them seemed to vibrate with tension. The minutes slid past. Joletta let her eyelids close with a snap. She leaned forward to prop her elbows on her knees and rest her aching head in her hands. "God," she said, "how long is this trip going to last?"

Caesar's love for his city and his country was genuine. It was in his voice as he pointed out the different buildings and monuments as they passed them on the way to dinner, and it was in his eyes as he gazed around him, looking for some other bit of stonework or rare architectural detail to bring to their attention.

Their water taxi took them to the Piazza San Marco, where they disembarked to walk to the restaurant located somewhere in the maze of streets beyond the square. The evening was advancing. The tourists were gone for the day; they had the square very nearly to themselves as they strolled over the gray paving stones and among the ancient buildings with their soaring Byzantine arches, carved stone fretwork, and hundreds of columns marching pale and ghostly in the light of an early-rising moon.

Caesar looked at Joletta's rapt face as he walked beside her. "*Bella*, no?" he said softly.

"*Si*," she said, grasping at the Italian since in that moment English seemed sadly lacking, "*bella, bella.*"

Rone, walking on the other side of her, chose that moment to point out a flight of pigeons wheeling in a perfect spiral about the campanile with the glow of moonlight captured under their wings. She smiled and nodded, and realized in some amusement that she had regained her enthusiasm for the trip.

It was heady stuff, having two tall, dynamic, knock-you-dead gorgeous men vying for her attention. Joletta enjoyed it, though she wasn't at all sure what she had done to deserve it. She had never thought of herself as the femme fatale type. She had no inclination whatever to play one off against the other; she was, in fact, afraid tempers might flare between them. Still, to have them both walking along with her did wonderful things for her spirits.

At the restaurant the waiters seemed inclined to enter into the competition also. They bowed and smiled and murmured compliments and followed her progress with their eyes until she began to wonder if she was wearing a permanent smirk. It was all too much. More was to come.

As the salad course was removed their waiter, a slender blond man in his late thirties who moved with swift, deft grace, picked up Joletta's serving plate along with her salad plate. She thought it was a mistake for a few moments, since both Caesar and Rone's plates of gray-veined marble had been left in front of them. Then the pasta appeared, fettuccine in a delicate seafood-and-cream sauce. As the only woman, Joletta knew she should have been served first, but it did not happen that way. Both men were given their portions while she sat with an empty space in front of her.

At last their waiter reached over her shoulder to set a square gold serving plate in front of her. Next came her serving of fettuccine, a generous portion twice as large as that of the men. Finally she was offered freshly grated Parmesan, something neither gentleman had been served.

"It's a compliment of the most sincere kind for a beautiful woman," Caesar said, his gaze amused as he sat back, watching the flush on Joletta's face. "All that is required is to say thank you."

She did that, of course; still, there was something compelling about the experience. Added to the presence of Rone and Caesar, it made her feel special, different, if only for the night. She could feel that difference in her smile, in her walk as she left the restaurant, in the way she felt inside. She was not sure how long it would remain with her, but it was nice while it lasted.

All true gondolas were black; it was not only a requirement, but a strict tradition, according to Caesar. The one he had reserved for their journey along the canals shone with polish from its high carved prow to higher stern. It seated five on seats covered with crushed burgundy velvet, and the sea horses that decorated the sides were of softly gleaming brass. If it was so splendid because of the tourist trade, Joletta didn't want to know; she preferred to think it was because it was typical of Venice and the Venetians.

The gondolier was good-looking in a Pan-like fashion in his shirt of black and white stripes. He was also deferential yet enterprising in the assured Italian manner she was coming to recognize. It was he who managed to hand her into the gondola while Caesar and Rone stood arguing politely about where they were going to sit. As he saw it, Rone looked at Caesar and the two shrugged. Rone turned immediately, then, to step into the boat, taking the seat beside Joletta. The other man threw up his hand before settling into the seat in front of her and turning to lean over its back to talk to her.

The Grand Canal was fairly well lighted, but not so brightly as most city streets; it was certainly dim enough to maintain the air of ancient romance. The night wind off the Adriatic Sea was fresh and cool without being strong enough to cause anything more than a slight swell in the water. The regular thump and splash of the gondolier's oar was hypnotic, while the glint of moonlight on the winding channel between the old buildings seemed almost stagelike in its perfection.

Caesar pointed out some of the more famous of the palaces as they passed them, also indicating Casanova's house and the place where Robert Browning and Elizabeth Barrett Browning had lived during their sojourn in the city. As he showed them the house of Marco Polo, indicating the water that lapped over the landing as a sign of the gradual sinking of the city, he rested his hand on Joletta's knee in a casual gesture. Her attention was so focused on the graceful old building that she hardly noticed.

Rone leaned to clamp his fingers on Caesar's wrist, transferring the other man's hand to the back of the forward seat. His expression in the dim light was pleasant yet with a trace of challenge as he met the Italian's gaze. Caesar said something under his breath that sounded less than complimentary, but the moment passed as he shifted immediately afterward to point out the Rialto Bridge looming up before them.

A short time later they turned into a smaller canal. At the same time they were joined by another gondola, this one carrying a soloist and an accordion player. While they idled slowly down this darker waterway the singer, a dark slim man with an operatic voice, serenaded them with "Santa Lucia," "O sole mio," and "Torna a Surriento," as well as "Non ti scordar di me," at Caesar's request. Strollers on the canal bridges stopped to listen as the gondolas swept past beneath them. People hung from the windows of houses for the free concert, while one man, walking on a short stretch of sidewalk running alongside the water, joined in the refrain in a quite creditable performance. His voice followed them for some time as they eased along.

The romantic songs, the uninhibited joining in of the stranger, the heart-tugging music were all such clichés they bordered on caricature. Torn between scorn and amusement for her own sentimental susceptibility, Joletta simply gave up and enjoyed it all. She lay back in the velvet seat, relaxing against the cushion. Discovering that Rone's arm was stretched out behind her, she used it for a pillow.

It occurred to her to wonder, after a time, if this could be the same canal where Violet and Allain had stayed; there was no reason to doubt that that building with its stained plaster and columned loggia was still around here somewhere. The place had been standing for three hundred years or so when those two had come to it; another hundred and forty could make little difference. Venice had changed in many ways, but much of it had also remained the same.

The gondola neared a cross channel. The gondolier called out his warning, then swung the long boat to enter the intersecting canal. This one was unlighted, closed in by blank stone walls. They rode into dimness that grew ever blacker. It became so dark that Caesar was no more than an indistinct blur, and it was impossible to see the prow of the gondola.

"Perfect," Rone said.

Turning, he placed his warm fingers at the jawline of Joletta's face, tilting her head. His lips, gentle, smooth, warmly possessive, touched hers.

The sweetness of it, the rightness in time and place, at that moment, was like a chime ringing inside her. She had been corrupted by the European lack of inhibition, she thought, for she did not care that the gondolier was directly behind them or Caesar ahead in the darkness. She turned to Rone, spreading her hand over his chest to feel the firm, sure beat of his heart. Relaxing against him, she accepted the impulses that drove them both with the same ready inevitability as she had accepted the music.

His hold tightened. He traced the sensitive surfaces of her lips with his tongue, probing, receiving the grace of entry. In delicate play, their tongues touched, the smooth-nubbed resilience of both meeting with exquisite abrasion. Their lips warmed, softened to conform yet more closely.

Joletta turned more completely against the hard length of his body as tingling pleasure invaded her senses. It rose higher, flooding like an Adriatic tide. Beneath it, fueling it, increasing it, was an exhilaration so wild it brought a prickling of goose bumps to the surface of her skin.

The light began to increase.

With slow reluctance, Rone released her.

The night was cool without the protection of his arms, Joletta discovered. She hadn't been ready for him to let her go. She could not remember when she had felt so alive, so desirable, so euphorically happy.

It was crazy and she knew it. There were people dogging her every footstep, maybe trying to harm her.

Maybe that danger was a part of what she felt, some primitive response to its threat.

Maybe it was just the freedom phenomenon, the effect of being far from home and the people who knew her, of being, finally, on her own.

Maybe it was simply that wine and male appreciation had gone to her head.

She didn't know, wasn't even sure she wanted to know. It was enough, for now, simply to feel it.

The sensations remained with her as the gondola ride came to an end. They were there as Caesar kissed her hand in a good-night salute before parting from them at the landing. They lasted while she and Rone strolled to the hotel and climbed the ancient winding staircase that led to their room. It was with her still as Rone unlocked the door.

Joletta, entering the room first, reached for the light switch. Rone caught her hand. For an instant she was afraid he had seen or heard something in the darkened room.

No.

He closed the door behind him and turned her to him. Placing her hand on his shoulder, he drew her into his arms.

His lips in the darkness were heated and heady in their sweetness. Joletta felt herself lifted, swung, carried toward the bed. Moonlight washed over her as he placed her in the patch of it that streamed across the mattress from the open window. As he loomed above her the broad width of his shoulders, the shape of his head, and individual strands of his hair were outlined in a nimbus of silver that left his face in shadow. He seemed, for the briefest possible instant, a stranger and threatening because of it.

Then he eased down beside her, joining her in the wash of light, and she was engulfed in the rich, barely tasted familiarity of him.

Silvered by the moon's steady glow, they melded together, mouth to mouth, thighs entwined.

There was something inevitable about the moment to Joletta, as if she had known from the second he had turned to her in the gondola that it must come. Or perhaps it had become inescapable before that, when he had pulled her from the wrecked car, or earlier, when he had kissed her on the bridge at Lucerne, or even as she had looked up to see him there in Paris. It seemed that she had been waiting a lifetime, waiting only for this. Now she need wait no longer.

Wine and rich languor moved through her veins. She touched his face, the faint bristles of his beard just emerging from his skin, the firm planes of his cheek and square turn of his jaw. He cupped her face in a strong hand, fingering the softness of her skin and the gentle perfection of the bones beneath it. For long moments their eyes met in the dimness, searching, dark and liquid with promise.

On a swift, indrawn breath, Joletta tightened her hold around him. The firmness of her breasts pushed against his chest and her lower body pressed the incredible heat and rigidity of his masculine form. Through the soft cotton of her skirt, she felt his need of her, and her heart swelled, thudding into the bones of her ribs. The muscles of his shoulder under the cotton of his shirt were taut yet fluid with movement as he stroked her back. The scent of him, of cotton and sandalwood, of warm male and the humid freshness of the Venetian night, was an incitement. It blended with her own Tea Rose scent to form an erotic rhapsody of fragrance.

He was not a novice; the sureness of his touch upon her breast, at the buttons of her blouse, proved it. But then, neither was she. The relationship she had shared with her fiancé had been hasty and, for the most part, none too satisfactory. Perhaps for that reason Joletta could not remember ever feeling this same compelling need before. She had never known this frantic impulse to hurry, to fling herself upon him and urge instant gratification while at the same time acknowledging a deep, internal yearning for slow and unending fulfillment. She wanted to be a part of Rone, to make him a part of her, to know him without reservations.

Was that ever really possible?

These thoughts flickering through her mind were banished as she felt cool air against her bare skin. Rone brushed aside the fine material of her blouse. The warmth of his breath, then the moist heat of his mouth, brushed across the arch of her throat. A tremor caught her as he flicked the hollow at its base with his tongue. It increased as he moved lower, trailing a moist path of warm kisses along the valley between her breasts while he unhooked her bra.

Heat flowed along the surface of Joletta's skin. The beat of her heart became a muffled drumming in her ears. She moved to help as he tugged her skirt from her hips, then gasped as he lowered his head to brush his mouth across the tense muscles of her abdomen. She caught his hair, tangling her fingers in its silken crispness as if to stop him, then, with a soft sound in her throat, she let him proceed.

Unhurried, certain in his movements, he buried his face in the concave hollow of her belly, breathing her rare scent, tasting the sweet hollow of her navel before moving upward once more. He circled the peak of a breast with his tongue, savoring the texture and resilience with meticulous care as he ascended toward the crest. Joletta ceased breathing as her senses expanded. Her skin radiated warmth. Then as she felt the heat of his mouth close on her nipple, she yielded to that searing caress.

She had not known it could be like this, had never felt such a hot flood of sheer, wanton delight. She lifted trembling fingers to his face, smoothing its strong planes, feeling the slight movement of his jaw as his tongue abraded the nipple he held. There was inside her a sense of giving, of bountiful fullness that brought an ache to her throat.

Leaving one nipple taut and wet, he gave the other the same slow and careful attention. He paused to press his lips to the firm curve where her heart throbbed in steady, shuddering pulsation beneath the skin. Shifting then, moving upward once more, he sought her mouth while he smoothed his hand in steady and deliberate descending circles, reaching inexorably toward the silken triangle at the juncture of her thighs.

How intimate a touch could be, invading privacy, destroying barriers, reaching deep into secret places that had been closely guarded, with a pleasure that both demanded and beseeched acceptance. Rone was insidious, undeniable, assured, constant. His ministrations brought the molten surge of unbridled desire. A soft sound vibrated in her throat. She moved against him, with him, drowning in sensation, afraid he would stop. Unbidden, in an ecstasy of giving, she eased her thighs open to allow greater access.

He took it, following his touch with his mouth. Joletta gasped, succumbing, answering in silent grace to his guidance. She ceased to think as the pleasure grew, only shifting slightly, reaching for him in wanton, passionate gratitude, reveling in the muscular hardness of his body that was so perfect a complement to her own softness.

There was magic in the exploration of tender hollows and sensitive curves and protuberances. It quickened inside them, blooming, while their breathing deepened and their hearts battered against each other. It banished past and present, leaving only blind need and its delicate tending, its deliberate, tendon-straining enhancement.

Then in sudden surrender, they turned, coming together.

He entered her; she received him, encompassed him with rhythmic internal welcome.

Magic, physical magic that was also in the mind.

They made it last, striving, rising, falling in tenuous rhythm, tumbling upon the sheets with trembling muscles and moist skin surfaces that glided upon each other like oiled silk. Joletta clung to his arms, hard-muscled with restraint, as he moved above her. She rose against him, taking him deep inside and deeper still with every plunge. The blood rushed through her veins, pounding in her ears. The shocks of his striving rippled through her, and she took them and gave them back again. Her senses stretched, soaring. Straining, they advanced in vital increments toward a goal neither was yet desperate enough to reach.

Then abruptly it was in their grasp.

Joletta felt her heart cease, then begin again with the sharp beat of a striking bell. She gave a low cry. The magic caught her in its vortex, spinning her out of control in a pleasure so piercing it was near unbearable, so endless it seemed to spread wider and wider until it lapped the very edges of eternity. She clung to the man who held her, feeling the shudder that shook him as he plunged into her one final time. She heard her name whispered like a benediction. They were still.

The wind off the Adriatic dried the perspiration from their bodies. Before their skin had cooled, they slept. Waking in the dawn in each other's arms, lying like spoons under the sheet, they heard the whine of a mosquito.

They turned to each other. It was like a homecoming.

Chapter 15

He hadn't meant to do it.

Rone let the shower spray pour over him in a hot, steady stream, chasing the sandalwood-scented lather off his body and down the drain while steam rose in a scented cloud. He should regret the hours just spent in bed with Joletta, he knew. But he didn't. He would have this much, if no more. The regrets he'd save for later.

She was like no woman he had ever known. No surprise there; he had recognized it from the start.

She had come to him the night before as naturally as some Roman nymph, without hesitation or pretense or trying to make him realize the honor she was conferring upon him.

And because of it, he did feel honored.

He felt a lot of other things, none of which he needed to think about now, not if he was going to let her sleep a little longer this morning.

God, but she had courage. And self-control. He had expected to have to deal with a full-blown case of hysterics yesterday after the accident. No such thing. And it wasn't that she lacked the knowledge or imagination to understand what could have happened. Her face had been pale and her eyes huge for a full five minutes; she had just refused to subject the people around her to the emotional fallout of her horror.

Earlier, before they had been run off the road, she had been well and truly irritated with him—not without reason. He would have felt better if she had screamed and called him choice names; he wondered if she knew that. But no, she had put him in purgatory and kept him there until he couldn't stand it anymore.

Not that he thought she realized it. He hoped she didn't. If she ever discovered how much she could hurt him, he was going to be very sorry indeed.

He had seen Venice before, but never with a woman who refused to pretend that she was blasé about it. Joletta had looked and absorbed in her quiet way, and her delight had sparkled like the sun glittering off the lagoon. Everybody around her had been enchanted, including every man in sight. Including Caesar Zilanti. Including himself.

To keep his hands and his inconvenient lust to himself had been impossible. The moment had been too right, Joletta too incredible in the Venetian moonlight.

He had been too jealous. Caesar was lucky he wasn't at the bottom of the Grand Canal. Smooth-talking son of a—

Self-control. He was the one who needed that. He had thought he could stick close to Joletta, watch her every minute, and play it cool. Idiot. He had set his own self up.

So now what?

So now he would act the Judas goat, take Joletta to St. Mark's Square, and wait. He would pretend innocence and feel like a treacherous bastard.

He turned off the shower and reached for a towel, pressing it to his face for a long moment. He breathed deep, once, twice, before letting the air seep from his lungs in a slow sigh.

Dear God, but he hated this. He really did.

He had known he would, just not how much.

There was still a short time left, another week in Italy before the tour was over, however. Stupid and selfish it might be, but he intended to make the most of it.

Joletta, watching through slitted eyelids as Rone emerged from the bathroom, smiled a little to herself at his attempts to be quiet. She was a light sleeper—the shift of the mattress as he had eased out of bed had wakened her—but there was no need to make him feel bad by letting him know it.

She had never actually lived with a man; never wakened in the morning to find one there, never seen one easing around in the gray dawn light clad only in a towel. It was interesting.

There were drops of water between his shoulder blades where he had missed them with the towel, and also a few caught in the dark and curling hair on his thighs. She watched in lazy appreciation for the way they shone with the movement of his muscles. And she thought, with a slight flush, of drying them for him.

He had been more concerned about privacy in Switzerland, she thought; he had dressed in the bathroom, then left the room altogether while she showered and changed. That he had abandoned such maneuvers this morning was a measure of the intimacy that had been established between them. It was disturbing, that sense of intimacy, but she thought she just might be able to get used to it.

He began to whistle under his breath, a blues rendition of "St. Louis Woman," as he pulled a change of clothing and what appeared to be a small coffeepot from his suitcase. He skimmed into briefs and a pair of jeans, then moved back into the bathroom to fill the pot with water. An instant later Joletta caught the aroma of fresh coffee grounds, followed by the soft sizzle of water beginning to heat.

Rone stepped back into the room, walking noiselessly to the window, where he leaned one shoulder against the frame. He crossed his arms over his bare chest as he looked out over the rooftops. The dim light gave his features a gray cast, so that he appeared pensive and even a little sad. What could be troubling him? Some business problem? Something to do with being with her?

Joletta thought of asking him what was wrong, but she didn't know him well enough to pry into his business. And if it concerned her, she was not sure she wanted to know.

She stretched, pushing herself up on one elbow. Her voice husky, she said, "Is that coffee I smell?"

Rone turned his head. His mouth curved in a slow smile as he gave a brief nod. "I hope it's not too strong for you."

"I'm from New Orleans, remember? Coffee doesn't come too strong for me."

He acknowledged that sally before he went on. "I'm sorry about last night."

"Are you? That isn't too flattering." The light tone wasn't too bad, if she did say so herself.

His smile faded as his face took on a serious cast. "All right, the only thing I'm sorry about is failing to protect you. I would have if I had expected—but at least it can stand as evidence that I didn't plan what happened."

"Oh," she said, lowering her gaze to the sheet that covered her as she realized what he was talking about. Pregnancy and the ways to prevent it had not crossed her mind. "I didn't either—that is, I don't—"

"I didn't think so," he said, coming to her rescue with a trace of humor in his voice. "That can be fixed, if we go looking for another pharmacy?"

It was subtle, the questioning inflection in his suggestion, the intimation that he was taking nothing for granted. Hearing it, Joletta recognized that she was being handed an excuse for drawing back from the new physical relationship he had established, if that was what she wanted. What could she do except return the favor?

"We can do that, of course," she said, "if you think we can find the time."

"Oh," he drawled, "I think we can manage it."

She laughed; she couldn't help it. A moment later she was being tumbled across the mattress as it bounced on its springs from his weight hurling down upon it. He rolled her to her back, lying across her with his weight on his elbows while he stared down at her with some dark exultation suspended in his eyes. She met his gaze for long moments, then reaching up, she slid her fingers along the strong column of his neck to the back of his head, and dragged his lips down to hers.

The pigeons had converged on St. Mark's Square, hovering in squabbling crowds around the grain sellers, fluttering and circling with the morning sunlight shining iridescent magenta and green on their heads and necks. They scattered in clouds as groups of tourists and Italian schoolchildren crisscrossed the paving stones from the quay to the Doges' Palace and the cathedral, and they rose with a fluttering of wings like a host of earthbound angels as the two moors on the old clock tower struck the bronze bell to mark the hour.

Joletta, watching the activity as she and Rone had a cappuccino at the sidewalk café on the square, thought the birds had the same red legs and amorous dispositions as the pigeons of Jackson Square in New Orleans. It seemed comforting, somehow.

The pigeons were not the only familiar sight. Joletta's lips tightened as she saw a tall, blond woman striding toward her, threading her way among the strolling groups and the vendors of postcards and head scarves. Natalie.

Joletta's main reaction was irritated anger. She couldn't be surprised that Natalie had found her, not after everything that had taken place, but it was hard to see how the other woman could dare face her.

She thought of getting up and walking away, of refusing to speak to her cousin. That didn't seem likely to be helpful. Something had to be done, that much was clear. She might as well make a beginning now.

Natalie lifted her hand to wave while she was still several yards away. She was boldly fashionable in a Versace dress in vigorous shades of teal and magenta and hot Italian yellow, yet she looked out of place there in the square with its muted colors and timeworn elegance. As she waggled her fingers the dozens of gold and enamel bangle bracelets on her arms made such a clanking noise that the pigeons were startled into flight for a good twenty feet around her.

"Good morning, cousin," she called in gay greeting as she came nearer. "I knew you had to show up here in the square sometime; everybody does."

Joletta gave her an unenthusiastic hello. Natalie was undaunted. As she came to a halt beside the table she appraised Joletta in a single sweeping glance. "You're looking well; Venice must agree with you." She turned toward Rone, who had gotten to his feet as she approached. "Or maybe it's the person you're traveling with. Aren't you going to introduce us?"

As Joletta complied Rone gave her cousin a brief nod. His features were a little stiff, as if he was less than thrilled with the interruption. They did not relax as Natalie spoke again with a sly glance at Joletta.

"Yes, I'd say a definite improvement over the types you usually have in tow, cousin, the bearded artists with nothing to say for themselves and the stuffy professors who talk too much."

Joletta seemed to hear an undercurrent of envy in the other woman's voice. The bright, clear light was not kind to her cousin; it exposed the sallow skin tones under her makeup caused by too many late nights and too much to drink, and etched the lines of discontent between her carefully arched brows with hard shadows.

Natalie reached for a chair to seat herself without waiting for an invitation. As Rone stepped to hold the chair for her, she gave him a brilliant smile over her shoulder. "Rone," she said musingly, "it sounds like a name for a cowboy. Are you one?"

"Not exactly," he answered.

"What does that mean? I'm dying to know." Natalie, catching sight of a waiter, snapped her fingers for service.

"I have all the cowboy instincts, just no horse."

The expression on the face of Joletta's cousin turned arch. "Which instincts are those?"

He gave her a bare glance as he returned to his chair. "An impulse to ride to the rescue, the urge to settle problems with a well-planted fist."

"A man of action. Dear me." The other woman propped her chin on her fist as she held his gaze.

Joletta gave her cousin a hard look. There was something odd about the exchange between her and Rone. Natalie's tone was openly mocking, and her smile had a predatory edge to it.

Natalie was the kind of woman who preferred the company of men and did not trouble to hide it. It wasn't unusual for her to concentrate on whatever man she might happen to be around, or even to attempt to attach any that happened to be available.

Rone's reaction was unexpected, however. He leaned back in his chair as if he would like to put distance between the two of them, while the muscles of his face were stiff.

As Rone failed to answer her last taunting comment, Natalie glanced at Joletta, then back to him again. She asked brightly, "Have you two just met, or is this a long-standing arrangement?"

"What difference does it make?" Joletta answered, her voice tight. "Unless you're afraid he'll be in the way?"

Natalie swung toward her with wide eyes. "You don't have to bite my head off. Anyway, I don't know what you're talking about."

"Oh, I think you do. I'm surprised you have the nerve to come near me after nearly getting us killed yesterday."

"Killed? Me? Aren't we being just a little melodramatic?"

Joletta held her cousin's gaze. "You may not have intended it, but the car we were in caught fire, you know, after the truck ran us off the road."

"Just a minute—" Natalie began, a frown drawing her arched brows together.

"It was a mean, underhanded trick, the next thing to attempted murder."

"You think I had something to do with this accident?"

The incredulity in her cousin's face seemed genuine, Joletta thought. But Natalie had always been good at pretense. "I saw you in Paris; I know you've been following me."

Natalie turned a wide stare toward Rone. He returned it without expression. She swung back to Joletta. "So you think that we—but that's ridiculous; we're family! As for following you, I have to tell you this jaunt of yours seems wild to me. I guess you must have found the diary—no surprise, since you knew Mimi and the house— but if there had been a formula in it, we would all know it by now. I figure you stumbled on something that brought you over here, but if there's a chance in a million of a real lead after all these years, I'll be amazed."

"Then what are you doing in Europe?"

Natalie gave a small laugh. "I do have a life of my own, you know. I was passing through and decided to see how you were doing."

Joletta didn't believe it, but there was no point in saying so. "And Aunt Estelle and Timothy?"

"I have no idea where my dear brother is; he took off on his own, though there was some mention of Cascais—or maybe it was Corfu. He thinks this deal is, and I quote, 'A waste of good beach time.' " There was real warmth in the other woman's voice before she went on. "As for mother, the last I heard she was on her way to New York to see Lara Camors. Camors Cosmetics has a great lab, where they not only concoct their own perfume, but can do chemical breakdowns of others. She's taking a sample of Le Jardin de cour to be analyzed and duplicated."

"It won't work," Joletta said, though her voice was strained.

Natalie made a careless gesture with one hand. "Mother seems to think it will, and she usually manages to get what she wants, one way or another."

That was too true to be argued. Joletta said, "You didn't say where you were going—that you happened to be passing through."

It was a moment before Natalie answered as she turned her attention instead to the waiter approaching to take her order. When the man had gone, she said, "Actually, I was to meet a friend for a few days at Saturnia, to recuperate from the winter season with a spa treatment. Something came up, and she'll be delayed for a few days."

"Too bad." There was a slight shading of irony in the comment.

"I don't suppose," Natalie said with her most sunny smile, "that you would mind if I hung around with you and Rone until she shows?"

"I doubt you'd be thrilled," Joletta said. "We're with a tour group."

Laughter gurgled in Natalie's throat as she turned toward Rone. "You mean with guides and chicken dinners and elderly women with blue hair and polyester suits?"

Joletta said, "Most of the ladies are in sand-washed silk and parachute nylon, but that's the idea."

"Ah, well," Natalie said with a shrug, "I suppose if you can bear it, I can."

"No."

The uncompromising sound of Rone's voice brought Joletta's head around. He was frowning as he met her cousin's incredulous gray-blue gaze. The thought that he would show so plainly that he preferred to be alone with her brought the heat of a flush to her face.

"I was speaking to my cousin," Natalie said, her voice rising with annoyance.

Rone gave her a tight smile. "I don't mean to be rude to a relative of Joletta's, but we would prefer to be alone just now. You understand."

"Oh, so that's the way it is?" The gaze Natalie turned on Joletta was measuring. "What a fascinating development."

"There's nothing unusual about it," Joletta said defensively. Natalie could not know she and Rone had just met, she thought, could she?

"I suppose not, for some people. But I never suspected you of enjoying this kind of fling, Joletta."

"And what kind of fling is that?" Rone asked, his voice hard.

Natalie lifted her brows as she turned a sardonic look on him. "So protective; I do love it. But really, Joletta and I have so seldom been able to talk, just the two of us. Surely you won't deny me at least a few hours this afternoon?"

"Not alone."

"Oh, we want you with us, of course." Natalie's voice was bland.

Rone said no more, only looking toward Joletta with a questioning tilt to his head.

Joletta said to the other woman, "We were just going to wander around until after lunch, then we'll be going out to the islands of

Tercello and Burano for the old church and the lace this afternoon.
You must have seen it all a dozen times."

"Never in such company," Natalie said firmly, and picked up
her coffee cup to drink as the waiter set it before her.

It was plain that Natalie had some reason for wanting to spend
time with them. What it might be, Joletta could not imagine. If her
aunt was having the perfume analyzed, then it could hardly matter
to Aunt Estelle and Natalie if the formula was discovered in some
other way. Unless, of course, they preferred to be in sole possession.

Her cousin's interest seemed centered on Rone. It was possible
she wanted to discover more about him, to decide just what effect
his presence was going to have on the quest. Since it seemed to
Joletta that it might be helpful if Natalie and everyone else knew
she was no longer a lone target, she ceased to make objections.

Natalie was determined to be charming. She talked nonstop as
they walked through the streets, making brittle, acidly amusing
comments about this passerby or that former resident, telling stories
about past trips to Venice and elsewhere in Europe, stories liberally
sprinkled with titles and nicknames of people she seldom bothered
to identify otherwise. She directed most of her comments to Rone.
His response was minimal, but the twitch of his mouth now and
then showed a ready acquaintance with many of those she mentioned.

Natalie had little interest in the merchandise in the shop windows that caught Joletta's attention; the hand-blown glass or the
painstakingly carved cameos in unusual gray and aqua stone did not
excite her. She showed no appreciation for the fine Gothic carving
on the buildings and was impatient with standing on the small arching bridges to absorb the vistas of mysteriously winding canals.
Since it was difficult to override Natalie's strident reminiscences in
order to speak to Rone, Joletta began to feel like the odd man out.

It was not unusual; Natalie had always been able to make her
feel that way with her sophistication and background of private
schools and moneyed friends. There had been a time when she suspected that Natalie did it on purpose. Now she was no longer sure.
It could also be a simple lack of comprehension of how other people
might feel.

Once, Joletta turned into a small shop for a closer look at a
collection of porcelain figures by Armani. They were so beautifully
done, so gorgeous in their romantic opulence, that she stayed longer
than she intended. She longed to own a particular piece showing

lovers in a gondola. It was not only fragile for shipping, however, but was far too expensive for her pocketbook. Leaving it and the engagingly kind shop owner with regret, she emerged once more into the street.

Rone and Natalie were standing some distance away down the sidewalk. Natalie was talking in quick phrases, shaking her finger in Rone's face while he stood with his head lowered and a look of tight-lipped resignation on his face.

A frown drew Joletta's brows together as she started toward them.

Natalie glanced in Joletta's direction. The anger was instantly smoothed from her face. She spoke a few final words under her breath even as she summoned a brilliant smile.

"Is something wrong?" Joletta asked as she walked up to them.

"What could be wrong?" Natalie said. "Rone has just decided that the three of us should form our own tour group, forget the island trip, maybe stroll along the Rialto, or better still, since it's so warm, go out to the Lido beach."

"Has he?" Joletta said.

She couldn't believe it, not after the disagreement they had been through the day before over the same sort of high-handed decision. She looked at him, her gaze inquiring. There was a grim set to his features and his eyes were dark, but he made no effort to defend himself.

Joletta had discovered a couple of things in the past hour. The first was that she did not want to be with Natalie for any length of time. She had had enough of trailing behind her cousin, watching her monopolize the conversation with Rone. She had also learned that she was a possessive woman. It was a disconcerting insight, but she didn't intend to fight it. What she intended was to do something about it.

"Are you sure," she said, giving her cousin a straight look, "that this was Rone's idea?"

"Who else's? Isn't it marvelous? We'll have so much fun!"

Joletta shook her head. "I'm not so sure. Rone, as you may have noticed, is a southern gentleman; he doesn't like to refuse a lady, and he's nearly always polite. But I think he was right the first time around. We will be better off alone."

"Oh, no, Joletta, how mean!"

"I'm sorry you feel that way. But it should be no problem for you to entertain yourself until your friend arrives. You know so many interesting people that I'm sure there must be a duke or prince you can call to help pass the time."

The last comment was catty, there was no way to get around it. Joletta couldn't help it; that was the way she felt.

Natalie stared at Joletta for a stunned instant before she swung to face Rone. "Tell her," she said in strident tones. "Make her see you don't mind. Persuade her; I'm sure you know how."

A flush of anger rose to Rone's face at the insinuation in Natalie's tone. The other woman lifted her chin as she met his hard stare. It was he who turned away first, his gaze clouded, a little unfocused, as he met Joletta's eyes.

The words quiet, almost without inflection, he said, "You know I would rather not follow the group."

That Natalie could influence Rone when he had been so positive before seemed strange. There was something wrong here. Joletta did not know what it was, but she could feel it.

Natalie gave her no time to reply. Her voice coaxing, she said, "You don't really want to do the same old touristy things, either, do you, Joletta? Of course, if you really prefer it, Rone and I can carry on without you."

"No," Joletta said slowly, "that's all right."

"It's settled then," Natalie cried. "This will be so much better."

They returned to the hotel to pick up bathing suits and inform their tour director they would not be going on the afternoon outing.

As they neared the entrance Caesar Zilanti came toward them with his arms spread wide.

"There you are at last. I knew you must return soon or miss the excursion you mentioned last evening." He caught Joletta's hand, carrying it to his lips. "Ah, lovely one, how is your head? Perfect, yes? I wanted to be certain to catch you before you left, to extend an invitation I thought you, especially, might enjoy."

"Invitation?" Joletta said inquiringly. She was aware of Rone's frown as he watched the other man, and of the surprise on Natalie's face, but ignored both.

"I have a cousin who owns a palazzo of some historical interest. She will be pleased to have you see it, if you come to visit."

It was the lingering turmoil of her feelings that caused the decision Joletta made in that instant. She knew it, but knowing made no difference.

"I would like that very much," she said, her smile bright-edged with rebellious pride. "I can't speak for Rone or for my cousin, of course; they may have other plans."

That had to be explained, naturally, and an introduction performed for Natalie. Joletta's cousin gave the Italian a warm smile and allowed her hand to linger in his for long seconds. Caesar acknowledged the gesture with suitable charm, but looked toward Joletta immediately afterward with a frown between his thick brows. He said, "You don't go to the islands then? But there won't be time after today, and it's a mistake to miss them."

"Oh, really, there's nothing so great to see out there," Natalie said.

"Venice is more than the Grand Canal and the basilica of St. Mark," Caesar declared, his face set in lines of disapproval. "The character of her is in her islands, in the glass factories, and other places that were set apart to prevent fires—and where the fishermen enjoy their isolation and paint their houses in colors bright enough to be seen from the sea."

To Joletta, it was all the incentive she needed. She meant to see as much of Italy as possible. She turned to Rone and Natalie. "You two can do what you like, but I think I prefer to go on to the islands after all."

Natalie divided a dissatisfied look between her and Caesar. "You're sure?"

"I am." Joletta's voice was firm.

"We can't prevent you, of course." Her cousin lifted a shoulder in a careless gesture.

Rone said, "I'll have to go with Joletta then. I suppose we could see if there's room on the tour for one more."

"Or perhaps two if you are making additions to your party," Caesar suggested with a confident smile. "It would give me great pleasure to be your guide once again."

"Wait a minute," Natalie said in rasping tones. "I refuse to set foot on a tour, and that's final. You promised me the Lido, Rone."

There was a small silence. It was Caesar who broke it. "There is no problem that I can see. I will take Rone's place with Joletta. He can then keep his word."

Joletta saw Rone make a quick movement that was instantly stilled. She met his gaze, her own questioning. He held that steady regard for only a second before he looked away, his gaze following a passing boat.

A hollow feeling began in Joletta's stomach and expanded,

crowding against her heart. Her face was somber and there was doubt in her eyes as she looked toward Caesar. "I'm sure you must have other things to do than follow me around."

"If I had a thousand things, I would cancel them, *carina* Joletta," Caesar said instantly. "It will be my great pleasure."

His ready acceptance and his gallantry were balm for Joletta's bruised spirits. She summoned a smile. "Well, that's all right then."

"It must be," Natalie said, though she did not look happy.

Rone was silent.

Joletta expected the afternoon to drag past; it flew instead. The trip across the lagoon was made in a water bus of shining wood and brass, beautifully clean and well kept. Boats, Caesar pointed out when she mentioned it, were the pride of the men of Venice, things to be polished as other men polished their cars or their weapons.

Of the two islands, Tercello was her favorite, mainly because it seemed so small and friendly, with so much unpaved land and gardens that seemed particularly Italian with their vigorous, hairy-leaved artichokes, rampant-growing peas, and paths where cats sat sunning themselves among the greenery.

She and Caesar walked on tiles in the ancient church, which had felt the footsteps of worshipers for more than a thousand years. Afterward, they ate a quick lunch under a grapevine that might have sheltered Hemingway during his stay at the Locanda Cipriani Inn where one fogbound and lugubrious winter he wrote *Across the River and Into the Trees.*

On Burano, Caesar insisted on buying Joletta a piece of lace, a small picture of a gentleman and lady in seventeenth-century costume holding a heart with an arrow thrust through it. Avoiding the square with its kiosks of tourist merchandise, they strolled among the houses washed in colors of rose and saffron, tangerine and brilliant azure and oxblood red.

Caesar took her hand, smiling down at her with admiration in his dark eyes while the sun gleamed in the blue-black waves of his hair and turned the skin of his face to gold. It meant nothing, she knew, or thought she did; still, she couldn't help being affected by his aura of confident masculinity and his appreciation of her as a woman. It was such a potent weapon, that manifest appreciation, so typically Italian or Latin. She wondered if he realized it. And wondered, too, why more men, especially American men, didn't use it.

In a curious way she was grateful to Caesar. His easy compliments and endearments, his ready flirtation, had helped to repair the damage done to her ego by Rone's defection. Caesar had also given her a respite from emotions that had developed too quickly, becoming too intense for comfort. She had needed time to step back and take note of what she was doing and why, and perhaps to reconsider her rush into intimacy.

Looking at Caesar, Joletta thought, too, about Violet and also about her Allain, who had had Italian ancestry. If history did in some manner repeat itself, she supposed it would be Caesar who was most similar to Allain. Not that she really believed in such things—reincarnation, past lives, the return of old souls who had lived before. And yet, she felt closer in time to Violet here in Venice than she ever had in New Orleans.

She was beginning to understand the impulses that had driven her great-great-great-great-grandmother, to understand them far too well.

They had reached the end of the street, one that had led to the sea and a grassy verge with a handy bench. Caesar headed toward the seat, ruthlessly cutting off another couple who had been making toward it. He seated Joletta, then dropped down beside her, ignoring with his customary aplomb the fuming irritation of the other man and woman.

They sat for long moments, feeling the sun and wind on their faces, watching the hazy, blue-green sea shift and sparkle.

After a while Caesar said, "Your cousin, Natalie, she is not much like you."

"In looks you mean?" Joletta said.

"Well, she is blond, which is always attractive, but I was speaking of her manner. She is very—determined."

"You saw that, when you were with her such a short time?" Joletta's glance was teasing.

A small smile tugged at his mouth. "A man notices these things."

"You like that, determination in a woman?" she asked.

"Sometimes yes, sometimes no. I object to being ordered to do this or that."

Joletta would have thought that Rone would object, too. Strenuously. He had not. Why? The question had been with her all afternoon, nagging at her like a dull toothache. The only answer she could see was that he had been attracted to Natalie, had wanted to spend time with her.

Her voice soft, almost contemplative, she said, "Do you think my cousin is more attractive than I am?"

"What a question, *carina*," he said, turning toward her and propping an elbow on the back of the bench. "Why would you ask it?"

She shrugged a little. It had been an impulse, one she hadn't even tried to resist.

"Is it for my sake, or because of Rone that you compare yourself to her?"

Caesar saw a great deal, more than she had expected. "Forget it," she said. "It isn't important."

"I think it is." He paused, then went on in low tones. "You are different, that's all. Her beauty is obvious, a bright fire that reaches out to a man. Yours is a softer glow like candlelight; one must come closer to appreciate its gentle light and its mystery. You are the kind of woman a man marries so that he may spend years tending the flame, warming himself in its constant heat. She is the kind he makes his mistress for the quick bonfire that just as quickly burns out."

Joletta met his steady gaze for long moments while a smile rose slowly into her brown eyes. She said, "And is that the only two types of women you recognize?"

"No," he answered with lazy, understanding humor and warmth in his dark eyes. "There are also mothers."

Joletta and Caesar did not go back to the hotel before the visit to his aunt, but stepped straight from the water bus to a gondola, which took them the short distance through the canals to the old house.

It was not a particularly impressive building from the outside, being rather plain except for a loggia of Gothic arches. It was rather like the house where Violet and Allain had stayed, but Joletta had discovered that there were many of those.

Inside, the decor was an eclectic blend of huge old gold-leaf mirrors and sleek torch floor lamps in black and chrome, of great majolica urns filled with masses of spring flowers, and of abstract prints the size of barn doors.

Caesar's aunt was not the bent old lady in lavender and lace Joletta had expected. She was, rather, a woman of intense charisma, wearing her hair slicked back in a firm bun to reveal yellow diamond earrings like small captured suns in her ears, and a dress in a pale gold silk with the indelible stamp of Armani.

The Italian woman was pleased to receive a friend of her nephew's, she said; she had not known he had such exceptional taste in women. More, she was delighted to show off her house, since it had just been redecorated after many years of neglect. She had married the house, so to speak; it had been in her husband's family for many years, but they had only moved in a year ago, when his mother had died. Many changes had been made, and they must see them all.

They were invited, even commanded, for dinner. It was a lovely meal, served on the loggia as the long twilight faded into night, but its courses were innumerable, an endless progression of food and wine and conversation.

It was late when Joletta and Caesar reached the boat landing near the hotel again. He would not leave her there, but insisted on walking with her along the side street, and even seeing her to her room.

She stopped in the hall outside her door. She thanked him once more for her lace picture, and also for the afternoon and evening. As she reached to unlock the door he prevented it by the simple means of catching her hand.

His smile rueful, he said, "I take it you are not going to invite me inside?"

"You take it right." The refusal was quiet but firm.

"I knew it," he said on a sigh. "I suppose I must be glad that you are not like so many, so hungry for love that you will accept the first man bold enough to offer it."

She frowned. "So many women, you mean, or just so many American women?"

"It's your countrywomen I speak of, *carina*, yes. You are surprised?"

She was and she wasn't. "I suppose it's the ones who are looking for something who come to Europe alone in the first place."

"Ah, my Joletta," he said, his voice low, "what is it you are looking for?"

She glanced up at him as she caught a note of tense inquiry, almost a demand, in his tone. He met her gaze, his own dark. Abruptly, he released her hand and stepped nearer, reaching out to clamp his arm about her waist. He bent his head to press his mouth to hers.

His lips were firm and muscular and tasted of wine; his movements were experienced. His hold was close without being tight. There was tentative pleasure in his touch, an inkling that it might, with care, be increased in some degree. And yet, it brought no consuming desire, no wild need to discover how much greater the enjoyment might become.

Why had she allowed the kiss? Gratitude? A disinclination to hurt him after his courtesy? A need to test her emotions where Rone was concerned? All these things had been a part of it. Was it fair to Caesar? That was unanswerable, since it depended on the solutions she found. No doubt he had been seeking his own answers, also.

She began to draw back, gently and without haste, so that it need not appear a complete rejection.

At that moment the hotel-room door opened. Rone, dressed only in a pair of jeans and holding a rolled magazine in his hand, stood scowling at them.

"Sorry," he said in clipped tones as his gaze rested on Joletta's pale face, "I didn't mean to interrupt, but I thought you might be having trouble with your key."

"No," she said, her voice tight.

"So I see. You might speed it up. I started your bathwater running." He stepped back inside and closed the door.

Joletta absorbed the import of his words, with their brazen advertisement of the intimate arrangement between them, in blank astonishment. There could be little doubt they had been intended as a warning for Caesar, though how Rone could dare make it after his conduct with Natalie, she did not understand.

She had noticed two other things as well. The bathwater was indeed running. And what she had taken at first for a magazine in Rone's hand were the last few pages of Violet's journal.

Chapter 16

August 10, 1854

    I was afraid to tell Allain about the destruction of the portrait he had painted. How painful it would be for him to know that Gilbert had taken out his rage on the canvas that he had worked upon so diligently. What would he say? Would I be forced to tell him what had followed? That had been humiliating to endure; it would be even worse to describe.

    It was nearly a month and a half after we had reached Venice before I gathered together the nerve to speak of the subject, and even then it was almost an accident.

Allain had been out all morning. He had formed the habit of shopping for the simple meals Violet sometimes arranged for the Signora da Allori's cook to prepare, dishes of squabs and larks, squid in ink, aubergines and mirlitons cooked with tomatoes and cheeses. Violet sometimes went with him; she enjoyed the ramble through the market, the haggling over fresh fruits and vegetables and, always, buying fresh flowers to scent their rooms. The outings, extended sometimes by visits to an antique shop or cloth warehouse, wine shop or shoe shop, and perhaps on to a sidewalk café for coffee and pastry, made the mornings fly past and provided tidbits for conversation for the rest of the day.

This morning, she had not felt well. Though the indisposition was minor, she had not liked the thought of the many raw smells in the market. Nothing was more uncomfortable than having to combat a stomach disorder while in a public place.

Allain returned carrying a painted canvas in a roll under his arm. He had found it at a junk dealer's stand, he said. The artist was Antonio Canale, known as Canaletto. His work was out of favor because he was said to have been too commercial in his lifetime, painting hundreds of views of Venice that had been bought as souvenirs by visitors to the city, primarily the English, during the mid-eighteenth century. Allain was enthusiastic over the draftsmanship of his find, which he claimed showed training as an architect. He exclaimed over the luminosity of Canaletto's colors and his masterly use of camera obscura that, apparently, formed the base drawing. These qualities pleased him, but that was not, he said, the reason he had bought the painting.

He looked, Violet thought, like a small boy with a secret. She smiled with love rising strong inside her as she put the question she saw she was meant to ask. "Why did you buy it then?"

Allain tapped the center of the canvas, which showed a stretch of the Grand Canal beyond the Rialto Bridge in softly brilliant shades of aqua and peach and gold, and every possible tint of blue. "This," he said.

It was a moment before she saw it. "Ah," she said, and smiled straight into his eyes with a brilliance to match the painting.

The scene showed the house where they were staying. It was only a partial view, it was true; the house was obscured by the walls of a palace. Still, there it was with its loggia and upper windows that opened onto the bedchamber where they slept and its walls that were still the same warm ocher with the same blue-brown water licking at its foundations.

It gave Violet a strange feeling to see it, and to know, as Allain told her, that the painting was at least a hundred years old. It did not seem right, somehow, that it had survived so many years past the life span of the man who created it.

"One day," Allain said as they stood looking at the canvas, "I would like to have a house where this can hang in the salon to brighten a dim corner—and with your portrait over the mantel to watch over the household."

Violet looked at him. She swallowed hard as she looked away

again. Her voice quiet, she said, "It would be lovely—but it's not possible."

"What do you mean?" he asked, his voice tight.

"The portrait—Gilbert ruined it, slashed it. He was sorry, I think, afterward, but the damage had been done."

"And you?" he said. "Was that when he hurt you?"

She couldn't answer; it wasn't possible. As he reached to tilt her chin so she must look at him, she shielded her eyes with her lashes.

He didn't insist. Taking her in his arms, he held her to his heart while the hard breathing of his pent-up anger stirred her hair. At last he said, "I should have killed him."

His understanding, his delicacy, and even his outrage were healing. Over the knot in her throat, she said, "He was sorry for the injury, too."

It was long moments before he spoke again. Finally he sighed, the tension going out of his hold. "Perhaps I should pity him. I might be violent in my anger, too, if I knew I was losing you."

She managed a small nod. "I am so sorry."

"About the portrait? I will paint another, and finer. But it comes to me that you would not have been hurt if not for me. I share your husband's blame."

"Why," she said in low, strained tones, "when all you have done is give me joy?"

"I have taken more."

"Nothing that I did not offer, willingly."

"Yes, of course, such a wanton as you are," he said with an ache in the soft, laughter-edged timbre of the words.

"Yes," she agreed seriously. "Will you take me to bed now?"

"Madame, you shock me."

"Impossible. Will you?"

"St. Mark's own bronze horses come to life couldn't stop me," he answered.

Afterward, as they lay naked in the warm wind from the sea that filtered through the shutters over the windows, Allain rose and left her lying half-asleep among the twisted sheets. He returned a moment later. His weight caused the mattress to shift, then something cool and heavy was placed between the pale and gently rounded mounds of her breasts with their rosy nipples and tracery of blue veins.

She thought at first it was a pendant necklace. The chain was of heavy links with the soft rich sheen of pure gold. Attached to it was a small object that looked much like the censers for the burning of incense used in churches. It seemed to be carved from a single large amethyst and set in gold bindings that were ridged with pearls and diamonds.

She sat up, taking the piece of jewelry in her hands. The workmanship was ornate and extremely fine, with scrolls, veins, and leaves forming the gold bindings, and a design of a bird with spread wings carved into one side of the amethyst. Her fingers trembled a little as she turned it this way and that in the light, for she could see it was no ordinary trinket.

She looked up at Allain. Her voice compressed, she said, "What is this?"

"Here, permit me," he said. Reaching for the necklace, he twisted the amethyst. A portion of one caplike end came away in his hand.

From the jewellike bottle rose the fragrance of a perfume so lovely, so complex yet simple, rich yet refined, so dense with dreamlike images that it struck the senses with purest delight. It was the essence of a summer's night in some exotic clime, redolent of hot breezes from hills where oranges and almonds grew. It was scent-heavy blossoms within a walled garden drenched in moonlight where could be heard the far-off whisper of the sea. It was deep kisses and moisture-dewed bodies amid crushed petals of roses. It was candied violets and roots of iris-orris and tangled fields of wild rosemary and narcissus. It was waving vetiver fans and twisting vanilla pods and snow-chilled wine. And still there was more, layer upon layer of evocative scents that rose in the mind like some ancient, half-remembered refrain.

"Cleopatra's perfume," Violet said, her voice quiet with wonder.

"And Joséphine's. And Eugénie's."

"But how—why?"

"The perfumer in the Rue de la Paix whom I spoke of before holds the empress's commission to make it. He risked much giving it to me, but he was indebted to me for past favors. Besides, he is a romantic, and could not refuse when he learned I wanted it for the special lady who rules my heart."

She met his gaze, and thought she might drown with ease in the measureless depths of love she saw mirrored there. She felt chastened by it, unworthy yet exalted, and warmed, even heated, by its force.

"I will be grateful for the power it's supposed to have," she said, "if it will bind you to me, and me to you."

"I pray it's so," he answered.

It was a vow that required a kiss, and more, to seal it. Later, as they lay with arms and legs entwined in the bed, Violet said, "I would thank you for my perfume—"

"You already have," Allain said, a low laugh shaking his chest, so that it rumbled under her cheek.

"Wretch," she said without heat, tugging a little at a clutch of curling hair on his chest that was tickling her nose, then immediately soothing the spot. She rested her hand on his arm, idly smoothing the tender red scar where the knife cut he had taken had healed. "I was going to say that I'm afraid I may enjoy the effects of this perfume so much that I don't know what I'll do when it's all gone."

"We'll have some more made," he answered comfortably.

"Isn't that a little extravagant, sending so far for it?"

"Thank you," he said in mock umbrage. "I see now what you think of my foresight. But, my dear love, if Napoléon brought his Joséphine the recipe for this perfume, do you suppose I would do less?"

"You have it?"

"Indeed. And you may have as much of it as you like made, enough to take a bath in, if that's your desire."

"My desire," she said with a wondering shake of her head, "is for you. You are amazing."

He hoisted himself up so that he rested on one elbow. Leaning over her so that his mouth was inches from hers, he said, "See that you remember it."

So the days passed, fading into each other in sunny, mindless splendor. They ate and slept and made love; they sat late into the evenings on their loggia, watching the sunset colors stain the city and shimmer away into the gray of night. They added to their meager wardrobes with visits to tailors and modistes. One day Allain bought a sword cane, for use, he said, when she was not near at hand with her trusty parasol.

Sometimes they hired a boat and took a basket of food and wine to the Lido or to one of the outer islands, where they fished and waded in the water, returning sunburned and ravenous for their dinner and each other.

Allain bought oils and brushes and began to paint again, concentrating on capturing the lambent light and delicate colors of Venice on small, easily carried canvases.

While he worked, Violet sometimes sat with him with her embroidery. Other times she visited with the widow Signora da Allori, a lady of sharp tongue and gentle heart who delighted in screaming out the window at her majordomo as he departed on his errands. Now and again Violet went shopping on her own, enjoying the freedom to come and go at no one's behest except her own. She learned the language spoken around her, became known to the shopkeepers, and made the acquaintance of a special gondolier, a handsome boy who watched for her appearance on the quay and shot his black craft forward to meet her, risking life and limb and volleys of insults to serve her.

Slowly, the things she and Allain bought on their outings—the fragile Venetian glassware, the small pieces of antique furniture, the paintings and bits of bric-a-brac—began to crowd their room. They arranged to take the entire top floor of the Widow da Allori's house. Spreading their possessions out in that spacious area, they hired a maid—a girl they were unsurprised to discover was the niece of the majordomo, Savio. With the slow passage of the days, the rooms began to take on the feel and look of something approaching a home.

By accident and incidental introductions, Violet and Allain met other expatriates in the city, most of them English. They began to attend dinner parties now and then, or else received an occasional visitor from among this circle. They made little effort to enlarge such contacts, however. Their own company was preferable at any given moment.

Violet was happy. There were times when her spirit sang with an ecstasy so intense she could hardly contain it. There were days so beautiful, so filled with color and laughter and pure, unrelenting grace that they brought tears.

There were also times when dread seized her with iron talons and would not let go, times when she stood staring out the window at nothing, or lay at night watching for the dawn and listening to the soft sound of Allain's breathing.

She sat one morning watching Allain paint. He had set up his work area in the end of a spare bedchamber with tall, north-facing windows. The light spilling in over his shoulder was clear and blue-tinted. In it, his face had a look of sober concentration not at all marred by a streak of azure paint on his chin where he had rubbed it with the side of his hand. He was so intent upon what he was doing that she thought he had forgotten she was there.

She shifted in the velvet slipper chair where she sat. He glanced up at once.

"Bored with embroidery?" he said, glancing at the half-finished cushion cover lying neglected in her lap.

She shook her head. "I just like watching you. You are so involved in what you do."

A slight flush of pleasure and something more rose to his face. "I didn't mean to neglect you."

"I haven't been neglected," she said, tilting her head slightly as she sent him a quick, smiling glance from the corners of her eyes. She went on: "But I wish sometimes that I had something, some kind of work, to absorb my time and thoughts in the same way."

"There's plenty of paint and canvas here if you want to try."

"Oh, I doubt I have the talent."

"You sketch well, I've seen the things you do in your journal," he said seriously.

She only shook her head with a smile. She had been doing a sketch of him on the back of a journal page at the same time he was painting her. It was a tolerably accurate likeness, but failed to capture the warmth of his personality, at least to her eyes.

He gave her a direct look. "What did you have in mind to do, then?"

"I don't know, really."

"Music? We could buy a piano for you. Or you might try writing, since you seem to enjoy keeping your journal."

"I like music very much, but prefer to listen to someone else. As for my journal, it's like second nature, spreading my thoughts out on paper, but I'm not sure I have stories or poems inside me."

"You underestimate yourself, I think," he said seriously. "But what shall it be, if not these things?"

"Maybe I'll take in needlework," she said, and laughed aloud at the look of total disapproval he gave her. "I was joking, but there may be something else just as tainted with trade that will take my notion."

He put down his brush and wiped his hands before coming to kneel beside her chair. "Do what you will, so long as you remain near me."

She reached out to wipe at the paint smear on his chin with the soft pad of her thumb. "As long as you want me."

"That won't be so very long," he said, catching her hand, carrying it to his lips, "only one or two short forevers."

Such phrases, as sweet as they might be to hear, were as close as they came to speaking of the future.

Violet wondered at times how long they would go on in this way, but when she tried to speak of it to Allain, he made some jest or proposed some treat, or went out and bought her another bonnet or bauble. She came finally to understand that it was not a subject he wanted to explore. She was not certain he had a plan or a timetable to give her.

There had been no more incidents such as the one at the train station. If they were being watched or followed, they could not tell it. The waterways did not encourage such things, of course.

Regardless, there was something not quite real to Violet about the procession of days. She thought of writing to her family, her two sisters and the wife of Gilbert's youngest brother, who had been a friend since childhood, but could find no words to explain what had happened. They would, she knew, want explanations. They would require to be told when she meant to return to Louisiana, if she would ever return. They would want to know about Gilbert, if he was going to divorce her, whether he would complete his sojourn in Europe. The answers to so many of these questions did not depend on her, and so she could not give them. The time for writing, then, never seemed right.

Because she had not contacted them, had told no one she had left Gilbert, given no one news of her whereabouts, she received no letters, no news from home. It was as if she had been cut off from the world and all she knew.

Allain was loving and constant and endlessly reassuring, yet she could not prevent herself from wondering what she would do if he left her. She had no resources of her own. She could send to Louisiana for the means to return there, but it could take weeks, even months, before her relatives could arrange for her passage, and how was she to live in the interim?

That was, if she could return to New Orleans at all. If she took up residence in that city again, she would be forced to live in disgrace, a fallen woman, one who had left her husband for a sordid affair with an artist. It hadn't really been like that, not at all, but she knew the gossip mongers of New Orleans well, and it would be impossible to convince them otherwise.

Somewhere deep inside, she was afraid. She didn't know why

she felt this buried edge of incipient terror; she only knew it was there.

That was, perhaps, the reason she was not surprised when, late one evening, there came a mighty hammering on the door of the house.

Savio answered the summons, then mounted up the stairs to see if Signor Massari wished to receive the two gentlemen who were below demanding his presence. Savio's thin face was stiff with umbrage as he handed over the visiting cards that had been presented to him.

Allain stood frowning down at the cards in his hand for long moments. He took a deep breath and squared his shoulders. Inclining his head, he said, "Inform them I will be with them shortly."

"What is it?" Violet said when Savio had disappeared back down the stairs. She put her hand on Allain's arm in unconscious supplication.

"Don't worry; it has nothing to do with Gilbert," he said as he covered her fingers with his own. "It's only something that should have been taken care of long ago."

She could not press him; she had no right to pry into the life he had lived before they met. Yet she didn't want him to go; every instinct forbade it.

"Is this really necessary? Suppose it's a trick?"

He drew her to him and took her face in his hands, pressing his lips to hers before he said, "I love your concern, but there is no possibility of deception. Trust me. I'll only be a moment."

He was gone considerably longer.

She did not mean to eavesdrop. It was the sound of raised voices that drew her out onto the loggia. The visitors had left the house and were standing almost directly below on the stone landing where their gondola waited. Allain had walked outside with them.

One of the callers, an older gentleman judging from his voice, was holding his raised fist before him and his face was twisted with frustrated anger. He spoke in French, yet with such an odd, guttural accent that it was almost unintelligible.

"You could have such power as you never dreamed. I say to you that the time will come when you will mourn what you have thrown away."

"I want no part of it, now or ever," Allain said, his voice edged with grim implacability. "Your country is not mine, nor has it ever been."

"Pigheaded fool. We would have risked all for you; it would have been an honor. The shame of this violation of trust is on your head."

"I will bear it."

"So will your country. Such a ripeness as is fast coming—you could have saved lives, changed everything. Everything!"

"Or nothing," Allain said, the words weighted with tiredness, as if it was an old argument. "Some things cannot be changed in decades, even centuries. My father tried."

"Ah, yes, your father. He promised freedom, justice, but they never came. Our hearts cry for them still, but must cry in vain. Remember it. Remember it well."

"That much," Allain said, "I can do for you."

The older man made an exclamation of disgust. Turning, he strode to the gondola and stamped down into it with the other man at his heels. As they emerged from under the shadows of the loggia's overhang, Violet saw that they were not the men from the train station as she had half feared. Nor did she think they were the pair who had followed Allain and herself in Paris.

They were substantial men, men who held themselves with dignified, almost military erectness. They were well dressed, their clothing correct from the silk cravats at their throats to the shine on the fine leather of their half boots. Regardless, there was about them an air of being uncomfortable in their present attire, as if something was missing, perhaps a weapon.

Standing in the gondola, the older man looked back at Allain once more. "Twice we have asked, and twice been refused. It is your right. Yet it is not so easy. There are others who will come."

"Yes," Allain said, his tone echoing as hard as the stone column where Violet rested her hand, "I know it."

"We will not trouble you again, then, exalted one; we look on your face a final time. Farewell."

Allain's only reply was a bow, a brief gesture of decorum that seemed to have a ceremonial dignity. As the gondola shot away into the channel of the canal, he turned and reentered the house.

Allain was more silent than usual for the remainder of the evening. He sat staring at nothing, starting when spoken to, turning to her now and then with a look in his eyes that was weary, indecisive, and even, at times, distraught.

Violet waited for him to confide in her; she wanted to help him, to share whatever was troubling him. He said nothing, not immediately after the men had gone, not while the wick in the oil lamp burned down as they read, not later as they made ready for bed. She thought he meant to spare her, but she did not appreciate it. She felt shut out of his thoughts, cut off from his problem.

She woke in the night. There was no moon; the room was dark except for a blue rectangle where the window stood open to the wind from the sea. Allain stood naked in the opening, braced with his one arm on the frame.

"What is it?" she whispered.

He looked over his shoulder at her pale form in the dimness of the great, curtained bed. "Forgive me," he said, his voice soft, "I should have left you unloved. It was selfish for me to take you, and to take you away."

"What are you saying?" She sat up, clutching the sheets around her with fingers that had gone cold and numb.

"I wronged you. I destroyed your quiet, safe life, and can offer nothing so fine in return."

His words had the sound of renunciation. A painful alarm constricted her throat, so it was hard to force words through it. "I need nothing more than we have."

"I need it for you. And for our child you carry."

The words, dropping so softly into the darkness, seemed for long moments to be without meaning. She drew a quick breath as they settled into her mind in patterns she could accept. "You know?"

"Some things announce themselves. The lovely ripeness of your body gives me pleasure beyond anything I ever dreamed; still, I wonder—"

"Yes?" She waited with held breath for him to complete what he had been saying.

"I wonder if Gilbert could be induced to believe the child is his."

The despair that swept in upon her held her mute for long seconds. At last she said, "Perhaps it is his."

"You have reason to think that it might be?" The words were tentative, but tight with doubt.

"Who can tell. I—had my monthly indisposition after Paris, while in Switzerland, but not since Lugano. There is reason to think that—that he could be."

"I understand." He turned toward her but moved no closer, instead resting his back against the heavy door facing. "It might be best," he said, his voice holding the rasp of steel on a whetstone.

"No!"

The cry broke from her, ripping from her throat with all the anguish she could not deny. Hearing it, he crossed to her in plunging strides. Springing up onto the mattress, he caught her close with murmured words of love and reassurance. She struggled in his grasp, fighting him, refusing the easy reassurance, while her brain was alive with horror.

"Don't, Violet, please," he said, taking her hands in a firm hold. "It isn't what I want! It's only what may be best for you, and for the baby. It's mine, I know that as surely as I know that it's my own heart beating inside my chest—it could not be otherwise. But I have to think of the danger. No one must know you are going to have my child. I could not live if anything happened to you because of me."

Her movements stilled as she heard the pain in his voice. "What danger?" she asked tightly. "Who were those men who came? What was it they wanted of you?"

A shadow crossed his face. "I would tell you if it would make it easier for you. It won't. Please believe me."

"I am to know nothing?"

"It will be better so." His voice was bleak.

She clenched her hands into fists, swallowing hard before she spoke again. "But if Gilbert is to think the baby is his, I will have to go away—be with him."

"Yes." The single word was barely audible.

"How can I?" she cried. "How can I, now?"

He dragged her against him, holding her tight to his chest, burying his face in the soft cloud of her hair, which spilled loose around her shoulders.

"Dear God," he whispered, "do you think I would permit it if there was any other way? The thought is like a dull knife tearing at my heart. You are mine, now and for all time; you will always be a part of my being, the partner of my soul. And yet, I would rather have you alive in his arms than dead in mine."

"Even if being alive there is like death?" She closed her eyes tightly, the better to savor his strength, the scent of him, the closeness that might soon end. "Have I no voice in this decision?"

"Not if you love me."

"That's unfair," she said on a ragged breath.

"What isn't?" he whispered. "Oh, my Violet, I thought this war in the Crimea had changed matters, distracted attention, so it was possible for me to lose myself in my own pursuits and joys. I was wrong. There are those who are more determined than ever that I not be allowed to be anonymous, or happy. Your misfortune is that you became a part of my error."

"I don't count it a misfortune."

She said the words plainly. She was growing more calm as she listened to the aching timbre of his voice, felt the trembling in his taut embrace.

"Nor I, in truth," he said in husky agreement, "though the regret remains."

She was still for the space of several breaths. Finally she said, "Is there nothing else we can do, nowhere we can go to—to get away?"

"Running, hiding, looking over our shoulders, is that what you want?"

"It's better than being apart." Her voice was low but firm.

The breeze from the open door drifted around them, shifting Violet's hair across her back. Allain caught the warm skein of it in his hand, lifting it to his lips. Finally he said on a sigh, "Perhaps. It may be that a place can be found."

Chapter 17

"Gilbert is in Venice."

Allain made the announcement on his return from the market. Violet was lying on a chaise longue in the salon, nibbling on a piece of the dry bread Signora da Allori had recommended for morning sickness. She sat up quickly, then closed her eyes as nausea swept over her. She choked a little as she said, "You saw him?"

"Not I. I had a report from friends I asked to watch for him at the frontier. He was seen going into the Hotel Principessa."

"You—had him watched?" Her voice sounded strange even in her own ears.

He paused in the act of removing a dress glove to search her pale face. After an instant he tugged the glove from his fingers and tossed it into the hat that he had set on a side table. He said deliberately, "It seemed a reasonable precaution."

"And only just, of course, since he had us followed before." She paused to give him time to comment. When he made no effort to do so, she went on. "Or did he, Allain?"

"What are you saying?"

There was a faint imperious shading in his tone as he spoke. Things had changed between them in the days since the two men came. They had both tried to pretend that the words spoken, and unspoken, made no difference. Both knew it was a lie.

224

"I have been thinking," she said slowly. "Were the men in Paris really sent by Gilbert, or were they a part of this—this danger you spoke of?"

"Does it matter?" He turned away as he removed his coat and took the button links from his cuffs before beginning to turn up the sleeves.

Her voice strained, she said, "You know it does."

He looked straight ahead for long moments before he faced her. "I suppose it does. If Gilbert did not send the men who followed us there, then you came to me because of a misconception."

It was a long moment before she answered. "I meant only that Gilbert was not quite the villain I had thought, that he had some reason for his failure to understand what took place."

"Ah," Allain said, his voice soft. He moved away again, going to the windows, where the heat of the sun was growing minute by minute. His face was quite blank as he reached to close the shutters, plunging the room into sudden dimness.

"That wasn't what you meant, though, was it?" Violet went on. "You must have guessed the men were not sent by him, yet you allowed me to think otherwise. Why?"

"How was I to tell you without explaining everything?"

"It was easier to keep me in the dark, and to accept whatever benefit might come of it."

"If by that you mean your surrender, then yes." He removed his hands from the shutter knobs and turned to meet her gaze without evasion.

"But don't you see that it changes everything?" she said earnestly.

"What I see is this," he said slowly. "If I had told you then, I would have lost you. Gilbert was going to take you away; I saw it in his eyes that evening at the ball. I thought that if I could have you for one night, just one, I would be able to support being without you for all the nights that would come after. That was a mistake, not my only one, but perhaps the most grave."

Her voice low, she said, "I had thought better of you."

"Did you?" A wry smile touched a corner of his mouth. "I'm flattered, and glad. But in my defense I will say that, though I may have guessed the men that night and later at the train station were not sent by your husband, I couldn't be sure—can't be sure even now. I have never been attacked before. The cause of it at this time might be the war and its consequences. Or it might not."

She put a hand to her face, rubbing at her eyes, pressing her fingers to her head that had begun to ache. "Or it could be that you are still making excuses."

"Oh, yes," he answered, his voice quietly reflective, drained of emotion, "and it could be you are searching for a reason to return to Gilbert, after all."

"No!" She drew back as if she had been struck.

"You see," he said as he moved toward her, "this doubt between us is a sword that cuts both ways. It hurts you, but I am not immune to its pain."

She nodded in weary agreement, exhaling softly as she lay back on the chaise. "I know. And I am sorry for it."

His clothing rustled as he knelt on the floor beside the lounge where she lay. He picked up her hand, carrying it to his lips, then cradling it between both of his. "I can't bear that we should hurt each other. It may be that in trying to keep you safe, I am destroying the love and trust between us. If I do that, then the sacrifice you made for me will be meaningless and the love we have shared without worth."

He stopped, his gaze wide as he searched her face. There was a sheen of perspiration on his forehead not caused by the heat of the day, and a faint tremor in his hands. He moistened his lips before he went on.

"Because of these things, I leave the decision to you, then, knowing that your concern for the child you will bear must be even more vital than my own. Will you hear who I am, and what, or will you remain in safe ignorance of it?"

She reached to spread the fingers of her free hand over his, where he clasped her other one. With love and resolve plain in her eyes, she said, "Tell me everything and tell me quickly, while my courage lasts. I want to know all of you, though it means the end of life itself. How else am I to know my child, if I never know his father?"

He drew a breath, then let it out in a single gust. He gave a fatalistic nod. His voice was not quite steady as he said, "It began nearly two years before I was born, in the year 1825—or perhaps it really began long before, but came to a head in that year. My father had been unhappy in his marriage and his position for some time. His wife was sickly, and he had no living children of the marriage. . . ."

· He went on, the words coming easier and with more clarity as the narrative took on shape and form. He presented the facts without embarrassment or pride, and without subterfuge. It was not a long tale in its essence. But it changed everything.

When he had fallen silent, Violet sat still, staring into space. She felt stunned, as if at some unexpected blow. She was not disbelieving so much as reluctant to allow herself to believe.

This was not a tale she could record in her journal. She might never be able to put it on paper, never speak of it to a single person, never even whisper it to the child in her womb when it was fully grown.

Her heart felt leaden inside her. She could sense all the half-formed plans and unfinished dreams she had not really known she was building begin to wither and fade slowly from her mind.

"Don't look like that," Allain said, his voice rough.

She brought her gaze back to his face. Her lips trembled into a smile as she lifted her hand, smoothing the lines of anxiety that creased the skin between his brows, trailing her fingertips through the damp curls at his brow.

"No," she said quietly, "it's all right. I'm all right."

His features eased only a fraction. "Tell me what you think. I must know."

"I think that I love you, that I'll always love you."

He bowed his head, and his lips were warm against the coolness of her fingers still in his clasp. As he looked up he answered, "No more than I shall love you."

She thought the words had the sound of a vow, the only one she was ever likely to hear. It was, in its way, enough.

"I also think," she went on after a moment, "that we should leave Venice at once."

"But your condition—what of that?"

"Is that why you have delayed? I am generally quite healthy. The morning sickness is normal, nothing to be concerned over."

"I've been thinking that perhaps the countryside would be best, instead of any city where I might be expected to go. Signora da Allori has a sister who owns a villa near Florence. Savio will take us there with a letter of introduction, and with suitable precautions and disguises, unless you would hate such things. It waits only for your approval."

It would be an easy journey, perhaps too easy. "If you are satisfied, then I give it my blessing, of course. But—you would not forfeit your safety for my comfort?"

"Willingly," he said, his gray eyes steady. "But you forget that your safety also depends on mine, and will until our child is born."

"Then," she said simply, "I will trust you to keep us all from harm."

It was at the villa that Allain finished the miniature of Violet that he had started in Venice. The small portrait was the best thing he had ever done, or so he maintained. The inspiration was in her smile, he said, that faintly superior and mysterious smile of interior knowledge.

Violet had not known she could look that way, so beguiling, so serene. She accused him of flattering her outrageously for his own purposes. He denied the charge with vehemence. The painting was perfect, he said, an exact likeness. The villa and the country life obviously agreed with her.

He was right about the last.

The villa was ancient, with broken roof tiles, tawny building stones that were crumbling to dust at the edges, and jagged cracks in the high walls that surrounded it. From the windows could be seen long views of rolling hills covered with gray-green olives, verdant vineyards, and with umbrella pines standing sentinel on the ridges.

Inside, the ceilings were painted with nymphs hiding among clouds, the walls were hung with tapestries that shivered in the cooling breezes through the open windows. Opening from the kitchen and its adjoining dining room was a walled garden. This retreat had the long arcade, the gnarled roses and luxuriant grapevines, and sublime silence of a cloister.

The villa could not be called convenient. Every drop of water for cooking and bathing had to be carried from the fountain in the center of the garden. The stable was a tumbledown ruin where chickens and ducks nested in the feed boxes. The nearest village was nearly three miles away and it was only a cluster of houses around a church. Violet loved the place anyway, loved it for its age, its imperfections, and its sense of having sheltered other lives, other lovers, over long ages.

She and Allain spent most of their days in the walled garden. He set up his easel under the grapevine arbor where the mosaic floor gave him a fairly level surface and the light was good. They had a table and a number of comfortable chairs set up there also, and ate their meals there as often as not.

There was such peace and security within the old walls where the only sounds were bird song and the hum of bees, and the cool trickle and splash of the fountain. The plants growing against the crumbling masonry and in large pots were kept clipped and watered by the villa's caretaker, a young man named Giovanni whose father and grandfather had also tended the house and garden in their time. Giovanni was always somewhere about, dipping water from the fountain and carrying it for the housekeeper, Maria, who was his mother, bringing eggs from the stable or onions from the kitchen garden beyond the wall, plucking yellowed leaves from the roses on the walls or cutting the grass under the huge silver-gray olive tree that grew in a corner. When Violet glanced in his direction, he always smiled and inclined his head in a gesture that seemed more a salute than an indication of subservience.

With Giovanni's help, she identified many of the plants that grew in and around the villa, from the ancient and enormous apothecary's rose to the sweet basil and oregano, sage and shallots and mint growing in the garden's geometric-shaped beds.

Giovanni was soft-spoken and exquisitely polite, a nice-looking youth near her own age with curling black hair, liquid brown eyes, and brawny shoulders developed by his outdoor work. He kept a market garden in his spare time, where he grew vegetables and flowers that a cousin took once a week to Florence, some twenty or thirty miles away. In the spring, he said, when the huge old roses in the garden bloomed, he collected the thousands of petals as they fell. He extracted their perfume, as had his father and grandfather before him, and this essence he bottled and sold also.

When Violet showed an interest in his extraction process, he told her about it in detail, and even requested that she go with him to look at the equipment he used. He was so starved for someone to talk to about his interest in the oil essences of perfumes that his tongue became tangled in his eagerness, though he was lyrical in his description of it.

The perfume making turned out to be a fascinating process. It did not seem possible that something so simple as pressing flower petals into cold oil, then later draining off the oil holding their essence and adding it to the aqua vitae distilled from wine, could have such wonderfully fragrant results. Violet insisted on trying it herself, using Giovanni's equipment and the blossoms of a night-blooming jasmine. The result was amazing, a revelation to her. It was as if in taking the scent from the flowers, one was preserving the souls of the blossoms, allowing them another life, a miraculous second blooming.

One evening after a visit to the shed where Giovanni made his perfume, she was returning with him to the villa through the side gate in the walled garden. She had been laughing at some droll remark he had made when she turned her head to see Allain standing under the grape arbor, leaning on one of its supports as he watched them.

Giovanni flushed a little under Allain's steady regard. He gave him a quiet greeting, however, then turned to incline his head to Violet. "Good evening then, madonna," he murmured, and walked away into the house.

Violet moved toward Allain, stepping into the circle of his left arm as he reached out to her. She waited until the young gardener had disappeared inside before she spoke.

"You don't mind that I spend time with Giovanni, do you? He enjoys showing me his flowers and perfumes, and you know how much I like such things. He is always careful to show me every courtesy, and to keep a proper distance."

"I should be jealous," he answered, smiling down at her. "Our Giovanni is, I think, more than half-inclined to be in love with you."

"Oh, no," she protested. "I have it on the best authority—his mother—that he flirts shamelessly with the village girls and has a dozen ready to marry him tomorrow."

"That may be, but I understand the signs all too well to be mistaken. He may flirt with others, but you he worships. Only consider the title he gave you just now—*madonna*, our lady. It's an old one of great reverence, used only for ladies of highest birth in times past, but reserved now, in the main, for the holy mother Mary. He can pay you no higher compliment, assign you no greater place in his heart."

"I can't believe it; I've done nothing to make him feel that way, I promise."

"It was not required. You have only to be you."

"But I'm with child!" she protested, shaking her head with a troubled look beneath the laughter in her eyes.

"So you are, and blooming like some lovely flower yourself, growing sweeter and more beautiful every day. Why should Giovanni not adore you? I cannot blame him, since I feel that way myself."

Allain was meticulous about saying such things. It was not, Violet thought, that he felt she needed to hear them just now, as the contours of her body began to lose their slender shape. And it was not that he was in any way insincere. It was more that he intended that no opportunity should pass that he might take to show her what he felt for her. She loved him for it, yet it gave her a strange sense of impermanence. It almost seemed that he feared there might come a time when he could not be there to say such things to her.

Nevertheless, they were happy. The days passed, and the nights. They laughed, they sang together in the evenings, they touched and held each other. They watched the soft, glowing sunsets over the hills and the even softer sunrises. They ate the wonderful roast meats and fresh vegetables cooked with virgin olive oil and seasoned with herbs, and they washed them down with a different wine each day. And the love they made in the great tester bed took on the feeling of a hallowed communion.

It was Giovanni who brought the news that destroyed their peace.

He had heard it from his cousin, who, when he went to the market in Florence, sometimes visited the lovely young daughter of the cook at the house of the elderly lady who owned the villa and was a sister to Signora da Allori in Venice.

Signora da Allori was dead. She had died of a heart attack after discovering a prowler in her house in the night.

The widow's sister, Giovanni said, insisted that she had died of fright. There were bruises on her body, and her little finger had been broken.

Was it only a coincidence? Or was the Signora da Allori's death connected with their stay in her house? Had the prowler been trying to force the energetic old lady to tell him where Violet and Allain were hiding?

"It's my fault," Allain said. "I should have foreseen something like this."

"Who could have guessed they would go so far?" Violet answered him with horror in her voice. "She was only an old woman who rented her house. Why would they think she could tell them anything?"

"They grow desperate. With so much political unrest everywhere, no country is immune to revolution. The fighting will begin at any moment in the Crimea. It makes a fine excuse, for everyone."

"I don't know what you could have done to protect the signora."

He shook his head. "I could have at least given her a stronger warning. I did try to make Savio understand—as well as I could without a full explanation. It was not, apparently, enough."

The widow and her majordomo had thought they were helping only to hide them from Violet's irate husband. It had seemed a sufficient excuse, at the time.

Violet said in tentative tones, "Do you think this so-called prowler got the information he wanted?"

"It doesn't seem so. Savio heard the widow's cries and arrived in time to frighten the man away. Even then, the poor lady was dying."

They had both grown fond of the elderly woman during the time they had spent in her house. For all her gruff ways and tirades at her servants, she had been kind of heart, and had given them privacy and company in equal measure. To think that she might have died because of them brought a weight of guilt that turned the days gray and without savor.

Allain grew silent and ceased to paint. The flowers for perfume had faded as the autumn crept nearer, but Violet had no interest in any case. Her morning sickness had passed and her appetite revived, yet nothing seemed to taste right or to be seasoned correctly.

There were nights when Violet woke to see Allain standing at the window, staring out over the hills that were pale blue in the light of the stars. There were mornings when she woke to find him lying beside her, watching her with a look on his face that was both absorbed and tormented. Sometimes he held her so tightly she could not breathe while he buried his face in the smooth turn of her neck or between the pale hills of her breasts. Often, he spread his open hand upon her belly, caressing, holding.

He liked to watch her wash her long tresses and to help her comb the tangles from them. He spread the shimmering mass out across her shoulders and, as it dried, gathered great handfuls and held them to his face while he breathed their fragrance. Later, he would move aside the warm strands to kiss the individual white bumps of her backbone above her shift.

One evening, when dinner was over and Maria and Giovanni had gone, Violet and Allain sat under the grape arbor watching the moon rise over the garden wall. The warm air smelled of fresh-cut hay and ripening grapes with just a taint of wood smoke.

The grapevines overhead rustled dryly in a quiet zephyr of a breeze. The shadows cast by the leaves against the moonlight moved in a rhythm as hypnotic as it was unending. Allain had been holding her hand, caressing the smooth skin over the bones with his thumb. When he spoke, his voice was quiet, reflective.

"There is something I have been meaning to say to you. The time never seemed right, or I—but never mind. Listen to me closely. If ever, for any reason, you find yourself alone, *carita*, you must go to a lawyer and man of business whose name and address I will give you. He will have funds for you—"

Fear made her voice sharp as she interrupted. "You mean money? But I don't want—"

"I know, believe me I do, Violet, but please hear me out. This is something I have arranged for my own peace of mind. You will permit me to tell you of it, please, and commit what I say to memory, for my sake."

"Do you think—" she began, then stopped, unable to put her fear into words. Her fingers tightened in his grasp.

"I don't know. I only know that this is one of the things I must do to protect you and our unborn child. Allow me, please."

There was such pain and pleading in his voice. How could she refuse?

"Good," he said in relief when she said no more. "Listen then."

She did as he asked. When he was certain she understood, he fell silent. The night gathered around them, deepening, while the brilliant moon seemed to hang huge and motionless above them.

Allain rose and moved to kneel at Violet's feet. He gathered her close then, while he placed his head in her lap. She smoothed her fingers through the crisp waves of his hair, touched the planes of his face with the palms of her hands, and enclosed as much of his shoulders as she could reach in the circle of her arms. They remained like that for long moments, until he whispered, "Come, lie with me."

He spread the cloth from the table over the ancient tiles, then drew her down beside him upon it. They lay for a long time with moonlight and shadows in their eyes. Gently, then, he turned to her and drew the pins from her hair. He kissed her eyelids and the hollows underneath, her forehead and earlobes and the point of her chin. With slow and gentle care, he eased her from her clothing and also removed his own until they lay with their naked skin patterned with the dark outlines of grape leaves.

His touch was reverent, his mouth warm and moist as he gave unhurried attention to every curve and each pulsating hollow of her body. Like a blind miser counting hoarded gold, recognizing its form and substance by sensitive exploration, he paid her his homage.

She clung to him, dissolving inside in molten joy. Desire ran in her blood, while keeping pace with it was a generosity so intense, so jubilant that it seemed a benediction, a loving sacrament.

He pressed against her, beseeching entry, and she took him inside her with slow care. Gently, gently they moved together, their breathing shallow, uneven, as they sought with rigorous will and steadfast consideration to regulate the force of the tempest building inside them. Trembling, shuddering under its ferocious onslaught, they conquered the impulses that drove them, refusing to jar the child they cradled between them. And they received their reward in the spreading heat of rampant glory that sprang, singing in their veins, rising to overflow their pounding hearts.

Afterward, Allain gathered her close, holding her while he whispered of love. When their skins had cooled, he gathered up their garments, then picked her up and carried her into the house. In their bedchamber, he lay with her close in his arms while she slept, breathing the fragrance of her body with closed eyes while he listened to the hard, regular pulsing of his own life's blood in his veins. He did not sleep.

Violet was alone in the tester bed when morning came.

She was not especially alarmed. She thought Allain might have gone to bring coffee back to her, as he sometimes did, or else that he had thought of some early-morning vista that he wished to capture on canvas, or perhaps gone for a walk. She expected to find him, surely, in the garden or at the breakfast table. She thought he might have gone to the stable to visit a litter of kittens that had appeared there a few days before. She expected that he had decided to go to Florence on some errand that had taken longer than planned, or else one that was to be a surprise for her. She felt sure that whatever note he might have left her had been misplaced, or perhaps blown from where it had been resting and fallen behind some piece of furniture.

She looked up at the sound of every footfall through the morning and started at every whisper of wind. She walked from the bedchamber to the garden a dozen times and made the trip down to the stable on at least three occasions. She questioned Maria, hearing her own voice grow sharp before she brought it back under control. She would have asked Giovanni what he knew, but the gardener had gone to take his vegetables to his cousin's house for the weekly market.

It was late afternoon when Giovanni returned. Violet was in the garden when she saw him approaching. His footsteps were slow and his gaze troubled as he came to a stop before her. In his hand was a bunch of flowers, though the blooms were too few and ill assorted to be called a bouquet.

"Forgive me, madonna," he said in low tones. "I was to bring these to you this morning, and would have, but you were sleeping and I did not like to wake you. It's a poor thing, this bouquet, but I was instructed to present just these flowers and greenery, and no other."

She took the bouquet in careful hands, turning it this way and that. There were marigolds, bright orange and aromatic. Twining around them was dark green ivy. The soft blue of forget-me-nots was half-hidden among the rough leaves of dandelion greens.

Her voice was hoarse as she forced it through her throat. "It was sent by Signor Massari?"

"Yes, madonna."

She closed her eyes, unable to bear the sight of the wilting bouquet. "Thank you, Giovanni," she said quietly. "That will be all."

"There is one thing more, madonna."

"Yes?" She looked up with hope springing inside her.

"I am to be your guard."

"My guard." The hope died away, completely.

"With my life. This is a privilege I had not expected. It gives me great pleasure, and honor."

What could she say to him while he stood before her with such unassuming pride, such readiness to serve. It was impossible to tell him she didn't want or need him, that she preferred the guard she had had before and wanted him back.

She forced her cold lips to curve, at least a little. "Thank you, Giovanni."

"It is nothing, madonna."

Nothing, and everything. Violet felt as if her breath, her life had been cut off. As the young gardener turned and began to walk away, a thought occurred to her. "Giovanni!"

He whirled at once, returning with quick steps. "I always come when you call."

Violet paused at the fervency of his tone. She could spare no thought for it, however. She said, "The signor, he gave you his instructions—when?"

"Last evening it was, before nightfall."

"I see. Thank you again," she whispered.

Giovanni went away then, though not without several frowning glances over his shoulder. Violet carried the bouquet with her to a chair beneath the grape arbor. She lowered herself into it, placing the flowers on her lap. She touched them with careful fingers while tears rose slowly to sting her eyes.

The forget-me-nots, for True Love.

The ivy, for Fidelity.

The marigolds, for Grief.

The dandelions, for an Oracle.

It was a message of its own kind, their own kind.

Allain was gone, had decided, perhaps, to leave to keep her safe after all. Or else for some reason that she might understand, but could not accept.

Just as she understood, but could not accept, his message.

He loved her.

He would love her unto death and would never love another.

He grieved at the parting.

Whether he would return, only the gods knew. And they would not tell.

Chapter 18

Joletta put down Violet's journal, which she had been studying, and walked into the hotel bathroom. She leaned close to look at herself in the mirror over the lavatory. Her eyes were indisputably brown, much like Violet's had been, also like those of her mother and her father both, as far as that went. Mimi's eyes had been gray. Natalie's eyes were gray blue, but perhaps more on the gray side. Timothy's eyes were hazel.

Gilbert Fossier had had hazel eyes. Allain Massari's had been gray.

None of which really counted for anything, since Mimi had married a distant Fossier cousin, a man descended from Gilbert's younger brother, whom Violet had mentioned in the journal. At least everyone had always thought Mimi and her husband, whom they called Pop, were distant cousins.

Mimi must have known it wasn't so.

Or perhaps not. Violet had not seemed too certain herself which man was the father of her child.

It was difficult for Joletta to think of her ancestors as hiding secrets or living with mistakes. They had for so many years just been names on the family tree, almost legendary figures.

Joletta had always had the idea that Violet and Gilbert's trip to Europe had been a typical grand tour, a sort of last hurrah before such extravagant gestures were ended by the Civil War. There had never seemed to be anything particularly unusual about it, never been any hint of scandal or suggestion that it might have greatly affected their lives afterward, except for the acquisition by Violet of the famous perfume. All Joletta had ever known, all she had ever heard mentioned, was that Gilbert and Violet had spent two years traveling and returned home with a baby girl.

Rone was already gone. He had showered and left the room early, well over two hours before. He had tried to move quietly, thinking she was asleep. Joletta had lain with her back to him and her eyes closed until she had the room to herself. She had reached for the journal then to be certain it was all there, that it was safe. Leafing through the pages, her attention had been snared by the entries concerning the early days of Violet's pregnancy.

She wondered what Rone made of it all. She was beginning to have a few ideas based on her knowledge of history, but they were too nebulous to be useful. She would like to see if Rone had come up with anything.

He would not finish the small portion he still had left to read. She intended to make certain the journal went into her shoulder bag right now, and stayed there. Rone must have taken it out the day before; there was no other way he could have had it to read last night. Somehow, with the upsets of the day, she had failed to notice.

With the journal safely tucked away, she returned to the bathroom to shower. Afterward, she pulled her hair back in a simple wooden clasp and applied a bare minimum of makeup. She didn't feel like fussing; besides, there was something about the clear light of Italy and the natural air of the Italians that made anything more seem too contrived.

Taking a T-shirt and cotton knit skirt in periwinkle blue from her suitcase, she tossed them on the bed. Her gaze rested a moment on the pillow that still bore the indentation of Rone's head. She looked quickly away.

She had been afraid he would expect to continue as they had begun when she joined him in the big bed the night before. He had not. It seemed that he had an unexpected appreciation for her moods, or else he had felt something less than passionate toward her himself, after seeing her with Caesar. He had kept to his own side of the bed.

As she skimmed into her clothes Joletta considered the situation between Violet and Allain once more. They had been so close, what they felt had been so certain, so fervent. How much of it had really been love, she wondered, and how much simple sexual attraction?

They had been lucky, those two, she thought. People in their time period had not been troubled by such considerations. They had accepted everything they felt as part of a whole. They hadn't analyzed their relationships to death, hadn't questioned their dependency on the person they loved, or fought it.

There was an affecting innocence about the passion that existed between them. It was pure in its way, untainted by decadent Freudian intimations or the constant bombardment of sexual innuendo from the media. There was sanctity in it, a whole other spiritual dimension that had been lost in the present day with its minute tracking of sexual arousal and response and its preoccupation with personal pleasure.

Joletta's reflections scattered as a knock came on the door. Assuming it was either Rone or the maid ready to clean the room, she moved to pull it open.

"Hi," the young man who stood there said. He lounged at ease with his hands in the pockets of his chinos and a grin of satisfaction on his face.

"Timothy!" Surprise and the pleasure of seeing a familiar face in a strange place made her reach out to hug him before she went on. "Where did you come from?"

"Corsica. Got in last night," he said, returning the hug with enthusiasm. He stepped back, sweeping the sandy blond hair out of his eyes with a hasty gesture. "You had breakfast? Natalie said I'd never catch up with you here at the hotel, but I bet her a twenty I would."

They made their way to the hotel dining room for the usual continental fare. The rolls and croissants with butter and jam were already on the tables, along with carafes of hot coffee and hot milk. By the time they served themselves the coffee, he had told her how he had got bored with sunning and sailing and looking at ruins and decided to see how she and Natalie were doing with the perfume. He felt he ought at least to show an interest.

"So, any luck?" he asked as he took a healthy bite of his croissant.

His directness, after Natalie's pretension, was refreshing. Joletta gave him an unvarnished answer.

He nodded as he swallowed. "Didn't think so. It's a lost cause, if you ask me. Tell you what I'd do if it was me; I'd just amble around and have a good time."

"Yes, well, I've been doing that," Joletta answered.

"I mean, really. What's the big deal, anyway?" he said reasonably. "How different can a perfume be? I don't see why we didn't just get our heads together, take something out of Mimi's stock, and tell this Camors woman here's the old family recipe. I mean, who's going to know the difference?"

"Lara Camors, if she has much of a perfumer's nose."

He shrugged. "If you say so. You could always say the smell was off because some flavor wasn't available anymore, something like that."

"That won't help me if I decide to keep the shop open. There are women in New Orleans who have been using Violet's perfume for decades, and I can guarantee you they would know if it wasn't the same."

"Well, something may have to be done if things don't look up pretty soon. Mother is fit to be tied. You'd think she was going to become a bag lady if this deal doesn't go through."

"I can just see that," Joletta said with a twitch at the corner of her mouth.

"Me too." His face turned gloomy after a moment. "She's threatening to cut my allowance and send me out looking for one of those terrible things called a J-O-B. She gets like that when the budget gets out of whack."

Joletta tilted her head. "Would that be so terrible, joining the rest of us in the work force?"

"I don't know, maybe not if I had been trained for anything. Trouble is, I never did the college bit. Mother couldn't decide what I should do, finally said I made a better beach bum than anything else."

"She wasn't, by any chance, the one who suggested you might cut short your beach time and come help Natalie check up on me?"

His thin skin showed a flush of color. "You know how she does—or maybe you don't. She never really said I was to come, just talked and talked until I got the hint."

Joletta sipped her coffee before she said, "I can't believe the money is that important to her."

"You have no idea. Folding cash. *Dinaro. Argent.* We always need it. We are expensive people, my mother and her children. It's a strain keeping up with the folks who have it in buckets." He gave a low laugh. "Poor Natalie may even have to get married again. She won't like that. Or maybe she will, depending on the man. She had a good prospect cornered this morning."

"Did she? Here in Venice?"

He nodded as he swallowed hot coffee. "The CEO of the Camors cosmetic conglomerate, actually the son of the woman who owns it. Natalie had a breakfast date with him at the Cipriani, where she's putting up."

"Did she?" Joletta said dryly. The Hotel Cipriani was not cheap by any standard. It was also interesting that someone from Camors was in Venice just now.

"That's how I knew you'd be free." Timothy looked at her, his gaze a little apologetic, as he took another roll.

"Oh?" Joletta considered putting apricot jam on her croissant, but decided against it.

"My darling sister seemed to think it was a coup of sorts; she was as pleased with herself as a biker with a new Harley. The guy had been hot for you, but she nailed him."

Joletta looked up. "For me?"

"So she said. Actually, he's just your type, I'd say; straight as they come, all-American, manners coming out his ears. Great boss, so they say: super efficient and even creative; oversees his own in-house advertising and promotion. It's a shame, but all's fair in love, war, and business."

Joletta put down her roll. Suddenly she had no appetite. Her voice sounded hoarse and not quite steady, as she said, "This CEO, what is his name?"

"Now let me think," Timothy said, chewing slowly. "Something a mile long that fairly shouts Four Hundred family. Adamson, I think it was, with a third or fourth or fifth tacked on maybe."

"You're sure?" she asked, though she already knew there was no mistake.

"Oh, yeah," Timothy said. "Tyrone Adamson, that's him."

Sickness rose inside her. She swallowed hard against it; still, it brought gooseflesh to her arms and a sudden chill around her heart.

"You all right?" Timothy was watching her, his gaze arrested. "Don't tell me you didn't know who Adamson was?"

She didn't answer directly, saying instead, "Why isn't his last name the same as his mother's?"

"He's supposed to be the son of a second husband or something; the woman has been married a million times at least."

"You know her?" Joletta asked. "You've met Rone?"

"I was introduced to the old lady when I was being my mother's 'walker,' last year, taking her around to parties and charity balls and so on in New York. I never spoke to her son until this morning; he didn't have a lot to do with that scene."

"I just can't believe it." The words were measured, and there was a glaze of pain in her eyes.

"You going to eat that last croissant? No?" Timothy reached across to take it from her plate. "People say his mother built the corporation, but she did it with his dad's money. After the divorce his dad hung on to a majority interest in the business. Rone got that when his dad died, which makes him the powerhouse in the corporation. He's the one who makes the final decisions these days."

"Such as whether to buy the perfume, and how to go about seeing that they wind up with the formula?"

"You got it." He shook his head in admiration. "And the guy's been traveling with you around Europe without letting on who he is, putting up with a tour bus when he's used to the Concorde. God, what an operator."

She couldn't stand it. She had to get away. She needed to think, to sort out the jumble of pain and rage that threatened to explode inside her.

She got to her feet and slung the strap of her big purse over her shoulder. "Look, I'm sorry, Timothy, really, I am, but I've got to go. I'll take care of your breakfast."

"You don't have to do that," he protested.

"I'll still get it. Will you be in Venice long?"

He lifted a shoulder. "Depends."

"Where are you staying?"

"The Cipriani with Natalie, for now," he said before he went on with his cheery grin. "I expect it'll be the hostel again tomorrow. I don't mind; the company is friendlier."

"That's good then. Maybe I'll catch you later." She started to turn away, then swung back. "You have enough money?"

He grimaced. "The funds are okay, they just have to be made to last. Not to worry, I'm fine."

She touched his shoulder, then walked quickly away. She was afraid to stay there, afraid that if she remained a moment longer, she would burst into tears. She felt like such an idiot. She couldn't do anything right, even fall in love.

The thought brought her up short, so that a waiter moving

behind her with a pot of coffee in one hand and one of hot milk in the other sidestepped with a sharp exclamation. She murmured an apology before she moved on again.

No. It could not be. She wasn't in love; she wouldn't allow it.

She wasn't some sheltered Victorian female who had to give her heart to a man before she went to bed with him. She was modern and sensible. Making love was an excellent antidote for stress, she knew, also a pleasant diversion for a Sunday afternoon and a dandy way to get to know a person. She had no need for lace and perfume and flowers, did not require desperate sacrifices and eternal vows of devotion.

All she really needed was a warm body, a little expertise, and some occasional conversation.

Yes. And stability.

A tiny bit of tenderness.

Humor, maybe.

Concern.

And honesty.

That was all. Really.

Damn the man.

Damn him, damn him.

She paused at the hotel desk long enough to leave a message that she would not be going with the morning tour; she just couldn't face it. Not now. She had turned away, heading toward the door that stood open to the street, when she saw a tall form approaching.

Rone. She stopped short. It was, however, too late to avoid him.

" 'Morning," he called. He stepped over the wide marble threshold as he spoke, at the same time dodging a rotund lady tourist in a sweater woven in a Stars and Stripes design. His voice was low and insouciant, and his smile for Joletta shaded with a hint of intimacy as he moved toward her.

Joletta gave him a look designed to freeze him in his tracks as she swept past without stopping. A moment later she was out the door, blending with the foot traffic of morose and sleepy-eyed Italians on their way to work. She turned in the direction of the nearby quay.

Swift, firm footsteps sounded behind her. Rone caught her arm, dragging her to a halt. His voice curt, he said, "What's the matter with you?"

She swung on him, her eyes black with anger. "Oh, nothing at all is wrong with me. I've just discovered the man who has been sharing my bed is a sneak and a liar."

His brows snapped together over his eyes. "What are you talking about?"

"You know very well what I'm talking about," she said with scalding scorn. "And I hope you found something useful for your mother in Violet's journal last night, because it's the last time you'll ever see it."

She jerked her arm from his grasp, whirling away from him to walk on. He reached her in two strides and clamped a hand on her forearm to stop her again. "Just a minute," he said, his features grim, "you don't understand."

The rage simmering inside her boiled over. "I understand just fine! Did you think I wouldn't find out? Did you think you could go on using me until you had everything you needed to know? And what about Natalie? I should have known something was wrong when you went with her yesterday like a pet poodle."

"It wasn't like that," he said. "I never intended—"

Joletta was aware of the interested glances cast in their direction by the people moving around them, a river of humanity dividing around an annoying obstruction. She ignored them.

"No? Oh, but once you started, it was so convenient to keep going, wasn't it? God, but when I think of it, I could die—or kill you with my bare hands!"

"Joletta, don't," he said in low-voiced concern. "Don't do this to yourself."

"Me? You're the bastard who did it. You did it with your low-down sneaking tricks. I should have known there was something fishy about you when your southern drawl started to disappear. I've had enough of you, New York Yankee. I want you out of my room, off this tour, and gone from my life. I don't want to see you again. Ever."

"Tough," he said.

She blinked at the stoniness of his tone. "What do you mean by that?"

"I mean that where you go, I go. Drawl or not, the blood of the Stuarts who produced Confederate General J.E.B. of the same name runs in my veins, and I'm as stubborn as you are any day. You don't take a step without me right behind you, until this mess is over. What in hell do you think it was all about?"

"If you think I'm going to let you stay anywhere near me, you can think again."

"You don't have a choice."

She lifted her hand and punched him in the chest with an extended forefinger. "You are dead wrong there."

"Am I?" he said, his voice even. "We'll see."

This time when she whirled to walk away from him, he made no move to stop her. Instead, he moved at her side, keeping pace with a long and effortless stride. The drop-dead look she gave him caused not even a flicker of expression. He only met her gaze with impassive determination.

She halted. "Go away," she said, "or I'll yell for a policeman and tell him you're molesting me."

"Do that," he said tightly, "and by the time one gets here, it may be the truth. Will you please stop long enough to listen to me?"

"What can you possibly say that I would want to hear? And how can you think I'd believe it even if you said it? Leave me alone!"

"If you'd just let me explain—"

"Explain what? How you just happened to be walking down the street near the perfume shop in New Orleans? It was probably you who was following me to begin with. Or maybe you'd like to tell me what a wonderful coincidence it was that you were around when my bag was stolen in London? I may have been gullible, but I learn fast. No, thanks."

She was breathing so hard as she swung and walked on that it felt as if she had been running for miles. She refused to look at the man who fell in beside her once more. She kept her face turned away, even as he began to talk.

"I followed you to the shop in New Orleans, all right. I didn't mean to give you such a scare, but I got too close because you reached the shop sooner than I expected. Later, I saw the creep who was following you, but had no idea exactly what he was up to, so I circled around and staged that little scene to scare him off. Since I was watching you, and getting concerned, when I found out you were going to Europe, I tagged along. I was at the airport because I was on the same plane, in a seat as far as possible from where you were sitting. I never meant to get so involved with your life; it just seemed, once I got to know you, that it would be easier to keep an eye on you if I was traveling with you."

"Right," she said waspishly, "and it just got easier and easier, didn't it?"

He drew a deep breath, as if striving for control. His voice was rough when he answered. "Yes. It did. But if you think I went through all that just to get Violet's perfume, you're wrong."

"Oh, I don't think that. You did it for Natalie, didn't you? She thought I was such a stranger to male attention that I would be bowled over by any handsome man who happened along. Well, she was right. I hope you enjoyed it."

"As a matter of fact—" he began, then stopped, folding his lips tightly for a moment before he started again. "It wasn't like that."

"No? Then you did it for my smile," she said in derision, though there was a stabbing ache inside her.

"I did it because I was afraid of what might happen to you."

"Oh, please." The sudden weariness in her voice also weighted her shoulders.

"I know it sounds crazy; I've thought several times that I must be out of my mind. But my mother hasn't been rational about this perfume since she first heard of it. She has been possessed with the idea that it could become the next Joy, a perfume so wonderful that it would take the country by storm. She meant to make it the best loved, most enduring—and not incidentally the most expensive— perfume in the world. A perfume with history and romance and a kind of grandeur that can't be found in some concoction out of a laboratory. But what bothered me most was not knowing exactly what she was willing to do to get her hands on it."

"You could have asked her," Joletta said. She was not sure when she had begun to listen to him. It didn't mean a thing that she had, of course.

"You don't ask Lara Camors much. She started her company out of her basement, a backwoods girl from Arkansas with an accent you could wade through who had been deserted in New York by a salesman who may or may not have been her first husband. She built it with guts and hard work, and a few convenient marriages. She didn't take it kindly when I used the shares my dad had been holding for years to muscle my way in after his death."

"Why not? You are her son."

"Her son whom she had deserted, along with his father, at the age of three."

The difference was small, but it was there. Her footsteps slowed. She met his gaze for long moments. A small portion of the tension that gripped her neck and shoulders began to ease.

"Anyway," he went on, "things began to really worry me after

I walked in on her in her office while she was speaking on the phone about the perfume. She shut up fast, but I heard her say something about it being too soon to celebrate just because Mimi Fossier was dead. There was still, she said, the other granddaughter."

"Meaning me."

"I had heard enough about the deal from her to know she wasn't talking about Natalie."

Joletta walked on a few steps. Finally she said, "Not saying I believe all that, but if you really thought I was in trouble, why didn't you tell me?"

"And admit I thought the great Lara Camors was dealing in extremely shady industrial espionage? Or worse? It would have sounded crazy; it still sounds crazy. I respect my mother; we've learned to work together over the last few years. I thought I'd fly down to New Orleans and check things out, then make up my mind. That turned out not to be so easy."

"But why lie to me about who you were later?"

"I didn't lie; I just didn't tell you the whole truth."

"You let me think you were some kind of adman, a producer of commercials."

"I am. I control the promotion for Camors, among other things. I just didn't spell it all out for you. It seemed entirely possible you would tell me to get lost, and I—didn't want to do that."

There was something in his voice that she refused to acknowledge. She said instead, "And I suppose you're going to tell me that you have no interest in the perfume, that nothing you did had any bearing on getting the rights to it for your company."

They had reached the quay. He stopped and shoved his hands into his pockets as he stared at the shifting waters of the canal, where a transport boat rumbled past with its decks piled high with cases of Coca-Cola. At last he gave an abrupt shake of his head. "No, I'm not going to tell you that."

"Meaning," she said with quiet disdain, "that it did have a bearing."

"Meaning I refuse to conceal any part of the truth from you, starting from this moment. I would like to see what can be done with the perfume if the formula ever comes to light. I wasn't too interested at first; in fact, I was skeptical that there could be anything to it. But reading Violet's journal, seeing that the whole story just might be legitimate, made a difference. There is potential there."

She wanted to believe him; that was the worst of it. But how could she? Her tone acerbic, she said, "I've decided to keep the formula for the shop if I find it."

"It would be a shame to bury it away again. You don't have the money or the organization to take advantage of what you would have."

"That doesn't make any difference. The perfume was fine just as it was for more than a hundred years."

He made a small gesture of negation with his head that he stilled abruptly. "All right. Whatever," he said. "But right this minute there are people trying to see that you don't get it. There seems to be a connection with Camors Cosmetics, and that makes me responsible if something happens to you. I don't intend to let you out of my sight until this thing is settled."

"Which will put you in a nice position to make a grab for it if it does turn up."

He looked at her with cold, quiet fury in his eyes. "I hope to hell you do find the formula. I promise that if you do, it's yours to do whatever you like with, as long as you like, if I have to camp on your doorstep for the rest of my life to see that nobody tries to stop you."

She gave him a straight look. "Now there's a real threat."

He made no move to disavow the words, which seemed to indicate that he meant to stick around whether she found the formula or not. After a moment he stepped closer. "I'm trying to help, that's all. Can't you believe that? Can't you trust me?"

She wished she could; it would have been so much easier. But there was too much doubt and pain and confusion inside her, and experience gave her no reason to think it was worth trying.

"I don't think I can," she said.

Rone felt as if he had been through a junk dealer's car crusher. That it was his own fault didn't make it any better. He had been trying for days to think of a way to tell Joletta who he was, especially since the meeting with Natalie. Joletta had every right to be angry. The way she had stood there flat-footed and let him have it had been something to see. He would have been even more admiring if her wrath had not been directed at him.

He wished that he could start over, from the beginning, there on the street in New Orleans. He would introduce himself and invite her out to dinner, then tell her in plain words exactly what she was up against. How would she have reacted if he had done that? he wondered. Would she have told him to hit the road, or would she have allowed him some sort of entrance into her life. Would she have trusted him enough to let him help her?

He wanted that trust with a desperation beyond anything he had ever dreamed.

Too late.

He couldn't worry about it now. It was going to take everything he had to keep Joletta from having him thrown into an Italian jail in the next few hours. Not that he intended to molest her, but he felt fairly sure that his idea of keeping a close watch on her and her own idea of it were two different things.

He would not think too much about the difference, or he might lose his sanity.

It was time he did something to try to redeem himself.

He said in neutral tones, "All right then. So what are the plans for today?"

"I have no plans," she said, her voice tight.

Rone had been prepared for the cold glance that went with her admission, but not for the dejection in her eyes. He frowned a little as he said, "I've been thinking about the Canaletto Allain bought, the one showing the house where he and Violet stayed. I'm not sure what good it would do to see it, but it might be worth a try."

"We have no idea what became of it."

"True, but if you'll remember, there was a small sketch of a house and a bit of the canal in Violet's journal, on a page next to where the painting was mentioned. Dollars to doughnuts, it was a detail from it."

A flicker of interest crossed her face. "If that's so," she said slowly, "we wouldn't have to find the same painting, just one that has the same stretch of canal, only with a few more identifying features."

Rone took his hand from his pocket and clasped the back of his neck, easing the tension that had gathered there as he gave a nod. He had been right in guessing that an interest in her search would be the way to reach her. His tone carefully neutral, he said, "I suggest we visit a museum or two, possibly the Palazzo Pesaro."

Joletta gave him a level look, but did not object. He was lucky, he knew, that she was a reasonable woman, and a fair one.

They wandered up and down gritty, marble-floored galleries, turning their heads this way and that until their necks were sore. It was amazing how much there was to see, and astonishing how little had been done to protect it all. There were few paintings or pieces of sculpture that one could not walk right up to and touch. It was almost as if there was such a wealth of artwork in Italy, and the problems of protecting it of such magnitude, that after safeguarding a few of the masterworks, the authorities simply threw up their hands.

It was Joletta who found the view that came closest to matching the sketch made by Violet. The painting was not a Canaletto, however, but one by J.M.W. Turner. She claimed to prefer Turner's more brilliant colors and blurred effects, as if the scene had been viewed through rain, over Canaletto's work, with its perfection of line and soft, clear colors. Rone declined to argue, since he was certain she was only trying to get under his skin. That she was succeeding was a fact he did his best to hide.

She was standing before the Turner with her hands clasped behind her back and a judicious pucker to her mouth that made him long to do things it would be best not to try in public. He did his best to listen to what she was saying.

"You realize that this may just be a house that looks like the one Violet drew? So many of these old palaces and houses are nearly alike, and one stretch of winding canal looks like any other."

"True," he answered.

"Besides that, Violet might have been sketching the house across the street."

Rone said, "If you have a better idea, I'm listening."

"No, no," she said. "I just wanted to be sure you realize we may be wasting our time."

We. It was, Rone thought, a nice little word. He said, "So do you want to go and knock on doors, or not?"

"We really need Caesar," she suggested.

"I think we can manage without him."

She gave him a dubious look. "Not unless you speak Italian." She paused a moment. "You don't, do you?"

A corner of his mouth tugged upward in a smile with more than its share of irony. "There are all sorts of things you don't know about me."

"I'm beginning," she said acidly, "to find out."

Just wait until tonight, he thought. Aloud, he said, "We have a couple of hours before lunch and the siesta hour to make a start. You ready?"

Chapter 19

It was not as easy to find the right house as it had appeared, even after it was located in the painting. The artist had taken liberties with the perspective, and even eliminated a building or two that did not suit him. Rone swore Turner had also narrowed the curve of the canal. Joletta told him there was something wrong with his eyes.

At the fourth house they tried, a young woman opened the door with a toddler on her hip. She wore a violent pink sweat suit and Reeboks with pink-and-green shoestrings and her hair was held back by a sweatband. She was talking in rapid-fire Italian over her shoulder to someone in the shadowed depths of a long entrance hall. As she turned to look at her visitors she paused, then switched to accented but perfectly grammatical English.

"This is not a museum or a hotel," she said. "Please go away."

She would have closed the door on them if Rone had not put out his hand to catch it. "We are sorry to intrude, but we aren't tourists. We are looking for information about a man and an American woman we think may have stayed here at this house many years ago."

"I know nothing of these people," the woman stated as she jiggled the little boy, who stared at them with huge black eyes under a tangle of golden-brown curls, like some living Botticelli cherub.

251

Joletta said quickly, "We have reason to think that the lady who owned the house then may have died because of them."

"Ah, *allora*." The young woman frowned. "One moment." She called something over her shoulder. There came the shuffle of footsteps, and an elderly man emerged from the dimness. He was, she said, her husband's grandfather, who had lived in the house all his days.

He was stooped and spare, so that the black wool sweater he wore to combat the dampness of the house drooped in front. His iron-gray hair had grown wiry as it curled and his smile had a few gaps in it; still, he had not lost his memory. The woman they spoke of had been his ancestress, a widow of small means like a thousand others who had taken in boarders in the last century, before the tourist hotels sprang up across the lagoon. She had died of a heart attack, so the doctors claimed, but in the family they knew better. A terrible tragedy, and a curious one. Money had been paid afterward, as though in reparation. It had caused an improvement in the fortunes of the widow's heirs. Such a thing was not easily forgotten.

There had been a sister, *sì*, with a villa near Florence. This villa had been razed during World War II and a new one built in its place. The garden? But yes, it was still there, if they cared to make the trip to see it. It was unaccountable, the things Americans desired to see.

Success.

Joletta could not quite believe it. To be able to find someone who could actually verify a detail from Violet's journal seemed a miracle. It was as if time had been made to contract upon itself, bringing the past closer. At the same time the meagerness of what they had been able to learn only pointed up how difficult it was to discover anything of importance about those long-ago events.

When she and Rone left the house, they turned in the direction of the Rialto Bridge. They had agreed to look for a place for a late lunch in the market area. They walked along in silence, past flower vendors and shops selling leather luggage, silk scarves, fans and clocks, and a thousand other temptations for tourists. The sun on the canal was blinding and the lozenges of shifting light it cast on the sides of the buildings had the sharp-edged brightness of mirror reflections. The breeze off the water was refreshing in its softness, and only slightly tainted with diesel fumes from the passing boats. There were few people on the sidewalk, as most Italians paused for their long meal and an hour or two of rest. Joletta and Rone moved along in silence, their urgency gone now that they had reached their objective for the day.

"You know," Joletta said suddenly, "I'm not sure there's any point in going on with this. It's not as if somebody is going to produce a piece of yellowed paper and say, 'Here, here's the formula your great-grandmother left here a hundred years ago because she knew you'd be along for it about now.' "

Rone glanced at her. "I thought you were looking for inspiration, something to help decipher a code that might be in the journal."

"Yes, and maybe I was only fooling myself. Maybe there's no chance of ever making sense of it."

"But think what a great thing it will be if you do. And even if you don't, are you any worse off than you were in New Orleans?"

"That's easy to say, but it's your time being wasted, too," she pointed out.

"If I don't care, I don't see why you should."

"Right, I almost forgot," she said in stringent tones. "If I find something, you want to be around."

He gave her a direct look. "Maybe I want to be around anyway."

"Don't!" she said sharply. "You don't have to say things like that."

"I know," he answered. "On the other hand, I don't have to stop, either."

She gave him a quick look, but sidestepped the issue, saying instead, "What I'm trying to tell you is that I'm thinking of quitting. I may try to see this garden, since the tour group is going to Florence anyway. Then again, I may just stick with the group. Two days in Tuscany, on to Rome for three days, and that's it; I head for home."

"Fine."

She gave him an exasperated look. "What do you mean, 'Fine'? I'm saying that you can go on about your business now."

"We've been through this already. You're stuck with me to the bitter end."

"Somehow I don't remember agreeing."

His attention seemed to be on a flower stall just ahead of them as he said, "Maybe I'm enjoying the whole thing."

"And maybe," she said deliberately, "I'd like to enjoy what's left of my trip."

He was silent a long moment. Finally he said, "Sorry, but it seems more important that you get home in one piece."

"So you intend to make certain that I'm miserable."

He gave her a slow smile. "That wasn't my intention, no."

There was an undercurrent in his words that she did not like. She stared at him, at the firm planes of his face and the opaque look in his dark blue eyes. She could make nothing of his expression, however. Her eyes narrowing, she said, "Look—"

"Later, if you don't mind. I'm starving, and besides, I need to make a phone call. We'll find a restaurant and argue while we eat."

He turned and moved on as he spoke. She stared after him a long moment while she thought strongly about turning and walking away in the opposite direction. Let him catch up with her if he could. And yet, escaping him did not, somehow, seem as satisfactory as telling him what she thought of his high-handed tactics. Compressing her lips in a firm line, she stalked after him.

They returned to the hotel after lunch. It was a free afternoon. Since they would be leaving for Florence early on the following day, however, Joletta intended to repack her suitcase and, just possibly, take a nap.

It chafed her to have him still at her side, but she couldn't think what to do about it. There was nowhere to run, no way to break away from him. What troubled her more, at the moment, was wondering what he was going to do in their small hotel room while she commandeered the bed.

As they walked toward the hotel desk to pick up the key, a couple rose from a bench further along the hallway.

"Finally!" Natalie said in laughing exasperation. "Caesar and I have gotten to be old friends while we waited for you two. We had about given you up."

"Nevertheless," the Italian added with his warm smile, "it's a pleasure to see you at last. The blue color you wear, Signorina Joletta, is *perfetto*, perfect for you."

Joletta saw Natalie give Caesar a glance that was both amused and sardonic. They were standing very close together, their shoulders almost touching, and there was an air about them of interrupted discussion. Joletta glanced at Rone. He was watching them also, and the look on his face could only be described as wary.

"Did we forget an appointment?" Joletta asked.

"No, no," Caesar answered. "I came to the hotel with an idea for a drive and met your cousin, who was waiting. We had a long lunch; this is Italy, so there was no problem. But it would have been better if we could all have gone to see the villas of the River Brenta together."

"Villas?"

"A little like the châteaus of the Loire Valley, you understand. They are country retreats built by the old Venetians to get away from the damp and play at farming with the profits made from sea ventures. Few tourists find them, which is a great pity."

"We could still go," Natalie said. "It's only twenty miles, not much of a drive. Caesar was telling me about a wonderful trattoria he knows in a town called Mira. We might wind up there for dinner."

"No, I don't think so," Rone said, taking Joletta's arm. "We have other plans."

"What other plans?" Joletta asked as, with deliberate movements, she removed her elbow from his grasp.

Natalie's gaze moved quickly from Rone's frown to Joletta's flushed face. Her voice was sharp as she said, "You have to eat somewhere."

"Not in a crowd," Rone said.

Joletta turned a chill stare in his direction. That he would try to arrange her time after everything that had happened was beyond belief. "I think," she said distinctly, "that this trattoria sounds interesting."

"You don't know the first thing about it," Rone said in clipped tones.

Caesar struck in quickly: "It's the best in the region, this I promise."

"Don't be ridiculous, Rone," Natalie said, her voice hard. "Perhaps we should have a little talk? I think I can persuade you to see reason."

Rone stiffened before he swung his head slowly toward the other woman. His voice hard, he said, "I doubt it, Natalie; I really do. Joletta already knows who I am."

Natalie's eyelids flickered. She looked from him to Joletta once more, her gaze lingering on his stance, the way he shielded Joletta both from view of the door and from direct eye contact with Caesar. Her lips twisted. "So that's the way it is?"

"That's it," Rone answered, the words abrupt.

"Does she also know," Natalie said softly, "what *good friends* we are?"

The stress she put on the words was suggestive, and was meant to be. Joletta felt the sting of distress behind her eyes. She forced a smile as she answered for herself. "He didn't tell me, but it wasn't necessary. I thought the two of you reached an understanding with amazing speed."

"Yes, indeed," Natalie drawled. "He is amazingly quick to make up his mind. You have to admire that."

"Not," Joletta answered, "when he's making up mine for me at the same time. I think the drive sounds great."

Caesar smiled with a lifted brow. "This means you will go? We can rent a boat and punt down the river; that's the best way to see the villas. But we should leave soon if we are to have the daylight."

It was not a comfortable outing.

Caesar was on his dignity with Rone. Natalie seemed annoyed with Caesar. Joletta had little to say to Natalie or Rone. Rone said nothing to anybody.

It was worth the trouble, however.

Many of the villas were quite literally Palladian, designed by Andrea Palladio himself. Classically pure of line and with perfect harmony in their proportions, they were more like palaces than villas, though their plastered facades of rich cream and gold and gray gave them a soft, airy look. The pediments and columns and arched windows glimpsed behind walls and greenery had very little of the *Arabian Nights* look so obvious in Venice.

The rowboats Caesar hired were designed for two people in each, with a pair of sweeplike oars that were used while standing, as in a gondola. Joletta was silently amused at the way Caesar maneuvered to hand her into the boat he had chosen for himself, leaving Rone to follow with Natalie.

The Italian tried to insist that Joletta remain seated while he sent the boat skimming down the river, but she refused. She felt the need for some kind of physical exertion to work off the irritation still bottled inside her. Besides, it was easier to see while standing, and much easier to avoid the pass she was afraid might come if Caesar decided to sit with her while letting the boat float along with the current.

"Ah, American women," Caesar said as he leaned on his oar in the rear of the boat, gazing with open admiration at the grace of her movements as she swung the sweep. "They can do anything, and so beautifully."

"I've seen Italian women rowing, too," Joletta pointed out.

"A few," he agreed with a grin, "but, like your cousin, most prefer that men do the work."

Joletta wondered briefly if there was some salacious undertone to that remark; with Caesar, she had discovered, there often was. She gave him a direct look, but he only met it with smiling sang-froid.

A moment later he said, "So you go on to Florence tomorrow. Such a pity to leave Venice so soon." The timbre of his voice dropped to a more caressing note. "I need not tell you, I think, *carina*, that I am at your disposal. Only speak, and I will drive you there, stay with you every moment."

"Rone wouldn't like that," she said dryly.

He flicked his fingers. "I care not even that much for what Rone likes or dislikes. It's what you want that's important."

His attitude was a refreshing change. That he had picked up on her dissatisfaction earlier and used it made no difference. An idea began to form in the back of her mind.

"You would have to get up very early," she said, a warning in her voice, though her smile was brightly quizzical.

"For you it would be no sacrifice."

"*Very* early."

"Joletta, *carina*, command me."

She glanced at the other boat that was some distance away but closing fast as Rone got the hang of the sweep oar. Keeping her voice low, she outlined what might be required. When she had finished, she asked, "Is it possible for you?"

Caesar spread his hands, letting the boat veer as it would. The look in his eyes several degrees warmer, he said, "How can you ask?"

She gave a slow nod. "Let me think about it a little more, and I'll let you know if we're on."

"Think quickly, Joletta, I can live only so long on hope," he answered in droll despair.

They had time after the river journey to visit the palatial Villa Pisani, which had been owned in succession by a doge of Venice, Napoléon I, and by the emperor's stepson, Eugène de Beauharnais. They were also able to wander through the house called *la malcontenta*, supposedly named for an erring wife who was shut away in the country to prevent indiscreet behavior. At last they made their way in the lingering twilight toward the Trattoria Nalin.

The food was everything Caesar promised, from the antipasto

of squid eggs, scampi, spider crab, and scallops to the delicate risotto and the crab fettuccine. To accompany it, they had a fine local wine, a Prosecco Conegliano, that tickled in its fresh astringency.

Because conversation with the others was still strained, Joletta and Caesar talked and laughed with each other. He paid her outrageous compliments and refilled her wineglass with practiced ease, in spite of her protests. When Rone objected to the amount she was drinking, Joletta stopped protesting and encouraged the Italian.

She came to her decision concerning the trip to Florence while ordering the dessert. Rone made one suggestion, Caesar another, and while she was making up her mind Rone ordered for her. It was a small thing, especially since he chose the gelato flavored with apricots and almonds that she was about to settle on herself. But she had had enough of having her decisions made for her, enough of having her wishes overruled.

Outside the restaurant, as they walked toward the car, she spoke to Caesar in quiet tones. The look he gave her was exultant.

It was late when they reached Venice again. Joletta and Rone parted company with Caesar and Natalie at the quay. At the hotel desk she asked for her key. Rone stood aside, waiting. She gave him a quick, warning glance, but said nothing until they had mounted the stairs and were outside her room.

"I thought," she said as she fitted her key into the lock, "that you would have asked for your own room key."

"I couldn't," he said evenly. "I turned it in, and they've already filled my room."

"You did check then?"

"Did you think I wouldn't?" he said, the words even.

She hadn't been sure. Just as she wasn't sure at that moment whether he was telling the truth.

She took a deep breath. "You know—"

"I know," he said abruptly. "You don't want me in your room, and you would like me to leave. I'm not going to do that. But I don't intend to entertain the rest of the hotel with the argument over it."

He reached above her head to push open the door she had unlocked. Stepping around her, he entered the room.

Joletta could stand in the hall or go join him. She moved after him into the darkened room. The door swung shut, latching behind them.

She noticed the smell even as she felt for the light switch. Spicy, fresh, it was a dense wave of fragrance reaching out of the darkness.

She pressed the button under her fingers, and the room sprang into brightness.

The tiny, old-fashioned carnations known as clove pinks were everywhere, hundreds of them massed in vases sitting on every available surface. Peach pink and bloodred, striped and white, their small, tattered-edge blossoms shed their scent on the air until the night was dizzy with the sweetness of it.

"What in the world?" she said in frowning amazement.

"Carnations. I saw them at the Rialto market and made arrangements."

"The phone call."

He agreed. "They are supposed to mean Blighted Love, or something like that according to the journal." His voice was abrupt, shaded with something near embarrassment.

"Alas My Poor Heart," she said in hollow recognition.

"Exactly."

It was absurd of her to allow herself to be affected by such an obvious appeal to sentimentality. Yet the generosity of the gesture, and the understanding of her needs and thought processes shown by it, indicated a level of awareness about her that was astounding. And disarming.

"What are you trying to do?" she asked quietly.

"Say I'm sorry, that I didn't mean to hurt you. Find out if there's some way we can try again."

"At least long enough for you to finish reading the journal?"

He took a harsh breath and let it out slowly. "I don't care if I never see the journal again."

"That's good," she said soberly.

She expected to see irritation in his face. There was nothing except iron determination. She moved toward a chair, where she slipped the strap of her shoulder bag down her arm and let it drop onto the seat.

"I love you, Joletta," he said, his voice low and husky.

"Don't!" she said sharply without looking at him, then added more quietly, "Please. Just don't."

"I know I've given you no reason to believe me, but it's important to me to tell you."

"It's certainly convenient that you discovered it just now," she replied, her voice steady.

"I've known it for a long time, since Bath at least, though it began before that, possibly even that night in New Orleans. It just didn't seem right to say it when I wasn't being honest with you. It would have been carrying false pretenses a little too far."

"Too bad you didn't feel like that about climbing into my bed."

"For that," he said, "I have no regrets. It seemed likely to be all I would ever have."

She really wanted to believe him; that was the worst of it. She couldn't. He had used her, and would continue if she let him. She wouldn't. Not again.

No doubt he thought there was still some chance she might manage to wring the formula from the journal and wanted to be around if it happened. When that time came, if it did, that would be the end of it; he would have what he wanted, and he would be gone. Or if she failed, if when this trip was over she had nothing to show for it, he would have no reason to stay. Either way she would lose.

It was this she couldn't face, as much as his lies told to please her.

Everyone always left her. Her mother and father, her fiancé. Even Mimi. But not this time.

This time it was she who would leave.

She moved to the bedside table, where several vases of the small carnations sat. Leaning to breathe deep of their rich scent, she allowed the cool petals to touch her eyelids, her chin, her mouth. With wine and fragrance simmering in her veins, she thought that, just possibly, Rone deserved at least a parting gift, something from her to remember later, to take away the sting of being abandoned.

"Joletta," he said, a pleading note in his voice.

She needed time to think, time to be sure this was what she wanted. Pure compassion, misplaced desire, or guilty sacrifice, there were all these things in the impulse rising steadily inside her. There was more, she knew, but she would not acknowledge it.

She wanted a last night with him, a last time in the security of his arms. Perhaps she needed a farewell after all, for herself. Who would ever know? Who would care? Except her.

He might think, when she surrendered, that he had won, but what of it? She would know the truth.

And so would he, soon enough.

Her voice not quite even, she said, "The luggage will have to be put out before we go to bed for collection early in the morning. I still have to repack. I think I'll shower first, if you don't mind."

He watched her for long seconds before he turned away with an almost inaudible sigh. "No," he answered, "I don't mind."

The smile that touched her mouth as she sent him a glance from the corners of her eyes was wry and fleeting, but tender.

Joletta did not take long in the bathroom. While Rone took his turn she laid out the slacks and shirt she meant to wear next day, set her packed suitcase outside the door, and stuffed the things she would be carrying with her down inside her big shoulder bag. She patted the bulky purse to be sure the journal was still where it should be; she had hardly thought about it all day. The feel of a sharp corner reassured her that all was well.

Wearing only a nightgown of much-washed white cotton embroidered in white around a design of open cutwork flowers, she moved to inhale the scent of the carnations once more. They really were delicious. She reached to cup a single blossom in her palm. Lifting it from the vase, she took it with her as she turned out the light, then moved to slip between the sheets.

When Rone emerged from the bathroom a few minutes later, she turned her head. He was tall and broad where he stood framed in the doorway before he turned out the light. She watched him in the dimness as he moved around the foot of the bed to the opposite side. The width of his shoulders and shape of his head were silhouetted against the window as he climbed in beside her. She waited, not quite patiently, while he stretched out and settled onto his back.

She could feel the uneven pumping of her heart in her chest, like a ball bounced by a clumsy toddler. Heat moved over her in waves, and the palms of her hands itched with the dampness collecting there. It was, she discovered, terrifying to become a temptress, nearly as terrifying as it was exciting.

Easing to her side, she supported herself on her bent elbow while she reached out to draw the carnation she held in her fingers across Rone's lips.

He snatched at the flower in a swift reflex, as if he thought it might be some invading insect. His movement stilled abruptly.

"What are you doing?" he asked in stifled tones.

"Shh," she said.

Tugging the carnation free, she touched his mouth once more, outlining its shape, before trailing the ragged petals down the strong jut of his chin and along the turn of his neck. She dipped it into the hollow between his collarbone, then brushed slowly back and forth through the glinting hair on his chest to the flat disks of his paps. As she touched one, teasing it to a nub of firmness, he turned his head toward her in the darkness.

"Joletta?" he whispered in entreaty.

She did not answer.

Leaving the carnation lying on his breastbone, she moved closer and leaned to touch the wet heat of her tongue to his tightened pap. She traced its circumference, applied adhesion, nibbled gently, then moved to the other one.

He said not a word as he reached for her, circling her body with his arms as he held her close, searching out the warm and sensitive curves of her body through the soft, thin cotton, finding areas of delicate sensation she had hardly known existed.

She tasted him without haste, and with rich delight growing inside as she felt the increased depth of his breathing that matched her own.

Blindly then, she sought the warm, chiseled shape of his mouth. Her soft lips molded to his as she traced the edges of his teeth and gently eased deeper to entice his response. Sweetly, generously, he gave it, twining his tongue with hers, following her lead.

He drew her closer, until the lower part of her body was pressed against the unyielding length of his thigh. Holding her there, he smoothed the slender concave of her waist, ran his fingers with exquisite care over the roundness of her hips, and drew the cotton of her gown tight to outline the shape. He smoothed his hand over that gentle curve before he began to inch the gown higher.

Joletta lifted her knee across his body, allowing access to his delicately probing touch. The heat that flushed her skin spiraled deep inside, coalescing in the lower part of her body. A soft sound left her as he sought and found its center. Molten inside with desire, she tasted the corners of his mouth and trailed a line of kisses across the hard plane of his face to his ear. She tasted the lobe, then in a rush of ecstasy, buried her face in his neck.

Shifting his attention, Rone cupped the fullness of her breasts in his hands, flicking the tender nipples with his thumbs, so the firestorm of sensation within her became nearly unbearable in its intensity.

Still, there was no hurry. Grasping at control, Joletta spread one hand to clutch at the muscled hardness of his shoulder before brushing lower to find and put aside the carnation that scented his chest. Her fingers trembled as she reached lower still, pushing away the sheet that covered him, slipping her hand under the loose waistband of his pajamas. Seeking to return the pleasure he was giving her, she increased her own a hundredfold.

When nerves and tissues and shivering minds could stand no more, he drew her on top of him. She lay for long moments with the firm contours of her breasts pressed to his chest and the surface of her belly flat against him while their hearts jarred in double rhythm.

Finally she rose above him with the glide of heat-oiled muscles and took him inside her in a slow, liquid slide.

Gently, they rode, gathering ease, gathering force, gathering speed. He moved with her, matching her rhythm, allowing her to set depth and pace while he held himself in stringent check.

Their breathing increased. Moisture dewed their skin. The clean scent of her hair and the warmth of their bodies mingled with the scent of clove carnations, mounting to their brains like an aphrodisiac. Joletta felt light, yet powerful, filled with grace and boundless caring, fecund and daring and eternally female.

Then she felt the contraction of her heart, her loins, her very soul. The silent magic burst like a firestorm inside her.

He heaved himself up, maintaining the contact as he swung her to her back among the rumpled sheets. He lowered himself over her, covering her with his welcome weight, plunging deep into the vital strength of her body. And once more he began to move.

Joletta held nothing back. She strove with him, breath for gasping breath, muscle against quivering muscle. The magic returned. Feeling its hot, tumbling grip, they clung, gasping, while they let it take them.

It was only later that Joletta, curled in the shelter of Rone's arms and staring wide-eyed into the dark, remembered that this loving was supposed to be a farewell. It had not, somehow, turned out as she had planned.

She thought of staying where she was, as she was, for as long as she was permitted. She considered accepting whatever pretense of love Rone cared to make.

It might be that the pretending could be made real, or at least that it could be enough.

No.

She couldn't do it. Her choice had been made, and bitter or not, she would follow it through. To fail would be to let Aunt Estelle and Natalie—and Rone—win by default. It would certainly mean discarding something she was beginning to realize was just as important, and that was her self-respect.

She would go. She must.

It was early when she woke; the gray light beyond the window was barely touched with gold. The church bells had not yet begun to ring. As she slid out of bed Rone stirred and stretched out his hand after her. If he woke, however, he refrained from making her feel guilty by letting her know it.

The bells began to clang as she finished dressing. She dragged her hairbrush through her hair a final time and fastened it back with a pair of bone barrettes. Moving into the bedroom, she crossed to the chair to push her brush into her shoulder bag, then picked up the heavy purse.

Rone was lying on his back with his hands clasped behind his head. His firm lips curved in a smile as he turned toward her. As his gaze drifted over her, settling on the shoulder bag, he said, "Where are you going so early?"

"There are a couple of female-type things I need. I'll only be a minute."

"There won't be any shops open," he pointed out.

His hair was tousled, his jawline shaded with beard stubble, and his eyes heavy with sleep. Perhaps it was the dark concern in his eyes, but he had never looked so fine.

Joletta swallowed on an obstruction in her throat before she said, "Maybe the concierge can help, then. Be right back."

She didn't wait for a reply, did not linger at all. She didn't kiss him, didn't say good-bye.

She was strong.

She went out the door and closed it behind her.

She made it as far as the stairs before the tears crowding into her eyes blurred her vision too much to see.

Chapter 20

Caesar sent his red Alfa Romeo hurtling toward Florence with all the élan of the chariot drivers whose blood ran in his veins. Joletta made certain that her seat belt was tight over her lap, then concentrated on trying not to clutch at the dashboard any more often than was absolutely necessary.

Her trepidation amused the Italian, she thought, and drove him to greater recklessness to prove to her that he was in complete control of the car. She didn't appreciate it, though she kept her protests to herself. She was grateful for his offer to drive her. More than that, she didn't have the energy or heart to argue just now.

She debated whether talking to him would be a dangerous distraction, or one likely to make him slow down in order to pay attention to her. She decided to chance it, mostly because she did not care for her own dismal thoughts. The place to start seemed to be with normal questions that had somehow never come up between them.

"Where do I live now?" he repeated, his smile expansive. "In Venice, most of the time, sometimes in Rome or on Capri. Paris, often. Or maybe Nice."

"Yes, but where is your home?"

"Ah, that. A village twenty miles from Venice; my mother and father still live there."

"You don't have a permanent residence? An apartment, maybe?"

"No, why should I?"

She stared at him in puzzlement. "But I thought you said you were from Venice. Where were you staying there?"

"I say I am from Venice and people say, yes, of course; everyone knows Venice. It's easier." He shrugged. "These last days I am at the Hotel Cipriani."

It was the same grand hotel where Natalie had been staying. Joletta felt an instant of disquiet, but pushed it away. "I don't think I ever heard you say what you do for a living."

"This and that, buying and selling. I was once a waiter on a cruise ship. It was long hours, hard work, but valuable. I learned to speak English, French, Spanish, German, a little Japanese, and I met many lovely ladies of wealth, widows, divorced ladies traveling alone."

She wondered if he was trying to tell her what she thought. She studied him with wide eyes, noticing once more the sleekness of his appearance, his careful grooming; the cream silk shirt he wore this morning, the Rolex on one wrist, and his heavy gold bracelet on the other.

"Did you think," he said with a lifted brow, "that I was a rich man because I drive this car? I am flattered, but no. At least not yet."

"You intend to be." Her voice was flat as she spoke.

"I work hard to make it so." He paused, then added in softer tones and with a warm glance from under his lashes, "But it isn't often that I get to do what I prefer with a lady who is as beautiful as you."

It was fine to hear, but she no longer believed a word of it. "You mean," she said slowly, "that you live by—making yourself useful to wealthy women."

"Joletta! I am insulted. I have investments, I make deals. I am no gigolo."

"No?"

"I am my own man. I am always myself."

"But what you do involves a certain willingness to be nice to—people?"

He gave her an earnest look. "There is always something pleasant that can be said to a woman; they are each beautiful in their own way."

"Are they?" she asked, her voice neutral. All that charm, all the blatant flattery and caressing attention. Just an act. She should have known.

"I would never say anything that was not so. I swear this to you, especially to you."

She smiled a little, but the look in her eyes was pensive. He had met her in Paris, then taken the trouble to follow her movements, even trailing her in his car as she neared Venice. Had that really been for his own reasons, or was there something else behind it?

She wished she knew, wished there was some way to be sure. There was so much that might depend on knowing.

The red and gold of the Apennine hills rose up to meet them. Gentle mountains, they rolled away on either side of the highway with their coating of gray-green olive trees, wildflowers, and aromatic herbs. As they neared Florence they passed farmhouses and orchards and vineyards without number, and also nurseries, where, along with the usual trees and plants being offered for sale, there were weather-beaten columns and gigantic flower urns of stone looking for all the world like relics from some old Roman garden.

They stopped at an autogrill for coffee and pastry. A silver Fiat with dark-tinted windows turned in after them, though it swung quickly around behind the building to park out of sight. Joletta had noticed the car in her side mirror for the last several kilometers. As she sat waiting at a table while Caesar stood in line to pay for their food and drink, then took the receipt to the counter to be served, she watched for the occupants to come inside. No one entered from that direction.

She mentioned the car to Caesar, but he shrugged it off. "Perhaps they had their own coffee and only needed a place to stop," he said, "or else there was a baby who needed a clean diaper. Shall I go see?"

"No, no," she answered. "You're probably right."

He propped his elbow on the table, fingering his chin with his thumb and forefinger. "Are you then an American spy?" he suggested with humor in his dark eyes. "If you are being followed, maybe you would like me to outrun this Fiat?"

"No, thanks," she said in haste. "That will be quite all right."

"I was afraid it might be. But I was only joking; your cousin, you know, mentioned to me that you are in search of a formula of some kind. I am assuming this is why we go to Firenze, Florence. You could have come on the bus, so I must guess there is somewhere you want to be driven besides your hotel. I am right?"

When she made no immediate answer, he went on. "It may be
that I should not ask; still, I am curious. And I must know sometime, if I am to take you."

It was not really fair to keep him in the dark. At the same time
she wasn't sure it was wise to tell him too much. The day before
she might have thought little of it. Today things were different, and
so was she.

She wished she knew a little more about this garden and the
place near Florence where it was located. She wondered, for instance, if it was isolated, or if the house nearby was occupied year
round. She had been so excited about finding it, and discovering
how to reach it, that she had not thought to ask.

After coming this far, however, it was nearly impossible to go
back. Anyway, she didn't think she could stand to bypass the opportunity in her grasp by going to the hotel and waiting for another
time. Inside her was a slow-building revulsion for taking the safe
way. That was, just possibly, what had been wrong with her life up
to now.

Turning to her shoulder bag, she took from it the map drawn
by the elderly man in Venice. She spread it out on the table as she
began to explain where it was she wanted to go, and why.

The silver Fiat was behind them when they left the autogrill. It
kept well back, but maintained the same pace, passing when they
passed, slowing when they slowed.

Outside Florence, they ran into a traffic jam caused by a combination of roadwork and an accident. They inched forward in the
midst of four lanes of cars trying to merge into a single line. Enterprising vendors of newspapers and razors, cold drinks, chewing
gum, and breath mints weaved among the stalled cars with a reckless
disregard for life and limb, considering the racing engines and blast-
ing horns all around them. Caesar was impatient, muttering and
stretching his neck to look, slamming his hand on the horn himself
whenever a driver threatened to invade the small area that was his
minimum distance from the car in front of them.

Once, the driver of a vehicle several lengths ahead nudged the
back bumper of the car in front of him. Men piled out of both
automobiles. There was a great deal of shouting and fist waving and
rude gestures. Then as traffic began to inch forward again everyone
wheeled around as at a signal and jumped back into their cars with
a great slamming of doors.

As entertaining as it was as a spectacle, however, the greatest benefit of the traffic jam was that it caught the Fiat behind them and held it back. When traffic finally cleared, and the Alfa Romeo began to pick up speed, there was no sign of the silver car.

The garden they sought might have been outside Florence in Violet's day, but the city had since reached out to embrace it and the farming village near where it had stood. Signora Perrino, the middle-aged lady who owned the modern villa built against it, had been warned of their coming. She met them at the door, a motherly woman with soft, well-cut dark hair, dressed for casual comfort in mulberry linen. She offered them the hospitality of her home, including a luncheon of crown roast of pork with *panzanella*, or bread salad, and an earthenware pitcher of chianti classico.

Joletta had not realized it was so near the noon hour, or she would have waited until a later time. The last thing she wanted was to impose on a stranger, or to sit trying to make conversation with someone she hardly knew. It was impossible to refuse, however. All she could do was make a mental note to send flowers, as required by Italian social custom, later.

The meal was served in the walled garden, which had been made into a terrace adjoining the new villa by the addition of a flight of wide stone steps leading from a wall of glass doors. A rustic air had been maintained, however, for the table was of weathered wood placed on a floor of old mosaic tiles under an arbor shaded by an ancient grapevine with a stalk as thick as a tree trunk. It was so obviously the spot in the garden that Violet and Allain had favored, the place where they had made love long ago, that Joletta was enchanted.

From her seat at the table, she could look out over the enclosure with its rambling roses, its geometric beds, and central fountain. While Caesar kept their hostess entertained with an effortless stream of pleasantries, she could breathe the scent of the rose blossoms and sun-warmed herbs, listen to the splashing tinkle of the fountain and the mumbling undertone of bees.

Sitting there, visualizing the way it had once been, Joletta felt a bountiful peace flowing around her. It almost seemed she could hear the low voices of Violet and her Allain, nearly see them there in the shadow of the olive tree where a gate gave access to the vineyards and the stables, and where Giovanni had once gone in and out performing his tasks.

Only there was no gate now, just a gate-shaped arch of stone in the wall where one had once been.

She shook her head. Imagination. She didn't know hers was so vivid.

But as she studied the walled space she could see what Violet had done. She had re-created this garden in New Orleans. She had built a memorial to love, and possibly to her lover, in the courtyard of her house.

"It gives me much pleasure to have you here, signorina," their hostess said, raising her voice a little as she addressed Joletta. "I have been fascinated all my life by the tragedy which occurred; there were members of my family who worked here at that time, you see. I have often wondered what became of the American woman who was at the heart of the story, and if those descended of her line in the States knew what took place in Italy. And then there is something that I—"

Somewhere inside the villa, a bell rang. Their hostess broke off, frowning. She was expecting no other guests, she said. After a few moments a fresh-faced maid, wearing a calf-length black dress with Joy Walkers, came out to confer with her mistress. Signora Perrino excused herself and rose to enter the house.

Caesar sat drinking his wine, his gaze resting on Joletta while the grapevine overhead cast shifting leaf patterns across the bronze skin of his face. He leaned forward to set down his glass, reaching at the same time for her hand. Holding it in both of his, he said, "What were you thinking of just now, before Signora Perrino spoke to you? You looked quite different, somehow, very sweet and mysterious, as if you had a secret."

"I was thinking of my great-grandmother," she said. It was the truth, but not quite the whole truth. It was impossible to say more, however.

"She must have been quite a lady. She loved an Italian, did she not?"

He held her gaze with his own dark, penetrating eyes as he lifted her fingers to his mouth. At the last moment he turned her hand to expose her palm. His lips were warm and smooth, and the tip of his tongue, as it flicked lightly over the sensitive surface, sent a small jolt of sensation along her arm to her shoulder.

"My, my," Natalie said in acid tones as she came to a halt in the doorway through which their hostess had disappeared. "Dear Caesar, I don't think I told you to be that charming to my cousin."

Caesar lifted his head while a flush rose under his skin. The look he gave Natalie was dark with resentment.

Joletta removed her hand from the Italian's tight grasp. As he turned a glance of remorse and pleading upon her, she said quietly, "Someone needing to change a baby diaper?"

Natalie laughed. "Did Caesar really say that? But I was afraid you might have seen us, since Rone was so bent on staying close. I'll never have another word to say about Italian drivers; Rone was like a maniac, especially when we reached the traffic jam outside town."

Joletta's cousin was not alone. Rone's tall form filled the doorway behind her. Joletta refused to look at him, though she had known from the first that he was there.

Their hostess hovered in the background beyond the other two with a perplexed expression on her face, as if she was wondering about the sudden interest in her garden.

"Too bad Rone didn't think to copy the map," Joletta said without inflection.

Natalie tossed her hair back away from her face. "He thought of it, but there was no time, or so he said. Luckily he has a good memory for detail."

Joletta risked meeting Rone's dark gaze then. It was grim and watchful. If he felt the slightest flicker of personal interest in what was taking place, he gave no sign.

They were all against her. There was not one of them who had her same interests and concerns, not one who did not want something from her. The truth of it was like a many-edged barb thrust inside her. There was no way to be rid of it without making the damage worse.

She turned back to her cousin. "You must have been glad to hear from at least one of your accomplices."

"Yes, well, but there would have been no need for them if you had just cooperated," Natalie complained. "I don't know why you have to be so disagreeable. Actually, they have both been a disappointment. I think Rone only let me come along with him because it was the only way I would tell him who you were with and where you were going."

"Extortion, Natalie, as well as theft and burglary?"

"Theft and what? I don't know what you're talking about."

Joletta eyed the other woman without expression. "All right, if that's the way you want to play it. I hate to give you the bad news after you went to so much trouble. The fact is, there's nothing here."

"Nothing?"

The letdown in Natalie's face was almost comical. Joletta waved at the garden in front of them as she said, "You have my notes. What do you see?"

Natalie put her hands on her hips while her thinly arched brows met over her nose. "Make sense, Joletta; I don't have anything and never did."

"Oh, come off it," Joletta said, rising to her feet and moving away from the table. "If you and Aunt Estelle didn't send somebody to steal my carryon and ransack my room, who did?"

"How should I know? All I've been doing is keeping track of you, and it hasn't been easy. I thought that somehow or other we could work this out."

Joletta didn't know whether to believe her or not. She sounded sincere, but then she had always been good at that.

Was it possible that Aunt Estelle had acted without her daughter's knowledge? She certainly had the strength of will, but whether she had the contacts or the sheer greed was hard to say. It might be that she was keeping the knowledge of it from her children in order to safeguard them. She had always been a protective mother, the kind who never admitted that her children could do wrong.

Or perhaps it was Rone who had paid someone to do those things. To discover someone in her room while he was with her would certainly be a way of directing suspicion away from himself.

There was still his mother, that shadowy woman known only by her publicity photos, Lara Camors. Was she the ruthless businesswoman her son claimed? Or had that all been a sham, a story concocted to give Rone an excuse for tracking her.

It made no great difference either way. Her part in the search for Violet's past and her formula was at an end.

"I believe," she said slowly, "that we have imposed on Signora Perrino long enough. We had better go."

"I'll drive you to the hotel," Rone said.

"She came with me," Caesar interrupted, putting his hands on his hips.

Rone gave him a hard look. "You can take Natalie back to Venice."

"Venice?" Natalie exclaimed. "But I don't want to go. Joletta and I have to talk. We have to decide—"

"Another time," Rone said.

Natalie narrowed her eyes as she stared at him. "Now, you look here, Rone Adamson. I've about had enough of you and your high-handed ways—"

But Rone wasn't listening. He turned toward Joletta as he said, "Coming?"

To be alone with Rone or with Caesar? Joletta was not sure which one she wanted least. Or which choice would take more courage.

"Coming," she said quietly, and moved to Rone's side. She met Caesar's dark gaze for a brief moment. His lips curved in a fatalistic smile and he sighed before he lifted his shoulders in a shrug.

Joletta thanked Signora Perrino for the meal, apologized for their abrupt departure, and promised to send her the little she knew about the death of the widow in Venice. With that done, she turned to go.

She looked back, however, just before she left the garden. The sun still shone and the leaf shadows still danced on the ancient tiles. The bees hovered among the herb flowers and the leaves of the old olive tree sparkled like silver. The grass, fine and dark green, bent with the spring wind, ruffling as at the tread of light footsteps. And a single, perfect blossom of the huge old red rose shattered, so the petals fell, spinning, whispering, to lie like drops of blood on the ground.

Joletta turned quickly and walked away.

The first thing she noticed, when they reached the street-side parking, was the car Rone was driving. It was a tan Volvo.

She had assumed the silver Fiat was his, a rental car picked up at the quay in Venice as the Volvo must have been.

More than likely, whoever was in the Fiat had not been follow-ing her at all. There was nothing strange about another car keeping the same pace over the relatively short distance from Venice to Flor-ence, especially since it had dropped behind after the traffic jam.

Rone did not speak until he had pulled up before the hotel in Florence. He turned to her then. "Tell me just one thing," he said, his voice harsh in its intensity. "Did the carnation you left on my pillow mean something, or was it just an impulse, or a joke."

She had expected many things, but not this. Panic surged through her as she searched for an answer that would not leave her exposed to more pain. The truth was always good, but she wasn't sure what that was at the moment.

"I don't know," she said finally as she stared ahead of her through the windshield. "I'm not Violet; I'm just a modern woman who prefers things nice and simple. Symbols are nice, but plain words and actions are better."

He thought that over. "Meaning?"

"I don't mean anything," she said, her voice rising. "I would just like to forget the whole thing. I would like to finish my trip, and then go home and get on with my life."

"It isn't going to happen," he said in low certainty, "even if I would let it, which I won't."

"Why not? I give up; I'm not even going to think about the perfume anymore."

"No one's going to believe it."

"Watch me," she said.

"I intend to," he answered, his voice grim. He hesitated, then went on. "But not, this time, at such close quarters. I had in mind a room next door."

She turned her head to meet his gaze without evasion. "Not adjoining."

"No."

"Good," she said under her breath. But it was not, in her mind, an agreement of any kind.

Almost immediately after she had checked into her room in the hotel, she left it again. She had no real plans, no special purpose; it was just that she was determined not to be kept under supervision and thought Rone would not expect her to make another move so soon.

It was pleasant to walk around the old city on her own, to visit the cathedral and the old squares, to climb steps to see the views, and to pay her fee for the privilege of standing and staring at Michelangelo's *David*.

She bought a jacket with a wide, flowing collar, one made of incredibly soft and lightweight leather of the kind used for the mild winters of Sicily and Capri. It should be just right for New Orleans. She found a pair of wonderful hoop earrings of eighteen-karat gold and several gilded leather comb cases as souvenirs for friends.

The exercise, solitude, and self-indulgence was what she had needed. Regardless, she still had to return to the hotel.

The first person she saw as she neared it was her aunt Estelle.

She almost didn't recognize her in her acid-green culottes with a braided jacket, Italian sandals, and a jaunty hat with an attached scarf that covered her hair. There were three other people with her, sitting at a table at a sidewalk café next door to the hotel. Timothy pushed awkwardly to his feet, smiling and waving at Joletta, resuming his seat only after she started in their direction. Natalie, next to her brother, looked self-conscious and a little worried. The fourth person was another older woman with beautifully styled white hair, perfect makeup including false eyelashes, and a stylish pearl-gray suit. There was in her smoky blue eyes an expression that was definitely measuring as she watched Joletta's reluctant approach.

"Joletta, dear," Aunt Estelle said, "here is someone I think it would be worthwhile for you to meet." She turned to the white-haired woman beside her. "Lara, my niece whom I've told you so much about. Joletta, this is Lara Camors."

Rone's mother. The owner of Camors Cosmetics.

The older woman smiled with an odd twist to her lips as they exchanged greetings. "So you're Joletta," she said. "I might have guessed."

Joletta looked inquiringly at the other woman.

"I had Rone's description, of course," Lara Camors said. "But you also have much the same style as Rone's grandmother who brought him up—his father's mother. Elegant, sensible, but with soft edges."

"Thank you—I think," Joletta said.

Aunt Estelle claimed Joletta's attention, demanding that she sit down, pressing a glass of wine upon her as she ordered another for herself.

"Natalie tells me," Joletta's aunt said as soon as the waiter had left them, "that she hasn't been able to really talk to you since she caught up with you. I thought it was time we remedied that."

"If you and Mrs. Camors came all this way for that reason, you could have saved yourself the trouble."

"She did say that you claim to have no leads on the perfume, but I find that hard to believe. You wouldn't have come, wouldn't have been visiting that woman here in Florence, unless there was a purpose."

"Did it ever occur to you, Aunt Estelle, that I might have other things on my mind?"

Timothy, lifting his beer to drink, nearly overturned it as he put it down again. Wiping at the spill with the edge of his hand, he said, "Be fair, Joletta. You know we're in the dark here, that we haven't had a chance to see this diary."

"Of course she knows," Lara Camors said, entering the discussion unexpectedly. "She's just being obstructive because you are all ganging up on her."

Joletta hardly knew whether to be flattered or incensed at this too accurate description. She turned a look of appraisal on Rone's mother.

The woman's hands, resting delicately on the rim of the wine-glass in front of her, were soft and exquisitely groomed, with oval nails painted a neutral color with only a hint of rose. Her facial skin was fine and unblemished, though with a network of tiny lines around the eyes. The expression in those eyes was understanding, but shrewd.

Lara Camors went on after a moment. "Your aunt was concerned to hear that you have been having trouble, stolen bags, break-ins, and so on. So was I, for that matter."

Joletta, returning the other woman's scrutiny with a steady gaze, said, "Your son has been taking care of me."

"So I understand from Natalie," Mrs. Camors said, her smile unperturbed. "I hope you have been getting on well with Rone? He can be extremely annoying at times."

"We've managed."

Rone's mother acknowledged that bare comment with only a faint quiver of her lashes. "As difficult as he can be, however, he is often right about things. He suggested, when this venture first came up, that there should be some way for all parties in this situation to reach an agreement. He has since convinced me, in a number of urgent transatlantic phone calls, that it would be wrong to negotiate with any one family member. I'm here to see if we can't discover some equitable settlement."

Joletta saw Aunt Estelle and Natalie exchange a long look. Judging from their faces, the things Lara Camors had just said came as an unpleasant surprise. Timothy glanced at his mother with a puckered frown between his brows.

Joletta said to Lara Camors, "But there's really no point, is there?"

"I refuse to believe that the formula to a perfume that has been made in a single shop in New Orleans for well over a hundred years can be lost. Businesses are simply not run that way." The older woman's tone was firm.

"Mimi's was," Aunt Estelle said. "But are you saying that you don't want the perfume, regardless of the report from the lab, unless Joletta is involved?"

"According to my legal department, I must have the consent of all living heirs of Mimi Fossier if I am to have complete and unrestricted use of this formula when it is finally presented. In that case, Estelle, I suppose the answer to your question is yes. But before we go that far, the background of the perfume must be documented. Without its colorful past, it's simply another nice scent. And Camors has enough perfumes of that kind already."

Joletta lifted her chin. "I have to tell you that I prefer to keep the perfume for the shop in New Orleans."

"Do you indeed? Now why?" Lara Camors said.

"Pride, tradition, the challenge of it," she answered.

"Oh, those," the older woman said with a knowing smile.

"You do realize that we're talking millions here, don't you?" Natalie asked as she looked at Joletta with an arched brow.

"I realize."

"If you are sitting on that journal, keeping it and everything we need to know from it to yourself, I—I'll kill you, cousin or no cousin." The other girl turned to Lara Camors with caustic amusement in her face. "Come to think of it, that's not a bad idea, since Mother is Joletta's next of kin under Louisiana's lovely inheritance laws. It would make matters so much easier, don't you think?"

The older woman looked blank for an instant before she got the joke. She didn't laugh, however, nor did anyone else.

Chapter 21

I wait.

I have waited through the last days of the fall, through the grape harvest and the grain harvest, and the faded, dreary days when the earth itself seems worn-out and ready for rest. I cannot believe that my dear Allain will not return for me. I will not believe that he can stay away.

This autumn, men have been dying in the Crimea at places that are mere names on a map as the allied sovereigns of England, France, Prussia, and Austria join battle at last to try to curb the ambitions of Czar Nicholas. I pity the poor soldiers of both sides, sent to die so far from home and family, but it is a surface sympathy only. I pity myself more. Yet, wishing to have faith in my love, I despise the weakness.

Sometimes Violet grew angry with Allain. What was he thinking of, to go away and leave her here alone among strangers? Had he no idea of the fears and fancies that beset a woman in her condition?

He had said he would never leave her. Yet he had. He had.

She told herself every day that he must return soon, that he did not intend to stay away forever. Every day the sun went down and night smothered the villa in shadows, and Allain did not come.

She was sure he must have had a good reason for going. There was someone he intended to see, something he meant to do to put an end to the surveillance of his movements. Or perhaps he planned to bring to justice whoever had terrorized Signora de Allori enough to cause her death.

But to leave her there alone in the villa after what had been done to the elderly woman who had taken them in seemed callous in the extreme. What would she do if the men returned, if they demanded to know where Allain had gone, and she could not tell them.

She felt so clumsy as the child grew, so unlike her usual self. Where once she had been quick and agile, she was forced now to move with care. And she felt vulnerable, not so much for herself as for the child she carried. If anything happened to her, it could not survive. To protect it, she must keep herself safe.

She was not really alone, of course. Giovanni was there.

He was always near, pruning, raking, or sweeping the tiles, when she was in the garden. Often he brought a bouquet for her, to place on her table at breakfast or luncheon. If she dropped her sewing, he was there to retrieve it. If she walked in the lanes around the house, he was ready to offer his arm for her support.

Since the night Allain had left, Giovanni had been sleeping in the house. He came every evening just after twilight and stayed until dawn. He took up a post outside her door, where he made himself a pallet. When he slept, however, she did not know. If she got up in the night, he was there, asking if she had need of him. If she rose early, he was up before her. In the long evenings of late autumn, Giovanni came and sat with her in the salon. He enjoyed having her read to him. He was not uneducated, having gone to the local priest for schooling, but his long workday left him little time for books or study. He liked hearing what was happening in the world from the news sheets, but was especially fond of Italian translations of Sir Walter Scott's tales of gallant men and fair ladies. When she caught him grinning quietly to himself at her mispronunciation one day, he began to help her with her Italian.

He always served her dinner when his mother had cooked it. He would not allow Violet to eat in the kitchen, however, but moved in and out of the dining room with the different dishes in the correct form. He made her laugh with his droll comments on his day or the life in the village, and he was always urging her to eat more, insisting she try this tidbit or that, offering food as if it were a substitute for love.

At first she had been disturbed.

"You must not neglect your work for me, Giovanni," she said, "or your family."

"No, madonna," he answered, his black eyes tender, "but I must be near in case you call."

"Yes, but you needn't watch my every breath."

His smile faded, replaced by concern. "It troubles you, having me near you?"

"Of course not, but you must have a life of your own."

"No, madonna; it is yours."

He had changed the subject then with so much firmness it was not possible to persist. She was left to wonder whether Allain had indeed left instructions for so much attention to her comfort, or whether Giovanni was stretching his instructions more than a little for his own reasons. She suspected it was some of both.

Another time she said to him, "Do you have someone special, a sweetheart, Giovanni?"

"No, madonna. If I had, I would not be here."

She absorbed that a moment. "Perhaps you should find a nice young girl and settle down?"

He met her gaze with a soft glint in his eyes and a meaningful tilt to his head. "It's very easy to find a nice young girl, madonna; it's much harder to find a beautiful woman."

Such devotion was pleasant to a woman growing larger every passing week with child. Violet felt some guilt for allowing it to continue when she had nothing to offer in return, but at the same time she was grateful for whatever prompted it. It soothed the feelings of desertion that sometimes crept in upon her and helped make the days pass.

Then came the winter rains.

The ocher and rust of the Tuscan hills turned gray, as gray as Violet's spirits. She stood one morning at the window of a small back bedchamber that she intended as a nursery, one that overlooked the path leading alongside the outside wall of the garden and down to the kitchen garden and stables. The rain had stopped, though the eaves of the house still dripped and the wind whipped fat drops from the tree limbs. Below her, Giovanni left the stable with a wheelbarrow loaded with stable straw that he was spreading under the roses in the garden. She lifted a hand to wave as he inclined his head in greeting. He turned to push open the gate in the garden wall and disappeared inside.

Behind her, Giovanni's mother, who was helping clean out the room, said, "He's a good boy, a hard worker, but he has a head full of nonsense and big ideas."

"I don't know what I would have done without him these last weeks."

Maria fluffed the feather pillow she was holding with more violence than seemed necessary. "Yes, you have much need. But I beg of you, take care. My Giovanni knows with his head that you belong to the Signor Massari, but not, perhaps, with his heart."

"Maria," Violet said in surprise, turning to face the other woman, "only look at me. I'm in no shape to appeal to a man."

"You have not grown ugly just because you are with child, my lady, and you are much alone and in need of protection. Giovanni sees these things."

Her voice low, Violet said, "I don't mean to encourage him."

"You do that by remaining here without your man."

"I would rather not be here alone, but I have noplace else to go." Violet hesitated before she went on. "What am I going to do, Maria, if he doesn't return?"

"I don't know, my lady. There is money, that is—you have means to live?"

"Oh, yes," Violet said tightly, "only nothing to live for."

"Don't say that!" Maria put her hands on her ample hips. "You have the bambino, and that is something very great. You must not make noises about not living, about death, or your baby will be marked by these terrible thoughts. You must be serene so the little one will be well and content."

"That's easy to say. Suppose—suppose Allain hasn't come back because he's hurt? Or worse? Suppose he has been dead for weeks, but there is no one to tell me, no one who knows I am waiting here?"

"There's time enough to think of such things if they happen, and no need to waste your strength fretting over them if they don't."

"I have to think of them. I have to decide what I'll do."

"You will do nothing until the bambino comes; that much is only wise. The signor was so excited, so proud to be a father; surely he will return for the birth if he has breath in his body."

"And if he doesn't, what will I do? Where will I go for help?"

"You will go nowhere, my lady, for I will come to you. You will send Giovanni for me; that is why he is here. And you are not to worry, I have had six children of my own and brought many more into the world. All will be well."

The autumn wore on. Reports from the Battle of Alma in the far-off Crimea claimed an allied victory. As more news trickled in, however, it became plain that it had been a costly and bungled fight.

The allies began a bombardment of Sevastopol, Russia's main port on the Black Sea, in mid-October. However, the French magazine blew up, and a final assault was postponed. This allowed time for increased defenses by the Russians. As a result the allies settled in for the prolonged siege that appeared necessary to take the city.

The Russians counterattacked at the main supply depot of the allies at Balaklava. During this engagement confusion in the relaying of orders given by the English high command resulted in a suicide charge led by Lord Cardigan's Light Brigade. The carnage was horrendous, but the incredible display of courage, aided by reinforcements of French cavalry, carried the day.

Some ten days later, in the midst of morning fog and rain, the Russians attacked the Anglo-French forces besieging Sevastopol. When the retreat was finally sounded, thirteen thousand men were dead.

Shortly afterward, the British supply ships, bringing not only arms and ammunition but food and medicine and winter uniforms, foundered in a storm in the Black Sea. The allied army went into winter quarters, waiting for springtime to resume active hostilities.

In the midst of the early Pyrrhic victories, a dispatch was sent by the war correspondent of the *London Times* detailing the horrible conditions prevailing in the British military hospitals. A woman named Nightingale was sent, along with thirty-eight female nurses and a commission from the secretary of war, to improve matters. She arrived in the Crimea just in time to set to work receiving the accumulated wounded from the fall battle, and to become a heroine in the press for her efforts toward saving lives.

So it went, bad news and good, as the season advanced and the long gray chill of winter closed in. The villa took on the smoke smell of wood fires, also the scent of drying herbs and curing garlic from the loose bundles and strings hanging from the kitchen rafters. These scents combined with the rich aroma of meat broth and pasta from Maria's huge iron stove. Maria taught Violet to knit, and together they made dainty little blankets and booties that Violet embroidered with tiny flowers. And she and Giovanni also made perfume.

He came across the formula one day where it was lying in Violet's chair in the salon. Violet had used the back of the piece of paper to write down the pattern for the baby blanket she was making. Giovanni picked it up and began to read it aloud.

"This is the perfume you wear?" he asked after a moment, glancing at her from under his curling lashes.

"The one I had been wearing. There are only a few drops left, and I'm saving them."

He nodded in perfect understanding. "For when the signor returns. But it would not be hard to make more."

"Wouldn't it?"

"The rose oil, I have. The others can be found at the shop of the apothecary in Florence, most of them. One, perhaps two, may have to come from Rome, but that would not take long."

"You are sure?" she said, an arrested expression on her face.

"Yes, certainly." He looked up at her, his gaze warm.

"Do you think I could do it?" There was suddenly nothing she wanted so much as to mix together the scents that would mingle to produce the lovely fragrance in the jeweled bottle.

"It would be my pleasure to show you," he said simply.

One night when Maria had gone to bed, they assembled the various precious oil essences and the pure aqua vitae whose alcohol content would bring out the fragrance. They took them into Violet's bedchamber, as far away as it was possible to get from the distracting food and herb smells of the kitchen. On a small table drawn near the fire, they set out everything they would use, including a glass beaker with a pouring lip and a small glass pipe that would be used to pick up the minute amounts of the oils and add them drop by drop to the beaker.

Giovanni, his manner serious and faintly superior, explained the process. He himself made the first mixture as Violet read out the ingredients and their proportions. After stirring it gently, he reached for Violet's wrist.

She pulled back instinctively.

He smiled at her as he retained his grasp, rubbing a thumb across the vein on the inside of her wrist. "It must go on your skin," he said, "for that is where it belongs."

As she ceased to resist he put a little of the volatile oil on her wrist, waited a few minutes, then inhaled the scent.

A frown of dissatisfaction creased his brow. "It isn't the same."

"Are you sure?" Violet breathed in the skin-warmed perfume

herself, closing her eyes as she concentrated on it. Finally she shook her head. "You're right. What's wrong?"

"A little too much of this, not enough of that. I thought I was being careful, but somehow I made a mistake."

She breathed deeply again. Abruptly, she smiled. She said, "I think—I'm almost sure it's too much of the narcissus."

"Yes?" He repeated her actions. "Ah, madonna," he said, "you have a wonderful nose."

She laughed; she couldn't help it. It was such a strange compliment to give her so much pleasure. "You think so?"

"I know it. Quickly, now. You must mix."

The batch she put together was perfect. She knew it even before she placed it on her wrist. The fumes rising from the stoneware beaker filled her head with their perfect bouquet, one resonant with spring narcissus and summer roses, of softly blowing orange blossoms and exotic musk and many other things, but also with power and beauty and, yes, with love.

Giovanni caught her wrist the moment the perfume had settled upon it, snuffling noisily of the warm, rich scent. A look of bliss smoothed his features and his lips curved at the corners.

"Yes," he whispered. "Yes."

He stepped close to take her in his arms. It was a spontaneous embrace of triumph and satisfaction and pure joy. There was nothing carnal in it, nothing of deviousness or guile. It might have been easier for Violet if it had been, easier for her to refuse, simpler for her to resist.

As it was, she leaned into his hard, young strength, accepting it and the support he gave without thinking, savoring the warm security and the sense of being at rest. Then she felt his lips on the soft wave of hair at her temple. And the child inside her shifted, as if in protest.

She released herself without haste, but with finality. Giovanni was sweet and dear, and seemed all too ready to allow himself to be used; still, it was unfair to encourage him by clinging to him. She felt a gentle affection for him. If things had been different—but they were not. Her love had been given to Allain and could never be retracted.

She knew then, as she stepped away from Giovanni, that the time had come for her to do something other than wait.

———

The letter of credit left in her name with a Florentine banker seemed to have no limit. She drew upon it heavily for traveling expenses for two.

She thought long and deep about asking Giovanni to accompany her. It was one thing to have him sleeping in the same house with her in the midst of a village where everyone knew him and the house of his mother was only a few yards beyond the garden, but quite another to be staying with him in inns and pensions, even when he would have his own small room at a distance from her own. It was not her reputation that concerned her, however; she was sure she no longer had such a thing. She was only doubtful about her continued reliance upon the young Italian and the ideas he might garner from such dependence.

Nevertheless, it would be foolish of her to start out on her travels without some support. She was not quite six months along, according to her best calculations, but she was already growing clumsy, and carrying heavy luggage would not be wise.

The problem, as it turned out, was not whether to permit Giovanni to go, but how to keep him from it once he discovered what she meant to do. His delight at the prospect was so transparent, his determination so steadfast, that she did not try too hard.

They went first to Venice, to the house of Signora da Allori. There was no one there; it was locked up and the knocker taken from the door. They inquired for Allain at every hotel and other place that took paying guests they could find, but no one had seen him; he was certainly not among the registered guests.

His house in Paris was the next destination. It, too, was shuttered and still. None of his friends had caught so much as a glimpse of him since the summer. They wondered where he had been keeping himself; he was much missed.

There was bright speculation in their eyes as they watched her. If any asked themselves why she was inquiring, however, or why she was accompanied by a handsome Italian with a pugnacious and jealous look in his eye, they kept their curiosity well hidden.

London was the last possibility on her list, one added only because it was where she had met Allain. Yet Violet had no idea where he had been staying while he was there, or if he had a permanent or even semipermanent address. In any case, she could conceive of no purpose he might have in crossing the channel. After having so little luck discovering anyone who had seen him elsewhere, it seemed useless to pursue so vague a possibility.

With nowhere else to turn, Violet began to think of finding Gilbert. She wondered if he was still in Europe, if he was holding to his original schedule, and what he had told their families in New Orleans. She wondered, too, if Gilbert was still trying to locate her. Most of all she wanted to know if he had seen Allain, by accident or design.

That last question troubled her increasingly, especially as she remembered Allain's suggestion made in Venice that she should, for her own safety, resume her place with her husband. Just over a week after her return to the villa, as soon as she had rested from her travels, Violet sat down and wrote a series of letters, directing them to the places she could remember that Gilbert had meant to visit in the first year of his grand tour. She was by no means sure he would take the trouble to reply, even if a letter of hers chanced to find him; still, she had to try. She did not give her own direction, beyond the letter office in Florence. She wished any contact between them that might come from her writing to be at a time and place of her own choosing.

Her answer came from Rome, where he was spending the winter. She was urged to travel there and discuss the questions posed in her letter at great length.

To go, or not to go?

The visit promised to be an uncomfortable one. She had thought the old guilt for profaning her marriage vows and forsaking the man she had promised to honor until death was forgotten, only to discover that it revived with the prospect ahead of her. However, the memory of the treatment she had received at his hands had faded, and she no longer feared him. She had also ceased to consider that he was responsible for the attack upon Allain at the train station.

If it was not for an opportunity to find out if Allain had contacted him concerning her, then why had she written him, after all? She had to go. It was her last hope.

Still, she put it off until after Christmas, and then again because she thought she was getting a cold. Finally, near the middle of January, she and Giovanni set out.

Gilbert was staying in a pension, a dreary place near the Forum that smelled of cats but was redeemed by a view of the Coliseum. He did not open the door to them himself. A pert young woman wearing a low-necked blouse and a skirt with no sign of petticoats under it let them in. When they had been seated and served cups of barely warm tea, the woman departed. Calling out a farewell that was far too casual for a mere maid, she clattered away down the stairs.

Giovanni looked at Violet with a wry smile and the quick, backward jerk of the head that showed his opinion of Gilbert's taste in women. Violet wondered if the presence of the young woman had been for her benefit, to show her that she was not the only one who could indulge in carnal behavior, or perhaps to arouse her jealous instincts. If so, it had missed its mark. She felt sorry for her husband that he would need to bolster his male pride by doing such a thing, and also glad that he had found consolation.

Gilbert appeared thinner. His face was more drawn and lined, so that he seemed to have aged ten years. There was a noticeable tremor in his hands, and the collection of silver-tagged liquor decanters sitting on the side table were all nearly empty.

He gave Giovanni a hard stare as Violet introduced him, then ignored him as if he did not exist. "So," he said, his voice rasping and his attention centered conspicuously on her belly, "I see you are well."

"Yes, and you also," Violet said politely. At the same time she sent a warning glance to Giovanni, who had shifted forward on his chair seat with his fists clenched on his knees.

"Since you have not until now seen fit to let me know you were still aboveground, I assume you want something very badly if it brings you here," he went on, his tone less than agreeable.

"News," she answered, "only news."

"Explain to me why I should give it to you."

Hope leaped inside her. "You have something to tell me?"

His voice grated as he went on with no regard for her question. "Did you never consider my feelings, my dear Violet? Did you never think that I would be worried about you? Did it never occur to you, leaving in that way, that I might wonder if you had been carried off by kidnappers or criminal fiends? Could you have not sent me at least a small message which said simply that you lived?"

Before he would attend to her, he must first castigate her for the anxiety and embarrassment she had caused him. He had not changed at all.

"I'm sorry if you were hurt," she said slowly, "but so was I."

"Were you? That's something, at any rate."

His concern was quite obviously with his own feelings, his own loss, with little left over for what she might think and feel. For an instant she could sense again the emptiness of her marriage, of knowing that she was loved, if at all, as an image in Gilbert's mind, an extension of himself, a possession, rather than as the flesh-and-blood woman she really was inside herself.

She said, "Have you heard from home?"

"A few lines, most inquiring why you have not written, or I. I pleaded the disruption of the mails due to the war, that and because there was nothing of interest to say, since I have made little progress with the purpose of my journey."

Nothing of interest to say.

It was better, perhaps, than being vilified to his relatives, and hers, by letter. She should be grateful to him, and might have been if she could have thought it had been done from any motive other than to save himself humiliation.

She said, "Do you mean to return to New Orleans in advance of your plans?"

"Because of your desertion? No, indeed. I don't see that one thing affects the other. The town house requires a few more sticks of furniture, regardless."

"I'm glad. I would not like to think I had—inconvenienced you." She paused, clasping her gloved hands together in her lap. "Now, if you please, I would like an answer to the questions you had in my letter. You must tell me—have you seen Allain at all since Paris? Has he, perhaps, spoken to you out of concern for me, made some suggestion in the event that he—that I should be left alone? I must know."

Gilbert stared at her for long moments. Finally he said in soft satisfaction, "He has left you."

"Not," she said tightly, "of his own will." The need to be supplicating for the sake of the information she wanted was becoming an unacceptable task. She could feel the wash of anger in her blood, driving out all other consideration.

"Why then? What could possibly force him from the side of the woman who is carrying his bastard?"

Giovanni was on his feet before she could put out a hand to stop him. He reached for Gilbert, clenching a toil-hardened hand in his cravat to drag him to his feet. Nose to nose with Gilbert, he said, "You will apologize to the madonna. On the instant."

Gilbert glared at Giovanni while his face turned brick red and the veins stood purple and blue in his forehead. His breath began to wheeze in his throat.

"Giovanni, please," Violet said, rising to her feet with difficulty, "for my sake."

Giovanni did not move or speak.

"Yes, I—was hasty," Gilbert managed to say through the whistling rasp of his breathing. "I should not have spoken so of a lady."

Giovanni did not release him, but shook him as a reminder. Gilbert's eyes bulged as he stared from Violet to Giovanni and back again.

"As for—Massari, I—have not seen him."

Giovanni opened his hand and let him fall. As Gilbert drew a gasping breath and flopped into his chair, the young Italian stepped back. Reaching out his hand to Violet, he drew her to his side. "I think," he said quietly, "that we have done all that can be done here."

Her eyes were dark with desolation as she met his steady gaze. "Yes," she answered, "let us go home."

Chapter 22

It had been a day of warm March winds and brilliant sunshine. The air had been balmy, the grass seemed to leap into growth, and the fruit trees unfurled white and pink blossoms like welcoming banners for the approach of spring.

The winter coolness still lingered inside the stone walls of the villa. Violet had taken her journal out into the garden as the day warmed toward the middle of the afternoon. Giovanni had brought a stool for her feet, to keep her ankles from swelling, and also a shawl to ward off any vagrant chilliness in the scant shade of the olive tree.

"You are comfortable now?" he asked, standing relaxed yet observant in front of her chair with one hand clasping the wrist of his other arm.

"Very." She smiled up at him.

His smile in return faded quickly. He said, "I should tell you—it's probably nothing, no need at all for alarm—but I have been told that a stranger was seen outside the villa late last evening."

The neighborhood was close-knit, she had discovered in the last few months; nearly everyone was related to everyone else and few things went unnoticed. If Giovanni said the man was a stranger, then he was.

"What was he doing?" she asked.

"Nothing. Idling. He moved on when some of the men asked what his business was here."

There were advantages to close neighborhoods. "Has there been any sign of him today?"

He shook his head. "Not that I know, but you are not to worry. I will be just beyond the wall, planting a few rows of beans. Call if you need anything. Call when you are ready to go into the house."

She grinned up at him, amused by his excessive concern, yet warmed by it at the same time. "I know, you always come when I call."

"Always," he said, his dark eyes serious in spite of his smile.

When he had gone, Violet sat bringing her journal up to date, trying to think what else to add other than complaints about the numerous aches and pains of her condition. She was eight months along and beginning to be anxious to be delivered of her burden.

She set down the news of the recent and unexpected death of Czar Nicholas from a chill, and its effect on the chances for peace in the Crimea. The Russian ruler had been a hard man and unbending autocrat; there had been many attempts to depose him during the years since he ascended to the throne following the mysterious death of his elder brother, Alexander, with bloody reprisals following the failed coups. It was felt that since the pride of this unpopular czar need no longer be considered, Russian diplomats might now find some pretext for ceasing hostilities. Negotiations could well begin soon.

The end of any war must be good news, but Violet could not see that she would be affected in any way. She would go on as she was, the lady in the villa who was eccentric enough to want to make perfume. The only difference was that soon there would be a child.

Violet picked up the jeweled bottle on its chain that she wore around her neck. The scent rising from it soothed her senses, making her smile. It had become a part of her once more, drifting around her as she moved, penetrating her pores, so that it seemed she exhaled it. It was still stronger near the bottle lid, however, strong enough to provide her own sense of peace.

She should, she supposed, be concerned about what was going to happen to her and her child, how they would go on from year to year if Allain never returned. She could not be. She had entered into that period of placid acceptance that comes to all women as they near their time. There was nothing she could do at this moment

to change what was to happen, and she had no energy to fret over
it.

The afternoon faded to a sunset of rose-and-gold splendor that
painted the stone walls around Violet in the magnificent hues of
Titian or Michelangelo. The shadows stretched long across the
tender new grass. The water in the fountain gurgled in the quiet.
Maria came out of the house and filled a kitchen bucket from the
fountain's basin. She smiled in Violet's direction as she lifted the
filled bucket, then turned and went inside.

On some not-too-distant hillside, a goat's bell tinkled. It seemed
a signal that set the church bells of the village to clamoring in evening song.

Violet could barely see to write. It was time to go into the house.

Still, she lingered. The afterglow was lovely. She was tired, and
it was too much effort to heave herself out of the deep chair of
woven wicker. If she waited, Giovanni would come to help her.

She heard his footsteps on the grass, a quietly purposeful approach from the direction of the garden gate. She sat very still,
absorbing the peace, reluctant to let it go.

He knelt at her feet, placing his warm hand upon her knee.

"Look at me, and forgive me," came Allain's voice in low and
strained resonance. "Let me hear your sweet voice, or I will be
forced to die from my longing."

She turned her head slowly, so that by the time she met his
upturned gaze, her own eyes glittered with tears tinted lavender
with twilight. Her hands trembled as she reached to touch his face
and trail her fingertips through the waves of his hair above his ears.

"Oh, my Allain," she whispered, "where have you been? Where
have you been?"

"Trying to preserve sanity and our lives, though I discovered
my own life was not worth the effort if I could not be with you.
Knowing your time was near, I had to return. I could not bear it to
be otherwise."

Maria had been right; she should have listened to her, Violet
thought. But what did it matter, so long as he was there?

"Help me up," she said, lifting her feet from the stool and holding out her hands.

He whipped off his hat and cast it aside with the cane he carried,
then leaned to encircle her waist in his strong, warm grasp.

A moment later she was in his arms while he rocked her and
the baby she carried inside her gently from side to side. She buried

her face in his shoulder while content washed over her in long, slow waves and her breath left her in a slow sigh. Then she raised her head.

He touched his mouth to hers as though he thought she might break. Then he was kissing her with desperate hunger, reveling in the taste and feel of her, holding her closer and closer until she tore her lips away in a gasp of protest.

He begged her pardon in frenzied phrases as he pressed his face against her hair, but he seemed inclined to begin again.

They came from out of the gathering shadows. There were four of them who came through the gate, four men with swords and knives that flashed silver in the last light of evening. Their faces were masked, so there were only pale, round holes for their eyes in the blackness under their wide-brimmed hats.

Violet saw them beyond Allain's shoulder. Her warning scream was choked with horror.

Allain whirled, leaping for his cane. The steel blade enclosed inside it sang as he whipped it from its sheath. He placed himself between Violet and the advancing men even as he dropped into a fencing stance.

"To the house," he said over his shoulder, the words low and terse, as if they must not be overheard.

But they were. One of the men detached himself from the others, circling to the side, trying to get beyond Allain's guard. Allain retreated a step or two to keep them all within range of his sword.

Violet stumbled backward as she tried to keep out of his way. A sword thrust could not be more painful than the slicing edge of cold terror inside her. She must not, she thought, become more of a hindrance to him than she was already.

She could not see how Allain could best them all. There must be some way she could help him, something she could do. She could see nothing, think of nothing. Behind her, in the door into the villa, she heard Maria begin to scream, glimpsed her standing with her hands clamped to her mouth.

Allain snatched the offensive, attacking with a smooth uncoiling of muscles. In movements too swift to follow, he engaged three swordsmen at once, feinting, parrying, gliding away from blows, whirling to prevent the fourth man from sliding past his guard of Violet. His face intent in the dying light, he settled grimly to his task.

Swords hissed and scraped, clanging as they clashed, tapping, tapping as one man sought for advantage against four others.

His assailants advanced and retreated, shoving one another as they stumbled together, or were pushed by Allain. They grunted and cursed, hissed commands at each other, cried out as they felt the biting slash of Allain's sword. Blood appeared here and there on their coat sleeves and hands. Their panting breaths grew harsh with fury and effort.

Allain fought with desperate brilliance and sweating strength. His wrist was tempered and pliant as he drew on skill and tricks learned with the best *maître d'armes* of Paris and Rome. His assailants were good, but they were no match for his consummate precision of movement, his exquisitely timed stratagems. A masked man gave a gurgling cry, falling to one knee with his body bent over Allain's shining sword.

Even as Allain dragged his blade free, the fourth man slipped past him, gliding toward Violet. The other two closed in as one upon Allain, trying to overcome him with their combined strength, so that for long moments he was engaged in a fight for life.

Violet retreated at a clumsy run, plunging under the grape arbor, twisting her body to circle the table and put it between her and her attacker. He gave a coarse laugh as he lunged across the table with his left hand to grab at the fullness of cloth over her breasts. She staggered back, but his hand caught the jeweled perfume bottle on its chain.

She was jerked toward him over the table. Her belly crashed into the edge and a moan broke from her lips. Violet grasped the table edge for support as her knees threatened to give way under her. The man drew back his sword with a gesture almost leisurely in its certainty.

Rage sprang white-hot into Violet's brain. She gripped the table and, almost without thinking, heaved it upward.

The necklace chain broke. Her attacker leaped away, but not fast enough. The table caught his shin. He swore, stumbling away. Freed, Violet staggered back in the attempt to keep her balance.

The man with the sword bared his teeth in a snarl as he flung the table aside and, limping, closed in on her.

Allain, watching even as he fought, cried out in despair.

Then there came a shout of outrage from the direction of the garden gate. Giovanni, his face twisted with fury, plunged toward Violet's attacker. In his hard fist was a hand-held scythe. Honed to a razor's edge, it was a formidable weapon, but no match in length and utility for a sword.

The attacker whirled to face the new danger. Giovanni had only one chance, to close in quickly and get within the man's guard. He leaped, the scythe whirling before him like some ancient weapon of godlike destruction. The two clashed together, grappling, twisting, flailing. The attacker stumbled, dragging Giovanni down. They both crashed to the tiles. The masked man dropped his sword. It went clattering as Giovanni kicked it. Slithering grittily over the tiles, it landed at Violet's feet.

She bent swiftly to pick it up, gasping in pain as she straightened once more. At the same time she saw the man who had attacked her strain to reach inside his coat, saw him wrench a glinting stiletto from within its folds.

She cried out a warning. Giovanni heard and lunged to fasten his hard fingers around the man's wrist. The two rolled on the ground, grunting, bringing strength to bear against strength and resolve against ferocity.

Violet took a quick step forward, trying to see in the growing dimness, ready to thrust with the weapon in her hand. But the men wrestling back and forth moved too quickly. She could not be sure of striking the right one.

They surged to their feet again. For an instant they pushed away from each other. They circled. The lingering light flashed blue along the scythe in Giovanni's hand, hanging like a starry drop at the tip of its half-moon shape. The attacker turned his stiletto in his grasp so the tapered blade had the look of a stinger.

As at some unheard signal, they sprang together, growling, panting with strain, slinging each other this way and that, slipping on the tiles. There came the thud of a blow. At the same time Giovanni brought the scythe down and around in a hard swipe.

The attacker fell back, half turning, his head lolling only half on his shoulders while blood spurted from the great gash in his neck.

Giovanni stood for a wavering instant, staring down. He looked up at Violet, his eyes dark with pain and remorse. "I would have come sooner, madonna," he said. "I heard your cry, but had no weapon—"

He reached then to grasp the stiletto protruding from his chest. He crumpled to his knees.

Violet stifled a cry with both hands while sickness rose up inside her.

"In the house! Run, Violet!" Allain gasped out behind her. The words were underscored by the clash of his sword as he held his two assailants at bay. Their blades whined, scraping together with a shower of orange sparks. Their breathing was labored. They advanced and retreated across the grass, stumbling over the limp body of the fallen attacker. They trampled the geometric herb beds, so the smells of basil and mint and shallots and trampled earth rose sharp in the air.

Violet, torn by pain and horror and terror, could not force herself to retreat to safety. As the struggling men danced back and forth they came between her and Giovanni's fallen form, so she could not help him. She could only stand, hefting the sword in her hand, seeking some way to be useful.

Allain flicked a harried glance at Violet. He redoubled his efforts. Driving the taller of the two men backward in a display of rigorous skill and tempered, tensile strength, Allain circled the other man's blade, slipped past his guard. The man cried out in terror as Allain struck like an adder, thrusting and withdrawing in a movement too swift to follow. Even as his opponent fell he whirled to face the last of the four.

The man had taken advantage of that bare instant of inattention to throw down his sword and plunge his hand inside his waistcoat. He brought out a pocket pistol, pointing it and pulling the trigger in a single, jerking movement.

The pistol boomed, a thunderous sound in the enclosed garden. Blue-gray smoke and fire exploded. Allain was flung backward like a puppet with cut strings. He clamped a hand to the crimson blotch on his shirtfront above his waistcoat even as he fell. Striking heavily, he rolled, sprawling in loose-limbed grace. He lay still with the fine curls of his hair mingling with the blades of the grass.

The last of the attackers threw the single-shot pistol to the ground in a fierce gesture of triumph. He flung a quick glance around him for his sword and he leaned to pick it up. He turned then toward Violet.

He halted abruptly as Maria, with three of their neighbors armed with rakes and pitchforks, poured from the kitchen doorway. He stared wildly around at his fallen comrades. His gaze fell on Violet's journal, which lay in the grass with its blood-spattered pages ruffling in the light wind. Sprinting forward, he scooped up the book. With a last backward glance in Violet's direction, he plunged toward the gate and skimmed through it.

In that instant everything seemed to stand out sharp and clear for Violet, so brightly crystalline that it hurt her eyes. The shape and outline of the garden and its bed, the silver glitter of the wind-tossed olive leaves were too perfect, too beautiful. The scents of herbs and bruised grass mingled with the smell of the warm blood that stained the mosaic tiles beneath her feet to form a sickening miasma. The feel of the soft spring air upon her skin was like a scourge. It seemed that if anyone touched her, no matter with what gentleness, she would flinch as from a blow.

Maria moved forward with an anguished moan to kneel beside Giovanni. She gathered her son to her, supporting him, reaching for the stiletto and dragging it free even as he smiled up into her eyes. Others gathered at his feet to lift him and carry him into the villa.

A kindly older woman came to Violet's side, timidly touching her arm, tugging her toward the house.

Violet shook her head.

She forced her muscles to move, to answer her commands. Slowly she moved to where Allain lay with his blood staining his shirtfront, seeping into the grass. She lowered herself awkwardly beside him. She picked up his hand, lifting the lax, boneless fingers to her cheek. She closed her eyes, rocking a little; still, the warm tears seeped through, wetting the calluses that marked his thumb and forefinger and the inside of his palm.

His eyelids fluttered, lifted. He stared up at her with such love and concentration in his gray eyes that it seemed he meant to imprint her image on their surface, a final lovely vision.

He winced a little, allowed his gaze to drift. His voice so soft she had to guess at his meaning, he said, "Gone?"

She nodded, unable to speak for the aching tightness of her throat.

"My fault. Followed me. Should have watched closer."

His hand was growing cooler. She swallowed hard. "Please," she said, "please don't." But she hardly knew whether she meant to keep him from talking, or to beg him not to leave her again in death.

His gaze wavered, steadied as if by a supreme effort of will. He tried to smile, though pain arrested the movement. "I—would have brought you—flowers—but for haste."

"Never mind," she whispered.

"Rosemary," he said, his voice no more than a finespun spider's silk of sound. "For Remembrance. Pray, love—"

She cried out as his voice stopped and his eyes fluttered shut. The piercing keen of it hurt her throat, but she could not stop.

The pain came from deep inside her, a rushing, pouring tidal wave of agony. She was engulfed in it, submerged by it, carried on it to some far shore of her mind where she was left stranded and exposed. Racked by the merciless anguish, every touch was an added ache, every sound an exacerbation of it. She tried to fight the hands that lifted her, tugging at her, removing her from where she wanted to be. She heard voices she could not recognize, felt her own blood hot and wet as it drained from her as from a wound.

Then came the glad darkness. She reached for it with both hands open and supplicating, for she could bear the pain no longer.

"Your daughter, how she is beautiful. *Bella, molto bella.*"

Violet turned her head as Maria spoke. She smiled as she saw the cherubic picture the small baby made, lying in a soft white knit blanket upon the lap of Maria's black skirt. The small face was relaxed in sleep, the perfect pink rosebud mouth still moist with milk. The tiny lids that covered the dark blue-brown eyes were finely fringed with curving lashes and made expressive by delicate, arching brows, and the fine hair that curled over her pink scalp was a soft light brown.

Yes, she was beautiful, and a joy, and a solace.

"Bella Giovanna," Maria went on in soft tones. "I am so proud you named her so. She is," the woman added in doting tones, "a very Italian-looking baby."

Violet closed her eyes against the pain. She could control it now, though barely, since she had learned that it would, eventually, ease.

"Yes," she answered just as quietly.

She turned back to her journal, a new one with an ornate cover of embossed burgundy velvet with brassbound edges that Maria's nephew had found for her in Florence. She had spent the past days writing into it everything that had been in the old one, painstakingly recreating the days, and reliving them. Perhaps even living in them, at least a little. It was one way to escape the intolerable present.

It gave her something to do, that endless writing and remembering. More than that, she wanted the record of the year just passed. She would not be cheated out of it by spite and the petty fears of some assassin that it might document her days with Allain. She needed it for herself, and for Allain's daughter.

Maria cleared her throat, her gaze still on the baby as she spoke again. "I have said nothing to you of the funeral. It was a solemn Mass, most moving; the priest said good things, true things of comfort. There were many mourners and—many flowers."

Violet drew a quick breath, holding it against the press of tears. She said quickly, while she still could, "And the burial?"

"On the hill near the church, among my people. The headstone is beautiful, large, nicely carved with blossoms of roses and sprigs of rosemary, and with a standing angel."

Violet could not answer.

They were silent for a long time. The gentle spring wind blew in at the window, stirring the bed curtains. There was a haze on the hills in the distance, though their colors of ocher and rust and gray green were bright in the sun.

Maria sniffed a little before she spoke at last. "The doctor has said you may walk a little today."

"May I indeed?"

Violet had sat up in a chair by the window the day before, but that was all. The birth had been difficult, with much loss of blood. They had feared for her life, or so Maria told her; she didn't remember. They had also feared for the baby, but Giovanna had come into the world screaming with rage at her early ejection from her warm cocoon. She had been a little pale at first, but had soon turned pink. Like a babe of normal time, she had suckled the first time the breast was presented to her, and had stopped only to sleep in the three weeks since.

"You must try," Maria said. "He has been waiting all this time, and not patiently. He will see you today, or he will get up himself. This he should not do, not for at least another week."

"He would do it if it killed him." Violet's voice trailed away and her smile faded slowly, like a candle burning out.

Maria reached out to press Violet's hand, though her own eyes were dark with tears of distress. "Men are fools, yes. But would we have them any other way? No, no. Come, let me put the little one down and I will help you."

Maria supported her as far as the bedchamber door. By then Violet had begun to feel less weak in the knees, had begun to get her strength back. It felt strange to be able to move with her usual supple grace, strange to put her hand on her stomach and feel the flatness. For the first time in ages she wondered what she looked like. Maria had brushed her hair for her and left it hanging down her back in a soft, brown-gold curtain, but she had not seen a mirror. She did not know if she was pale and sallow or flushed from her efforts.

It didn't matter, of course. But it seemed that the fact she could care might be a good sign. She really was getting better.

Maria opened the bedchamber door, gave Violet a small, encouraging push, then left her.

Violet moved inside with the soft folds of her gown and dressing gown of batiste and lace flowing around her feet. The man on the bed had been dozing. His lashes quivered, then opened in sudden alertness. He saw her.

A slow smile gathered at the corners of his mouth, spreading over his face to shine in his eyes. He reached out to touch the chair that sat nearby, before he held his hand out to her. His voice warm and low, he said, "Come. Sit here, close beside me."

Her heart shifted a little inside her. She felt the need to cry, but would not. There had been so many tears, so many.

She moved to do as he asked. As she placed her hand in his and felt the strong grip of his fingers, her own closed convulsively, holding tight, as if she would never let go.

"I wish," he said, his voice vibrant with longing, "that you could lie beside me. So I might comfort you."

"Yes," she whispered from a full throat.

"If that cannot be, then speak to me. Tell me how you are, and how you feel. Talk to me of Giovanna—I have seen her and she is as lovely as her mother, as small as she is. I want to hear your voice and know you are here, when I was so sure, for a terrible moment, that I had failed to guard you, that you were lost to me—"

He stopped because she had leaned to place her fingers on his lips. Under the sensitive fingertips, she felt his smile, felt the movement of his lips as he turned the smile into a kiss.

"Tell me what will happen now," he said.

She swallowed hard. "When we are better, both of us, we will go away. Perhaps to Egypt, if you like."

"That should be far enough so that you will be safe."

"And you also, perhaps."

His smile was indulgent. "My safety doesn't matter, so long as I am with you."

"You will become strong again there, and brown by the sun."

"Something to be wished. And then?"

"God knows. I cannot say."

He made no reply, only lay playing with her fingers. Some minutes passed. His grasp on her hand tightened briefly and was released before it could become hurtful. He whispered, "Call me by my name. Say it. I want to hear it, now, on your lips."

"I—can't," she answered with slow tears rising in her eyes in spite of all she could do.

"You must, for my sake. Please."

How could she refuse? It was impossible. Still, she searched for even a small delay. She said, "Please, madonna?"

"Ah. As you wish, always. Please, madonna—my madonna."

The pain was acute. Her lips trembled a little as she said, "Very well then. Yes, love, yes—"

"Giovanni," he said for her, the word soft with pleading.

"Yes, Giovanni," she repeated in gentle, musical tones.

She slid to her knees beside the bed then. Holding his hand with both hers, she rested her forehead on his good shoulder away from his bandaging. As her hair drifted forward to cover her face, she allowed the healing tears to fall.

April 24, 1855

I received a visit from Gilbert today. He came to offer his condolences. He had heard, he said, of the death of the artist. He heard it when he arrived in Florence. I asked him how long he had been in the town. He claimed only two days. I wonder.

I am amazed. He suggests that we return to New Orleans together. He will continue with his buying while I do as I please until the time comes that was set for his return in his original itinerary. A year from now we will sail for home. In the meantime I may do as I please.

I intend to. My plans have been made.

Once in New Orleans, Gilbert will accept the child I have borne as his and will never open his lips again to speak otherwise. He will make me a gift of the town house and will visit me there from time to time, in the daylight hours. In return I am to pretend that all is as it was before between us.

How cynical I have become, and how hard. I agreed. Why not? It makes matters so much easier.

Gilbert seems chastened.

Poor man. He thinks it is possible that everything may one day be the same as before.

I know better. I know far better.

Chapter 23

Joletta sat holding the journal pages against her chest. She wiped away a little moisture that had gathered under her eyes. She had read the end of Violet's odyssey before, but not in Italy where it had happened. That made it more poignant somehow.

A large part of her sadness was for Violet, but a portion was also for herself. The losses in her life had been so many. The latest of these was someone who might, had things been different, have been a lover like Violet's Allain.

No. She wouldn't think about that.

Violet's last cryptic entry troubled her just as much now as it had the first time she saw it. It didn't seem quite like her at all. More, she could not quite understand Violet's easy agreement to return home with Gilbert after everything that had gone before. Violet had done just that, she knew, however; everything Joletta had ever heard about her great-great-great-great-grandmother's life told her it had happened exactly that way.

Had Violet agreed to the reconciliation in order to return home to New Orleans and her relatives and friends without the necessity of explaining an estrangement? Had it been for the sake of her baby, so that little Giovanna could have an unsullied name and the benefits of a close-knit family? Was it for security, perhaps, for herself and her child, or had it been from the need to leave the sorrow she had found in Europe behind?

What had happened in Egypt in that lost year? Why had Violet not stayed on in Italy as she herself had hinted she might?

Another question was why Gilbert had asked her to return with him. Was it for love, or only to save his pride? Had it been to gloat over her, or to test her attachment to Italy, forcing her to choose between it and her old way of life?

And was the reason Violet agreed, perhaps, because she thought it a just revenge that her husband be forced to give his name to the child of the man he may have had murdered?

Still, Joletta wanted to know more, such as why Violet had stopped writing in her journal, and how she had felt about taking up life again, however changed, with Gilbert.

There was also Giovanni. Joletta had a great need to know what had become of him. She suspected, but she did not know.

There was no way to tell these things at this distance in time, and so there was a sense of things left unsaid, unfinished.

As irritating as it might be, the real world was like that, she thought, untidy, with loose ends left quietly flapping down the years.

And yet, there was an idea taking shape in Joletta's mind about the journal. It was fascinating that the original of the pages she held in her hands was not the book that Violet had begun when she started out on her grand tour. That fact opened up possibilities that had not been there before. Anything could have been done to the revised edition; events and dates could have been changed, things added or omitted or twisted slightly to suit Violet's purpose.

There was no real reason to think Violet might have done such a thing. She had been keeping the journal for herself after all; there was no one she needed to impress, nothing she need have concealed. If she had been trying to keep her clandestine affair from posterity, all she need have done was to destroy that record of it.

Regardless, there were things Joletta wanted to check, both in Italy and back home in New Orleans.

The sound of a knock at the door interrupted the quiet flow of her thoughts. She knew who it was. She not only recognized the knock, but had been waiting for it, both consciously and unconsciously, ever since she returned to the hotel.

Rone stood with one hand propped on the door frame as she

opened the door. He looked her up and down, an appraisal that seemed to satisfy him, since he gave a slow nod.

"Think you're smart, don't you?" he said.

"Excuse me?"

"You know very well what I'm talking about." He shouldered past her and stopped in the middle of the room to look around before he went on. "It's enough to make a man wonder if you didn't do it on purpose."

She shut the door with a snap. "I didn't ask you to watch over me like a mother hen. I'm a grown woman and have a perfect right to leave my hotel room without your permission."

He kept his back to her, surveying the twin beds with which the room was furnished as he said with deliberation, "You must have known when you did it that all bets would be off."

"Meaning?"

"Exactly what you think it means. I'll move my things in here before bedtime."

She moved around to face him. "Try it, and I'll have the hotel manager call the police. I really will."

"Fine. I'll tell them it's a lovers' quarrel. And you can explain to Italian males with amorous dispositions why you're objecting in Florence to something that was perfectly fine in Venice."

"Even Italian women can change their minds!"

He looked thoughtful. "Maybe I'll tell them you're holding out for marriage and won't let me back in until I agree."

"You wouldn't."

"Try me." His blue eyes appeared steel gray with determination.

She breathed deep and let it out slowly before she said, "Maybe I'll tell them you're a con artist who seduces women for what you can get out of them."

His eyes narrowed. "Is that what you think?"

"Why not?" As he stood scowling without even attempting an answer, she went on: "But you don't have to go through this charade just to get Violet's journal. You stay in your own room, and you can have it. To finish reading, I mean, not to keep—for what good it will do you."

"You mean that?" The challenging tone was abruptly gone from his voice.

She nodded as she turned away. Her tone flat, she said, "Allain died."

"No." He sounded as if the death had happened at that moment, to a close member of his family.

She gave a slow nod as she moved to sit on the foot of one of the beds. It struck her as odd that she had known how he would be affected by the news. But she had known; that was why she had thrown it at him.

"I suppose it had to be," he said. Glancing toward the other bed, he stepped nearer to lower himself to the foot of it. "There was never any mention of him in Violet's life in New Orleans. It was always possible that she broke off with him, but I couldn't see her doing it. And he didn't seem the type to let her."

She sent him a quick look, but he was staring at his hands. A vague idea surfaced in her mind. Before she could stop herself, she said, "Do you remember what you said in England, when I asked you about the language of the flowers?"

"Not really; probably the first thing that came into my head."

"You mentioned rosemary."

"Oh, everybody knows that one," he said with a dismissive gesture. " 'Pray, love, remember.' *Hamlet*."

"Not everybody knows it." The words were dry.

He looked at her, his gaze suspicious. "What are you driving at?"

"Nothing, nothing at all."

She should have known better. Things didn't work like that, reincarnated lovers born again to be together. It was just entertainment for people with overactive imaginations, nonsense that was not at all helpful in dealing with the present problem. Eyewash, as Mimi would have said.

"Who killed Allain?" Rone asked.

She lifted a brow. "How do you know he was killed?"

"People's cholesterol counts must have been sky-high in those days, but he didn't seem the kind to keel over with a heart attack. Besides, somebody had tried to do him in at the train station."

"Well, apparently it was the same people, but I don't know that; Violet doesn't say and I'm not sure she ever knew. I think Gilbert was skulking around, myself—somebody was seen watching the villa. I wouldn't put it past him to have hired men to do the job. He wasn't rational."

"Old Gilbert didn't seem to know much about women; he brought a lot of his problems on himself. But he did have a thing or two to try his temper."

"You're defending him?" she said in disbelief.

"I'm just saying it's the dull, uptight men who are sometimes the most jealous. And a jealous reaction to a wife's straying was not only to be expected back then, but excused a lot in the way of mayhem."

"So Gilbert seemed to believe."

"I'll grant you he went about getting his wife back the wrong way."

"But he got her back. That's what I find so hard to believe."

"Yes and no," Rone said.

"What do you mean?"

"He didn't exactly get her back, I'd say, since they never really lived together afterward."

"Who told you that?" Joletta's question was as sharp as the frown between her eyes.

"Natalie's mother, when she was explaining how Violet got into selling perfume," he answered without altering his look of concentration. "Anyway, it seems to me that to be married to a woman but not allowed to touch her because of something you did yourself would be a form of torture."

The parallel was there, she thought, if she wanted to accept it. Rone was not allowed to touch her because of something he had done also.

Or was that what he was saying? Maybe she was reading too much into it. She should really stop using her imagination and listen only to the words.

"You feel sorry for Gilbert?" she said.

"Don't you, at least a little? Sure, he was a prude with the personality of a stump, your typical Victorian man. But he went off to Europe with a beautiful young wife and his dreams for a nice town house and a family, and he came back with nothing. A year later he puts a chased-silver dueling pistol to his head and tries to blow his brains out. He makes a mess out of that, too, winding up an invalid."

"I always thought he was hurt in some kind of accident."

"It was called an accident. According to Estelle, the story was that he was cleaning the pistol. Had to keep the scandal quiet, I suppose."

"He lived for years," Joletta said, her voice low as she reflected on old deaths, old tragedies caused by hasty words and acts undertaken in anger. After a moment she said, "I think I'll see if I can find Allain's grave tomorrow."

"You know where to look?"

"A church near the villa, though where exactly, I don't know. I can call Signora Perrino."

"Or drive out and look around," he said, his tone tentative. "I still have my rental car."

It was an offer if she cared to accept it. She couldn't do it. He was from the enemy camp. Before she could answer yes or no, however, he went on.

"Are you hungry? If you went out for dinner, I missed it."

"I didn't think about it," she answered. "I started reading the journal and didn't want to quit."

He shook his head in disapproval. "Not to worry. You want to eat late? Thesse ees Italy, *bella signorina.* No problem. As for me, I'm starving."

"You missed dinner because of me?"

"The dedicated guard. Don't you feel sorry for me?"

"I feel irritated and outdone, but not a shred of pity."

"But you'll eat with me anyway?"

It was a mistake to allow herself to be cajoled by a show of concern and an appealing smile. She knew it, but could not seem to help herself.

Regardless, even as she ran a brush through her hair and applied a little lipstick, her brain was busy with ways to keep him from spending the night in her room. She wasn't sure how she was going to do it, short of creating the kind of scene that made her cringe to contemplate. But she was not going to stay in that room with him. She would get rid of him before bedtime, no matter what it took.

An opportunity of sorts presented itself before the evening was over.

The restaurant was small and less than five blocks from the hotel. The food was northern Italian with a French accent, robust but with a refined presentation.

The place was full in spite of, or possibly because of, the hour. There were a few obvious tourists, but most of the tables were occupied by local residents. Their waiter appeared ready to take it as an insult to both the restaurant and himself personally if they did not order at least five courses. By the time they had worked their way through soup, salad, pasta, an entrée of spit-roasted lamb with baby carrots and aubergines, and dessert of crème caramel—with appropriate wine and a liqueur flavored with almonds—they could begin to guess why the Italians walked everywhere they went. It was necessary to counteract all that food.

They had set out for the hotel again when they saw Natalie and Timothy coming toward them.

"The concierge said he had recommended this place to you two," Natalie said, "but I couldn't believe you were operating on Italian time."

"Another week," Rone said, "and we'll be more Italian than the Italians."

"You two can stand it, you're both so slim; I'd have to go straight to a spa. But I wanted to ask Joletta what in the world she said to Caesar? He called me, totally strung out about it. He wasn't making much sense."

"I didn't say anything," Joletta answered.

"You must have. He was raving about going back to his home-town, some little place near Venice with an unpronounceable name, to become his own man again. He didn't like the way you saw him, didn't like the way he saw himself because of you. At least I think that's what he said."

"Oh," Joletta said.

"You do know what it's all about. Caesar was such a marvelous man. Really, I'm sorry I asked him to be nice to you."

"So am I," Joletta said quietly.

Natalie looked contrite. "I shouldn't have said that, I guess, though I don't know what difference it makes now. It just seemed like a good idea to have somebody move in on you, stay close to find out what you were up to."

"Lord, Natalie," Timothy said in brotherly disparagement.

Joletta felt the blood rush to her head. She curled her fingers slowly into fists. "It was an underhanded trick. Did you stop to think that maybe Caesar recognized it, and felt guilty?"

"Caesar?" Natalie arched a brow. "I wouldn't think he could feel guilty about anything."

"I think you underestimate him," Joletta said seriously.

"But not you?" Natalie said with a brittle laugh. "Honestly, I don't know what you're complaining about; knowing him didn't hurt you any. I thought you might even enjoy a little attention from a good-looking man, *amore* Italian-style."

"So kind of you. Maybe I should be grateful." Joletta tried hard to keep the embarrassment, the hurt and anger, from her voice, but was not sure she succeeded.

Natalie flushed a little and there was still an edge to her tone as she said, "Anyway, I should be the one upset. I had a great thing going with Caesar, but he hardly knew I was alive after I threw him at you in Paris. He fell for you, I think, maybe because he thought he saved your life in that ridiculously providential near accident. You made him feel all gallant and worthy or something, I guess."

"Sorry," Joletta said, "I didn't mean to ruin your romance."

Natalie gave her a moody look. "Yes, well, I suppose it was my own fault. But how was I to know that Rone had come up with the same idea, all on his own?"

Rone's voice was stringent as he broke in. "Thank you very much, Natalie, but I can make my own confessions."

"Yeah," Timothy said. "I think enough's been said anyway. Joletta will want to drum us out of the family, and I wouldn't blame her."

"Thanks, dear brother." Natalie's sarcasm had a tired sound.

The younger man ignored the comment as he turned an earnest look on Joletta. "Look, I'm sorry about all this. I'm sorry things didn't work out, too—Natalie tells me you've traced things as far as the journal goes, and found zip. Not to worry. We'll all get by. But families have to stick together. So if there's any way we can make this up to you, just say the word."

"I think," Joletta said slowly, "that there just might be."

"Hey, great."

Joletta met Natalie's wary gaze. "You're at our same hotel here, aren't you? Do you have twin beds in your room?"

"Joletta, wait, please." There was urgency in Rone's touch as he placed his hand on her arm.

"There's something wrong with your room?" the other woman asked.

"Not the room, but the security system."

"I don't think I understand."

"She means," Rone said in exasperated tones, "that I've been keeping too close an eye on her."

"You mean—in the same room? Wasn't that a little above and beyond—" Natalie stopped as her gaze rested on Rone's set face. She added hastily, "Oh, never mind."

"He seemed to think I was in danger," Joletta said.

"You were in danger," Rone answered shortly.

"There's been no problem since we got to Venice."

"You mean since I took up night duty."

"Good Lord, Joletta," Natalie said, "I never knew you were such a heart breaker."

"I'm not. This has nothing to do with me personally, as you ought to know."

"Doesn't it now?" Rone asked, his voice soft.

Timothy held up a hand like a traffic cop. "Come on, enough," he said. "I'm sure Natalie won't mind you sleeping over with her."

"You forget, Tim," his sister corrected him. "The hotel was short of rooms. Mother is with me."

"Oh, right." He turned back to Joletta. "But, hey, I could come bed down in the other twin, if that would make you feel better."

"It won't be necessary," Rone said, the words brusque.

"Now wait a minute," Natalie said slowly. "Joletta is my cousin, and if she doesn't want you in her room, I think you had better stay out."

"Your concern is touching, but a little late," Rone said.

"Just what do you mean by that?" Timothy asked.

"Your cousin was nearly killed. Where were you then? Joletta is perfectly safe with me—at least from anything I might do—so put your minds at ease on that point. For the rest, I've been looking after her, and I'll keep right on doing it. If you think you can stop me, go ahead."

Timothy narrowed his eyes, but after an exchange of glances with Rone, he swallowed and was quiet. Natalie said nothing either, only stood watching Joletta's protector with quick and rather surprised consideration in her blue-gray eyes.

Rone did not wait for more, but touched Joletta's arm in a gesture that suggested they move on. She went with him, partly because there seemed no point in standing there in the middle of the block, and partly because her mind was so busy that she started moving by reflex action.

When she realized what she was doing, she stopped. She said baldly, "You can't move in with me tonight."

He halted. He ran his fingers through his hair and clasped the back of his neck as he looked toward the night sky as if for inspiration. Finally he said, "Why? What is it you're so afraid of? What is it about me that makes you prefer to take your chances with the creep who ransacked your room in Lucerne and put you in a ditch near Bologna than have me in the same room with you?"

"You're an overbearing, manipulative—"

"Those are character faults, not reasons."

She gazed at the display of fine leather shoes in the store window behind him until the bright, yet soft, clear colors began to blur. "All right," she said, her voice a little thick from the constriction in her nose and throat. "What is it you want me to say? Do you think I'm afraid of what I might feel for you? Fine, I'm saying that. I don't like having somebody play with my emotions for the sake of what they can get out of me. I hate starting to feel something for somebody, then finding out I'm being used. I can't stand the thought of maybe learning to care about someone and waking up to find them gone. You say you're trying to protect me. That's great if it makes you feel big. What I'm trying to do is protect me, too. I'm—I'm just trying to keep myself safe, from you."

"Joletta," he said, the word a soft entreaty as he reached to take her hand.

"Don't!" She jerked away, stepping back from him. "Don't say sweet things, don't bring me flowers, please! And don't make love to me. I don't need that. I don't want it. All I want is to be through with this trip, and then to get as far away from you as possible."

His blue gaze was somber with strain as he searched her face. Abruptly, he said, "I didn't mean to hound you."

"People do a lot of things they don't mean." She refused to look at him.

A car went past in the street with the wafted blast of a radio and a shriek of laughter. Neither of them noticed. The atmosphere between them had the heated fragility of a piece of hand-blown glassware just before it was struck from the pipe.

Rone set his jaw, then deliberately relaxed it. He said, "If you want to get rid of me, you don't have to wait for the trip to end."

She turned her gaze on him then. His face was a little pale in the dimness of the streetlights, but its planes were hard and unreadable and his lashes shielded his eyes.

"You mean it?" she asked.

"Beginning now."

The words could not have been more firm. Regardless, there was inside her a strange reluctance to test them. It had to be done, however.

She took a step backward. He made no move.

She took another step. He put his hands in his pockets.

"Good-bye, then," she said.

He did not answer.

There was nothing left to do but turn and walk away.

That was what she did.

But as she walked she could feel the ache inside her growing. She should have felt better; she was rid of him, wasn't she? That was what she had wanted.

Wasn't it?

Rone watched Joletta as she left him, moving with her back straight, shoulders set, and head up. He loved her grace and dignity, the sense of class about her. He even loved the way she had told him to get lost. God, he just loved her.

He wished he had never heard of the perfume. Better still, he wished his mother had never heard of it. There had been a time when he had thought it could be a huge success. Now he didn't care if it was ever resurrected. He thought, in fact, that it would be a good thing if it was lost forever. What did it really matter? All good things had to come to an end sometime.

Maybe his pursuit of Joletta was another one?

Maybe it was time he moved on, did something else, thought of something else.

She didn't want him sticking around, didn't need him.

There seemed no way to break through to her, nothing he could say or do to convince her that he wanted her for herself, needed her with a deep, slow ache that twisted his insides into knots and made his heart feel as if it had a ten-pound weight hung on it.

So that was it. Farewell. Good-bye.

The kiss-off without the kiss.

At least he still had the carnation.

Chapter 24

The cemetery was walled with golden stone and lined with the somber green of cypress trees. The graves, marked with their slabs of marble and stone, were turned so that each faced the view afforded by the hillside on which they lay. Swallows swooped in the warm, still air, while in the gently waving grass a grasshopper clicked and sang quietly to itself.

Joletta stood with Signora Perrino beside a marble marker whitened by sun and scoured by wind and years to such a fine brightness that the carvings of trailing flowers and an angel with drooping wings were barely visible. With careful fingers, she traced the sprigs of carved rosemary and petals of the old-fashioned roses exactly like the ones that grew on the wall of the villa garden. She also outlined the name and dates:

ALLAIN ALEXANDER MASSARI
17 DECEMBER 1827–9 MARCH 1855

Violet had never mentioned his middle name. It had, Joletta supposed, been unimportant to her.

"He was very young," Signora Perrino said from where she stood on the other side of the grave.

Joletta gave a nod. "They both were, really, he and the woman who was here with him."

"Indeed. I must tell you that there are always flowers placed on this grave when the others of my family buried here are honored."

"Are there?" Joletta looked up in surprise. "How thoughtful."

"We had just begun to speak of this when your cousin arrived the other day. I know nothing of a perfume formula you seek, as I told you then, but the story of how this man and the woman he loved came to Florence has great importance for me and those of my blood who have lived since then. I heard it a thousand times as I was growing up. I tell my children, and they tell theirs."

"I don't think I understand," Joletta said slowly.

"Before these two came, we were peasants working as servants to the Franchetti, who owned the villa. Afterward, we were—not wealthy, precisely, but well-off. In the next generation we came to own the villa and its surrounding lands. We still do; the present villa was built by my father and came to me, since I had no brothers. My husband, God preserve his soul, thought it a fine dowry, and lived there because I wished it. The place will go to my sons when I am gone."

"I think—I suspect your family prospered because of a man named Giovanni, who went to America. Is that it?"

"That's only a part of it. There was payment before for a great service done for the American lady. We had lost her name after all these years; it is a great joy to discover it again, and to speak to one of her family."

"It's lovely to be here," Joletta said with a smile. "I've been reading about Giovanni and his mother, Maria, and I'm glad to know that everything turned out well for those who came after them."

The older woman looked at Joletta a long instant before she gave a sharp, decisive nod. "There is another thing."

She took a purse from her arm and opened it. From inside she drew out something that flashed gold and brilliant sparkling light in the sun. It was a necklace.

"This belongs by right to you, I think. It's been hidden away for years by the women of my family. I know it was the property of the American lady who was here, but how we came to own it, I'm not sure. There has always been such secrecy about it that I fear it may have been stolen. Or if not that, then taken for safekeeping by my great-grandmother Maria, who was housekeeper at the time, but for some reason never returned. I would like to give it to you now."

Joletta took the heavy necklace in her hand. The clasp, she saw at once, was broken. It could not have been worn since the evening in the village garden when it had been torn from Violet's neck during her struggle with her attacker. Had Maria picked it up after that terrible night, then forgotten it? Or had it been given to her? There was no way to know.

It was still beautiful, a little dingy with age and clogged with lint from some cloth it had been kept wrapped up in, but remarkably unchanged from the description of it in the journal. The diamonds encrusting the gold bands surrounding the perfume bottle caught tiny blazes of light and reflected them into Joletta's face. She blinked a little as she stared down at the huge amethyst, and at the design of a bird with spread wings etched into the side of the jewel. It really was exquisite, almost like a piece by Fabergé.

She turned the piece slightly. The edges of the small design on the side caught the sunlight. The etched bird sprang into relief.

She should know the design. It was familiar, and yet—

She did know it.

Thinking back over history lessons half-forgotten, bits and pieces studied during graduate work, she saw, quite suddenly, why Violet had not been able to record who Allain had been in her journal. She saw, too, why he had died.

Tears stung her eyes and pressed into the back of her nose in abrupt, unexpected grief for Violet and the man she had loved and the inescapable fate that had been theirs.

"Are you all right, signorina?" the other woman asked in soft-voiced concern.

"Yes, I think so," Joletta said. She managed a smile, though she could not quite meet the eyes of Signora Perrino. She wished that she could tell someone what she knew. Not just someone, but someone who was as interested in Violet and Allain as she was, someone who knew their story. She wanted to tell Rone, wanted to hear what he would say and what he thought about it.

There was a small amount of gold-colored liquid in the bottle.

With fingers that trembled, Joletta tried the top. It was stuck, frozen by time and age and ancient perfume crystals. She tightened her grip, afraid to force it and risk damaging the bottle, and yet overwhelmed by a need to inhale whatever vestige of fragrance remained.

The top came free in her hand.

She lifted the bottle, breathing in gently, drawing the scented air deep into the back of her nose.

Roses, that was the top note. Orange blossoms. Musk. Amber. Narcissus. Vanilla orchid. Violets.

Soft, warm, flowing, familiar yet exotic in their combination, the scents merged in the forefront of her mind.

She was amazed at the freshness of it. By all rights the perfume should have changed, should have lost its true fragrance with time and evaporation. That it had not was due, surely, to the fact that all the ingredients must have been pure and natural, instead of the volatile synthetic chemical compounds used so often in modern perfumes, and also because the necklace had been kept hidden away in some dark place all these years.

It was a lovely scent, beautifully made, evocative in a haunting fashion.

But it was not Le Jardin de cour.

She inhaled again. No. It was not the perfume they were looking for.

Roses—orange blossoms—musk—amber—narcissus—orchid—violets.

There was no vetiver. There was no jasmine, no lilac.

A slow, wry smile curved Joletta's mouth. Of course. How foolish they had all been.

She saw it.

The truth about the formula. And where it was to be found.

It had been there all along, but she had not recognized it because she had been expecting the impossible, a miracle in total disregard for the quirky twists and personal predilections of human nature, and in defiance of everything she had been taught about the evolution of perfumes.

She also saw something else.

A sound left her that was a laugh and a gasp of pain at the same time. The tears in her eyes overflowed, though she smiled through them with a shake of her head.

"Are you sure you're all right?" Signora Perrino said, her voice anxious.

"I'm fine," Joletta said. "Really. I just—thought of something." Her grasp tightened for an instant on the necklace, then she held it out toward Signora Perrino. "It was kind of you to show me this, but it doesn't belong to me. I think it's likely that it was earned, or else given in return for a great favor."

The older woman took the heavy piece of jewelry in her hand. "You're certain, signorina?"

"Yes," Joletta said, "quite certain."

The perfume shop was still open when Joletta arrived. It appeared to be fairly busy even this late in the evening, nearly closing time; there were customers browsing at the counters and the saleswoman at the cash register was ringing up perfume for a pair of women with the stamp of tourists. The place was bright and cheerful, and the smell of a dozen different fragrances wafted from the open door of the back mixing room to welcome her.

Joletta had meant to be at the shop earlier, but after the long flight routed through New York and Atlanta with delays in both places, she had been so tired that she had fallen into bed at her apartment and slept the clock around. By the time she had dragged herself up again, found something to eat, unpacked her suitcase, and searched out something to wear, the day was half over. Several hours at the university library doing research into the Crimean War and Russian history had taken care of the rest of the afternoon.

Now she only waved a greeting as she passed through the shop and the mixing room, then out to the courtyard. It seemed forever since she had been here. Nothing looked quite the same; it was as if it had changed subtly, though she knew it was she who had changed.

It also seemed forever since she had begun to guess at Violet's secrets. She couldn't wait to see if she was right.

She had been so sure, and so excited, that she hadn't finished the tour. After talking to Signora Perrino, she had gone straight back to the hotel. She had packed her suitcase, left a message for the tour director, and taken a taxi to the airport.

She had intended to leave a message for Rone also, telling him, briefly, what she had discovered. The man at the hotel desk told her it was not possible; he had checked out early that morning. He had left no forwarding address, but had mentioned in passing that he was on his way home.

Home to New York.

Joletta had been stunned to find him already gone. She had given him no reason to think that she was interested in his leaving; still, she would have expected him to say good-bye. She could only suppose he had finally decided she didn't need him.

She should be glad. It made no sense that she felt stymied and let down, and even depressed.

Joletta glanced at the courtyard garden as she passed through it. That, too, looked different, vaguely Italian now, with its columned arcade, its fountain and grapevine-covered arbor of stone, and the sweet olive in the corner where no true olive could tolerate the dampness. She shook her head a little as she climbed the outside stairs. Letting herself into the salon, she put down her shoulder bag and passed through into Mimi's bedroom.

She knew exactly what she wanted, thought she remembered where to find it. Going directly to Mimi's memory chest, she set the outer doors wide, then pulled open the top drawer on the left, turning over the contents. It was in the bottom where she had seen it for years, a packet of tintypes and glass negatives and faded photographs.

Joletta took the packet to the bed and untied the stringy ivory-colored ribbon that held them. With delicate care, she sifted through them until she found the one she wanted. She took it out, holding it to the light.

Taken at some time in the late 1870s or early 1880s, judging from the style of the clothing, it was a stiff photograph showing the front of the perfume shop. In it was Violet Fossier standing near the door with a female shop assistant on her right, both of them with their hair in pompadours and wearing shirtwaist blouses buttoned to the throat and bustled skirts that swept the ground. On Violet's other side was a man, while just beyond him could be seen the sign for the pharmacy that had stood next door to the perfume shop until the proprietor's death just before World War I, only a few months before Violet herself had died. On the sign in small letters was a name: GIOVANNI REDAELLI, PROPRIETOR.

The man who stood next to Violet was half-turned from the camera, as if he did not particularly care to have his likeness taken. Broad of shoulder and well proportioned, he was handsome in the fashion of another age, with side-whiskers and a fine mustache. He wore a dark suit and carried a cane in his gloved hand, and on his head was a low-crowned hat with a wide brim that shaded his eyes. In avoiding the camera lens, he had turned to look at Violet. Even with his partially concealed expression, the grainy print of the photograph, and the yellowing of the years, the look on his face was near adoration.

Violet herself stared at the camera with clear eyes and only a hint of a smile on her mouth. She had aged since the miniature was done, but she was still a beautiful woman in a serene, self-contained style. Though she was giving her attention to the photographer and the moment, it was plain she was also aware of the man who stood next to her. She gave the impression that as soon as the time passed when movement would not blur the photograph, she would turn and speak to the man so near her, perhaps even place her hand in the bend of his arm and walk away at his side.

Joletta gave a low, satisfied laugh.

With the photograph still in one hand, she returned to the chest and took out the heavy velvet-and-brassbound journal from the drawer where she had hidden it before she went to Europe. She carried both of them to the French windows that gave out onto the upper gallery overlooking the courtyard. Opening the doors for the added light, she turned through the journal to a page just past the middle of the book, to a small pen-and-ink drawing of the head and shoulders of a man. She held the two images up together for comparison.

Yes.

They were the same.

She sighed and moved slowly to seat herself in a wicker chair on the gallery. Letting the book and photograph drop into her lap, she stared out over the courtyard. Somewhere inside her, tension she had not known she was carrying seemed to ease.

How long she sat there, she had no idea. When next she noticed the time, the light of evening was fading away and there was no sound from the shop below. The evening wind off Lake Pontchartrain was stirring the leaves of the sweet olive below, sending its fragrance in drifting clouds to where she sat.

Her gaze was resting on a gate in the wall of the courtyard, a gate that had always been there. It led into the courtyard of the building next door, the building that was today a part of some bachelor lawyer's pied-à-terre, but which in other years had belonged to the owner of the pharmacy.

How many people, she wondered, had known about that gate in the past? How many had gossiped about the woman with the invalid husband who had tried to kill himself, the woman on such close terms with the good-looking Italian pharmacist whose shop was next door?

A pharmacist in those days was required only to have some knowledge of the concoction of pills and elixirs and mouthwashes, the money to buy ingredients, and the integrity not to adulterate the products he mixed together. The man in the photograph had appeared prosperous. Joletta did not doubt that he had been respected in the city, or that conjecture about him had been rampant among the female members of the community. That no whisper of ancient scandal had echoed down through the years to Violet's descendants was a tribute to his discretion and, perhaps, his devotion.

What must it be like, Joletta wondered, to be loved in that way, by a man who would risk everything, sacrifice everything, to be with you?

She would rather not think about it.

Joletta got to her feet and moved back into the salon. Leaving the photograph lying on a side table but carrying the journal, she went back downstairs and into the rear workroom, where the perfume was mixed and bottled.

Beyond the doorway that led into the shop, everything was quiet. The shop was closed and locked for the day. That was good, the way she wanted it.

She placed the journal on the long counter that ran down the center of the room. Taking a glass beaker and a series of pipettes from a shelf, she set them beside it. She used a couple of the smaller account books from under the counter to hold the pages of the small brassbound book open to the first entry that had one of Violet's small sketches at the top of the page.

It was really very simple, the code Violet had used to mark the formula for her perfume. It was in the drawings and the dates. Violet had made a lot of sketches, but most of them were on blank pages or in the margins. The ones that meant something were those placed at the dated headings of pages. The flowers and small animal figures she had drawn indicated the oil essence to be used. The numbers for that particular month and day gave the proportion of the oil shown to the whole.

Joletta studied the page a moment, then moved to the shelves holding the brown bottles filled with precious oils. Walking along it, following the labels with the tips of her fingers, she began to pick and choose.

With the bottles lined up in front of her, each corresponding to a journal page, Joletta picked up a pipette and began.

Within moments, the scents began to rise around her. She hardly noticed them individually, so great was her concentration. The combined effluences had a rightness that satisfied her, rather like a baker smelling the yeast of his rising dough and knowing the bread is proceeding according to the recipe.

She worked with care and exactness, adding just so many drops of each oil and not a lingering droplet more to the beaker, reaching for the next one, and the next, in their proper order. She took pains, just as she had been taught by Mimi, was careful not to plop the oils in any old way, not to shake or joggle the mixture so the scents were bruised. She treated the oils with respect, and even with love.

She was in her element, she realized, as she watched the pale green, light yellow, and golden orange-red drops meld and blend together and smelled their mingling essences. Always before, she had been watched over by Mimi as she mixed perfume; this was the first time she had undertaken to create something on her own. It made a difference in the way she felt, the way she thought of it.

She loved the way the glass jars and vials and other equipment felt in her hands, the weight and smoothness of them. She enjoyed the sense of experimentation and creative power that working with them gave her. The uniqueness of her task pleased her, the fact that she was making a formulation that had not scented the air, perhaps, in over a hundred years. She felt like a sorceress concocting some mystical imitation of life, one that required only a warm body to work its power, to become real for a few fleeting hours.

She knew what she wanted. She was going to make perfume.

She was going to create new and different fragrances, just as Mimi had done, and Violet, and all the other Fossier women who had gone before. It was in her blood, but most of all it was in her heart.

At last she had completed the measuring. Gently, she stirred in the pure alcohol that would make the oils volatile so they could become airborne and more available to the olfactory sense. She waited a moment, then applied the perfume to a piece of clean white paper. She let the molecules set, then inhaled the fragrance.

She had done it. She had re-created Violet's perfume exactly, the perfume that had been in the necklace.

Regardless, it still wasn't Le Jardin de cour. It was similar, very similar, but not quite right.

She had known it could not be.

To be sure beyond a doubt, she put a drop of the perfume on her wrist and let it settle, then brought her wrist to her nose.

No, definitely not.

She heard the scrape of a footfall on the stone floor. She began to turn, jerking around so quickly that the glass pipette she was still holding struck the beaker of perfume. The beaker tipped over. Perfume splashed in a wide sweep over the counter, spreading like water, its exotic oils gleaming with a rich sheen in the light from overhead.

The fragrance exploded on the air, overpowering, almost sickening in its strength, even before the voice sounded in the still room.

"I thought the perfume was supposed to be lost," Natalie said. "I should have known you were lying."

"Don't be ridiculous," Joletta snapped. She reached to snatch up the journal. Its thick pages had become saturated with perfume for a fourth of their width. The odor would be permanent, ineradicable.

"What do you call this then?"

The question came from Timothy, who had crowded into the room behind his sister. Aunt Estelle, her face grim with her enmity, was standing just beyond the door.

"I call this a false hope," Joletta said, cradling the journal protectively against her chest. "As you would surely understand if any of you had a perfumer's nose."

"Don't take that tone with me, my girl," her aunt said, her face set with anger. "I want an explanation for what you're doing and I want it now."

The temptation to tell them all where they could go with their demands and accusations was so strong for a moment that Joletta felt the blood rush to her head. There had been enough secrecy and misunderstanding, however; there was no point in carrying it any further.

"I'm telling you that the perfume you smell isn't Le Jardin de cour, and therefore isn't the famous old perfume we've been hearing about for years. I suspect this blend I got out of the journal may be based on it, but I think Violet changed it to suit herself, for reasons that—well, for her own reasons."

"How can that possibly be?" her aunt inquired in icy tones. "My mother and her mother before her are supposed to have used Violet's recipe; I've heard the story so often I could recite it in my sleep."

"They may have, but I think they changed it, a little here, a little there, according to what they liked, or maybe the oils they had available. For instance, there's no vetiver in Violet's formula, but you know yourself it's one of the main oils that Mimi used because people in New Orleans like the fresh wood scent."

Estelle exchanged a quick look with her children. As she saw the acute disappointment close over the faces of all three, Joletta went on.

"But I don't think it ends there, not by a long shot. I doubt that the perfume Violet discovered in Europe, the perfume used by the Empress Eugénie, is exactly the same as the one used by Joséphine. It's unlikely that either woman could have resisted adding her own favorite oil essences to it over a period of time. A heavy violet scent, for instance, was a passion with Joséphine, and was included in the formula I just used, but it's doubtful violet oil would have been available to Cleopatra several hundred years before in the heat of ancient Egypt. As for Cleopatra's version, I feel sure she included her two cents' worth, too. The incense of the priestesses of the Moon Goddess that she was supposed to have copied should have been a very simple compound, one strong on wood notes. More than that, the Egyptians loved perfume—"

Aunt Estelle held up a hand heavy with rings. "That's enough. I was raised with perfume, too; I do get the picture."

"Don't you think it's reasonable?" Joletta asked quietly.

"Very likely." The older woman's agreement was vicious.

"Are you saying we can never make Le Jardin de cour?" Natalie asked in sharp tones.

"I'm saying it won't do any good to make it, not for the purpose Lara Camors wants. Le Jardin de cour bears very little resemblance to the fabulous perfume of history's fabled women that she has been promised."

"That can't be true!" Natalie said as she clenched a hand into a fist and brought it down on the counter. "There's too much at stake for it to be true."

"Well, it is," Joletta said, "and there's nothing any of us can do about it."

"Except for you," her aunt said in astringent contempt. "You can use Violet's recipe to go on making something close to Le Jardin de cour."

Joletta gave a thoughtful nod. "That's true, not the same blend exactly, but something close."

"So you win."

Joletta made no reply. As quiet fell she turned from the others and reached for a paper towel from the roll at one end of the counter. Leaning as far as she could reach, she began to mop up the spilled perfume.

"Actually," Timothy said in his light voice, "it doesn't make any difference."

"Don't be stupid," his mother snapped, "of course it does."

"Why?" he inquired with clear-eyed simplicity from where he had slouched against the door frame. "We're the only ones who know that the perfume isn't the same."

Natalie looked from Timothy to her mother. The older woman was staring at her son with a heavy frown between her thin eyebrows. Natalie switched her attention to Joletta. Her gaze grew bleak before she shrugged.

"It won't work," she said. "Joletta knows, and she'd tell the first person to ask her point-blank, even if she didn't want the formula for herself. Since she does want it, all she'd have to do is place a call to Lara Camors."

Aunt Estelle pursed her lips before she spoke. "Dear Lara loves money, but she's a stickler for truth in advertising; she guards the good name of Camors like a hen with one chick. That would be the end of it."

"Unless there was a way to keep Joletta from talking." Natalie turned a speculative look upon Joletta as she spoke.

"What did you have in mind?" Timothy asked in lazy humor. "A ride to the Mississippi and cement shoes? Good planning, sis; we wouldn't have to split the two million with her, either, or worry about her signing the consent agreement."

"Very funny," his mother said. "You might bend your mind to something helpful, if you can manage that."

"What about a nice bribe?" her son asked. "What do we have that Joletta wants?"

"Nothing," Joletta said, her voice tight. "I don't want a bribe or anything else. I don't want anything to do with Camors Cosmetics."

Natalie's face lighted with eagerness. "You mean you'll give us the use of the formula and back off, not blow the whistle on it?"

"I—didn't say that." Joletta tossed the paper towel she had used into the trash can under the counter before turning to look from one to the other of her relatives. "Have you thought what would happen if somebody found out the perfume was a hoax after it went into production? Fossier's Royal Parfums would be completely discredited; it would be the end of the shop, not to mention the reflection on our good name in the city."

"You sound positively Victorian, Joletta," Natalie said on a laugh. "We would have the money, wouldn't we?"

"Joletta doesn't care as much about money as you do, sis," Timothy said softly. "But she might prefer not to make her family look like a bunch of fools."

"Now that is the most sensible thing you've said in a long time, Timothy," his mother said. She looked at Joletta. "Can we count on it, I wonder?"

"Personally, I wouldn't risk it," Natalie said. "But I've got another idea."

"Here, here." Timothy's gaze on his sister held as much resentment as irony.

Natalie sent him a scathing glance before she went on: "Look, Joletta, you say the old perfume recipe is no good. Fine. But would you want to make Le Jardin de cour again using the formula from the chemical analysis?"

"I suppose that would be all right." Joletta leaned against the counter behind her and folded her arms as she spoke.

"Great. Then let us have the old one out of the journal. We'll just say everything was fine until Mimi came along, that she was the one who made the changes, added the vetiver and so on. In other words we split the formula, turn it into two perfumes, one for you at the shop and one for us."

It was, Joletta saw, the bribe Timothy had suggested. They were so transparent in their greed. Didn't they realize it? Or was it just that they didn't care enough to hide it with her because she was family and didn't count. She said, "You think Lara Camors will go for that? Or Rone?"

"I think they might, especially if you explained it. If it would make you feel better, we could even admit that the formula was changed from the days of Cleopatra. French perfume is where it's at today anyway; it will be impressive enough for advertising purposes if we just throw in Joséphine and Eugénie. Besides, it's true, isn't it?"

"I don't know if it's true or not. Violet didn't say."

"But it's close enough to being true that you could claim it, couldn't you?" Natalie's tone was exasperated and the frown lines between her eyes grew deeper.

Joletta hesitated, but at last she shook her head. "I don't think I could, not to someone like Lara Camors, and especially not to Rone."

Chapter 25

Joletta locked the door behind her relatives with a sigh of relief. They could have seen themselves out, as they had let themselves in, but it gave her satisfaction to escort them from the premises.

She was exhausted. The argument over the formula, covering the same ground again and again, had gone on for what seemed like hours.

She didn't really think this was the end of it. Her aunt and her cousins would try again to convince her, no doubt, or would come up with other schemes to bring her around to their way of thinking. It didn't matter; it wasn't going to work.

She had tried hard to be fair. But she knew now what she could and could not do, knew what she wanted, and she would have no part of defrauding Camors Cosmetics or the public. She would mix and sniff and sniff and mix, trying to recreate Le Jardin de cour on her own. But if she couldn't, then that was all right. She would have done her best. There must have been thousands of perfumes lost over the ages, just as millions of valuable lives had been destroyed, cut off like snipping loose threads from a beautiful piece of embroidery. The loss was felt, but people kept right on living, right on loving again, making up their lives as they went along.

And that was what she would do, just as Violet had, all those years ago.

Joletta moved back through the shop. She would finish clearing away the mess she had made with the perfume, then it was time she headed for home.

She had left her shoulder bag and car keys upstairs. As she passed through the courtyard on her way to get them a short time later, Joletta stopped to breathe fresh, unperfumed air. She felt as if she were moving in a miasma of fragrance, that it clung to her skin and hair and clothes, and especially to the soaked journal she carried. She would have loved it ordinarily, but it was a bit much just now.

It was pleasantly warm. The moisture in the atmosphere gave it the softness of breathable silk. A gentle wind stirred the leaves of the huge old sweet olive in the corner and the grapevines on the stone arbor, so they made a rustling whisper. The pressure in the fountain was low, so it barely splashed as it fell into the basin. Under the old porte cochere that led from the courtyard through the lower floor of the house to the street, the roosting pigeons made noises like drowsy toddlers grumbling themselves to sleep.

For an instant Joletta was transported to Venice and St. Mark's Square with the pigeons wheeling in battle formation around the campanile, with Rone on one side and Caesar on the other.

"*Bella, bella,*" she said softly, smiling to herself with a bittersweet twist of her lips.

This garden had also been the scene of many a memory with Mimi, however, including her fall on the outside stairs. Now it carried shadings of that other tragedy in Florence as well because of its resemblance to the garden there.

Abruptly, she shook her head and turned to mount the stairs.

It was then that she saw the shadow move under the sweet olive in the far corner.

"Who's there?" she called, her voice sharp.

No one answered. The moments stretched as she strained to see. She was beginning to think it had only been a cat after the pigeons when a man stepped forward, into the light.

"It's just me," Timothy said.

She let out her breath in a rush. Irritable from ebbing fright, she said, "What are you doing here? I thought you'd gone."

"Mother and Natalie did go, but I had to come back to see you. I want the journal, Joletta."

"We went through this before. I thought it was settled, at least for tonight."

He moved a step closer. "Nothing was settled at all. I really need that journal for Camors, since they won't deal until they see it. I'm not leaving without it this time."

There was something flat and unemotional about his tone that sent a chill along Joletta's spine. Regardless, she held her place. "Why you? I thought you hardly cared."

"Money, honey, two mil, to be exact. Besides, there's mother. She'll be furious if she doesn't get it and the old formula you were making. She expects me to do something. I can't let her down."

"Oh, Timothy, I'm sorry, but don't you see it's impossible for me to go along with you?"

"Yeah. That's why I came back to kill you," he said quietly. "I don't want to, really; that's just the way it is."

As he took another step toward her she sidestepped, putting the table between them. At the same time the evening breeze brought a strong whiff of lime scent to her nostrils. Timothy's cologne; she could smell it here as she had not been able earlier in the mixing room with the overpowering scent of spilled perfume on the air. Lime. She had smelled that harsh, nose-tingling scent before.

Her voice stuck in her throat, so she had to swallow before she could speak. "You," she said. "It was you who tore up my room in Switzerland, and upstairs here before I left."

"Fat lot of good it did me, sneaking around, scaling up and down walls like some Outward Bound idiot. All I got was a stupid notebook with scribbles that didn't mean a thing without the journal." He circled around the table as he spoke.

"You ran us off the road, me and Rone." She moved again to keep the barrier between them while a memory flashed across her mind like a film image of the careening car, the fire and thunder of its explosion.

"I got mad. I almost ran you down in Paris, too, but that dumb Italian was there, not to mention old Rone. It's a mistake to cross me. Mimi found out. I only gave her a little push when she started down the stairs over there, but she died anyway."

Her grandmother, frightened to death like the Signora da Allori, Joletta thought as a shiver of horror moved over her. Or more likely, struck down by grief. That terrible ordeal may have been something else Mimi had been trying to tell them.

"Does Aunt Estelle know you did that?" she asked. "She doesn't, does she?" she went on as an uneasy look crossed his face.

"She hasn't been able to keep up with where I am or what I'm doing for years. Or Natalie either, though she thinks she can."

"Kill me, and they may begin to wonder about a few things."

"They won't care, so long as I get hold of the journal. That's the thing they really need, the thing that will make people sit up and take notice. But you'll give it to me. You'll be glad to give it to me."

As he spoke he slid his hand into his jeans pocket and took out something black and tubular like a large pocketknife. He held it away from his body. There came a metallic snap and click, and a switchblade sprang out, glinting in the dimness.

At that moment the scrape of footsteps came from the direction of the porte cochere. A hard voice spoke from out of the darkness.

"Hold it right there."

Timothy whirled, his face contorting as he muttered a curse. "Where did you come from? How did you get in here?"

"You left the street gate open," Rone answered.

Joletta had recognized his voice even before Rone walked out of the tunnellike area. She couldn't believe it. He was there in spite of everything she had said. He was there as he had sworn, on self-imposed duty.

He was breathing hard, as if he had been running, and beads of perspiration stood out on his forehead. Shrugging out of a light jacket, he wrapped it over his arm as padding as he walked. If he was armed in any other way, there was no sign of it.

"I can take you, man." Timothy's eyes widened as he made the boast. He settled into a street fighter's crouch.

"Try it," Rone said. "I don't mind." He moved toward the younger man, his gaze watchful, ready.

"Wait," Joletta cried. "Don't do this."

She felt as if she had wakened from a deep sleep only to find herself in a nightmare. Her chest jarred with the beat of her heart. Sickness clenched her stomach.

Rone had come to help her when she needed him. He was getting ready to lay his life on the line for her. Because of Violet's perfume. She couldn't let it happen. There had to be something she could do.

The heavy journal was in her hand. She thrust it out toward Rone. Her words tumbling over themselves in her haste, she said, "This is what he came for. You take it, take it for Camors. The code for the old perfume is in it, proof of where it came from, everything you need."

"Shut up!" Timothy shouted, stepping between her and Rone

before the other man could reach for the journal. His voice dropped to a growl and he took a pace toward her as he said, "What do you think you're trying to do?"

As he snatched at the journal Joletta jerked it back, retreating a quick pace. "If Rone has everything, then Aunt Estelle will be satisfied, and there will be nothing for you to do but go home."

Timothy turned the knife he held over in his hand. He turned it over again. He said, "Or I could kill you both and take everything to mother and Lara Camors myself."

Hard on his words, he moved to the attack.

Rone sprang to meet him. The two men came together with hard grunts. Rone blocked Timothy's first blow, and a ragged tear, rapidly darkening, appeared in his jacket. Then they were grappling, their staggering footsteps grating on the stone paving, as Rone's fingers bit into the wrist of Timothy's knife hand. Timothy clawed with his free hand at Rone's face, reaching for his eyes.

Rone struck a hard blow at Timothy's chin. Timothy wrenched from Rone's grasp and stumbled back, but recovered in an instant. They circled each other, watching for an opening.

Rone wrapped his arm once more where the jacket was flapping loose. The material had turned wet and shining. Timothy bared his teeth in a grin as he saw it. He leaped once more, driving the knife toward Rone's stomach.

Rone twisted away from the thrust, letting it slide past him before he closed with the younger man. They strained together, chest to chest, lips pulled back in effort.

Joletta couldn't stand it. Her eyes burned with the effort to see. The need to scream was so strong that it hurt her throat. Her muscles felt frozen in place, while her hands trembled with the cold rush of the blood in her veins.

She had to do something. She had to, or she would go crazy. She took a step toward the two men.

She drew back the journal and threw hard, with all her strength, straight at Timothy's head.

Her cousin saw the movement. He dodged the heavy book, so it only struck him a glancing blow on the shoulder as it sailed past him with pages flying.

In that moment of distraction, Rone shifted his weight, twisting. Timothy threw himself in the opposite direction, trying to get his shoulder into Rone's chest so he could free his knife hand. Rone gave ground, sidestepping. Timothy followed in a plunging tangle

of legs, and the two men went down. They rolled from the flag-
stones to the grass square around the fountain, each seeking purchase, straining to bring the knife blade to bear.

There came a sodden thud, a hoarse expelling of breath, and a
sigh. Then silence.

Joletta stood still while her heart ceased its beat inside her. Then
as Rone detached himself from the long form on the grass and
pushed up to his knees, she stumbled toward him. He caught her,
dragging her against him, holding tight.

They stood like that for long, shivering seconds. Joletta, feeling
the warm seep of his blood against her back, stirred first.

"Your arm," she began.

"It'll do, but we have to see about your cousin."

She drew back, a question in her eyes she didn't want to put
into words.

He shook his head in answer. "If you'll call an ambulance, I'll
look at him, but I think he'll be okay."

The crew of the ambulance that appeared in due time were more
guarded in their opinions than Rone, but none of them went into
the kind of action reserved for extreme cases. Nor did any suggest
that the police should not, eventually, ask Timothy their questions.

It was morning before the official business of explanations and
statements was over, before the last of Aunt Estelle's screams was
heard, or her claims that the violence was the fault of everyone
except her son and herself. She would get Timothy the best lawyer
in the state, she said. She could not believe he had actually tried to
harm Joletta; certainly he could not have hurt Mimi. It was all a
terrible mistake. They would fight this thing, claim insanity, but
they would need money. Joletta had better think about what she
was doing by denying the wealth from the perfume to them all.

The sun was rising as Joletta and Rone walked along the Moon
Walk, the raised viewing platform that overlooked the Mississippi
River in front of Jackson Square. The haze over the expanse of
yellow-brown water was shafted by spears of light. The Algiers
ferry made a sturdy track across the current while the foam of its
spreading wake drifted slowly downstream.

The smell of coffee and beignets hung in the still, warm air,
coming from the Café du Monde, which was located only a few
blocks from the perfume shop. They had already made their early
morning breakfast there. It was Joletta who had suggested that they
walk along the river afterward.

Rone moved beside her with his hands clenched into fists in his pockets and the fine line of a frown between his brows. He had not touched her since he had taken her in his arms in the garden. That restraint was deliberate, Joletta thought. He had been helpful and efficient in dealing with the police; he had been considerate and endlessly understanding. But he had said nothing personal. As for the perfume, it had not been mentioned.

Joletta had a great deal to say about it. She waited until the moment seemed right, until they were quite alone on the walkway, leaning on the railing looking out over the water, before she began.

She told him first about the code to the old perfume, then she went on. "There's something else. Violet was playing games with the formula, I think, though I'm not sure what was in her mind. Maybe she was afraid she might be killed and was determined to leave a record of who Allain had been, however concealed; maybe she had a Victorian preference for hidden messages and meanings— as in the language of the flowers. Or maybe the whole thing gave her some kind of comfort and satisfaction, I don't know. All I know is that she changed things as she was rewriting everything that had happened."

"Rewriting?" The expression in his eyes was keen as he gazed down at her.

"Exactly."

It was easy enough to continue from there, going back in the story of Violet and Allain to the point where he had stopped reading and catching him up on what had taken place up to the day the last entry was made in Violet's journal. She told him, too, the details she had not had time to tell her aunt and her cousins the night before, about her visit to Signora Perrino, and the many ways that Violet, and everyone else, had changed the formula.

"Violet sketched a lot of flowers and I did wonder about them, but there were too many for them to have any meaning; the blossoms and other sketches, you remember, were almost like idle work, doodling done while she paused to think. It was only after Signora Perrino showed me the necklace that they began to make sense. There was a design etched into the amethyst. It was the double-headed eagle with spread wings of the royal family of Russia."

"Not a phoenix?"

She shook her head. "That was a false trail, almost. No, this was the symbol of the Romanovs. As soon as I saw it, I remembered a series of small drawings all about the same size that had been placed

in the heading above a scattering of journal dates. One thing that
had thrown me off about them was that they were not all of flowers.
The drawings were of a rose, an orange blossom, a musk deer—"

"A fly trapped in amber," he suggested with a shake of his head.

"You see it, don't you?" she said in quick agreement. "Roses, R.
Orange blossom, O. Musk, M. Amber, A. Also a botanical narcissus
on the bulb, the orchid flower of the vanilla bean vine, and, finally,
a wood violet."

"Romanov." He repeated the name quietly as he acknowledged
the sense of the combined letters.

Joletta agreed. "I think Allain was the son of Alexander the First
of Russia. The one bit of concrete information he gave about his
father certainly fits, the meeting with Napoléon Bonaparte at Tilsit
in 1807—only a few years after the Egyptian campaign—when Napoléon is supposed to have given the perfume to Allain's father."

"But wouldn't everyone have known if Allain had this connection?" Rone objected.

"Apparently, they did know, a lot of them; it seems to have
been an open secret around the courts of Europe. That knowledge
explains Allain's unofficial standing with Louis Napoléon and Parisian society, as well as his supposed recognition elsewhere. And
remember Napoléon the Third telling Violet that Allain and the Duc
de Morny had something in common? I thought when I first read
it that he was suggesting Allain was an illegitimate son, like Morny.
But you may recall that Morny's wife was the illegitimate daughter
of Czar Alexander the First? That would have made her Allain's
half-sister. Allain would have been brother-in-law to Morny, therefore a connection, by marriage, to Napoleon the Third."

"You think Allain was legitimate then?"

"He must have been, otherwise he would have been no danger
to anyone."

"But if he was Alexander's legitimate son, why wasn't he in
Russia on the throne, instead of that idiot who started the Crimean
War?"

"I don't think he would have been recognized as the heir apparent. You see, Alexander the First is supposed to have died in
1825, something like two years before Allain was born. Since he
had no legitimate children at the time, his brother Nicholas became
Czar."

Rone stared at her a moment. He took his hands from his pockets, not quite touching her arm as he indicated a bench just down

from where they stood. As she moved to sit down he lowered himself beside her with his arm along the back behind her. He lifted his hand, as if he would clasp her shoulder, then curled the fingers into a closed fist. Joletta waited, barely breathing, but he only looked away out over the river with set features while he slowly opened his fingers again.

"All right, let's back up a minute," he said in quiet tones. "You're telling me Alexander the First was supposed to have died, but didn't?"

It was an instant before Joletta could marshal her thoughts once more. Finally she went on. "That's it. The death of Alexander the First is one of history's unsolved puzzles. From all accounts he had been disenchanted with his position for some time and had made numerous threats to abdicate. He was unhappy in his marriage to a sickly wife who could not give him a legitimate heir and depressed over the death of an illegitimate daughter. He was heard to say several times that he would give anything to be relieved of the burden of the life he was leading. Then he died, so the official record shows, in a small town on the Sea of Azov. Because of bad weather, his body did not arrive in St. Petersburg for proper burial until over two months later. By then, identification was difficult."

"I can see how that might have been a problem," Rone said dryly.

"Yes, and to make matters worse, his wife, the illness-prone czarina, died from shock and the rigors of the long funeral journey from Azov, leaving no one of high position who had seen him die. Rumors began to circulate immediately that the czar's death was faked, that some poor courier of the same general size and appearance who died in an accident was passed off as his corpse. Alexander was supposedly taken away in the yacht of the Earl of Cathcart, an Englishman and former ambassador to Russia. The Cathcart family has never refuted the story and has, in addition, refused to make their family papers public. And the Russian government has always declined to permit the body to be exhumed for tests which might settle the question."

Rone nodded his understanding. "After Alexander gets away, then, he lands in Italy and marries a diva of the opera who becomes Allain's mother?"

"One whom he may or may not have known before his escape," Joletta added in agreement.

"So Alexander, like the mythical phoenix, rose from the ashes of his own death."

"That's the way it looks. The insignia Allain wore may have been a new Romanov symbol, a phoenix within the laurel leaves of victory."

"So what became of Alexander later? The way I remember it, a year or so after Allain was born, his old man is supposed to have tired of domestic bliss and skipped."

"Or else he developed a great need to see Mother Russia again. There was a famous hermit at that time who was said to be the image of Alexander. People from the court at St. Petersburg were supposed to have visited him regularly for advice, and to have gone into mourning when he finally died in 1864."

"Which means this hermit, Alexander, would have been alive in 1855, when his brother Nicholas the First died," Rone suggested.

"Therefore able to confer some kind of legitimacy on Allain if there had been a movement to bring him to power. Alexander had been a popular ruler; Nicholas was not. Nicholas spent his entire reign putting down revolutions of the kind that shook Europe in those years and brought Napoléon the Third to the throne. He learned to watch for the least sign of rebellion and crush it before it spread. He would not have looked kindly on a usurper—and neither would the faction which wanted to continue in power after his death with Nicholas's son, Alexander the Second."

Rone stared out over the water. "Nicholas might not have officially recognized Allain as his brother's son, but he would have been aware of his existence and could possibly have paid men to keep tabs on him. The men who came to see Allain in Venice, then, might have been members of some group who wanted him to try for the throne. He refused them because he wasn't interested, but also because he knew he was being watched."

"Things were heating up because of the Crimean War," Joletta added. "It looks as if assassins were sent after Allain earlier in Venice to remove him before he could make trouble. He became worried about them trying again, especially after the visit from the two men who may have proposed that he lead a revolt to gain the Russian throne. That's when he hid Violet away in the country. Later, when Signora da Allori died, he became so fearful for Violet, and for the child she was carrying, that he left her while he tried—what? To make contact with Nicholas and renounce any claim he might have to the throne? To give himself up and accept imprisonment of some kind in exchange for safety for Violet and her baby? He never told Violet, so we don't know."

"The baby would not have been legitimate," Rone objected.

"No, and I'll admit that puzzles me. But the child was unborn at the time of the death of Nicholas the First, and Gilbert would not have been the first husband to die in the nick of time when a crown was at stake. That possibility was removed when Allain fell to the assassins in the garden—which is why the last man left standing that night made no great effort to kill Violet afterward. If there could never be a marriage, then she and her child ceased to be a threat."

"So Allain came back to be with her and protect her and the baby," Rone said, his voice reflective, "and, by dying, made certain that they would live."

"No."

Joletta let the word stand alone for long seconds. She couldn't be sure of what she was about to say, and yet nothing else made sense, nothing else fit all the facts.

Rone gave her a deliberate look. "No," he repeated quietly. "It was Giovanni who died, wasn't it?"

She tried to smile, though it was a poor effort. "It must have seemed so perfect, a repeat of what had happened with Allain's father, like some strange, macabre joke played by time. Giovanni and Allain were close in age and size and description. They died for the same cause, the same woman. Maria was there to lay out her son and wrap him in his winding sheet. Why else would Violet have left the necklace with the housekeeper and been so generous with the family, unless it was because Maria allowed them to bury Giovanni under Allain's marker, Allain's name?"

"While Allain became Giovanni."

"And traveled to New Orleans to become a pharmacist and live beside Violet all his days. They never married because Gilbert had the last laugh after all. Violet might have forced him to agree to a divorce if he had been hale and hearty, but she could not publicly abandon an invalid husband who had tried to kill himself."

"Could be they decided it was best that way, one less thing to fear in case Allain's identity was ever discovered."

"There is that," Joletta agreed.

Rone drew a deep breath, letting it out with a shake of his head. "Do you really think that's the way it was?"

"I looked it all up when I got back. The dates match. More than that, there's an old picture of Giovanni taken in New Orleans. It's not a very good one, but there's a strong resemblance to the sketches of Allain that Violet made in her journal."

"And yet," Rone said with his eyes narrowed in thoughtfulness, "it stands to reason that the agents of the czar could have traced him to New Orleans through Violet; they must have had a dossier on her by that time. But I suppose that if they believed the fiction of his death, then there would have been no further interest in her."

"And certainly none in a child who was publicly recognized as the daughter of Gilbert Fossier."

Rone looked at her and quirked a brow. "Which means you are—what? The how-ever-many-times-great-granddaughter of Czar Alexander the First of Russia?"

"Something like that, I guess," she said, "for what difference it makes. There must be thousands of people walking around with odd pedigrees; just look at all the presidents who are suddenly discovered to be the descendants of royalty after they are elected."

"And if you're not, if what happened to Violet and Allain was really about something else entirely, I don't suppose anyone will ever know it."

"No," she agreed, her voice pensive, "I guess not."

He was quiet for long moments, though his gaze, stringent and assessing, still rested on her face. When he spoke again, it was with an abrupt change of subject. "I left Florence before you did, though not by much, apparently. There was something I had to see about in New York. I wanted to pick up this, before somebody else got to it."

From his pocket, he took a folded sheet of paper and two small bottles, one the familiar type used by Fossier's Royal Parfums, the other of deeply cut crystal with an ornate silver top. He reached to take Joletta's hand and press them into it. He released them quickly, as if afraid she might shove them back at him, or as though he was afraid to prolong the touch.

She looked down at the things she held. With the perfume in one hand, she opened the paper.

It was a report, the breakdown of a chemical compound with the exact formulation for each component. Next to the figures was a color graph divided into pie-shaped wedges with numbers showing the percentage for each component.

It was the formula for Le Jardin de cour.

"The report Aunt Estelle ordered," she said quietly.

"That's right," he answered, his voice steady. "It's yours, and there won't be another one made at Camors. One of the bottles is the perfume Natalie's mother brought to New York. Do whatever you want with it."

She had given him the information she had; he had given her what she needed. Both had deprived themselves for the benefit of the other. It was funny if you thought about it. Joletta did not feel like laughing.

"You don't have to do this," she said. Her voice was without inflection. All reaction, all feeling had been erased by fear. Such gifts sometimes signaled good-bye.

"Yes, I do. You wanted it; you went to a lot of trouble to find it."

"You wanted it, too," she said through the tightness in her throat.

"It doesn't mean a thing to me if I have to lose you to keep it."

The constriction inside her loosened a little. She swallowed hard before she spoke. "Do you—is it possible that we could both use the perfume? You could take the older formula for what you need; I could have the newer version, Mimi's version, for the shop."

"You searched it out and nearly died for it; you should have it all."

There was no reservation in his voice as he made the sacrifice. Hearing that, Joletta knew a deep need to show a matching generosity. "No," she said. "You risked your life for it, too. I was so afraid Timothy would kill you. He had the knife, you had nothing. I thought there would be no reason for him to try to kill you if you had the journal—but I only made things worse. I was so afraid—so afraid."

Rone watched her while the river wind stirred their hair and brushed like warm fingers over their faces. Finally he said in quiet urgency, "Why, Joletta? Why were you afraid?"

She met his gaze, her own wide and dark. Her chest and her heart and her whole being were crowded to bursting with the love she held inside. But though she opened her lips, she made not a sound. She had walked away from him in Florence and he had let her go, had given his word that he would leave her alone. It was up to her to ask him to stay with her now.

The words wouldn't come. The risk was too great. To say them and have him walk away in his turn would be a loss from which she might never recover.

A slow smile curved his lips while the promise rising in his eyes deepened, grew steadier. He said in soft entreaty, "Can't you trust me, even now?"

"Yes, I could—I do. It's just that—" She stopped, unable to go on.

"That's good enough for me," he said, his voice deep and not quite steady. "Open the other perfume bottle, Joletta."

She obeyed mechanically, with fingers that were numb and a little clumsy. The silver top was stiff; it needed such an effort to remove it that Joletta almost spilled the bottle as the cap came away, suddenly, in her hand. A small amount of liquid splashed out, running over her fingers.

The scent was rich, piercingly sweet, ethereal yet passionate and positive; common yet rare, and extravagantly satisfying. She had no need to breathe deep of it to identify it, or to love it.

"For Violet and Allain," Rone said, his tones deep with emotion, as rich as the perfume, "it was the language of the flowers. For us, I thought the message of the perfume would be best. So I won't fill a room with red roses for you. But because you wear Tea Rose, I thought you, of all women, might recognize the meaning of the essence of a thousand Bulgarian roses."

Bulgarian roses, the most expensive, most prized in the world of perfume, and always rose red.

Red roses, for Love.

The scent mounted to her head, burgeoning inside her, settling in her mind and heart, inescapable, indelible, easing fear, erasing doubt.

She smiled with joy and confidence shining in her face. "I love you, Tyrone Kingsley Stuart Adamson the Fourth," she said.

He caught her to him, safe in the haven of his arms, holding tightly, smoothing his hands over her back as if he meant never to stop touching her, never to let her go.

"I adore you," he said against her hair. "I've been half-crazy trying to think of some way to make you believe me. I've loved you since the moment I kissed you on a dark New Orleans street, loved you more with every desperate step I took following after you over half of Europe like a devoted hound. And I mean to go on loving you and hounding you until you get so sick of it that you're ready to marry me to shut me up."

"If that's a proposal," she said, her voice muffled against his shirtfront, "I don't think much of it."

He drew away enough to look at her. "You don't?"

"It may be a long time," she said with dancing eyes, "before I get tired of being loved, or hounded."

"Shall we see?" he said in tones rough with tenderness and mock anger.

And began.

ABOUT THE AUTHOR

Jennifer Blake was born near Goldonna, Louisiana, in her grandparents' 120-year-old hand-built cottage. She grew up on an eighty-acre farm in the rolling hills of northern Louisiana. While married and raising her children she became a voracious reader. At last she set out to write a book of her own. That first book was followed by thirty-five more and today they have reached more than nine million copies in print, making Jennifer Blake one of the bestselling romance writers of our time. Her most recent novel is *Joy & Anger*.

Jennifer and her husband live near Quitman, Louisiana, in a house styled after old Southern planters' cottages.